Anonymous

Wonderful Deeds and Adventures

Anonymous

Wonderful Deeds and Adventures

ISBN/EAN: 9783337340018

Printed in Europe, USA, Canada, Australia, Japan

Cover: Foto ©Andreas Hilbeck / pixelio.de

More available books at **www.hansebooks.com**

WONDERFUL DEEDS
AND ADVENTURES

A Collection of Stirring Scenes and Moving Accidents

Illustrated

NEW YORK

CASSELL PUBLISHING COMPANY

104 & 106 Fourth Avenue

CONTENTS.

LIST OF ILLUSTRATIONS.

LIST OF ILLUSTRATIONS.

INTRODUCTION.

It is the love of adventure that makes the world's heroes. If men preferred inaction to action, what would historians have to write, what scientists to record? If Christopher Columbus had been satisfied to sail the Mediterranean the world would not have united to celebrate his greatest achievement, nor would our delightful Washington Irving have immortalized his memory. If Stanley had remained a *Herald* reporter to the end of his days, he would not have explored the "dark continent"; if George Washington had been content to carry the rod and chain, instead of leading an army, he would not be the father of this great country. The spirit of the men who made the charge at Balaclava is the spirit of bravery and daring that is one of the most admirable qualities in man.

All the world loves a lover, says Emerson, which is true enough, and it is also true that all the world idolizes a hero. It is the heroic deed that wins the quickest recognition. The man who plunges into the sea to save a fellow-man, a fireman who dashes through the flames to the rescue of a human being, either one of these is a hero, possessed of the same spirit that discovers continents or leads armies to victory. In the breast of every man, woman, or child that ever lived the love of the heroic burns. Every man may not be a hero himself, but he is a craven soul, indeed, if he does not admire the heroic quality in other men.

Stories of adventure by land or sea are the sort of reading to place in the hands of boys. True stories of adventure, of heroism—this is the intellectual food to give the young. Let them become saturated with such stories as the charge of the Light Brigade, for bravery; the adventures of Alexander Henry among the Indians, for long suffering; Captain Webb's Channel swim, for courage; the "Hunt for a Murderer," for perseverance under difficulties.

It will be a good thing for girls to read these stories of adventure too, for they will learn that heroines are plentiful as well as heroes. Women do not have the opportunities of showing their heroic qualities that men do, but when the occasion arrives they are not found lacking in courage, as this volume will prove. From Joan of Arc to Ida Lewis women have done deeds of daring.

> Lives of great men all remind us
> We can make our lives sublime,
> And, departing, leave behind us
> Footprints in the sands of time.

Lives of heroes also remind us that we may be heroes too. If it be not ours to discover new worlds, to lead soldiers to victory, or even to fight grizzly bears, it may come in our way to do some less conspicuous deed of heroism which will make us none the less heroes, even though our names may not be filed on "Fame's eternal beadroll."

The man who has "the courage of his convictions" may be as great a hero as the great general. It took no less courage on the part of William Lloyd Garrison to declare himself against slavery than it would have taken to penetrate the forest primeval or face the enemies' guns. Indeed, when he appeared alone upon a platform before a howling mob, any one of whom would have shot him dead at a signal, he showed the highest qualities of courage, for he faced his enemies alone. He was the one target for their insults, for their stones. Now the cause for which he fought is won, and it was won by a hero and a martyr—the brave and noble Abraham Lincoln. The history of our country is a history of adventure and heroism. The pioneers who, with their wives and families, settled in the wilderness, "snatched a fearful joy" between the tomahawk and the torch. We can scarcely realize it now, but this book of "Wonderful Deeds and Adventures" brings it graphically before our eyes, and stirs and thrills us as we read.

WONDERFUL
DEEDS AND ADVENTURES.

THE CHARGE OF THE LIGHT BRIGADE.

(BALACLAVA. OCTOBER 25TH, 1854.)

1.

THE Heavy Brigade—General Scarlett's "Three Hundred"—had made its charge. The horde of grey-coated horsemen, into which it had so gallantly pierced, had broken, turned, heaved up the slope of the Causeway Heights, over the ridge and down into the North Valley behind, and were now scampering up it in full retreat, their artillery lumbering after. The victors re-formed upon the slope. In a few moments of glorious life they had turned the fortune of the day, and to the penetrating eye of Lord Raglan, as he sat amid his staff high on the ledges of the Chersonese upland, the Battle of Balaclava was as good as won. For affairs stood thus :—Below on the plain to his right lay the small sea-port of Balaclava, behind its inner line of field-works. This town, the main object of the Russian attack (for upon it the Allied forces besieging Sebastopol depended for all their supplies), was now out of danger. In the valley before it—the South Valley—and on the slopes that led up to the low ridge of the Causeway Heights, no enemy was to be seen. For a few minutes the dusky cavalry had gathered there to swoop down on it as on a sure prey, but now, riven and scattered by the red-coated "Heavies," they had melted away, and the little force stationed about the inner line of works saw them no more.

The Causeway ridge—the outer line of fortification—was, it is true, still mainly held by the Russians. The three redoubts to westward, captured from the Turks on the first advance, were, with their guns, in the enemy's hands. But now a brilliant chance offered itself for their recovery.

On the other side of the Causeway Heights, between them and the acclivity of the Fedioukine Hills, lay another valley—the North Valley, as it was called —running roughly parallel to the South Valley. A few minutes before, this hollow had been full of cavalry and artillery; but now, with these in full flight towards the eastern end, it was left more and more empty of troops.

As a consequence, the Russian infantry and gunners that lined the heights on either side were left protruding—two weak and assailable heads—to any attack that the Allies might choose to make. According to Kinglake's apt comparison, the Russian array had resembled the closed fist of a pugilist: it was now rather like an open palm with the middle fingers bent back, and the fore and little fingers impotently protruding, these two fingers being the battalions on the Fedioukine Hills and those occupying the captured redoubts on the Causeway Heights.

Obviously the Allies were mainly concerned with these latter—to recapture the outer line of the fortifications with the lost guns. Indeed, before this, Lord Raglan had made his arrangements for such an attempt, ordering Sir George Cathcart to advance upon the redoubts with the 4th Infantry Division, and H.R.H. the Duke of Cambridge to support him with the 1st Division upon the southern slope. The Duke of Cambridge was in time, but Sir George, for some reason, was not. Fearing, therefore, to lose the precious moments which the fortune of war had given him, Lord Raglan bethought him of his cavalry.

The cavalry camp stood at the western extremity of the North Valley, just under the heights where Lord Raglan sat. The whole of the cavalry was under Lord Lucan; under him General Scarlett commanded the Heavies, Lord Cardigan the Light Brigade. Of these two brigades, the former was just re-forming after a charge that would vie with any in the annals of war. But the Light squadrons stood ready; chafing, indeed, at the inactivity to which they had been condemned throughout the morning. Close to their right rose the Causeway slope—its line of redoubts inviting recapture. Naturally Lord Raglan's thoughts turned to them. He wrote off an order and despatched it to Lord Lucan.

The order ran:—"Cavalry to advance and take advantage of any opportunity to recover the heights. They will be supported by the infantry, which have been ordered to advance on two fronts."

II.

Minute after minute passed. The precious opportunity was slipping from the grasp of the Allied Generals, and yet the order was not obeyed. From the heights, indeed, Lord Raglan and his staff saw the cavalry squadrons set in motion for a minute—then halted again. All that Lord Lucan had done was to move his Light Brigade to another position facing down the North Valley, and to halt the Heavies on the slope, there to await the infantry which, as he afterwards explained, "had not yet arrived."

Now the order had unmistakably and unconditionally ordered the cavalry to advance. The infantry was only spoken of as a support; and in delaying as he did, Lord Lucan deliberately sat in judgment on the command he had received from headquarters, and condemned it. On such a course two obvious comments must be made:—In the first place, it was an offence against discipline; secondly, it was an offence against common sense. Subsequently Lord Lucan explained his conduct thus: that, having taken up his position, he was "prepared to carry out the remainder of his instructions by endeavouring to effect the only object, and in the only way that could rationally have been intended, viz., to give all the support possible to the infantry in the recapture of the redoubts, and subsequently to cut off all their defenders."

Thus by weighing Lord Raglan's order in the scales of his own judgment he actually inverted its meaning Being told that the infantry would support his advance, he waited to support the infantry. And by his theory of what was "rationally intended" he sinned against common sense. For how could he upon

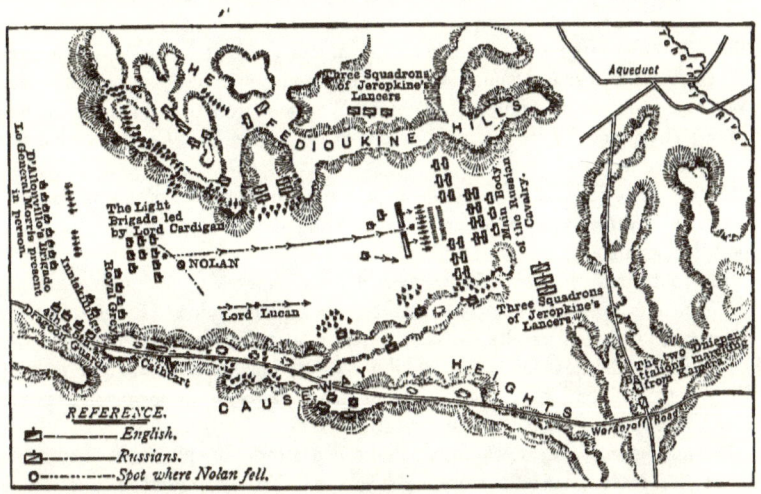

PLAN.

the plain have the same opportunity of judging what was necessary as Lord Raglan, who from the ledges of the Chersonese could overlook the whole field of battle ?

The murmurs of the staff around the Commander-in-Chief may be imagined as the minutes went by and still the cavalry did not budge. And now some of them, sweeping with their field-glasses the ridge of the Causeway Heights, perceived—or so they thought—some teams of Russian artillery horses, with the lasso tackle attached, coming along it. Clearly before the enemy retreated he meant to carry off as trophies the English guns in the redoubts taken from the Turks.

Lord Raglan's patience was worn out. He determined to repeat, more imperatively, his order for the advance of the cavalry. Turning to the Quartermaster-General at his side, he asked him to write such an order at once; and General Airey, placing a slip of paper on his sabretache, scribbled it with a pencil; but, before the paper went, Lord Raglan read it and dictated some further words, which were at once inserted. This slip of paper was what has afterwards been known as the "fourth order."

A Major Calthorpe, one of Lord Raglan's aides-de-camp, was standing ready for the mission, but the Commander-in-Chief called for General Airey's own aide-de-camp, Captain Nolan, and desired that the order should be carried by him. The young soldier took it, and, spurring his horse, dashed down the slope.

<h2 style="text-align:center">III.</h2>

While he is on his way it will be worth while to inquire for a moment what kind of man this young aide-de-camp was; for it happens that on his character the history of what is to follow greatly depends. To eliminate the individual in the soldier when executing an order of his superior; to evoke it in the highest degree when the same soldier is dashing into the enemy and grappling hand to hand—this is the first problem of military discipline. We have seen that Lord Lucan was anything but a machine in executing an order; let us see what Captain Nolan was like in delivering one.

He was, to begin with, a young man; he was an ardent lover of his profession; he was an enthusiast, with a theory and a blind devotion to it; and he was a superb horseman.

His youth and his zeal for warfare did not, however, prevent his holding the commands of his superior officers at their highest value. Rather, he had a reverence for tacit obedience that was, if possible, overstrained; and for the last forty minutes, like many another on the heights, he had been secretly boiling with indignation at the neglect of Lord Raglan's authority which was implied in the inaction of the cavalry arm.

The enthusiasm—the faith to which he had sworn his judgment—served to inflame this indignation still more. He believed that the fate of battles turned upon the right use of cavalry. Proud beyond measure of that arm of the service to which he belonged, holding that from the moment when he met the enemy the English trooper was an unequalled warrior, he steadfastly believed that the true value of cavalry had always been stupidly underrated, and that if intelligently used it could work miracles. He had watched with burning joy the feat of Scarlett's "Three Hundred"—a feat that confirmed his theory, and even did more than confirm it. He had watched with burning scorn the vacillation (as he thought it) of Lord Lucan, a General whom he secretly held in unmitigated contempt, and to whom, in his private journal, he attributed the inactivity of our troopers throughout the invasion. It may be conceived with what inner joy such a man bore down the message of reproof and urgent command to the plain below.

And he was a superb rider. Afterwards men who foreboded nothing at the time had little difficulty in remembering how that messenger rode upon his errand. The slope of seven or eight hundred feet which divided the staff upon the heights from the army in the plain was, to use Kinglake's words, "of just such a degree of steepness that, whilst no rider of mere ordinary experience and boldness would like to go down it at a high rate of speed, and whilst few of those going slowly would refrain from somewhat easing the abruptness of the path by a more or less zigzag descent, the ground still was not so precipitous as to defy the rapid purpose of a horseman who had accustomed himself in such things to approach the extreme of what is possible." Nolan went down it as a hawk swoops on its prey — hot, eager, and sure—upon the plain where Lord Lucan dallied with his squadrons.

IV.

Our cavalry yet stood in two masses : the Heavy Dragoons on a slope of the Causeway Heights, not far from the scene of their victory ; the Light Brigade in two lines, so placed as to face straight down the North Valley.

LORD LUCAN.

And still the Causeway Heights and the Fedioukine Hills were occupied with Russians inviting attack. Between them the valley lay, offering death to any that should enter raked on either side by artillery and lines of Russian riflemen, ending in a Cossack battery, with the defeated cavalry standing thick behind it.

Lord Lucan was seated in the saddle between his two brigades, and a little in advance of them, when Nolan came galloping up and delivered the paper. The message, as we have seen, was in General Airey's handwriting; the bearer was General Airey's aide-de-camp. Lord Lucan, it appears, had for some time persuaded himself that the Quartermaster-General was often responsible for orders which, in fact, he only transmitted. But at any rate the message was clear enough. The words were :—

"Lord Raglan wishes the cavalry to advance rapidly to the front, and try to prevent the enemy carrying away the guns. Troop of horse artillery may accompany. French cavalry is on your left. Immediate.

(Signed)   "R. Airey."

Read now, out of the heat and confusion of battle, this famous "fourth order" is as clear as day itself. Read in connection with the order preceding it, it seems impossible of misapprehension. The "third order" requested Lord Lucan to advance and take any opportunity of *recapturing the heights* —clearly the Causeway Heights taken by the Russians early in the day; there were no others to *recapture*. The "fourth order" directed him to "advance rapidly" and "try to prevent the enemy carrying away the guns." What guns could possibly be meant except those on the heights—those English guns of which the enemy were now in possession? Indeed, though it has since been argued that Lord Lucan was in doubt as to which were "the guns" intended, his own words disprove this: "being instructed," he writes in his despatch to Lord Raglan two days after the battle, "to prevent the enemy carrying the guns lost by the Turkish troops in the morning, I ordered," &c. The order was plain enough.

But Lord Lucan had no sooner read the order than he chose to condemn it. He afterwards declared that he "read the order with much consideration" —perhaps consternation would be the better word—"at once seeing its impracticability for any useful purpose whatever, and the consequent great unnecessary risk and loss to be incurred." This was, at least, a strange attitude of mind for a subordinate to assume, and stranger when we remember that Lord Raglan could see the whole field, whereas to Lord Lucan, from his position, neither enemy nor guns were in sight. But he did more than mentally condemn the order; he turned to Nolan, and began to urge the futility of it.

Nolan, though still more impatient and indignant, was yet conscious that Lord Lucan was his superior officer. Comrades who knew him well, believed him to be the last man who would show disrespect to one in such a position. Yet being equally conscious that Lord Lucan was guilty of this very fault in his treatment of Lord Raglan's order, he answered coldly—

"Lord Raglan's orders are, that the cavalry should attack immediately."

Lord Lucan turned sharply upon him—

"Attack, sir! Attack what? What guns, sir?"

Nolan was a man, not a statue; his blood had gradually, by the events and impatience of the morning, been worked up to boiling-pitch. At this last address he flung his hand back, looked the other in the face, and pointing with his hand in a direction which, Lord Lucan has averred, was towards the left-front corner of the North Valley, he answered haughtily—

"There, my lord, is your enemy; there are your guns!"

It was, no doubt, insolent. It was a taunt inflicted on a lieutenant-general in the face of his own troops. Nolan's gesture and manner was, doubtless, as Lord Lucan says, "disrespectful and significant." But at the worst it was a breach of discipline, and should have been avenged on Nolan himself. The aide-de-camp should, perhaps, have been put under arrest. But more-than ever should Lord Lucan have been eager to carry out the order to the letter.

Instead of this he allowed it to upset his reasoning faculties altogether. He chose to resent Nolan's gesture as a taunt, yet at the same time he took it for topographical guidance. Practically the angle of divergence between the two paths before him—the path up to the heights and that down into the fatal valley—was very slight, not above twenty degrees. Nolan was not looking down the valley when he flung his arm back; nor had he sight of enemy or guns to guide his hand. But, on the other hand, the aide-de-camp was fresh from the uplands of the Chersonese, where he could see every detail of the plain. It is absurd to suppose that such a man, with such recent knowledge of the enemy's position, would have sent our men down the North Valley.

Blinded with anger at the taunting gesture, Lord Lucan yet made up his mind to follow it as a cool indication of the direction he was to take. Alone, and putting his horse at a trot, he rode up to Lord Cardigan, who sat in his saddle in front of the 13th Light Dragoons.

Here we may use his own words:—"After giving to Lord Cardigan the order brought me from General Airey by Captain Nolan, I urged his lordship to advance steadily, and to keep his men well in hand. My idea was that he was to use his discretion and act as circumstances might show themselves; my opinion is that, keeping his four squadrons under perfect control, he should have halted them as soon as he found that there was no useful object to be gained, but great risk to be incurred; it was clearly his duty to have handled his brigade as I did the Heavy Brigade, and so saved them from much useless and unnecessary loss."

Whatever were the words used, Lord Cardigan took them to mean that he was to ride down the North Valley for more than a mile between two flanking columns of the enemy, and at the end to charge, and in front, the battery that was drawn across its further end.

He brought his sword down to salute and replied—

"Certainly, sir; but allow me to point out to you that the Russians have a battery in the valley in our front, and batteries and riflemen on each flank."

"I know it," said Lord Lucan, with a shrug of the shoulders; "but Lord Raglan will have it. We have no choice but to obey."

Lord Cardigan made no further question. He turned quietly to his men and said—

"The brigade will advance."

V.

They stood thus:—The front line was formed of two regiments: the 13th Light Dragoons, commanded by Captain Oldham; and the 17th Lancers, commanded by Captain Morris. With them at first stood the 11th Hussars, under Colonel Douglas, but these now moved back to form the second line. The third consisted of the 4th Light Dragoons, under Lord George Paget; and the greater part of the 8th Hussars, under Colonel Shewell. Each regiment extended in line, two deep. And it must be particularly remembered (Lord Raglan having ordered "the cavalry" to advance, without distinction of brigades) that Scarlett's Heavy Dragoons were to charge with them; and having brought two regiments of that brigade, the Greys and the Royals, in

"'THERE, MY LORD, IS YOUR ENEMY'" (p. 6).

advance of the other regiments, Lord Lucan determined to be present. The link which joined the two divisions of the English cavalry was afterwards —we shall see how—allowed to be broken; but the charge contemplated was a charge by the whole body of English horse.

Before them lay the valley—where for a full mile these men would have to ride, raked by a slaughtering cross-fire, without being able to strike a blow; and then, at the end, for such as survived, there awaited a battery, and behind this a dense mass of horsemen, almost the whole strength of the Russian cavalry.

Everything stood ready for the sacrifice—no circumstance absent, no pre-

caution omitted to make it full and complete. And no man questioned: " Not,"
as the Laureate says in his famous ode,

> " Not though the soldier knew
> Some one had blundered:
> Theirs not to make reply,
> Theirs not to reason why,
> Theirs but to do and die."

Least of all did that man question who now, his arrangements complete,
rode forward and put himself at the head of his brigade.

Lord Cardigan was in many respects an exceptional man. A soldier trained
rather to the rigorous and pedantic discipline of Aldershot and Hyde Park
than to the varied emergencies of actual warfare—an English nobleman with
more than a feudal conception of the differences between chief and follower,
General and trooper—his character as a commander had many startling defects,
but of these cowardice was not one. Indisputably he was, as Lord `Raglan
afterwards expressed it, " brave as a lion." Whatever faults are to be found
with him, his ready acceptance of a task which he knew to be deadly in
the highest degree of deadliness, his composed self-sacrifice, his absolute steadiness as a leader in this bloody tragedy, must for ever, in the eye of any
but a War Office martinet, be held to weigh against them. From the moment
he received Lord Lucan's order, to the moment when he leapt in, stern and
grim, between the Russian guns, his behaviour is flawless.

But as soon as a cavalry charge has once begun, owing to the impossibility
of giving verbal commands intelligibly and efficiently in the galloping din, the
behaviour of the men must necessarily adapt itself to the behaviour of their
leader. They look, and, looking, imitate. Throughout he sets to the front
rank the example which the hinder troops—insensibly, perhaps, but certainly—
follow. And so, in any account of a cavalry charge, the very physique of the
commander becomes important.

Lord Cardigan was a tall man ; long in the legs, yet sitting high in the
saddle. Fair and slender, he wore the uniform of his old regiment, the 11th
Hussars ; and wore his pelisse, not loose about the shoulders, but—as was the
fashion during the Crimean winter—tightly buttoned about the body, emphasis-
ing yet further his height and slimness. He rode a thorough-bred chestnut,
with two white " socks "—both high, and both on the " near " side. And
though, of course, to the men riding after him, only the " sock " on the hind leg
was conspicuous, yet it was high and marked enough to catch and arrest the eye.

About two lengths behind Lord Cardigan, and nearly three lengths in
front of the first line, stood his staff, Lieutenant Maxse and Sir George
Wombwell being the only officers present.

Lord Cardigan, though the enemy in front was far away, was yet aware
enough of the heavy fire that would await him before he had moved a

hundred yards, to look upon the advance from the first as a charge. Followed by his men, he moved forward at a trot in a direction straight down the North Valley for the battery, which lay a mile and a quarter away.

VI.

But before he had ridden a hundred yards he was destined to be shocked —amazed.

Before him he saw Captain Nolan, riding frantically across his front from left to right, waving his sword violently, and shouting as if he would that the whole brigade should hear him.

Lord Cardigan imagined that this audacious junior was cheering *his* men on. Alas! we know the young aide-de-camp's motive was altogether different. He rode right across the brigade. He saw that it had not changed its front —was not riding towards the Causeway Heights—was going down to irredeemable disaster. Already in imagination he saw, not only the utter failure of the Commander-in-Chief's plan, but the destruction of that noble body of men on whom the enthusiastic hopes of his life were fixed. We can too grimly interpret his shouts now. They conveyed this dread warning—"You are wrong; you are madly, hopelessly wrong! The direction in which I am riding is the right one. Here lie your enemies, your guns; down there is useless death!"

But to Lord Cardigan all this was unintelligible. It was vile want of discipline; it was the extremity of impudence. He was just going to raise his voice in hot rebuke—

The first Russian shell came and burst in front of him. As it exploded a fragment flew straight at Nolan, shattering his chest, burying itself in his heart. Down from his hand dropped the sword, but the arm remained erect, uplifted; the rider's knees still grasped the saddle; the charger, missing his master's hand, scared by the dropping reins, wheeled round and began to gallop towards the charging squadrons.

Then—from the dead man with the uplifted arm—there broke one agonising unearthly shriek—a sound that will never be forgotten by its hearers, unique and most awful amongst all the horrors of that awful ride. The corpse rode on and passed through the 13th Light Dragoons in the first line, then dropped from its saddle upon the turf.

This was the first Russian shell that met our squadrons; for, in truth, the behaviour of the Light Brigade was filling its very enemies with wild astonishment. Even the Russian private on the heights saw the stark madness of it—saw it, indeed, so clearly that 'it was only with difficulty he awoke to the golden opportunity thrust into his hands. Every moment those on the heights expected to be attacked, to be driven out of the redoubts they had captured. Instead of this they were in a position to fire, with an aim near and sure, straight into the masses they had feared. In fact, they were already

"THE CORPSE RODE ON" (p. 10).

falling back before the anticipated charge; far better than Lord Lucan they foresaw the step which the English should take—when, incredulously, slowly —for the blunder was too monstrous to be understood—they took to their guns again.

The distance between our Light Brigade and the Heavies was momentarily increasing. Lord Lucan, indeed, whatever he had done with Lord Cardigan's squadrons, evidently intended to use his own judgment with the Heavy Brigade, which he himself accompanied—"to keep his squadrons," in fact (to use his own words), "in perfect control, and halt them as soon as he found that there was no useful object to be gained."

As soon as the Light Squadrons had advanced far enough to reveal their wild purpose, there opened on them from the Causeway Heights and the Fedioukine Hills a deadly, double-flanking fire, with an efficiency that increased from moment to moment, of round-shot, grape, and rifle-bullets.

VII.

Meanwhile, straight for the battery ahead, for the cloud of smoke riven every now and again with tongues of flame, rode Lord Cardigan's brigade.

It was a ride condemned by one of the first principles of cavalry practice. To charge a battery in front, even without any added disadvantage, is a thing which all military writers have acknowledged to be beyond the fit employment of cavalry. Yet so determined was Lord Cardigan to fill up the full measure of his heroic sacrifice, that he chose out the very centre of the battery ahead and rode straight for it.

For a time the pace was steady. As a rider fell, or a horse dropped, the lines behind would open for a moment as they passed on either side and then close up again. And now so often did this happen that, to the spectators on the Chersonese upland, the alternate expansion and contraction of the lines seemed to work as regularly as if by machinery. Still the order was well maintained, though now two or three fell at each fresh moment. Faster than the seconds came the singing bullets past them to right and left, the hurling fragments of exploding shells, the twanging noise of the round-shot, and the hideous and indescribable sound with which it beds itself in the trunk of trooper or horse. And as yet they rode steadily, almost without gathering speed.

For before them was a soldier schooled to rate order above all things, and as long as by example he could, he kept the pace down. In such a strait it is natural in the bravest of the brave to wish to be through with it, to come swiftly to the grapple where at length he may let his lust of battle loose and strike. Yet when Captain White, of the 17th Lancers, anxious to get out of the murderous fire and into the guns, as being the better of the two evils, forced the pace until he came almost level with his leader, Lord Cardigan extended his sword across the captain's breast, as a reminder that discipline must be kept in whatever circumstances.

Otherwise this grim leader on the chestnut horse made no sign. Stiff, straight, erect, he rode for the guns; and behind him the brigade never faltered, but followed blindly, doggedly, through the storm of murderous missiles.

Nevertheless, the pace behind was increasing; and insensibly (for he never turned his head) the General's pace increased also. The regiments were becoming men—fierce, impatient individual riders. Now and then the troopers would dash past their officers. Nor, although it broke the order somewhat, was it under these conditions unpardonable. It was instinct; for now of the 13th Light Dragoons, Captain Oldham and Goad were dead, and Cornet Montgomery; in the 17th Lancers, Captain Winter and Lieutenant Thomson. Sir William Gordon was down, and White and Webb. But sixty at most remained of the third line.

The three regiments behind followed, but at slightly different paces. The second line, as we know, was formed of the 11th Hussars. Behind them came the third, which was originally formed of the 4th Light Dragoons and the 8th Hussars together. But in announcing the intended charge to Lord George Paget, who commanded the former regiment, Lord Cardigan had said, "I expect your best support; mind, Lord George, your best support." With this sentence in his ears, Lord George rode through the North Valley; and as he rode, Lord Cardigan's words and tone repeated themselves in his brain with gathering emphasis. Consequently, the dominant desire that went with him was rather to keep close up to the first line than to maintain his alignment with the 8th Hussars. On the other hand, Colonel Shewell, who commanded this last-mentioned regiment, resolutely kept down the pace of his men.

As a result, the three supporting regiments were soon in echelon, thus—

> 11th Hussars.
>> 4th Light Dragoons.
>>> 8th Hussars.

And although, of course, they suffered far less from the battery in front, yet the flanking fire treated them even worse than it did the first line, for the men on the heights were now more fully prepared for them. And they could see, what the first line could not, the full horror of the carnage—the saddles emptied; the plunging, falling horses; and (worse yet) were compelled to witness those of the officers and men that had been wounded, yet not too effectively to be still able to crawl or drag themselves along; or the chargers rolling in their last agony, or convulsively staggering up on their fore-legs and trying to drag along their hinder quarters that, shattered and paralysed, trailed powerlessly behind.

Those of the riderless horses that were unhurt also gave trouble; for a horse in battle, though brave enough as long as a guiding hand is on its reins, becomes a pitiable sight as soon as it misses the commanding presence of man. Suddenly all the appalling terrors of the battle-field seem to break on it; it winces, cowers, runs wildly with staring eyeballs. In such a case it seeks protection, not by wild retreat, but by ranging up in line and following the troopers. Often, too, it will piteously seek out its proper place in the ranks, and insist on pressing in. Lord George Paget, who rode a little in advance of his regiment, at one time had three or four of these riderless chargers galloping beside him and pressing in until his overalls were smeared with the blood on their flanks — blood from the wounds of their late riders.

And still to the old parade-cries of "Keep back!" "Look to your dressing!" "Keep back, right flank — keep back!" the devoted regiments followed. And still ahead the first line —every moment weaker—rode in their might. And still in front of all Cardigan on his chestnut charger — stern and relentless — drove straight for the guns.

LORD CARDIGAN.

VIII.

What do men think of at such a moment? Of death, in the nature of things, they must think; but how? Here are the reflections of one of the Six Hundred, told in the words of the historian of the Crimea, to whose narrative of Balaclava this account—as, indeed, all other accounts—must be indebted; for to no other historian of this century has been given at once such charm of style, combined with scrupulous care for exactness :—

"One of the most gifted," says Kinglake, "of the officers now acting with the supports was able, whilst descending into the valley, to construct and adopt such a theory of Divine governance as he judged to be the best fitted for the battle-field. Without having been hitherto accustomed to let his thoughts dwell very gravely on any such subjects of speculation, he now all at once, while he rode, encased himself, body and soul, in the iron creed of the fatalist; and connecting destiny in his mind with the inferred will of

God, defied any missile to touch him, unless it should come with the warrant of a providential and foregone decree. As soon as he had put on this armour of faith, a shot struck one of his holsters without harming him or his horse; and he was so constituted as to be able to see in this incident a confirmation of his new fatalist doctrine. Then, with something of the confidence often shown by other sectarians not engaged in a cavalry onset, he went on to determine that his, and his only, was the creed which could keep a man firm in battle. There, plainly, he erred; and, indeed, there is reason for saying that it would be ill for our cavalry regiments if their prowess were really dependent upon the adoption of any high spiritual or philosophic theory. I imagine that the great body of our cavalry people, whether officers or men, were borne forward and sustained in their path of duty by moral forces of another kind—by sense of military obligation, by innate love of fighting and of danger—by the shame of disclosing weakness — by pride of nation and of race—by pride of regiment, of squadron, of troop—by personal pride; not least, by the power of that wheel-going mechanism which assigns to each man his task, and inclines him to give but short audience to distracting irrelevant thoughts."

This, at any rate, we know—for he has disclosed it himself—of the leader in this race through the grim valley. Every moment he looked for death, and yet the feeling that was uppermost with him throughout was the feeling with which he began—one of consuming anger against the young aide-de-camp that had dared to ride across and shout to his brigade. He had heard—who could help it?—Nolan's shriek, yet somehow failed to connect it with the bursting shell. Down into the battery-smoke he carried his wrath, and on coming out from the charge his first words were of anger against this breach of discipline. General Scarlett stopped him, saying, "You nearly rode over Nolan's body."

IX.

But let us return to the brigade that is now within a few hundred yards of the battery—within the grey cloud that partially hid them from the object of their attack, the goal towards which, for more than a mile, they have been riding.

At length the leaders saw behind this veil the red brass muzzles of the guns, and the Russian artillerymen behind. By this time the regiments had been accumulating speed, and were now going at a rate that has been set down at seventeen miles an hour. The Russian gunners, on the other hand, stood firm. Aware of the immense mass of cavalry behind them, they had no intention of abandoning their post.

The moment arrived. Lord Cardigan, we have seen, had ridden all the while for the very centre of the battery, which consisted of twelve pieces of cannon. Not for one moment did he dream of "halting his men as soon as he found there was no useful object to be gained." It was not his "to reason why," even though his acutely developed sense of what was fit and proper must have revolted from the violation of all traditions involved in charging a battery so. He was within two or three lengths of one of the guns when the piece was fired; a flash of flame burst out in the direction of his chestnut's off shoulder. But it left horse and rider unscathed. The charger swerved but a little—then, borne on by his impetus, Lord Cardigan, still about two lengths in advance of his brigade, swept in between the guns.

With the exception of a few of the 17th Lancers on the extreme left, the whole of the first line was full in front of the battery, and drove in after their leader. The long interval of waiting was over. At length they could strike in return, and well they utilised their power. Some, carried on perhaps by their own speed, dashing through the artillerymen, tore yet further forward to assail the grey cavalry behind. Others did battle for the solid prize of the burnished cannon—sabring, cutting, hewing—though the Russian gunners, with fine tenacity, still clung to their posts. Some, indeed, crept under the wheels of their tumbrils, but the rest, showing their white teeth and hissing with rage as only a Muscovite can, bore up as brave men against the shock.

That portion of the 17th Lancers which outflanked the battery was under the command of Captain Morris. They were about twenty men in all, and found themselves confronted with a large body of Russian horse that over-lapped the guns and stood connected with the right wing of the great mass of cavalry posted behind. Luckily for the English their antagonists were standing still—the greatest, perhaps, of all mistakes for cavalry in such a position, and undoubtedly one of the chief causes of their defeat by Scarlett's dragoons earlier in the day. Morris, seeing this, half-turned in his saddle, and crying, "Now, remember what I have told you, men, and keep together," gave his charger, "Old Treasurer," the spur and broke into the opposing squadron with such force that his sword went through the trunk of the first Russian up to the hilt in such a manner that he could not dislodge it. While he was still tugging to get it free he caught a sabre-cut on the left side of the head, and another that pierced both plates of his skull across the very top. He dropped and lay unconscious. But his handful of men were before this in the thick of the Russians—"intermingled, the few with the many—the twenty gay glittering Lancers with the ranks of the dusky grey cavalry."

In a moment or two the Russians heaved back, and with few exceptions galloped off. But now from the flanks came pouring a crowd of Cossacks, cutting off the English retreat, and occupying the ground where Morris and his men had just charged.

As could not but happen, the glittering remnants of what had once been the first line were now struggling in small detached groups with the hordes of their foes. At one point was Cardigan nearly alone, facing the main body of Russian cavalry with his sword at the slope. At another Lieutenant

Chadwick of the 17th Lancers, unhorsed and so hideously wounded that he could scarce stir a foot, was defending himself with his revolver against a ring of Cossacks. To the left, Morris, who by this time had regained his senses, was keeping another ring at bay by ceaselessly whirling his sword and cutting at the thighs of his assailants. In other places the Cossacks were despatching such of our men as were down but still breathing. Here, again, the few left of the first line were still cutting and hewing at the artillerymen, when Brigade-Major Mayow, justly believing that if they remained here they would be an easy prey for the Russian cavalry if it charged, called off his men who were under the guidance of Sergeant O'Hara, preventing the gunners from dragging off their twelve-pounders, and shouting " Seventeenth! this way!" led them against the Russian cavalry, which with fifteen men only he broke and drove back on to their second reserve, when he heard a merry shout behind—" The Busby-bags are coming!" The three supporting regiments had come up, and were pounding through the battery.

X.

Of the doings of these three regiments—of the 11th Hussars, the 4th Light Dragoons, the 8th Hussars—we have not space to speak at length. They, too, plunged after their comrades—in the case of the 8th Hussars even to the accompaniment of a wild "Tally-ho!" There was one young officer who, when once in, coolly dismounted and began to cut away the tackle by which the Russian artillerymen were striving to carry off a gun. There was another, redly besmeared, who raged with an attack of blood frenzy, and, when the fight was over, broke into tears like a little child. Others were plying their revolvers right and left.

Then the three regiments under Colonel Douglas, Lord George Paget, and Colonel Shewell went on. The undisabled numbered now about 230, of which but 170 were in any order.

Oddly enough, the Russian cavalry fell back before them. The few beat back the many; the hinder regiments were accomplishing what the front line had begun. Crippled, shattered, and ravaged, the Light Brigade was wresting victory out of one of the most heinous blunders ever committed in war. To make that victory complete, they only wanted fresh troops.

Lord Lucan had followed with the Heavies for some distance. But—wisely or not—he refused to fling his second brigade after the first. When, as he led, he looked back and saw the Greys and Royals already amid the cross-fire, he halted his squadrons. " They have sacrificed the Light Brigade," he said ; " they shall not the Heavy, if I can help it."

Keeping his men halted, he saw Lord Cardigan and his men fade into the smoke at the end of the valley. It was a disruption—a denial of support that it must have been hard to make. Lord Lucan was no coward. He had generous feelings, too. On the whole, it must have been harder for him to decide as he

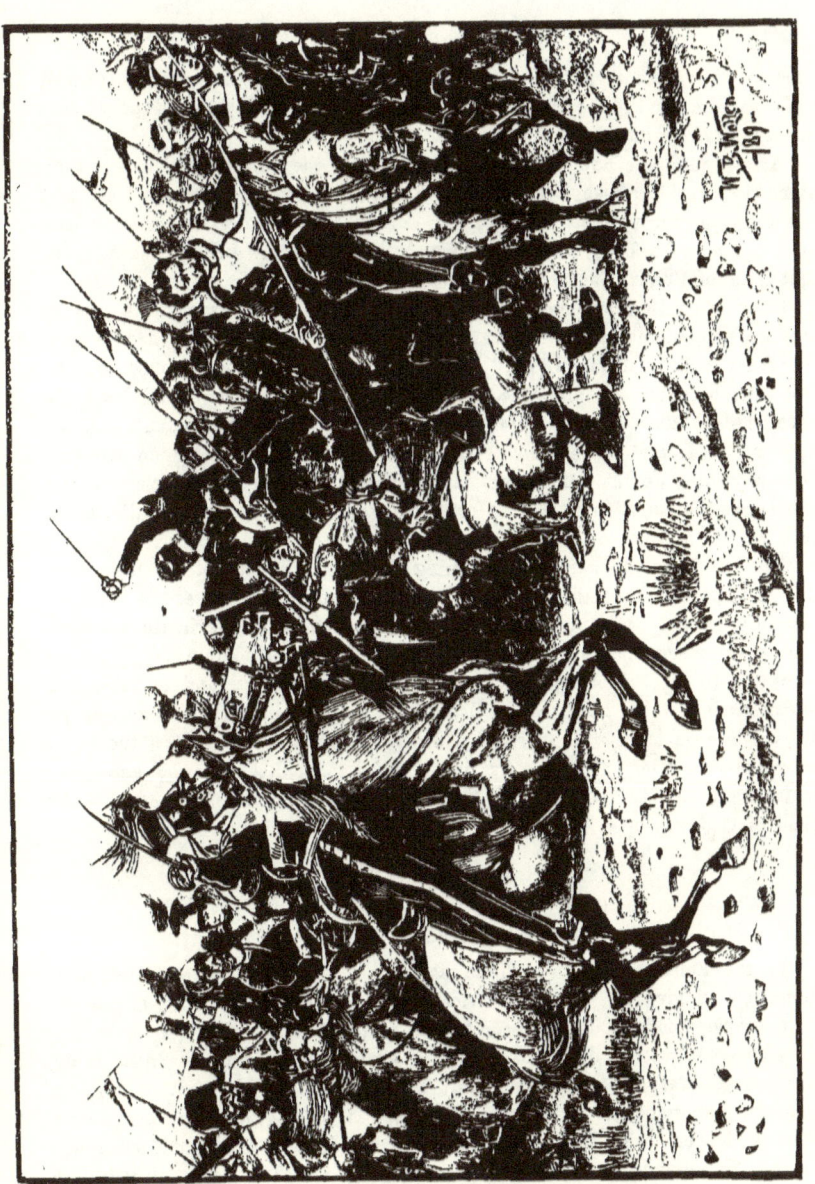

"HE LED THEM AGAINST THE RUSSIAN CAVALRY" (p. 16).

deemed right than to follow where Lord Cardigan was leading; and it seemed right to him to keep back the Heavies to protect the Light Brigade against pursuit on their return.

At any rate, the now victorious handful down the valley could look for no other support. Cardigan, by this time, in the confusion had lost his men and was returning through the battery; but Colonel Shewell, now the senior officer, in command of a body of seventy men, looking suddenly behind, found three squadrons of Russian lancers forming in his rear.

Of his duty in this emergency he did not doubt. Reluctant as he was to give up his pursuit of the now retreating masses of Russians, he had to give the order " Right about wheel! " His men faced round, and looked for the first time back towards the Allied camp. Then with the Colonel and Major de Salis in front they galloped straight for the three squadrons—seventy against three hundred—and drove them to right and left in rout. Seeing no relieving force anywhere up the valley, and having cleared a retreat for themselves and the rest of the Light Brigade, they continued their direction up the valley again back to the camp.

The 4th Dragoons were also returning from their pursuit of the foe. Lord George Paget, too, was retiring, having once faced about and checked the Russians that now in their turn were pursuing, when he too discovered, in the distance, a body of lancers flanking his line of retreat—a double column of squadrons —that is to say, a formation with two squadrons abreast, and at least two squadrons in depth. Lord George determined to dash past them, and this he did, warding off lance with sabre—for luckily the Russians were upon the right or sword-arm, side. " We got by them," wrote an officer; " how, I know not. It is a mystery to me. . . . There is one explanation, and one only—the hand of God was upon us! "

XI.

" Then they rode back, but not,
Not the Six Hundred."

In the limits to which such an account as this must be restricted, it is impossible to give any but the haziest picture of this fatal charge during its later developments. But the magnificence of the feat, the desperate gallantry, the hopeless miracle of devotion—all this is an heirloom which the British army, and indeed every British citizen, must continue to rate high. With lapse of time the importance of the Crimean struggle is gaining its right perspective. It is no longer to be reckoned with such campaigns as those of Marlborough in the Netherlands, or Wellington in the Peninsula. The Battle of Balaclava is, we now see, in most respects unworthy to be rated beside Blenheim and Vittoria; but it stands unique in one respect—the exhibition of personal valour by our cavalry.

As the wreck of what twenty minutes before had been the superb Light

Brigade came straggling back to the first muster on the slope that looks towards Balaclava, Lord Cardigan rode up to his troopers. "Men," he said, "it is a mad-brained trick, but it is no fault of mine." "Never mind, my lord," the men called out; "we are ready to go again!" "No, no, men! you have done enough."

There is no fear that we shall ever hold it less than enough. Of the 673 horsemen who rode down the valley, the first muster revealed but a mounted strength of 195. The 13th Light Dragoons consisted now of ten troopers only. Later, it was found that 247 men had been lost to the brigade; and that of the chargers 475 were killed and 42 wounded. By far the greater number of casualties had occurred in the ride down the valley. We have all heard how stern soldiers on the heights of the Chersonese burst into tears as they saw this noble body of men plunge into destruction; we have heard, too, how Lord Raglan afterwards described the onset as "perhaps the finest thing ever attempted." But the judgment which has lasted, and which will continue to prevail, is contained in the sentence uttered at the time by the French General Bosquet on the heights of the Chersonese. So exact is it that it has passed into a byword—"C'est magnifique · mais ce n'est pas la guerre."

THE STORY OF "DOC."

COAL-DUST, cinders, oil, and smoke, usually make 'firemen' (stokers) on duty rather grimy-looking personages. Perhaps few among the thousands of passengers who ride in the railroad cars behind us would care for our acquaintance. But we are useful—as useful perhaps as any other class of men; and certainly we have our full share of the hard disagreeable things in life, including frequent peril and much exposure to weather.

"Working up from fireman to engine-driver—or engineer, as we are usually

"'SHAN'T YOU JUMP, DOC?'" (p. 22).

called in America—is often a slow process. There are men on our line—the Hudson River R. R.—who have been firing eleven years with no promotion yet, though they are no doubt fully competent to run an engine; for promotion depends almost wholly upon vacancies occurring, or some special influence at headquarters.

"A man ought to be thoroughly familiar with a locomotive in eleven years. I thought that I knew every screw of mine after firing two years. Yet it takes a good deal of time to learn to fire well, so as to get the most steam out of the least fuel, and have the highest pressure at the grades where it is most needed. To do this, a man should know the road, every rod of it, as well as the engine.

"It is while 'firing' that the practical knowledge of running an engine is gained. A fireman is the groom, so to speak, of the 'iron horse.' He must, morning or evening, have the engine polished, 'fired up,' and ready for his superior, the engineer, to step into the cab and start off. Usually the engineer does not make his appearance till the moment of connecting with the train.

"When I began to fire under 'Doc' Simmons, I scarcely knew enough to build a good fire in a cook-stove, and could not have found a quarter of the oil-caps. I must have been a trial to him the first week or two. But he never gave me a sharp word, though he often had to tell me things over and over again.

"'Doc,' as the railway men all called him, was a superior engineer. He knew every pound of metal in a locomotive; just where it lay, and how much it was good for. He was one of those men who seemed to feel just what there is in a locomotive the moment he takes hold of the levers and starts up. He was a good-hearted fellow, and always had a pleasant word or joke all along the line; and it is generally the case that such men do not fail the company or the public at a critical moment.

"I went home and cried like a baby the day 'Doc' was killed. If it had been my own father, I could not have felt half as badly. I actually wished that I had gone to the bottom of the river with him.

"It was the night of the 6th of February, and fearfully cold. We had 'No. 117' then, and took out the Pacific Express, as it was called, from New York City up the line to Albany. It was a bitter night, and the line was frosty and slippery.

"The express was always a heavy train. That night we had three baggage and express cars, and eight passenger coaches; and we were late out of New York, to begin with—about fifteen minutes, I think.

"Such cold weather is always demoralising to a railroad. It is much harder to make time; all metal works badly; and though the fire appears to burn brighter, it takes more coal to make steam. The train seems to hang to the line. Then, too, the cutting wind is enough to freeze the marrow in a man's bones.

"It might have been mostly fancy on my part, but I thought 'Doc' had an odd look in his face that night as he got into the cab. He was more serious than usual, for we both knew that we had a hard run before us, and a cold one. Both of us were muffled up in fur caps and old overcoats.

"'Shove in the coal, Nick, and shake her down smart. We want every ounce of steam to-night,' says Doc. 'Fifteen minutes behind, and eleven cars on! Those sleeping-coaches are as heavy as a whole block, too. I'm glad this is a double-track line, and all clear ahead.'"

"We pulled out, and from the way Doc handled her I knew that he meant to pick up that fifteen minutes if it was in the old machine to do it. I suppose we made thirty-five miles an hour, perhaps forty, on the level stretches.

"On we went, reeling off the dark bleak miles, with the sharp wind cutting into the cab, till near New Hamburg Station, where the line then crossed Wappinger Creek on a trestle-bridge which had a 'draw' in it. It was a comfort to think that the draw would certainly not be open on such a night—for the creek was frozen up—and that there would be no delay there.

"Ah! if it were only permitted to train-men to know just what is ahead on the tracks on these bitter black nights! But we can only see what the head-lights show us; and often the signals seem strangely obscure in a fog, or in the driving rain and snow.

"One of those always possible 'breaks' which may not occur for years, but are yet constantly liable to happen, had occurred that night. One of the south-bound night freight-trains, running down to New York, broke an axle, and got one of its middle cars off the rails before reaching the bridge.

"How far they dragged the car in that condition no one knows, for it was so cold that the conductor and all the brakemen were huddled in the caboose behind. But they found it out after a time, and slowed down just as the train got on to the bridge.

"As they came to a standstill, two or three other cars jumped the track; and one of these, an oil-car, with a long tank on it, broke its couplings and was shoved over on the up-line of track—*our line*—where it stood sidewise across the rails.

"The accident made great confusion with the men on the freight, but they claimed that they got out their signal lanterns as soon as they could, and that it was not a minute before we came up.

"As we shot along past the dark station, and out towards the bridge, I saw the white steam of the freight train.

"'We shall pass No. 19 right by the bridge,' Doc said.

"Both of us were looking, Doc on his side and I on mine.

"Suddenly, right ahead, we saw a red lantern swinging on our track, at the end of the bridge.

"'God save us, Doc!' I shouted; 'the draw's open!'

"'Spring the patent brake,' he said to me—that was what we called the air-brake then—and in a moment we had shut off, reversed, and whistled for the hand-brakes.

"But we were going at a great speed. In a moment more we had come alongside the freight engine, and out on the bridge we saw the oil-car right across our rails. It had a look of death in it. I swung out on the step.

"'Shan't you jump, Doc?' I cried.

"He stood with his back to me, looking ahead, but turned when I called out. I never shall forget that last look he gave me. He did not speak, but his look seemed to say, 'Yes, you may as well jump, but I must stick to my post.'

"He barely looked round to me, but made no answer, then looked ahead again.

"Then I jumped, went heels over head along the side of the embankment leading to the bridge, rolled over and over, and landed down on the ice of the creek near the abutment, which I had scarce touched when I heard the crash as our engine struck the oil-car.

"With the collision came a sudden brilliant flash of light. Everything above me, the whole bridge and the cars on it, seemed wrapped in a blaze of fire!

"At the same instant, too, there was a dull, long, tearing crash! The trestle had given way beneath the strain.

"Down came our engine, the three baggage-cars, a passenger-car, and I don't know how many freight-cars of the other train, on to the ice. The whole wreck, as it fell down, seemed enveloped in flames; for the oil had splashed over everything, and the blazing coals from the fire-box exploded it on the instant.

"When the engine struck the ice, it broke through, and with a hiss went to the bottom of the deep water there, and on top of it came tumbling down all the other cars.

"For a moment following the crash there was an almost complete silence, then agonising screams and prayerful cries for help from the imprisoned passengers.

"We who were not disabled did what we could. The seven rear cars did not run into the chasm, but two of them burned on the track, along with a number of freight-cars. Twenty-one of the passengers were killed outright, and a still greater number were injured.

"As we worked there in the noise, heat, and awful confusion of that night, I cast many an anxious glance round for Doc, hoping and half expecting that he had got clear and would be at work with us trying to get out the passengers. But I saw nothing of him, and by daybreak I felt sure that he had gone down with his engine.

"The locomotive was not hauled up out of the water till the next week. Then we found his body, jammed down under the engine on the bed of the creek. His hands, face, and clothes had been scorched, but whether he was drowned or burned to death we could not tell.

"He had met death at the post of duty, gone out of the world with his hand on the lever, giving his own life that the lives of others might be saved —a man of whom any people may be proud."

THE FALLS OF THE MISSOURI.

THE STORY OF A FLOOD.

VALLEY OF THE MISSOURI, 1881.

IT is not often that the newspaper-reader is deeply moved by the heading "Terrible Catastrophe in America." Our sentiments have a perspective of distance, and we are—selfishly, but very naturally —apt to be stirred by a fit of hysterics next door far more acutely than by the engulfing of a town or swamping of a territory on the other side of the Atlantic. We lazily put down our *Times* or *Daily News* and remark that "they do things on a big scale over there;" which tribute being paid, we dismiss the subject.

Now and then, however, an appalling catastrophe wakens us out of this state of easy acquiescence. The burning of Chicago is a notable instance; and now (in 1889) our ears are still tingling with the awful tale of Johnstown. While they are, it may be that some melancholy interest will attach to the story of another great flood; or, rather, to a re-read page in the history of the wide ruin which, just eight years ago, swept down the valley of the Missouri.

Imagine, then, on the Nebraska bank of that wide stream a slight framehouse standing in a grove of large trees that spread beside the river. Behind, a level stretch of cultivated fields, which, dark brown at the time of ploughing, and deep in corn towards the summer, reach up the valley not far above high-water mark. The pastures by the water-side are green and well stocked, and nothing troubles the prosperous farmer but the thought of the spring

"IZAH WAS DANGLING IN MID-AIR" (p. 30).

freshets. Are these wide lands safe in case of flood? The oldest settlers affirm that they have known floods in the Missouri before now, yet have never seen this tract quite submerged; and Mr. Wilson (that is the farmer's name) can safely say that all his experience confirms them.

By the spring of 1881 these misgivings have grown very hazy indeed—so hazy that though he hears of gigantic snowfields in the mountains by the River Plate, that, melting, must in time sweep down into the Missouri, he is not particularly troubled. The river is already swollen very nearly to the high-water line; but this is not serious enough to prevent his starting off one morning with his wife for the nearest railroad town, where he has some pressing business. The town is thirty miles off; so the farmer and his wife intend to sleep the night there and return on the following day.

Mrs. Wilson took her youngest child with her. The frame-house was left in charge of Henry, a boy of fifteen, who promised faithfully to look after the rest of the family—two little daughters, Izah and Jennie, of ten and six years old. To help him in the necessary work of the farm-buildings there was a "hired man," Rudolph by name. This Rudolph, however, had relatives near —a mile or two back from the river—to whose house he had been invited that night. And as soon as the work of the day was over he left Henry in charge alone.

"I'm just going over to look up the folks," he explained.

"How soon will you be back?"

"Oh! I don't mean to be long. Look out for me about ten."

Henry was an independent boy. He had been left alone of an evening before this, and did not mind it in the least. So he watched Rudolph striding away across the fields, and turned to amuse his sisters till bed-time.

They had "a good time," telling tales and speculating on the presents their parents would bring home to them. Izah chose a doll, Jennie a picture-book "with giants inside," and Henry elected for a "real" derringer—"that would kill a man," he explained, "if he came foolin' round." As it was, he had an old fowling-piece, and there was his father's gun hanging by the chimney; so that he felt quite able to cope with robbers and such cattle should any come "foolin' around" before Rudolph returned, which was unlikely.

The children, in fact, went off to bed by nine o'clock; and within ten minutes all three were sleeping a perfectly tranquil and fearless sleep.

Henry awoke to find the sun already up and shining in at the window. Running to the door he called for Rudolph, as was his father's custom.

No Rudolph answered.

"Rudolph! Rudolph! The fellow can't be sleeping still. More likely he's dressed and out doing the chores," thought the boy. To make sure, he called again.

It was odd. There seemed to be a roaring sound, quite continuous, in his ears this morning. His own voice sounded faint beside it. The family in that frame-house, accustomed for years to the noise of the river, now no longer noticed it. It had become a part of their life. "Something wrong with my head," thought the boy; and then—"No; it's the river, I do b'lieve. What's the matter with it this morning, anyway? It sounds as if it was all round and round us. Goodness, if it is!"

He ran to the window, and saw a sight that brought his heart up with a jerk. All around was water—water spread all over the pastures, the cornfields, the fences; swirling round the trunks of the great trees, hiding the stockyard, rushing past in one wide, foaming, turbid torrent. Dotted here and there he saw the heads of the cattle as they were borne past, battling piteously; then the floating carcases of other cattle from higher up the river; then a jumble of logs, branches, and barrels and splintered wood, that spun round like a great raft as the flood hurried it along. There were tall trees, too, torn up by their roots, and huge lumps of white ice from the mountains, and then the battered roof of a house, sailing dismally down.

The terrified boy thrust his head out at the window and looked down. The foundations of the frame-house stood well above the cattle-yards, but already the doorsteps were under water, and the angry waves furrowing and eating away the earth around. It seemed to melt like snow before them. It dawned on him that their safety was a matter of minutes.

At first the knowledge petrified him. He stood as if rooted beside the window, his eyes glued to the work of devastation, watching the waves surging higher and higher, the gutters broadening, the soil running down and mingling with the flood. Then, at last, tearing himself away from the fascinating horror, he ran to the door and shouted "Rudolph! Rudolph!" again and again. Again no Rudolph answered. But now from their room his little sisters came running out in their night-gowns. They had been awakened by his screams; had heard the loud roaring; had looked out of their windows and seen the same awful sight; and now they clung to him, crying and sobbing.

"Rudolph!—Where is Rudolph?"

The sight of helplessness even greater than his own braced the boy somewhat. He told them to run and dress as quickly as they could, and ran downstairs to see how high the water had risen.

He dashed into the kitchen. Already big pools were gathering on the floor, the water gushing up through every chink and crack. Even while he looked, it rose fast—rose till the boards were covered—rose till the legs of the table and chairs were an inch deep. It seemed to rob him of all power of thought, this stealthy unrelenting force, gathering and growing to destroy him. It seemed he must stand there and wait till the flood rose up—up—until it swallowed him. "Father!" he cried once, and then leant back in the doorway with the stream pouring round his ankles.

"Thud!" It was the sound of a big ice-cake bumping outside against the door, and it roused him. *Thud! thud!* He pulled himself up, though his knees were still trembling, dashed the weak tears from his eyes, and tried to think.

How was it possible, without Rudolph's help, to save his little sisters and himself? He waded across to the kitchen window and looked out. Just before it stood a huge elm-tree, and under the shade of it a grindstone. The trunk was but six or seven feet from the doorstep—a giant elm, about sixteen feet in girth. Against it now the flood was surging and beating. The grindstone had gone—overturned and now covered by the waters.

In an instant the boy's mind was made up; his plan was conceived.

The old elm had many thick out-reaching branches, and one of the largest of these stretched well over a corner of the kitchen roof. This roof was flat, and built out from the first storey of the house, so that from the second-storey windows one could step straight out upon it. Time upon time had the boy got on to the roof, straddled the branch, and pulled himself along to the stem. From the fork where the branch joined it, one could even climb to the top of the tree, though it was only once or twice he had done so, and then with his heart in his mouth.

"The old elm is the thing," he thought to himself. "If only we can get among the big limbs! No flood will dig the old tree up, even if it sweeps away the house. But how about Izah and Jennie?"

This was the question. A boy could climb the tree well enough, though even for him, with that giddy water eddying and swirling underneath, it would be no pleasant job to climb along the branch. But for a little girl of six? She would grow dizzy and tumble, to a certainty. It was not a new sensation to him to pity a girl as a poor creature that couldn't climb a tree; but his pity now was of another kind altogether to that which he had felt before.

In another moment his plan was worked out.

Wading across the kitchen floor, where the water now reached nearly to his knees, he gained the wood-shed, and there equipped himself with an old door, a clothes-line, a coil of thicker rope, and a pile of old boards that were stacked against the corner. Slipping the coils of rope over his neck, he shouldered the door and the boards, and waded back across the kitchen again.

At the top of the stairway his sisters were now standing, dressed, and wailing for their father and mother. The boy tottered up with his burden.

"Now look here, Izah and Jennie," he said; "the first thing of all is to stop crying. Pap's coming back, you bet, as soon as ever he can get a boat. I guess he'd ha' been here before now, only boats, you see, would nat'rally be rather hard to get, these times. But he's coming all right; and till he comes I'm goin' to look after this family. Now just you listen: you don't see a flood like this every day, and so we're goin' to get up on the big elm and build a house there, so's we can watch this thing properly—see it *out*, I mean. We'll be safe enough there. The water isn't going to say much to *that* tree; it's stood there hundreds and hundreds of years, and you don't think it's goin' to take much account of a flood—eh? So what you've got to do is to bustle about and find something to eat up there. What's the use of girls if they can't look after the larder?"

With this, he pushed the old door and the loose boards out on the kitchen roof. His sisters, catching some of his courage, now began to hurry about and help. Making another descent to the kitchen, where by this time the water was waist-high, he managed to secure a smoked ham, some dried beef, and some loaves of bread. A second visit gave him a panful of dough-nuts and some more loaves. As he brought these safely up the stairs, he met

Izah and Jenny laden with a pile of blankets that they had pulled off the beds. Henry judged that this was enough in the way of provision.

He now helped his sisters out on to the flat roof, tied the clothes-line about his waist, and climbed out along the branch to the trunk of the tree. It was dizzier work than he had ever found it before; and the rushing water, twenty feet below, seemed to tempt him to fall. But his heart was now nerved. He climbed up till he found a place where two stout branches forked out close beside each other, and then turned to his sisters.

ON THE PLATFORM (p. 32).

Before starting he had told them carefully what they were to do; so now when he had uncoiled the rope from his waist and flung the end to them they at once caught it and securely tied it to the old door.

The door was pulled up, the rope untied and again flung. One after another, in this way, the boards and the remaining coils of rope were hauled up by the boy. When this was done, he set to work laying the boards across the fork of the tree, parallel and close to one another, and fastening them at either end with his rope securely to the branches. At the end of twenty minutes he had rigged up thus a rough platform, about eight feet square, and quite large enough for them all to sit or lie upon.

It was now the turn of the food and the blankets, which were soon safe on the platform. But there still remained the gravest question of all. How was he to get his little sisters up to this giddy height?

He had kept the longest and strongest of the ropes with this purpose in view.   But he must hurry, for now the masses of ice are thundering against the frame-house, gathering against it and pounding with every wash of the flood, so that it seems as if the frail timbers can hardly hold out another five minutes.

Looping one end of his stout rope around the branch, he flings the other to the children, shouting to them to catch and hold it for a minute.   His voice is scarcely heard above the roar of the waters.   By this time, too, the little ones, dismally terrified by the shaking and quivering of the whole building, are sobbing again and almost helpless.   Once, twice, three times, the rope is flung.   Twice they miss it; the third time they catch it, but it slips from between their fingers and dangles over the water.   But the fourth time they clutch and hold it.   What is the next step?

The boy climbs down to the branch below, straddles it, and is soon across and on the roof again.   Firmly tying the end of the rope round Izah, he is off again and climbing back to his old position on the platform.   But now comes the real work.

Unlooping his end of the rope from the branch, he winds it twice round his wrist, kneels down where his knees can get a good grip of the boards, shuts his teeth, and pulls.   A scream is the answer; but soon Izah is off the roof and dangling in mid-air.   She is a plump little girl, and the tension on the boy's arms is far more than he looked for.   The sweat breaks out all over him, his knees tremble, his arms are almost pulled out of their sockets; but he holds on, and with short quick breath manages to tug hand over hand at the rope until Izah, sobbing and screaming still, is high enough to catch hold of the jutting boards, and in a moment he has her safe.

Now it is Jennie's turn.   Again the end is looped; again the boy is scrambling across the branch; again he gains the roof; and, having fastened Jennie to the rope, again returns.

Jennie is four years younger than Izah, but, all the same, she is heavier. But now there are two to help with the pulling.   It is two minutes at least, though, before they have the youngest safe beside them, for by this time the boy is almost tired out.   At length they are safe together—for the moment, at least; and he turns to look at the house.

The waves are steadily rising, and are now lapping at the kitchen window-sills.   A brief terrifying thought flashes across the boy's brain.   What if the waters should in time rise right over the roof and up the tree to the platform on which they are resting?   But, no; their perch is surely too high.   He does not breathe this fear to the girls.   They are trembling now, worse than ever.   The excitement has passed, and despair is taking its place.

Fearing that they might tumble off the platform, Henry now managed to tie them to the tree behind, leaving them enough rope to allow them to move about.   And so the three sat, scanning the waters desperately, and finding no boat in sight, no chance of succour.

Faster came the flood, driving more lumps of ice against the elm, and jarring its old trunk till it shook to the roots. Great logs of drift-wood were crashing into the windows of the house; around, a few of the cattle were still swimming, lowing all the time most pitiably—and these were the most agonising sounds of all. Though the boy kept it to himself, gradually it was borne in upon him that no help would come, that no boat could venture across amid the ice and rushing timber. It would be shivered to matchwood. There was no hope; no outlook—but to perish.

So resistless seemed the water that he began to doubt for the old elm itself. It quivered wofully from time to time. The mere fact of being helpless there, of simply sitting and looking at the curling eddies below, and the blank lake around, at last began to work upon the boy's nerves. The monotony was torture. He felt that he must *do something*, or go mad. At first he busied himself about the platform, setting their small stores in order, arranging and re-arranging a dozen times. Then, growing weary of this, he looked down towards the house, and began to consider if it were possible to make one or two more journeys there, to save the bedding and the furniture. For if only he dared to venture, he saw that much of the household stuff might be hung or tied to the branches of the elm. Izah and Jennie would be able to pull some of it up to the platform, if only he went across and descended into the building. It was worth trying.

But, on second thoughts, no; it was not worth the risk. At any moment the house, already shattered and rocking, might be swept wholly away. And if he should chance to be on it at the time, who would look after the little girls? There was nothing for it but to sit mournfully and watch. Indeed, it began to dawn upon him that, for his life, he *could* not cross that branch again.

Instead, to employ himself, he proposed to the little ones that they should continue telling the stories that they broke off last night when they went to bed. And Izah and Jennie being too frightened to tell any coherently, he invented a wonderful tale, mixing it up with the story of Noah and the Ark, of a terrific flood, and a family that had taken shelter in a tree, and tied themselves there like "ponies picketed out to grass," and all their adventures, and how the father and mother of the family came at last in boats and rescued the little ones. And desperately through a whole hour he dragged the story out, to cheat his companions of their present terror, and only stopped at length to suggest that he was hungry, and they might as well eat; and, as they were housekeeping on their own account now, Izah should be cook, and Jennie parlour-maid; and then again dragged out the meal to an unconscionable length, while all the time his own heart kept sinking lower and lower.

And so long did the meal continue, that by the end the girls had eaten quite a large amount, notwithstanding their desperate plight, and rose to "wash away" (ominous term!) with quite a glow of courage in their little hearts. ·

And the long morning passed, and the longer afternoon drew towards sundown. By this time the waters had crept to the top of the second-floor windows of the house, and were still rising. Yet the house stood. And the ponderous lumps of ice kept pounding and crashing at the tree. Yet that, too, stood; and, though it nodded with each blow, never cracked.

Once they thought they heard the sounds of shouting, far away. Henry strained his ears, but could make nothing of it. Night drew on; he wrapped the blankets around his sisters, and lay down on the boards again to watch— to watch with all his eyes during the short half-hour that was yet to elapse before darkness should cover the face of the earth.

Still he saw water—nothing but water: saw no boat, nor heard any shouting. Night came without succour. And now there was blackness all around, and the sound of the water—monotonous, cruel, insatiable—eternally in his ears. The girls had cried themselves to sleep, their heads resting on their brother's knees. The boy could not close an eye; and so through the night, as through the greater part of the day, he sat listening to the roar around, bending his ear to catch the steady breathing of Izah or Jennie, and hoping on, against hope.

Soon after dark he heard a crash below him, louder than any before. The foundations of the house had given way at last. In the glimmering darkness he saw the whole building melt away, and vanish headlong down the stream.

Then came Egyptian gloom for hours, and at last, with a premonitory chill, the cold bleak paling of the dawn. As the sky passed slowly through the innumerable shades that divide black from grey, and grey from blue, Henry saw of all the old familiar landmarks not one, except the tree-tops. Even of the trees, many smaller ones had been crushed and broken by the masses of ice. Their downfall, one by one, had broken the night into intervals as a city clock chiming the hours.

The little girls opened their eyes. They had been dreaming; were again, in imagination, in the cosy room that now had vanished for good and all. They awoke, expecting to see again the familiar furniture, the well-known pictures and texts on the wall. It was a bitter moment as the truth broke on them.

The boy bent down, haggard and desperate himself, to cheer them and wipe their tears away.

"Hark! What was that?"

It was the sound of shouting. Or was it a trick of the fancy? No, indeed, it was no trick; for now, peering between the tree-tops, the boy could spy a boat cautiously picking its way towards them among the floating logs and ice-cakes. There were half a dozen forms in the boat, and, yes, there was Rudolph, standing up in the bows, waving to them. The boy stood up, waving a blanket madly in reply; and then, sinking upon the platform, broke into that flood of weeping which now for twenty-four hours he had repressed.

The neighbours had seen them the day before—had shouted—and had worked for many hours, without success, to get a boat across to them amid the floating ice. In the morning, looking out, they had, to their great joy, seen that the small trio were still safe and sound upon the platform. By this time the ice-cakes, the logs, and drifting trees were fewer. The rescuers put off with better hope.

Within an hour the plucky boy and his two sisters were safe within the boat, and moving slowly, but cautiously, towards firm ground.

Mr. and Mrs. Wilson, knowing nothing of the flood, had lengthened their absence till the evening of the same day; nor did they know anything of their children's peril till they found the three, safe and well, in the house of a hospitable friend.

"A BOAT CAUTIOUSLY PICKING ITS WAY" (p. 32).

A LEAP FOR LIFE.

N the August of 1854 I quitted the mounted police force of Victoria, and entered that of New South Wales. I do not know why I took this step; perhaps it was that yearning after "fresh fields and pastures new" which seems to be an instinct of human nature. Anyhow, one bright spring morning I found myself on board the steamship *Illawarra*, clearing the calm blue waters of Hobson's Bay (the largest harbour in the known world), with Queen's Cliff and Point Nepean some three miles ahead, and beyond them the snow-crested waves of Bass's Straits.

I shall not inflict upon my readers a narrative of my voyage, which, if barren in incident, was full enough of discomfort and misery. I was a second-cabin passenger, and the sea was so rough during the entire voyage that after tumbling into my bunk when off Cape Patterson, I never emerged from it until, forty-five hours later, we entered Port Jackson Bay, and consequently were in calm water.

It was about six o'clock in the evening when I landed at Sydney. I immediately hastened to report myself at headquarters, where the letters of introduction and commendation from the officers of the Victorian force, of which I was the bearer, had due weight. I was politely requested to attend the following morning at ten o'clock, in order to be sworn in. This I accordingly did; the ceremony was duly performed, and I retired to the barracks to don my new uniform and hold myself ready for orders.

I was destined not to have a long stay in Sydney, for the very morning following my admission into the force I was ordered for out-station duty, and received instructions to start at once, in company with another trooper younger than myself, for a place called Dunewatha, which lay at some distance on the other side of the Blue Mountains, and was a good three days' journey from the metropolis.

It was nine a.m. when we received our orders, and by eleven we were in the saddle and descending Elizabeth Street at a trot. We turned round Hyde Park Corner into Paramatta Street, and in another quarter of an hour the straggling suburbs of the city were left in our rear.

It was a most unpleasant day. A regular brickfielder* was blowing, and even before we had cleared the town our white shako-covers and snowy buckskin breeches were powdered thickly with reddish dust, which the furious

* Hot wind.

north-west wind, hot as the breath of a furnace, blew against our faces with such force as to cause intolerable pain; while the fine gritty sand would penetrate eyes, ears, and nostrils with a persistency anything but agreeable. The thermometer, when we left Sydney, marked 115 degrees in the sun; and as that luminary rose higher and higher in the pale, steel-grey, cloudless sky, the intensity of its rays became more and more unbearable. I tried to picture the verdant pastures, shady woods, and rippling streams of England, but that rendered the sufferings I endured still more unpalatable.

It was too hot to talk, and. my mate was as glum and discontented as myself; and so we slowly trotted along the solitary bush-road, silently and spectre-like, our poor horses black with sweat, their heads drooped, and their tails as limp as a shirt-collar without starch. Around us the straw-coloured vegetation was unvaried by the slightest tint of green, and the tall white trunks of the gum-trees, with their scanty vertical foliage, mingled with sombre peppermint and stringy bark, formed about as dreary a scene as it is possible to imagine.

As to the road we were travelling, they talk of *corduroy* roads in America, but I should like to show a Yankee a mile or two of the one we that day travelled over. Imagine a stony plain, the surface entirely covered with large swampy holes, filled with water, slush, and glutinous mud; then throw into these hollows a number of angular blocks of stone, half concealed by the muddy waters; and let mud and water turn into dust (twelve hours will in New South Wales effect the metamorphosis), and you will have a faint conception of our road. At length the scrub on either side grew less thickly, and we gladly quitted the rugged path for the open country. We had not ridden on for more than a couple of miles, however, congratulating ourselves that we had bidden farewell to dust, if not to heat, when a far greater annoyance than either befell us. This arose from the pertinacious attentions of the sand-flies, which are a kind of midge—small filmy things, like the midges at home, but much more lively, bloodthirsty, and venomous. They were as numerous as the grains of sand in the sterile Iron Bark ranges. They covered the whole ground for miles, and as we advanced, would rise up and get on our horses' legs and chests, puncturing them in such a manner that their legs were completely covered in a few minutes with blood. The poor animals of course became quite frantic, not being able to brush them off. It was often no trivial matter to keep one's seat, owing to their rearing and kicking from the pain. My mate told me in another month the birds would have eaten the midges up; it was only in spring they were so numerous. The effect of the bite on man is much worse than on horses. Wherever they bite, the part swells excessively, and becomes a great livid boil as large as a walnut. He had been bitten on the wrist the preceding spring, when riding on the banks of the Murray. The next day his hand was swelled enormously; it settled into one of those boils which are very sluggish and difficult to cure. It was not well, in fact, for a month, and would not heal till treated with caustic. Another, only a month ago, had bitten his other hand; the venomous puncture had gone exactly through the same process. As a proof of his words, he showed me a scar on each hand, which no doubt would never wear away.

About midday we reached a creek, where we watered and bathed our horses, to their great relief, and on whose banks we encamped to eat luncheon. It was a lovely spot; on account of the moisture the grass was green, and adorned with myriad-tinted flowers, while forty miles in our front rose the purple peaks of the Blue Mountains. Close to where we sat grew some grass-trees, but only dwarf ones, splendidly in flower. The flower is on a rod of two or three feet high, which rises perpendicularly from the centre of the tree, and surrounds some half a yard of it in the manner of the flower of the club-rush, but white, and the florets resemble those of the water tussilago.

During our meal we were terribly persecuted by "jumping ants." They were about half an inch long, and jumped surprisingly. They were great fly-catchers, and so far proved themselves our benefactors; but we soon found that it was only one pest giving place to another. These little black flies were, even in this comparatively cool and shady spot, the most impertinent, persevering vermin possible. The moment we produced our meat from our saddle-bags, they covered it. They also managed to settle on our hands and faces, where they raised up blood-blisters, and then sucked at them till they burst. The moment the spots were raw, they thrust as many of their heads in as they could, and so continually irritated and enlarged the orifice. What was a mere scratch, became a sore under their incessant operations; and unless such sore was speedily defended by handkerchiefs or gloves, it would soon become a wound. Plaster was not enough, for they would suck and envenom the wound through it.

After we had discussed our beef and damper, enjoyed a delicious drink from the creek, and had half an hour's draw at our pipes, we remounted and resumed our journey, making another twelve miles before sunset, when we encamped for the night, unsaddled our horses, hobbled them, lit the fire, boiled some tea in our billy, and sat down to enjoy our evening meal. Then we again had recourse to our pipes, and at length rolling ourselves in our blankets and with the saddles for pillows, soon sank into slumber both sound and deep.

The second day's journey was but a repetition of the first. There is great monotony in bush-travelling. The heat, the thirst, the mosquitoes and other insects, were the same; the only difference in the scenery was that every hour the towering mountain range we had to cross seemed looming larger and mightier before us; their summits, glittering in the sunlight three thousand feet and more above the level plains we were traversing, presented only a little deeper azure tint than did the cloudless firmament above. Well did they deserve their name of Blue Mountains.

On the afternoon of the second day after leaving Sydney, we were at their

"THE ANIMAL PLUNGED HEADLONG INTO SPACE" (p. 41).

base; and upon the earnest assurance of my mate that he had crossed them at this point before, and knew every inch of the way, I consented to attempt the ascent at once, fully expecting, as it was only three o'clock and the evenings getting long, we should encamp by sunset on the western side.

We were soon riding along a steep narrow gully, with almost precipitous sides, rising in lofty ridges that were covered with loose rocks and scraggy gum-trees, charred and disfigured by frequent bush-fires. It was a dreary scene, though here and there relieved by groups of pines and other eucalypti, with the jointed horsetail foliage of the shea-oak, and the gaudy blossoms of the blue wattle, while the towering peaks of Mount Gwallior rose gloomy and cloud-wreathed above all.

"Are you sure you will find the pass, Rootes?" I asked; "because, unless you are, it would be wiser to ride a matter of twenty miles round and follow the regular waggon-track."

"Oh! I'm all right. "I know it, never fear," retorted the young trooper, with a laugh. "Why, 'tis not two years since I travelled it, man, and on my road to this very same Dunewatha, too. It saves a round of very nearly nineteen miles by crossing the mountain here."

"And is it a pretty fair road for horses all the way?" I asked.

"Why, as to that, I shouldn't care to ride an unbroken colt or a broken-kneed old coach-horse over some parts of the track; but with such nags as ours, there is no hazard. In fact, there is only one dangerous place, and that does not continue for more than half a mile or so."

"And what is the nature of the danger, mate? I am unused to mountain-scaling, and like to calculate my risks beforehand."

"The place is called 'The Devil's Ridge.' It is a passage along the side of one eminence which a cataract divides from another. It is seldom broad enough for two horses to pass each other, and often not room enough for one. It is bare of all rail or fence; in fact, it is impossible to fix any."

"And how deep is the precious precipice which this narrow pathway over-looks?" I asked nervously.

"Deep? Oh! perhaps a thousand feet; but, owing to the narrowness of the gorge, the bottom is invisible."

"And into this gulf the slightest trip of a horse would precipitate its rider —a worn shoe, a loose pebble, a nervous twitch of the rein, would be certain death?"

"Decidedly so; and I can tell you of a very curious adventure on this very same Devil's Ridge."

"The devil you can! Well, then, fire away, for you can scarcely make me more nervous than I feel already."

Rootes laughed. "It happened in this way," he said. "Two horsemen met in the narrow pass. Such a thing doubtless never occurred before, and perhaps never may again, the road is so rarely traversed; but this once it did so happen. Neither of the parties had space to back his steed, and so make room for the other to go by. They tossed up which should sacrifice his horse. It fell to the lot of the man ascending the ridge. He dismounted, pushed his horse over the precipice into the gulf below, and then, snake-like, crept between the legs of the descending horse and continued his journey on foot."

By the time my mate had concluded his story, which I have narrated in as few words as possible, we had ascended some three hundred feet of the mountain's height, and beheld a prospect of sea and land to the extent of a hundred and twenty miles. Almost beneath was a roaring cataract; to look down upon and listen to its hoarse brawl was enough to appal more daring natures than my own. Still up and up we went, the pathway having a zigzag tendency that made the ascent anything but laborious. As we attained a higher and yet a higher altitude, the change from heat to cold became very apparent; and by the time we had left the level plains some nine hundred feet below us, it was easy to imagine one's self transported from a tropical summer to a bracing northern winter.

Australian mountains differ very much in appearance from those of Europe and this difference mainly consists in their being wooded to such an altitude. In the Northern Hemisphere it is rare to find a mountain bearing trees for more than a few hundred feet of its height, whereas the hardy and sombre eucalypti of Australia and Tasmania frequently flourish to the very apex of mountains three thousand feet in altitude. This, in my opinion, although it *sometimes* gives a peculiar beauty of its own, in most cases detracts from the majesty and awe-inspiring grandeur that would otherwise distinguish the mountain ranges of Australia, while to the eye it decreases the effect of their height by at least one-third.

Rootes and I spoke little during the ascent; he looked meditative, and I felt nervous, for an indescribable feeling had taken possession of me, to the effect that something terrible would happen to one or both of us before we descended to the level plain again. The very elements seemed impressed with my ill-omened forebodings, for the sky, which had been so blue and sunny when we commenced the ascent, was now flecked with heavy roofy clouds that appeared to be hurrying to a common centre; great drops of rain began to fall, and presently the dull rumble of a distant thunder-peal fell upon our ears.

"I fear we are in for a ducking, mate," said Rootes, turning in his saddle; "the rain comes down here in bucketfuls when it once begins. Thank God, our upward course is at an end, for we are at last opposite the pass. We now skirt the mountain, passing between it and its less lofty neighbour on our right. In five minutes we shall be descending the Devil's Ridge."

"And suppose our horses are startled at a thunder-clap, or shy at a lightning-flash in such a spot?" I asked.

"Why, then 'twill be a long good-night to Marmion," he answered, laughing. "But don't be afraid, friend; I think the storm will hold off for another

half hour; and if is   our horses are o d stagers and won't o fright ned in
a h_rry."

As he spoke the sky momentarily brightened, and somewhat reassured I
replied, "Well, go ahead, old fellow. You appear to know the way; and where
you lead, you won't find me far behind."

. "IT WAS A DIAMOND SNAKE" (p. 43).

We had now done with ascents, and had to round the mountain at about
half the distance to its summit, in order to descend on the opposite side. Our
peril was now about to commence. Rootes was right; in five minutes we were
on the Devil's Ridge, amidst all the horrors of perhaps the most dangerous
and terrible mountain-pass in the world.

We rode, of necessity, Indian file, Rootes at forty paces in advance. The
pathway was a yard wide, certainly never more, and often somewhat less. On
our left rose the precipitous mountain-side, a sheer cliff, to a height of at

s a thousand feet. (o. it yawned a dir ch i, apparently bottom-...s—to a depth, as I afterwards learned, of nine hundred and fifty feet; while from the bottom arose the roar c water, as though se thing and boiling from a subterranean Niagara. I do not hesitate to affirm that at any part of the pass, had I raised my arms in the shape of the letter T, the middle finger of my left hand would have touched the black cliff; and a pebble dropped perpendicularly from between the forefinger and thumb of my right would have fallen into the whirling torrent below.

Luckily the path was good, being of rough rock, without a loose stone to be seen.

Terrible and dangerous as the pass was, it seemed to instil no alarm into the breast of my companion, who in the most narrow parts would turn in his saddle to see how I was getting on. His jet-black steed stepped out as gaily and as steadily as though on a broad coach-road. Suddenly, however, just when he was traversing one of the narrowest ledges of the rock, a burst of thunder crashed through the narrow defile, and a flame of forked lightning shot and danced before his horse's eyes. The animal reared, beat the air for a moment with his fore-hoofs, and then plunged headlong into space, precipitating himself and rider into the abyss below!

In an instant—in the twinkling of an eye—horse and horseman had vanished for ever from my sight; and with my steed reined in until his haunches pressed the dark mountain-side, whilst his fore-feet were planted in the rocky path within a couple of inches of the precipice, I gazed in agony at the fathomless grave that had so remorselessly swallowed up my unfortunate companion.

How can I describe my feelings when I beheld this awful spectacle, this hapless fate of one who, a moment before, in all the pride and strength of manhood, was riding so gaily along only a few yards before me? The blood that, but a minute before, had been coursing healthfully through my veins, seemed to freeze and suspend its functions, while my brain appeared to reel about with lightness. It was a mercy that I did not lose my seat in the saddle and fall headlong after poor Jim Rootes. For at least an hour I must have remained stationary at this spot, gazing with horror-stricken yet almost imbecile stare down that dark abyss, until my heart and head seemed on fire, and I was almost a maniac; but, thank God, my reason at length returned, and I awoke to all the dangers of my own position.

I found the rain pouring down in torrents; the lightning was one continuous blaze of light; while the heavy thunder-peals, re-echoing again and again amid the mountain-peaks and stormy ravines, sounded like the roar of heavy artillery. My horse was black with sweat, and quivering with fear, as with dilated nostrils and glaring eyes he, too, gazed into the depths below him, as though terror was prompting him to essay the leap.

I saw that his fore-legs, from being kept so long in one position, were trembling, and the muscles strained. His sure-footedness was no longer to be depended upon; so, after a moment's consideration, I reined him round with his head down the pass, and freeing my feet from the stirrups, let the bridle fall loosely on his neck, and then slipped to the ground over his tail.

Even at this moment I tremble to think to what a terrible fate a kick or even the slightest movement on his part would have consigned me whilst I executed this manœuvre; as it happened, it was accomplished in safety, and I prepared to descend the ridge on foot, driving my charger before me. It was very slow progress. Sometimes the poor animal was so frightened that neither threats nor coaxings had any effect upon him, and he would stand trembling and whining most piteously for some minutes without moving a step. The rain, too, had made the rocky path slippery, and every dozen paces or so he would slip out and nearly topple over the precipice. Nevertheless, after another half-hour's torture, such as I never experienced before, and trust I never shall again, I could see the end of the Devil's Ridge about a quarter of a mile before us, and the sloping mountain-side beyond.

Hope now reanimated my bosom, and I do believe the poor horse felt it, too, for he never loitered in his advance until we were within a few yards from the end of the ridge. Then he stopped short, and no effort of mine would induce him to move forward. Not knowing the cause of this seeming obstinacy, I looked over his back at the road in front, and, to my horror and despair, perceived that a flash of lightning had cleft the solid rock, and caused some couple of yards in length of the pathway to slip into the gulf.

To scale the mountain-side was next to impossible. My horse could not do it; and to manage a clear six-foot leap without a run and in my present nervous state was a matter of no great certainty. I must, however, do this, or retrace my way along the Devil's Ridge over the path already traversed. This I could by no means make up my mind to do. Anything seemed preferable to re-crossing that terrible pass. I made up my mind to sacrifice my horse, and then essay the *leap for life!*

I could scarcely summon the heart to consign my noble charger to so terrible a doom, but his death was a necessity, and I steeled my heart for the sacrifice. I pushed him over, and with one wild shriek (for horses can shriek when in extreme terror, and the sound, though indescribable, if once heard, can never be forgotten) he disappeared from sight, though his heavy rebound from rock to rock in his descent, and ultimate dull splash into deep water at the bottom, rose plainly to my ear.

I now divested myself of my sword, belt, and coat, and threw them across the chasm; then I braced myself for the leap, keeping my eye steadily fixed upon the firm ground on the other side, and refraining from glancing below, lest I should turn giddy. At length I sprang, gained the opposite bank, but my foot slipped; I lost my balance and fell backwards, luckily clutching the spreading branches of a shrub in my descent, and thus saving myself from instant death.

Was I saved? or was it a few minutes' respite only?

The shrub to which I clung grew from out a cleft in the rock. It was about a yard below the surface. Beneath me yawned the terrible chasm that divided the two mountains. Did the branch give way, or my strength fail, I knew that I should drop like a plummet into the torrent that roared beneath me. Then arose the thought, "Could I scale the cliff, and so reach the pathway above?" Alas! one glance at the dark slippery rock, without a single excrescence to aid foot or hand, forbade the thought. Death seemed inevitable.

Suddenly I perceived a shelving cliff, upon which it might be possible to obtain a foothold. The question was, how to reach it; it was a desperate resource, even for one so fearfully situated as myself. I glanced at the base of the shrub that bore me; it appeared to be firmly rooted, and not likely to give way. The branch which I grasped was long, sinewy, and tough. The idea struck me that I might, by swaying my body to and fro, give it and the branch the momentum of a pendulum, increasing it gradually so as at last to be able to swing myself on to the shelving cliff.

This notion had scarcely occurred to my mind when a new horror appalled me. Close to the roots of the shrub two small glittering eyes met mine; their metallic lustre seemed to fascinate me. Then I saw a forked tongue, and a flat wedge-shaped head, which presently began to undulate from side to side as it approached me. The next instant I was aware of the dreadful fact that it was a diamond snake, one of the most venomous of its species; it had marked me as its victim.

My failing strength would not allow me to raise a hand to guard my face; the reptile was about to spring. At that moment a voice seemed to whisper in my ear, "The shelving rock—leap, and you are saved." As the voice prompted, so I acted: by a vigorous jerk I gave the branch a sudden impetus; two swings, and I sprang boldly from it, alighting on the jutting crag in safety.

I now clambered up the rough side of the shelving rock, an angle of which presently hid the Devil's Ridge and its dread ravine from view. Then my steps tottered, my eyes grew dim, myriads of fiery stars seemed to sparkle around me, and I fell to the ground in a swoon.

I must have lain thus for hours—yes, the whole night. When I recovered consciousness, the sun was just rising over the mountain-tops. It was a glorious morning. A thousand feet beneath spread a vast level country, with white stations dotted here and there, few and far between. I felt very weak, but was able to crawl down the mountain-side, and about an hour later reached its base. Here, happily—for I was almost dying of thirst and hunger—I came across a shepherd's hut. I stayed there the day and night. The next morning at dawn I set out for Dunewatha, and reached the out-station of mounted police, to which I was bound, about an hour before sundown.*

---

* For permission to use this story, which is told by Mr. J. S. Borlase in his "Daring Deeds," we have to thank the publishers, Messrs. Frederick Warne and Co.

VIEW OF MADRID.

A SPANISH PRISON.

(MADRID, 1838.)

THE prison of Madrid stands in a narrow street, not far from the great square. We entered a dusky passage, at the end of which was a wicket door. My conductors knocked; a fierce visage peered through the wicket; there was an exchange of words, and in a few moments I found myself within the prison of Madrid, in a kind of corridor which overlooked at a considerable altitude what appeared to be a court, from which arose a hubbub of voices, and occasionally wild shouts and cries.

Within the corridor, which served as a kind of office, were several people; one of them sat behind a desk, and to him the alquazils went up, and after discoursing with him some time in low tones, delivered the warrant into his hands. He perused it with attention; then rising, he advanced to me. What a figure! He was about forty years of age, and his height might have amounted to some six feet two inches had he not been curved much after the fashion of the letter **S**. No weasel ever appeared lanker, and he looked as if a breath of air would have been sufficient to blow him away; his face might certainly have been called handsome had it not been for its extraordinary and portentous meagreness; his nose was like an eagle's bill, his teeth white as ivory, his eyes black (oh, how black!) and fraught with a strange expression; his skin was dark, and the hair of his head like the plumage of a raven. A deep quiet smile dwelt continually on his features; but with all the quiet it was a

crı sn 'e such   ıe 8ı w lc have g ɯɜd the cou ɹnance o ɩ 'cro.
" Ma.. eɩ. ɩ .anche perɹonnɹ n'eɯiɩ plus honnéte.'

"Caballero," said he, "allow me to introduce myself to ᵧou as the alcayde
of this prison. I perceive by this paper that I am to have the honour of
your company for a time, a short time doubtless, beneath this roof; I hope you
will banish every apprehension from your mind. I am charged to treat you
with all the respect which is due to the illustrious nation to which you belong,
and which a cavalier of such exalted category as yourself is entitled to expect.
Caballero, you will rather consider yourself here as a guest than a prisoner;
you will be permitted to roam over every part of the house whenever you
think proper. You will find matters here not altogether below the attention of
a philosophic mind. Pray issue whatever commands you may think fit to the
turnkeys and officials, even as if they were your own servants. I will now
have the honour of conducting you to your apartment—the only one at present
unoccupied. We invariably reserve it for cavaliers of distinction. I am happy
to say that my orders are again in consonance with my inclination. No charge
whatever will be made for it to you, though the daily hire of it is not unfrequently an ounce of gold. I entreat you, therefore, to follow me, cavalier,
who am at all times and seasons the most obedient and devoted of your
servants." Here he took off his hat and bowed profoundly.

Such was the speech of the alcayde of the prison of Madrid: a speech .
delivered in pure sonorous Castilian, with calmness, gravity, and almost with
dignity: a speech which would have done honour to a gentleman of high
birth, to Monsieur Bassompierre of the Old Bastille receiving an Italian prince,
or the High Constable of the Tower an English duke attainted of high treason.
Now who, in the name of wonder, was this alcayde? One of the greatest rascals
in Spain. A fellow who had more than once by his grasping cupidity, and by
his curtailment of the miserable rations of the prisoners, caused an insurrection
in the court below, only to be repressed by bloodshed and by summoning
military aid: a fellow of low birth, who, only five years previous, had been
drummer to a band of royalist volunteers!

But Spain is the land of extraordinary characters.

I followed the alcayde to the end of the corridor, where was a massive
grated door, on each side of which sat a grim fellow of a turnkey. The door
was opened, and turning to the right we proceeded down another corridor,
in which were many people walking about, whom I subsequently discovered
to be prisoners like myself, but for political offences. At the end of this
corridor, which extended the whole length of the *patio*, we turned into another, and the first apartment in this was the one destined for myself. It
was large and lofty, but totally destitute of every species of furniture, with
the exception of a huge wooden pitcher, intended to hold my daily allowance
of water.

"Caballero," said the alcayde, "the apartment is without furniture, as you see.

It is already the third hour of the *tarde;* I therefore advise you to lose no time in sending to your lodgings for a bed and whatever you may stand in need of; the *navero* here shall do your bidding. Caballero, adieu, till I see you again!"

I followed his advice, and, writing a note in pencil to Maria Diaz, I despatched it by the *navero*, and then, sitting down on the wooden pitcher, I fell into a reverie, which continued for a considerable time.

Night arrived, and so did Maria Diaz, attended by two porters and Francisco, all loaded with furniture. A lamp was lighted, charcoal was kindled in the *brasero*, and the prison gloom was to a certain degree dispelled.

I now left my seat on the pitcher, and sitting down on a chair, proceeded to despatch some wine and viands, which my good hostess had not forgotten to bring with her; and, flinging myself on my bed, was soon asleep.

I shall not attempt to enter into a particular description of the prison of Madrid; indeed, it would be quite impossible to describe so irregular and rambling an edifice. Its principal features consisted of two courts, the one behind the other, intended for the great body of the prisoners to take air and recreation in. Three large vaulted dungeons or *calabozos* occupied three sides of this court, immediately below the corridors of which I have already spoken. These dungeons were roomy enough to contain respectively from one hundred to one hundred and fifty prisoners, who were at night secured therein with lock and bar, but during the day were permitted to roam about the courts as they thought fit. The second court was considerably larger than the first, though it contained but two dungeons, horribly filthy and disgusting places; this second court being used for the reception of the lower grades of thieves. Of the two dungeons one was, if possible, yet more horrible than the other; it was called the *gallineria*, or " chicken-coop," and within it every night were pent up the young fry of the prison, wretched boys from seven to fifteen years of age, the greater part almost in a state of nudity. The common bed of all the inmates of these dungeons was the ground, between which and their bodies nothing intervened, save occasionally a *manta* or horse-cloth, or perhaps a small mattress; this latter luxury was, however, of exceedingly rare occurrence.

Besides the *calabozos* connected with the courts were other dungeons in various parts of the prison; some of them quite dark, intended for the reception of those whom it might be deemed expedient to treat with peculiar severity. There was likewise a ward set apart for females. Connected with the principal corridor were many small apartments, where resided prisoners confined for debt or for political offences. And, lastly, there was a small *capilla* or chapel, in which prisoners cast for death passed the last three days of their existence in company of their ghostly advisers.

I shall not soon forget my first Sunday in prison. Sunday is the gala day of the prison—at least, of that of Madrid—and whatever robber finery is to be found within it. is sure to be exhibited on that day of holiness. There is not a set of people in the world more vain than robbers in general, more fond of cutting a figure whenever they have an opportunity, and of attracting the eyes of their fellow-creatures by the gallantry of their appearance. The famous Sheppard of olden times delighted in sporting a suit of Genoese velvet, and when he appeared in public, generally wore a silver-hilted sword at his side; whilst Vaux and Hayward, heroes of a later day, were the best-dressed men on the *pavé* of London. Many of the Italian bandits go splendidly decorated, and the very Gypsy robber has a feeling for the charms of dress. The cap alone of the Haram Pasha, or leader of the cannibal Gypsy band which infested Hungary towards the conclusion of the last century, was adorned with gold and jewels to the value of four thousand guilders. The Spanish robbers are as fond of this species of display as their brethren of other lands, and, whether in prison or out of it, are never so happy as when, decked out in a profusion of white linen, they can loll in the sun, or walk jauntily up and down.

Snow-white linen, indeed, constitutes the principal feature in the robber foppery of Spain. Neither coat nor jacket is worn over the shirt, the sleeves of which are wide and flowing; only a waistcoat of green or blue silk, with an abundance of silver buttons, which are intended more for show than use, as the vest is seldom buttoned. Then there are wide trousers, something after the Turkish fashion; around the waist is a crimson *faja* or girdle, and about the head is tied a gaudily coloured handkerchief from the loom of Barcelona; light pumps and stockings complete the robber's array. This dress is picturesque enough, and well adapted to the fine sunshiny weather of the Peninsula; there is a dash of effeminacy about it, however, hardly in keeping with the robber's desperate trade. It must not be supposed that it is every robber who can indulge in all this luxury; there are various grades of thieves—some poor enough, with scarcely a rag to cover them. Perhaps in the crowded prison of Madrid there were not more than twenty who exhibited the dress which I have attempted to describe above. These were *jente de reputacion*, tip-top thieves; mostly young fellows who, though they had no money of their own, were supported in prison by their *majas* and *amicas*—females who supplied them with the snowy linen, washed perhaps by their own hands in the waters of the Manzanares, for the display of the Sunday, when they themselves would make their appearance, dressed *à la maja*, and from the corridors would gaze with admiring eyes upon the robbers vapouring about in the court below.

Amongst those of the snowy linen who most particularly attracted my attention were a father and son; the former was a tall athletic figure of about thirty, by profession a housebreaker, and celebrated throughout Madrid for the peculiar dexterity which he exhibited in his calling. He was now in prison for a rather atrocious murder, committed in the dead of night, in a house at Cara-manchel, in which his only accomplice was his son, a child under seven years of age. "The apple," as the Danes say, "had not fallen far from the tree;" the imp was in every respect the counterpart of the father, though in miniature. He, too, wore the robber shirt-sleeves, the robber waistcoat with the silver buttons, the robber kerchief round his brow, and, ridiculous enough, a long Manchegan knife in the crimson *faja*. He was evidently the pride of the ruffian father, who took all imaginable care of this chick of the gallows; would dandle him on his knee, and would occasionally take the cigar from his own moustached lips and insert it in the urchin's mouth. The boy was the pet of the court, for his father was one of the *valientes* of the prison; and those who feared his prowess, and wished to pay their court to him, were always fondling the child. What an enigma is this world of ours! How dark and mysterious are the sources of what is called crime and virtue! If that infant wretch became eventually a murderer, like his father, is he to blame? Fondled by robbers, already dressed as a robber, born of a robber, whose own history was, perhaps, similar. Is it right?

The most ill-conditioned being in the prison was a Frenchman, though probably the most remarkable. He was about sixty years of age, of the middle stature, but thin and meagre, like most of his countrymen; he had a villainously formed head, according to all the rules of craniology; and his features were full of evil expression. He wore no hat; and his clothes, though in appearance nearly new, were of the coarsest description. He generally kept aloof from the rest, and would stand for hours together, leaning against the walls, with his arms folded, glaring sullenly on what was passing before him. He was not one of the professed *valientes*, and yet all the rest appeared to hold him in a certain awe; perhaps they feared his tongue, which he occasionally exerted in pouring forth withering curses on those who incurred his displeasure. He spoke perfectly good Spanish, and, to my great surprise, excellent Basque, in which he was in the habit of conversing with my servant Francisco, who, lolling from the window of my apartment, would exchange jests and witticisms with the prisoners in the court below, with whom he was a great favourite.

One day when I was in the *patio*, to which I had free admission whenever I pleased, I went up to the Frenchman, who stood in his usual posture, leaning against the wall, and offered him a cigar. The man glared at me ferociously for a moment, and appeared to be on the point of refusing my offer, with perhaps a hideous execration. I repeated it, however, pressing my hand against my heart, whereupon suddenly the grim features relaxed, and with a genuine French grimace and a low bow he accepted the cigar, exclaiming. "*Ah! monsieur, pardon, mais c'est faire trop d'honneur à un pauvre diable comme moi.*"

"Not at all," said I; "we are both fellow-prisoners in a foreign land, and, being so, we ought to countenance one another."

"Ah! monsieur," exclaimed the Frenchman in rapture, "you are right. *Tenez!*" he added in a whisper; "if you have any plan for escaping, and require

SUNDAY IN THE PRISON (p. 48).

my assistance, I have an arm and a knife at your service. You may trust
me, and that is more than you could any of these *sacrés gens ici*," glancing
fiercely round at his fellow-prisoners.

"You appear to be no friend to Spain and the Spaniards," said I. "I
conclude that you have experienced injustice at their hands. For what have
they immured you in this place?"

"For nothing at all—that is, for a mere *bagatelle*."

"Perhaps you are here for your opinions?"

"*Ah! mon Dieu*, no. I'm no such fool. I have no opinions. I—— But never
mind; here I am, and dying of hunger. I see by your look that you wish to
know my history. I shall not tell it you; it contains nothing remarkable."

Nothing remarkable in his history! Why, or I greatly err, one chapter
of his life, had it been written, would have unfolded more of the wild and
wonderful than fifty volumes of what are in general called adventures and hair-
breadth escapes by land and sea. A soldier! What a tale could that man
have told of marches and retreats, of battles lost and won, towns sacked,
convents plundered! Perhaps he had seen the flames of Moscow ascending
to the clouds, and had "tried his strength with Nature in the wintry desert,"
pelted by the snow-storm, and bitten by the tremendous cold of Russia; and
had plied his trade of robber in Biscay and the Landes, of which the latter is
more infamous for brigandage and crime than any other part of the French
territory.

I gave him a cigar and a dollar; he received them, and then once more
folding his arms, leaned back against the wall, and appeared to sink gradually
into one of his reveries. I looked him in the face and spoke to him, but
he did not seem either to hear or see me.

He was executed about a month from this time. The *bagatelle* for which
he was confined was robbery and murder by the following strange device :—In
concert with two others he hired a large house in an unfrequented part of the
town, to which place he would order tradesmen to convey valuable articles,
which were to be paid for on delivery; those who attended paid for their
credulity with the loss of their lives and property. Two or three had fallen into
the .snare. I wished much to have had some private conversation with this
desperate man, and in consequence begged the alcayde to allow him to dine
with me in my own apartment; whereupon Monsieur Bassompierre, for so I
will take the liberty of calling the governor—his real name having escaped my
memory—took off his hat, and, with his usual smile and bow, replied in purest
Castilian—

"English cavalier, and, I hope I may add, friend—pardon me that it is
quite out of my power to gratify your request, founded, I have no doubt, on
the most admirable sentiments of philosophy. Any of the other gentlemen
beneath my care shall, at any time you desire it, be permitted to wait upon
you in your apartment. I will even go so far as to cause their irons, if

irons they wear, to be knocked off in order that they may partake of your refection with that comfort which is seemly and convenient; but to the gentleman in question I must object; he is the most evil-disposed of the whole of this family, and would most assuredly breed a *funcion* either in your apartment or in the corridor, by an attempt to escape. Cavalier, *me pesa*, but I cannot accede to your request. But with respect to any other gentleman, I shall be most happy; even Balseiro, who, though strange things are told of him, still knows how to comport himself, and in whose behaviour there is something both of formality and politeness, shall this day share your hospitality if you desire it, cavalier."

This Balseiro was confined in an upper storey of the prison, in a strong room, with several other malefactors. He had been found guilty of aiding and assisting one Pepe Candelas, a thief of no inconsiderable renown, in a desperate robbery perpetrated in open daylight upon no less a personage than the Queen's milliner, a Frenchwoman, whom they bound in her own shop, from which they took goods and money to the amount of five or six thousand dollars. Candelas had already expiated his crime on the scaffold, but Balseiro, who was said to be by far the worse ruffian of the two, had, by dint of money, an ally which his comrade did not possess, contrived to save his own life; the punishment of death, to which he was originally sentenced, having been commuted to twenty years' hard labour in the *presidio* of Malaga. I visited this worthy, and conversed with him for some time through the wicket of the dungeon.

Upon my telling him that I was sorry to see him in such a situation, he replied that it was an affair of no consequence, as within six weeks he should be conducted to the *presidio*, from which, with the assistance of a few ounces distributed amongst the guards, he could at any time escape. "But whither would you flee?" I demanded. "Can I not flee to the land of the Moors," replied Balseiro, "or to the English, in the camp of Gibraltar; or, if I prefer it, cannot I return to this *foro* (city), and live, as I have hitherto done, *choring* the *gachos* (robbing the natives)? What is to hinder me? Madrid is large, and Balseiro has plenty of friends, especially among the *lumias* (women)," he added with a smile. I spoke to him of his ill-fated accomplice Candelas; whereupon his face assumed a horrible expression. "I hope he is in torment," exclaimed the robber. The two worthies had, it seems, quarrelled in prison; Candelas having accused the other of bad faith and an undue appropriation to his own use of the *corpus delicti* in various robberies which they had committed in company.

I cannot refrain from relating the subsequent history of this Balseiro. Shortly after my own liberation, too impatient to wait until the *presidio* should afford him a chance of regaining his liberty, he, in company with some other convicts, broke through the roof of the prison and escaped. He instantly resumed his former habits, committing several daring robberies, both within and without the walls of Madrid. I now come to his last, I may call it his master crime—a singular piece of atrocious villainy. Dissatisfied with the proceeds of street-robbery and housebreaking, he determined upon a bold stroke by which he hoped to acquire money sufficient to support him in some foreign land in luxury and splendour.

There was a certain Comptroller of the Queen's Household, by name Gabiria, a Basque by birth, and a man of immense possessions; this individual had two sons, handsome boys, between twelve and fourteen years of age, whom I had frequently seen, and indeed conversed with, in my walks on the bank of the Manzanares, which was their favourite promenade. These children, at the time of which I am speaking, were receiving their education at a certain seminary in Madrid. Balseiro, being well acquainted with the father's affection for his children, determined to make it subservient to his own rapacity. He formed a plan, which was neither more nor less than to seize the children, and not to restore them to their parent until he had received an enormous ransom. This plan was partly carried into execution; two associates of Balseiro, well dressed, drove up to the door of the seminary where the children were, and, by means of a forged letter, purporting to be written by the father, induced the schoolmaster to permit the boys to accompany them for a country jaunt, as they pretended.

About five leagues from Madrid, Balseiro had a cave, in a wild unfrequented spot between the Escurial and a village called Torre Lodones. To this cave the children were conducted, where they remained in durance under the custody of the two accomplices; Balseiro, in the meantime, remaining in Madrid for the purpose of conducting negotiations with the father.

The father, however, was a man of considerable energy, and instead of acceding to the terms of the ruffian, communicated in a letter, instantly took the most vigorous measures for the recovery of his children. Horse and foot were sent out to scour the country, and in less than a week the children were found near the cave, having been abandoned by their keepers, who had taken fright on hearing of the decided measures which had been resorted to. They were, however, speedily arrested, and identified by the boys as their ravishers. Balseiro, perceiving that Madrid was becoming too hot to hold him, attempted to escape, but whether to the camp of Gibraltar or to the land of the Moors I know not. He was recognised, however, at a village in the neighbourhood of Madrid, and, being apprehended, was forthwith conducted to the capital, where he shortly after terminated his existence on the scaffold, with his two associates, Gabiria and his children being present at the ghastly scene, which they surveyed from a chariot at their ease.

Such was the end of Balseiro. A celebrated robber with whom I was subsequently imprisoned at Seville spoke his eulogy in the following manner:—

"Balseiro was a very good subject, and an honest man. He was the head of our family, Don Jorge; we shall never see his like again; pity that he did not sack the *parné* (money) and escape to the camp of the Moor, Don Jorge."

I remained about three weeks in the prison of Madrid. The heaviest loss which resulted from my confinement, and for which no indemnification could be either offered or received, was the death of my affectionate and faithful Basque, Francisco, about which I may tell the following story:—

It was at Madrid one fine afternoon in the beginning of March, 1838, that as I was sitting behind my table in a *cabinete*, as it is called, of the third floor of No. 16 in the Calle de Santiago, having just taken my meal, my hostess entered and informed me that a military officer wished to speak

to me, adding, in an under-tone, that he looked a *strange guest*. I was acquainted with no military officer in the Spanish service; but as at that time I expected daily to be arrested for having distributed the Bible, I thought that very possibly this officer might have been sent to perform that piece of duty. I instantly ordered him to be admitted; whereupon a thin, active figure, somewhat above the middle height, dressed in a blue uniform, with a long sword hanging at his side, tripped into the room. Depositing his regimental hat on the ground, he drew a chair to the table, and, seating himself, placed his elbows

" HE CONFRONTED ME."

on the board, and, supporting his face with his hands, confronted me, gazing steadfastly upon me, without uttering a word. I looked no less wistfully at him, and was of the same opinion as my hostess as to the strangeness of my guest. He was about fifty, with thin flaxen hair covering the sides of his head, which at the top was entirely bald. His eyes were small, and, like ferrets', red and fiery; his complexion like a brick, a dull red, chequered with spots of purple.

"May I inquire your name and business, sir?" I at length demanded.

Stranger.—"My name is Chaléco, of Valdepeñas; in the time of the French I served as brigante, fighting for Ferdinand VII. I am now a captain on half-pay in the service of Donna Isabel; as for my business here, it is to speak with you. Do you know this book?"

Myself.—"This book is St. Luke's Gospel in the Gypsy language; how can this book concern you?"

Stranger.—"No one more. It is in the language of my people."

Myself.—"You do not pretend to say that you are a Caló?"

Stranger.—"I do. I am Zincalo, by the mother's side. My father, it is true, was one of the Busné; but I glory in being a Caló, and care not to acknowledge other blood."

Myself.—"How became you possessed of that book?"

Stranger.—"I was this morning in the Prado, when I met two women of our people, and amongst other things they told me that they had a *gabicóte* in our language. I did not believe them at first; but they pulled it out, and I found their words true. Then they spoke to me of yourself, and told me where you live, so I took the book from them and am come to see you."

Myself.—"Are you able to understand this book?"

Stranger.—"Perfectly, though it is written in very crabbed language; but I learnt to read Caló when very young. My mother was a good Calli, and early taught me both to speak and read it."

Myself.—"How came your mother, being a good Calli, to marry one of a different blood?"

Stranger.—"It was no fault of hers; there was no remedy. In her infancy she lost her parents, who were executed; and she was abandoned by all, till my father, taking compassion on her, brought her up and educated her; at last he made her his wife, though three times her age. She, however, remembered her blood, and hated my father, and taught me to hate him likewise, and avoid him. When a boy, I used to stroll about the plains, that I might not see my father; and my father would follow me and beg me to look upon him, and would ask me what I wanted; and I would reply, 'Father, the only thing I want is to see you dead.'

"When I was about twelve years old, my father became distracted, and died. I then continued with my mother for some years; she loved me much, and procured a teacher to instruct me in Latin. At last she died, and then there was a *pléyto* (law-suit). I took to the sierra and became a highwayman; but the wars broke out. My cousin Jara, of Valdepeñas, raised a troop of brigantes. I enlisted with him and distinguished myself very much; there is scarcely a man or woman in Spain but has heard of Jara and Chaléco. I am now captain in the service of Donna Isabel—I am covered with wounds—I am —ugh! ugh! ugh!——"

He had commenced coughing, and in a manner which perfectly astounded me. I had heard whooping-coughs, consumptive coughs, coughs caused by colds and other accidents, but a cough so horrible and unnatural as that of the Gypsy soldier I had never witnessed in the course of my travels. In a moment he was bent double, his frame writhed and laboured, the veins of his forehead were frightfully swollen, and his complexion became black as the blackest blood; he screamed, he snorted, he barked, and appeared to be on the point of suffocation—yet more explosive became the cough; and the people of the house, frightened, came running into the apartment. I cried, "The man is perishing; run instantly for a surgeon!" He heard me, and with a quick movement raised his left hand as if to countermand the order; another struggle, then one mighty throe, which seemed to search his deepest intestines, and he remained motionless, his head on his knee. The cough had left him, and within a minute or two he again looked up.

"That is a dreadful cough, friend," said I, when he was somewhat recovered. "How did you get it?"

"I am—shot through the lungs—brother! Let me but take breath, and I will show you the hole."

He continued with me a considerable time, and showed not the slightest disposition to depart; the cough returned twice, but not so violently. At length, having an engagement, I arose, and, apologising, told him I must leave him. The next day he came again at the same hour, but he found me not, as I was abroad dining with a friend. On the third day, however, as I was sitting down to dinner, in he walked, unannounced. I am rather hospitable than otherwise, so I cordially welcomed him, and requested him to partake of my meal. "*Con múcho gusto*," he replied, and instantly took his place at the table. I was again astonished, for if his cough was frightful, his appetite was yet more so. He ate like a wolf of the sierra; soup, *puchero*, fowl, and bacon, disappeared before him in a twinkling. I ordered in cold meat, which he presently despatched; a large piece of cheese was then produced. We had been drinking water.

"Where is the wine?" said he.

"I never use it," I replied.

He looked blank. The hostess, however, who was present waiting, said, "If the gentleman wish for wine, I have a *bota* nearly full, which I will instantly fetch." The skin bottle, when full, might contain about four quarts. She filled him a very large glass, and was removing the skin, but he prevented her, saying, "Leave it, my good woman; my brother here will settle with you for the little I shall use."

He now lighted his cigar, and it was evident that he had made good his quarters. On the former occasion I thought his behaviour sufficiently strange, but I liked it still less on the present. Every fifteen minutes he emptied his glass, which contained at least a pint; his conversation became horrible. He related the atrocities which he had committed when a robber and brigante in La Mancha. "It was our custom," said he, "to tie our prisoners to the olive-trees, and then, putting our horses to full speed, to tilt at them with our spears." As he continued to drink, he became waspish and quarrelsome; he had hitherto talked Castilian, but now he would only converse in Gypsy and in Latin, the last of which languages he spoke with great fluency, though ungrammatically. He told me that he had killed six men in duels; and, drawing his sword, fenced about the room. I saw by the manner in which he handled it that he was master of his weapon. His cough did not return, and he said it seldom afflicted him when he dined well. He gave me to understand that he had received no pay for two years. "Therefore you visit me," thought I. At the end of three hours, perceiving that he exhibited no signs of taking his departure, I arose and said I must again leave him. "As you please, brother," said he; "use no ceremony with me; I am fatigued and will wait a little while." I did not return till eleven at night, when my hostess informed me that he had just departed, promising to return next day. He had emptied the *bota*, and the cheese produced being insufficient for him, he sent for an entire Dutch cheese on my account, part of which he had eaten and the rest carried away. I now saw that I had formed a most troublesome acquaintance, of whom it was highly necessary to rid myself, if possible; I therefore dined out for the next nine days.

For a week he came regularly at the usual hour, at the end of which time he desisted. The hostess was afraid of him, as she said that he was a *brujo* or wizard, and only spoke to him through the wicket.

On the tenth day I was cast into prison. Once during my confinement he called at the house, and, being informed of my mishap, drew his sword and vowed with horrible imprecations to murder the Prime Minister, Ofalia, for having dared to imprison his brother. On my release I did not revisit my lodgings for some days, but lived at an hotel.

I returned late one afternoon with my Basque servant, Francisco, who had served me with the utmost fidelity during my imprisonment, which he voluntarily shared with me. The first person I saw on entering was the Gypsy soldier, seated by the table, whereon were several bottles of wine which he had ordered from the tavern, of course on my account. He was smoking, and looked savage and sullen; perhaps he was not much pleased with the reception he had experienced. He had forced himself in, and the woman of the house sat in a corner, looking upon him with dread. I addressed him, but he would scarcely return an answer. At last he commenced discoursing with great volubility in Gypsy and Latin. I did not understand much of what he said. His words were wild and incoherent; but he repeatedly threatened some person. The last bottle was now exhausted; he demanded more. I told him, in a gentle manner, that he had drunk enough. He looked on the ground for some time, then slowly, and somewhat hesitatingly, drew his sword and laid it on the table. It was become dark. I was not afraid of the fellow, but I wished to avoid anything unpleasant. I called to Francisco to bring lights, and, obeying a sign which I made him, he sat down at the table. The Gypsy glared fiercely upon him. Francisco laughed, and began with great glee to talk in Basque, of which the Gypsy understood not a word

The Basques, like all Tartars, and such they are, are paragons of fidelity and good-nature; they are only dangerous when outraged, when they are terrible indeed. Francisco to the strength of a giant joined the disposition of a lamb. He was beloved even in the *patio* of the prison, where he used to pitch the bar and wrestle with the murderers and felons, always coming off victor. He continued speaking Basque. The Gypsy was incensed, and, forgetting the languages in which, for the last hour, he had been speaking, complained to Francisco of his rudeness in speaking any tongue but Castilian. The Basque replied by a loud *carcajáda*, and slightly touched the Gypsy on the knee. The

THE COMBAT BETWEEN THE GYPSY AND FRANCISCO.

latter sprang up like a mine discharged, seized his sword, and, retreating a few steps, made a desperate lunge at Francisco.

The Basques, next to the Pasiegos, are the best cudgel-players in Spain—and in the world. Francisco held in his hand part of a broomstick, which he had broken in the stable, whence he had just ascended. With the swiftness of lightning he foiled the stroke of Chaléco, and in another moment, with a dexterous blow, struck the sword out of his hand, sending it ringing against the wall.

The Gypsy resumed his seat and his cigar. He occasionally looked at the Basque. His glances were at first atrocious, but presently changed their expression, and appeared to become prying and eagerly curious. He at last arose, picked up his sword, sheathed it, and walked slowly to the door; when there he stopped, turned round, advanced close to Francisco, and looked him steadfastly in the face.

"My good fellow," said he, "I am a Gypsy, and can read *baji*. Do you know where you will be at this time to-morrow?"*

Then, laughing like a hyæna, he departed, and I never saw him again.

At that time on the morrow Francisco was on his death-bed. He had caught the gaol-fever, which had long raged in the Carcel de la Corte. In a few days he was buried, a mass of corruption, in the Campo Santo of Madrid.

* The hostess, Maria Diaz, and her son, Juan José Lopez, were present when the outcast uttered these prophetic words.

THE VISION OF SUDDEN DEATH.

By Thomas de Quincey.

THE incident that follows, so memorable in itself by its features of horror, and so scenical by its grouping for the eye, occurred to myself, in the dead of night, as a solitary spectator, when seated on the box of the Manchester and Glasgow Mail, in the second or third summer after Waterloo. I find it necessary to relate the circumstances, because they are such as could not have occurred unless under a singular combination of accidents. In those days the oblique and lateral communications with many rural post-offices were so arranged, either through necessity or through defect of system, as to make it requisite for the main north-western mail (i.e., the *down* mail), on reaching Manchester, to halt for a number of hours—how many I do not remember—six or seven, I think; but the result was that, in the ordinary course, the mail re-commenced its journey northwards about midnight.

Wearied with the long detention at a gloomy hotel, I walked out about eleven o'clock at night for the sake of fresh air, meaning to fall in with the mail and resume my seat at the post-office. The night, however, being yet dark, as the moon had scarcely risen, and the streets being at that hour empty, so as to offer no opportunities for asking the road, I lost my way, and did not reach the post-office until it was considerably past midnight; but, to my great relief (as it was important for me to be in Westmoreland by the morning), I saw in the huge saucer-eyes of the mail, blazing through the gloom, an evidence that my chance was not yet lost. Past the time it was; but, by some rare accident, the mail was not even yet ready to start.

I ascended to my seat on the box, where my cloak was still lying, as it had lain at the "Bridgwater Arms." I had left it there in imitation of a nautical discoverer, who leaves a bit of bunting on the shore of his discovery, by way of warning off the ground the whole human race, and notifying to the Christian and the heathen worlds, with his best compliments, that he has hoisted his pocket-handkerchief once and for ever upon that virgin soil, thenceforward claiming the *jus domini* to the top of the atmosphere above it; and also the right of driving shafts to the centre of the earth below it; so that all people found after this warning either aloft in upper chambers of the atmosphere, or groping in subterranean shafts, or squatting audaciously on the surface of the soil, will be treated as trespassers—kicked, that is to say, or decapitated, as circumstances may suggest, by their very faithful servant, the owner of the said pocket-handkerchief. In the present case it is probable that my cloak might not have been respected, and the *jus gentium* might have been cruelly violated in my person; for in the dark, people commit deeds of darkness, gas being a great ally of morality. But it so happened that on this night there was no other outside passenger; and thus the crime, which else was but too probable, missed fire for want of a criminal.

Having mounted the box, I took a small quantity of laudanum, having already travelled two hundred and fifty miles, viz., from a point seventy miles beyond London. In the taking of laudanum there was nothing extraordinary, but by accident it drew upon me the special attention of

STARTING (*p.* 61).

my assessor on the box, the coachman. And in *that* also there was nothing extraordinary, but by accident, and with great delight, it drew my own attention to the fact that this coachman was a monster in point of bulk, and that he had but one eye. In fact, he had been foretold by Virgil as

"Monstrum horrendum, informe, ingens, cui lumen ademptum."

He answered to the conditions in every one of the items:—(1) A monster he was; (2) dreadful; (3) shapeless; (4) huge; (5) who had lost an eye. But why should *that* delight me? Had he been one of the Calendars in the "Arabian Nights," and had paid down his eye as the price of his criminal curiosity, what right had *I* to exult in his misfortune? I did *not* exult; I delighted in no man's punishment, though it were even merited.

But these personal distinctions (Nos. 1, 2, 3, 4, 5) identified in an instant an old friend of mine, whom I had known in the south for some years as the most masterly of mail-coachmen.

He was the man in all Europe that could (if *any* could) have driven six-in-hand full gallop over *Al Sirat*, that dreadful bridge of Mahomet, with no side battlements, and of *extra* room not enough for a razor's edge, leading right across the bottomless gulf. Under this eminent man, whom in Greek I cognominated *Cyclops diphrelates* (Cyclops the charioteer), I and others known to me studied the diphrelatic art. Excuse, reader, a word too elegant to be pedantic. As a pupil, though I paid extra fees, it is to be lamented that I did not stand high in his esteem. It showed his dogged honesty (though, observe, not his discernment) that he could not see my merits. Let us excuse his absurdity in this particular, by remembering his want of an eye. Doubtless *that* made him blind to my merits. In the art of con-versation, however, he admitted that I had the whip-hand of him. On this present occasion great joy was at our meeting. But what was Cyclops doing here? Had the medical men recommended northern air, or how? I collected, from such explanations as he volunteered, that he had an interest at stake in some suit-at-law now pending at Lancaster; so that probably he had got himself transferred to this station for the purpose of connecting with his professional pursuits an instant readiness for the calls of his law-suit.

Meantime, what are we stopping for? Surely we have now waited long enough. Oh, this procrastinating mail, and this procrastinating post-office! Can't they take a lesson upon that subject from *me*? Some people have called *me* procrastinating. Yet you are witness, reader, that I was here kept waiting for the post-office. Will the post-office lay its hand on its heart in its moments of sobriety, and assert that ever it waited for me? What are they about? The guard tells me that there is a large extra accumulation of foreign mails this night, owing to irregularities caused by war, by wind, by weather, in the packet service, which as yet does not benefit at all by steam. For an *extra* hour, it seems, the post-office has been engaged in threshing out the pure wheaten correspondence of Glasgow, and winnowing it from the chaff of all baser intermediate towns.

But at last it is finished. Sound your horn, guard. Manchester, good-bye; we've lost an hour by your criminal conduct at the post-office; which, however, though I do not mean to part with a serviceable ground of complaint, and one which really *is* such for the horses, to me secretly is an advantage, since it compels us to look sharply for this lost hour among the next eight or nine, and to recover it (if we can) at the rate of one mile extra per hour. Off we are at last, and at eleven miles an hour; and for the moment I detect no changes in the energy or in the skill of Cyclops.

From Manchester to Kendal, which virtually (though not in law) is the capital of Westmoreland, there were, at this time, seven stages of eleven miles each. The first five of these, counting from Manchester, terminate in Lancaster, which is, therefore, fifty-five miles north of Manchester, and the same distance exactly from Liverpool. The first three stages terminate in Preston (called, by way of distinction from other towns of that name, *Proud* Preston), at which place it is that the separate roads from Liverpool and from Manchester to the north become confluent.*

Within these first three stages lay the foundation, the progress, and termination of our night's adventure. During the first stage I found out that Cyclops was mortal: he was liable to the shocking affection of sleep—a thing which previously I had never suspected. "Oh! Cyclops," I exclaimed, "thou art mortal. My friend, thou snorest." Through the first eleven miles, however, this infirmity betrayed itself only by brief snatches. On waking up, he made an apology for himself, which, instead of mending matters, laid open a gloomy vista of coming disasters. The summer assizes, he reminded me, were now going on at Lancaster; in consequence of which, for three nights and three days, he had not lain down in a bed. During the day he was waiting for his own summons as a witness on the trial in which he was interested; or else, lest he should be missing at the critical moment, was drinking with the other witnesses, under the pastoral surveillance of the attorneys. During the night, or that part of it which at sea would form the middle watch, he was driving.

This explanation certainly accounted for his drowsiness, but in a way which made it much more alarming; since now, after several days' resistance to this infirmity, at length he was steadily giving way. Throughout the second stage he grew more and more drowsy. In the second mile of the third stage he surrendered himself finally and without a struggle to his perilous temptation. All his past resistance had but deepened the weight of this final oppression. Seven atmospheres of sleep rested upon him; and, to consummate the case, our worthy guard, after singing "Love amongst the roses" for perhaps thirty times, without invitation, and without applause, had, in revenge, moodily resigned himself to slumber—not so deep, doubtless, as the coachman's, but deep enough for mischief. And thus at last, about ten miles from Preston, it came about that I found myself left in charge of His Majesty's London and Glasgow Mail, then running at the least twelve miles an hour.

What made this negligence less criminal than else it must have been thought, was the condition of the roads at night during the assizes. At that time all the law business of populous Liverpool, and also of populous Manchester, with its vast cincture of populous rural districts, was called up by

---

* "Confluent:"—Suppose a capital Y (the Pythagorean letter): Lancaster is at the foot of this letter; Liverpool at the top of the right branch; Manchester at the top of the left; Proud Preston at the centre where the branches unite. It is 33 miles along either of the two branches; it is 22 miles along the stem—viz., from Preston in the middle to Lancaster at the root.

ancient usage to the tribunal of Lilliputian Lancaster. As things were at present, twice in the year* so vast a body of business rolled northwards, from the southern quarter of the country, that for a fortnight at least it occupied the severe exertions of two judges in its despatch. The consequence of this was that every horse available for such a service, along the whole line of road, was exhausted in carrying down the multitudes of people who were parties to the different suits. By sunset, therefore, it usually happened that, through utter exhaustion amongst men and horses, the road sank into profound silence. Except the exhaustion in the vast adjacent county of York from a contested election, no such silence succeeding to no such fiery uproar was ever witnessed in England.

On this occasion the usual silence and solitude prevailed along the road. Not a hoof nor a wheel was to be heard. And to strengthen this false luxurious confidence in the noiseless roads, it happened also that the night was one of peculiar solemnity and peace. For my own part, though slightly alive to the possibilities of peril, I had so far yielded to the influence of the mighty calm as to sink into a profound reverie. The month was August, in the middle of which lay my own birthday—a festival to every thoughtful man suggesting solemn and often sigh-born thoughts. The county was my own native county —upon which, in its southern section, more than upon any equal area known to man past or present, had descended the original curse of labour in its heaviest form, not mastering the bodies only of men as of slaves, or criminals in mines, but working through the fiery will. At this particular season also of the assizes, that dreadful hurricane of flight and pursuit, as it might have seemed to a stranger, which swept to and from Lancaster all day long, hunting the country up and down, and regularly subsiding back into silence about sunset, could not fail (when united with this permanent distinction of Lancashire as the very metropolis and citadel of labour) to point the thoughts pathetically upon that counter-vision of rest, of saintly repose from strife and sorrow, towards which, as to their secret haven, the profounder aspirations of man's heart are in solitude continually travelling.

Obliquely upon our left we were nearing the sea, which also must, under the present circumstances, be repeating the general state of halcyon repose. The sea, the atmosphere, the light, bore each an orchestral part in the universal lull. Moonlight, and the first timid tremblings of the dawn, were by this time blending; and the blendings were brought into a still more exquisite state of unity by a slight silvery mist, motionless and dreamy, that covered the woods and fields, but with a veil of equable transparency. Except the feet of our own horses, which, running on a sandy margin of the road, made but little disturbance, there was no sound abroad. In the clouds and on the earth prevailed the same majestic peace; and in spite of all that the villain of a school-

* "Twice in the year." There were at that time only two assizes even in the most populous counties—viz., the Lent Assizes and the Summer Assizes.

master has done for the ruin of our sublimer thoughts, which are the thoughts of our infancy, we still believe in no such nonsense as a limited atmosphere. Whatever we may swear with our false, feigning lips, in our faithful hearts we still believe, and must for ever believe, in fields of air traversing the total gulf between earth and the central heavens. Still, in the confidence of children that tread without fear *every* chamber in their father's house, and to whom no door is closed, we, in that Sabbatic vision which sometimes is revealed for an hour upon nights like this, ascend with easy steps from the sorrow-stricken fields of earth, upwards to the sandals of God.

Suddenly, from thoughts like these, I was awakened to a sullen sound, as of some motion on the distant road. It stole upon the air for a moment; I listened in awe; but then it died away. Once roused, however, I could not but observe with alarm the quickened motion of our horses. Ten years' experience had made my eye learned in the valuing of motion; and I saw that we were now running thirteen miles an hour. I pretend to no presence of mind. On the contrary, my fear is that I am miserably and shamefully deficient in that quality as regards action. The palsy of doubt and distraction hangs like some guilty weight of dark unfathomed remembrances upon my energies when the signal is flying for *action*. But, on the other hand, this accursed gift I have, as regards *thought*, that in the first step towards the possibility of a misfortune I see its total evolution; in the radix of the series I see too certainly and too instantly its entire expansion; in the f syllable of the dreadful sentence I read already the last. It was not that I feared for ourselves. *Us*, our bulk and impetus charmed against peril in any collision. And I had ridden through too many hundreds of perils that were frightful to approach, that were matter of laughter to look back upon, the first face of which was horror, the parting face a jest, for any anxiety to rest upon *our* interests. The mail was not built, I felt assured, nor bespoke, that could betray *me* who trusted to its protection. But any carriage that we could meet would be frail and light in comparison of ourselves.

And I remarked this ominous accident of our situation. We were on the wrong side of the road. But then, it may be said, the other party, if other there was, might also be on the wrong side; and two wrongs might make a right. *That* was not likely. The same motive which had drawn *us* to the right-hand side of the road—viz., the luxury of the soft beaten sand, as contrasted with the paved centre—would prove attractive to others. The two adverse carriages would, therefore, to a certainty, be travelling on the same side; and from this side, as not being ours in law, the crossing over to the other would of course be looked for from *us*.* Our lamps, still lighted,

---

* It is true that, according to the law of the case, as established by legal precedents, all carriages were required to give way before royal equipages, and therefore before the mail, as one of them. But this only increased the danger, as being a regulation very imperfectly made known, very unequally enforced, and therefore often embarrassing the movements on both sides.

would give the impression of vigilance on our part. And every creature that met us would rely upon *us* for quartering.* All this, and if the separate links of the anticipation had been a thousand times more, I saw, not discursively, or by effort, or by succession, but by one flash of horrid simultaneous intuition.

Under this steady though rapid anticipation of the evil which *might* be gathering ahead, ah! what a sullen mystery of fear, what a sigh of woe, was that which stole upon the air, as again the far-off sound of a wheel was heard! A whisper it was—a whisper from, perhaps, four miles off—secretly announcing a ruin, that, being foreseen, was not the less inevitable; that, being known, was not, therefore, healed. What could be done—who was it that could do it—to check the flight of these maniacal horses? Could I not seize the reins from the grasp of the slumbering coachman? You, reader, think that it would have been in *your* power to do so. And I quarrel not with your estimate of yourself. But from the way in which the coachman's hand was viced between his upper and lower thigh, this was impossible. Easy, was it? See, then, this bronze equestrian statue. The cruel rider has kept the bit in his horse's mouth for two centuries. Unbridle him, for a minute, if you please, and wash his mouth with water. Easy, was it? Unhorse me, then, that imperial rider; knock me those marble feet from those marble stirrups of Charlemagne.

The sounds ahead strengthened, and were now too clearly the sounds of wheels. Who and what could it be? Was it industry in a taxed cart? Was it youthful gaiety in a gig? Was it sorrow that loitered, or joy that raced? For as yet the snatches of sound were too intermitting, from distance, to decipher the character of the motion. Whoever were the travellers, something must be done to warn them. Upon the other party rests the active responsibility, but upon *us*—and, woe is me! that *us* was reduced to my frail opium-shattered self—rests the responsibility of warning. Yet, how should this be accomplished? Might I not sound the guard's horn? Already, on the first thought, I was making my way over the roof to the guard's seat. But this, from the accident which I have mentioned, of the foreign mails being piled upon the roof, was a difficult and even dangerous attempt to one cramped by nearly three hundred miles of outside travelling. And, fortunately, before I lost much time in the attempt, our frantic horses swept round an angle of the road, which opened upon us that final stage where the collision must be accomplished, and the catastrophe sealed. All was apparently finished; the case was heard; the judge had finished; and only the verdict was yet in arrear.

Before us lay an avenue, straight as an arrow, six hundred yards, perhaps, in length; and the umbrageous trees, which rose in a regular line from either side, meeting high over head, gave to it the character of a cathedral aisle. These trees lent a deeper solemnity to the early light; but there was still

---

* "Quartering." This is the technical word, and, I presume, derived from the French *cartayer*, to evade a rut, or any obstacle.

light enough to perceive, at the further end of this Gothic aisle, a frail reedy gig, in which were seated a young man and, by his side, a young lady. Ah! young sir, what are you about? If it is requisite that you should whisper your communications to this young lady—though really I see nobody at an hour and on a road so solitary likely to overhear you—is it therefore requisite that you should carry your lips forward to hers? The little carriage is creeping on at one mile an hour, and the parties within it, being thus tenderly engaged, are naturally bending down their heads. Between them and eternity, to all human calculation, there is but one minute and a half.

Oh! heavens, what is it that I shall do? Speaking or acting, what help can I offer? Strange it is, and to a mere auditor of the tale might seem laughable, that I should need a suggestion from the "Iliad" to prompt the sole resource that remained. Yet so it was. Suddenly I remembered the shout of Achilles, and its effect. But could I pretend to shout like the son of Peleus, aided by Pallas? No; but then I needed not the shout that should alarm all Asia militant; such a shout would suffice as might carry terror into the hearts of the two thoughtless young people and one gig-horse. I shouted—and the young man heard me not. A second time I shouted—and now he heard me, for now he raised his head.

Here, then, all had been done that by me *could* be done; more on *my* part was not possible. Mine had been the first step; the second was for the young man; the third was for God. "If," said I, "this stranger is a brave man, and if indeed he loves the young girl at his side—or, loving her not, if he feels the obligation pressing upon every man worthy to be called a man, of doing his utmost for a woman confided to his protection—he will at least make some effort to save her. If *that* fails, he will not perish the more, or by a death more cruel, for having made it; and he will die, as a brave man should, with his face to the danger, and with his arm about the woman that he sought in vain to save. But if he makes no effort, shrinking without a struggle from his duty, he himself will not the less certainly perish for this baseness of poltroonery. He will die no less: and why not? Wherefore should we grieve that there is one craven less in the world? No; *let* him perish, without a pitying thought of ours wasted upon him; and, in that case, all our grief will be reserved for the fate of the helpless girl who now, upon the least shadow of failure in *him*, must, by the fiercest of translations—must, without time for a prayer—must, within seventy seconds, stand before the judgment-seat of God."

But craven he was not; sudden had been the call upon him, and sudden was his answer to the call. He saw, he heard, he comprehended the ruin that was coming down; already its gloomy shadow darkened above him, and already he was measuring his strength to deal with it. Ah! what a vulgar thing does courage seem when we see nations buying and selling it for a shilling a day. Ah! what a sublime thing does courage seem when some fearful summons on the great deeps of life carries a man, as if running before a hurricane, up to the giddy crest of some tumultuous crisis, from which lie two courses, and a voice says to him audibly, "One way lies hope; take the other, and mourn for ever!" How grand a triumph if, even then, amidst the raving of all around him, and the frenzy of the danger, the man is able to confront his situation—is able to retire for a moment into solitude with God, and to seek his counsel from *Him!*

For seven seconds, it might be, of his seventy, the stranger settled his countenance steadfastly upon us, as if to search and value every element in the conflict before him. For five seconds more of his seventy he sat immovably, like one that mused on some great purpose. For five more, perhaps, he sat with his eyes upraised, like one that prayed in sorrow, under some extremity of doubt, for light that should guide him to the better choice.

Then suddenly he rose—stood upright—and by a powerful strain upon the reins, raising his horse's fore-feet from the ground, he slewed him round on the pivot of his hind-legs, so as to plant the little equipage in a position nearly at right angles to ours.

Thus far his condition was not improved, except as a first step had been taken towards the possibility of a second. If no more were done, nothing was done; for the little carriage still occupied the very centre of our path though in an altered direction. Yet even now it may not be too late. Fifteen of the seventy seconds may still be unexhausted, and one almighty bound may avail to clear the ground. Hurry, then, hurry! for the flying moments, *they* hurry! Oh, hurry, hurry, my brave young man! for the cruel hoofs of our horses, *they* also hurry! Fast are the flying moments; faster are the hoofs of our horses.

But fear not for him, if human energy can suffice; faithful was he that drove to his terrific duty; faithful was the horse to *his* command. One blow, one impulse given with voice and hand by the stranger; one rush from the horse; one bound, as if in the act of rising to a fence, landed the docile creature's fore-feet upon the crown or arching centre of the road. The larger half of the little equipage had then cleared our over-towering shadow: *that* was evident even to my own agitated sight. But it mattered little that one wreck should float off in safety, if upon the wreck that perished were embarked the human freightage. The rear part of the carriage, was *that* certainly beyond the line of absolute ruin? What power could answer that question? Glance of eye, thought of man, wing of angel, which of these had speed enough to sweep between the question and the answer, and divide the one from the other? Light does not tread upon the steps of light more indivisibly than did our all-conquering arrival upon the escaping efforts of the gig. *That* must the young man have felt too plainly. His back was now turned to us; not by sight could he any longer communicate with the peril; but by the dreadful rattle of our harness, too truly had his ear been instructed—that all was finished as regarded any further effort of *his.* Already in resignation he had rested from his struggle, and perhaps in his heart he was whispering, "Father, which art in heaven, do Thou finish above what I on earth have attempted!"

Faster than ever mill-race we ran past them in our inexorable flight. Oh, raving of hurricanes that must have sounded in their young ears at the moment of our transit! Even in that moment the thunder of collision spoke aloud. Either with the swingle-bar, or with the haunch of our near leader, we had struck the off-wheel of the little gig, which stood rather obliquely, and not quite so far advanced as to be accurately parallel with the near-wheel. The blow, from the fury of our passage, resounded terrifically. I rose in horror to gaze upon the ruins we might have caused. From my elevated station I looked down, and looked back upon the scene, which in a moment told its own tale, and wrote all its records on my heart for ever.

Here was the map of the passion that now had finished. The horse was planted immovably, with his fore-feet upon the paved crest of the central road. He, of the whole party, might be supposed untouched by the passion of death. The little cany carriage—partly, perhaps, from the violent torsion of the wheels in its recent movement, partly from the thundering blow we had given to it—as if it sympathised with human horror, was all alive with tremblings and shiverings. The young man trembled not, nor shivered. He sat like a rock. But *his* was the steadiness of agitation frozen into rest by horror. As yet he dared not to look round; for he knew that, if anything remained to do, by him it could no longer be done. And as yet he knew not for certain if their safety could be accomplished. But the lady!

But the lady! Oh! heavens, will that spectacle ever depart from my dreams, as she rose and sank upon her seat, sank and rose, threw up her arms wildly to heaven, clutched at some visionary object in the air, fainting, praying, raving, despairing? Figure to yourself, reader, the elements of the case; suffer me to recall before your mind the circumstances of that unparalleled situation. From the silence and deep peace of this saintly summer night—from the pathetic blending of this sweet moonlight, dawnlight, dreamlight,—from the manly tenderness of this flattering, whispering, murmuring love—suddenly as from the woods and fields—suddenly as from the chambers of the air opening in revelation—suddenly as from the ground yawning at her feet, leaped upon her, with the flashing of cataracts, Death, the crowned phantom, with all the equipage of his terrors, and the tiger-roar of his voice.

The moments were numbered; the strife was finished; the vision was closed. In the twinkling of an eye our flying horses had carried us to the termination of the umbrageous aisle; at right angles we wheeled into our former direction; the turn of the road carried the scene out of my eyes in an instant, and swept it into my dreams for ever!

A STRANGE DUEL.

ON a scorching day in July, 1830, whilst I was seated under a venerable live oak, on the evergreen banks of the Teche, waiting for a fish to bite, I was startled by the roaring of some animal in a cane-brake a short distance below me, apparently getting ready for action. These notes of preparation were quickly succeeded by the sound of feet

"BRUIN SEIZED ONE OF HIS LEGS IN HIS MOUTH" (p. 71).

trampling down the cane and scattering the shells. As soon as I recovered from my surprise, I resolved to take a view of what I supposed to be two prairie bulls mixing impetuously in battle, an occurrence so common in this country and season.

When I reached the scene of action, how great was my astonishment to behold, instead of bulls, a large black bear reared upon his hind-legs, with his fore-paws raised aloft, as if to make a plunge! His face was besmeared with white foam, sprinkled with red, which, dropping from his mouth, rolled down his shaggy breast. Frantic from the smarting of his wounds, he stood gnashing his teeth and growling at the enemy.

A few paces in his rear was the cane-brake from which he had issued. On a bank of snow-white shells, spotted with blood, in battle array, stood Bruin's foe, in shape of an alligator, fifteen feet long.

He was standing on tip-toe, his back curved upwards; and his mouth, thrown open, displayed in his wide jaws two large tusks and rows of teeth. His tail, six feet long, raised from the ground, was constantly waving, like a boxer's arm, to gather force; his big eyes, starting from his head, glared upon Bruin, whilst sometimes uttering hissing cries, then roaring like a bull.

The combatants were a few paces apart when I stole upon them, the "first round" being over. They remained in the attitudes described for about a minute, swelling themselves as large as possible, but marking the slightest motions with attention and great caution, as if each felt confident that he had met his match.

During this pause I was concealed behind a tree, watching their manœuvres in silence. I could scarcely believe my eyesight. "What," thought I, "can those two beasts have to fight about?" Some readers may doubt the tale on this account; but if it had been a bull-fight, no one would have doubted it, because everyone knows what they are fighting for. The same reasoning will not always apply to a man-fight. Men frequently fight, when they are sober, for no purpose except to ascertain which is the better man. We must, then, believe that beasts will do the same, unless we admit that the instinct of beasts is superior to the boasted reason of man. Whether they did fight upon the present occasion without cause I cannot say, as I was not present when the affray began. A boar and a ram have been known to fight, and so did the bear and the alligator, whilst I prudently kept in the background, preserving the strictest neutrality betwixt the belligerents.

Bruin, though evidently baffled, had a firm look, which showed he had not lost confidence in himself. If the difficulty of the undertaking had only deceived him, he was preparing to resume it. Accordingly, letting himself down upon all fours, he ran furiously at the alligator.

The alligator was ready for him, and, throwing his head and body partly round to avoid the onset, met Bruin half-way with a blow of his tail, which rolled him on the shells.

Old Bruin was not to be put off by one hint. Three times in rapid succession he rushed at the alligator, and was as often repulsed in the same manner, being knocked back by each blow just far enough to give the alligator time to recover the swing of his tail before he returned. The tail of the alligator sounded like a flail on Bruin's head and shoulders; but he bore it without flinching, still pushing on to come to close quarters with his scaly foe.

He made his fourth charge with a degree of dexterity which those who have never seen this clumsy animal exercising would suppose him incapable of. This time he got so close to the alligator before his tail struck him that the blow came with half its usual effect.

The alligator was upset by the charge; and before he could recover his feet, Bruin grasped him round the body below the fore-legs, and holding him down on his back, seized one of his legs in his mouth.

The alligator was now in a desperate situation, notwithstanding his coat of mail, which is softer on his belly than his back, from which

"The darted steel with idle shivers flies;"

and, as Kentuck would say, "he was getting up fast."

Here, if I dared to speak, and had supposed he could understand English, I should have uttered the encouraging exhortation of the poet—

"Now, gallant knight, now hold thy own;
No maiden's arms are round thee thrown."

The alligator attempted in vain to bite. Pressed down as he was, he could not open his mouth, the upper jaw of which only moves; and his neck was so stiff he could not turn his head short round. The amphibious beast fetched a scream in despair, but was not yet entirely overcome. Writhing his tail in agony, he happened to strike it against a small tree that stood next the bank: aided by this purchase, he made a convulsive flounder, which precipitated himself and Bruin, locked together, into the river.

The bank from which they fell was four feet high, and the water below seven feet deep. The tranquil stream received the combatants with a loud splash, then closed over them in silence. A volley of ascending bubbles announced their arrival at the bottom, where the battle ended. Presently Bruin rose again, scrambled up the bank, cast a hasty glance at the river, and made off, dripping, to the cane-brake. I never saw the alligator afterwards, to know him; no doubt he escaped in the water, which he certainly would not have done had he remained a few minutes longer on land.

Bruin was forced by nature to let go his grip under water to save his own life; I therefore think he is entitled to the credit of the victory. Besides, by implied consent, the parties were bound to finish the fight on land, where it began; and so Bruin understood it.

THE TALE OF THE "KENT," EAST-INDIAMAN.

DESTROYED BY FIRE, IN THE BAY OF BISCAY, ON MARCH 1st, 1825.

N Saturday, February 19th, 1825, a fresh north-easterly wind blew merrily down the Channel, driving the clouds from a steel-blue sky; and before it, her white sails bellying, her bulwarks bright with fresh paint, went the *Kent*, East-Indiaman, a handsome new ship of thirteen hundred and fifty tons, on her voyage to Bengal and China. As she sailed out of the Downs she carried on board a crew of one hundred and forty-eight men including officers; and twenty officers, three hundred and forty-four soldiers, forty-three women, and sixty children belonging to the 31st Regiment, besides twenty private passengers: in all, a total of six hundred and thirty-five souls.

Ten days after, on the night of February 28th, the stately ship was in lat. 47° 30′, long. 10° when a furious storm overtook her from westward. Buffeted and bewildered, she lay-to, her top-gallant yards struck, under triple-reefed main-topsail only. The gale continued and increased as the night dragged on, till with every lurch the main-chains were under water. The rolling was rendered threefold worse by the shifting weight of several hundred tons of shot and shell in the hold. A dozen or so of the sailors were just descending from the yards, where by prodigious efforts—for the sails were like sheet-iron—they had just succeeded in reefing the vessel snug. The passengers were below, sea-sick and horribly frightened, the children wailing, the women moaning in the midst of their endeavours to soothe. The three hundred and forty soldiers were huddled on deck and attached to life-lines run along the length of the vessel; among them the sailors were working hard to carry out the orders of their commander, Captain Henry Cobb, who through his speaking trumpet could hardly make his voice heard above the din of the elements.

By twelve o'clock, the pitching and rolling were at their worst. The best fastened furniture in the principal cabin was flung from side to side and smashing right and left with the most formidable violence. So it lasted till just before the dawn, when one of the ship's officers, wishing to satisfy himself that all was safe below, descended, with two sailors, into the hold. The men carried with them, for safety, a light in a patent lantern, but seeing that the candle of the lamp was burning dim, the officer took the precaution to hand it up to the orlop-deck to be trimmed. Having afterwards discovered that one of the rum-casks was adrift, he sent the sailors for some billets of wood to make it fast. While they were away, the ship gave a terrific lurch; the lantern was knocked out of the officer's hand. He let go the cask to catch

THE SCENE ON DECK (p. 75).

at the lantern; the cask stove, and out poured the rum. In a moment the light caught it, and the hold was in a blaze!

The spot where the fire broke out was surrounded by water-casks, and the men whom the officer called to help for some time believed that the flames would soon be drenched out. But their hopes were idle. The light blue vapour was followed by dense volumes of brown smoke, curling and heavy, stifling the men as they fought to keep the fire under, and driving them out of the hold. Now the flames ascended through all the four hatchways, and licked their way along to right and left, to quarter-deck and forecastle. The ship was doomed; there was no hope of hiding it from the passengers. And now someone cried, " It has reached the cable tier!" The alarm was too surely true, as was proved by a dense smell of pitch that pervaded the ship. The fire had reached the partitions and sides of the hold.

What meanwhile was the scene above, among the frightened wretches whose ignorance could only grasp the horror, not the hope, of the catastrophe?

Major M'Gregor, who had been reading the Bible to a friend whom the storm had unduly frightened, was interrupted by the whispered news that a yet more awful foe than the tempest was upon them—an enemy against which human foresight could provide little protection—"The after-hold is on fire!" He rose quietly, steadied his thoughts in an instant, and tapping at the cabin door, quietly whispered all his information to Colonel Fearon, the commanding officer on board. For the "cabin" in which he sat was a large dining-room on a level with the quarter-deck, and here most of the women were now gathered. The major looked about to see that none of these had heard the whisper. They had not. He resumed his seat and endeavoured to go on with his reading.

But they read the anxiety in his face and his restless glances towards the cabin door. Several women asked if the gale were not worse, and refused to be satisfied by his assurances. But the truth came to them presently, as the smoke crept in and grew thicker, and the planks beneath grew hot.

It was at this crisis that Captain Cobb showed himself not a hero only, but a born commander. He had been on deck directing the sailors and the men of the 31st Regiment, who, forgetting their sea-sickness and their terrors at the storm in the face of this deadlier foe, were throwing wet sails and drenching water over the fire. But as soon as it grew evident that the flames would never be quenched by such means, the captain resolved on a desperate measure, and did so with a prompt decision of character which seemed to increase with the imminence of the peril. He ordered the crew to get out their axes, scuttle the lower deck, cut the combings of the hatches, and open the lower ports for the free admission of the waves. There was one chance of saving the six hundred and thirty-five souls on board, to meet the fire with the waves and let the two battle it out.

It was an order at once merciful and cruel; for some lives must be knowingly sacrificed to carry it out. The seamen fell to work, their axes crashed through the timbers, and in poured the sea—swamping and drowning at its first rush several of the sick soldiers, one poor woman, and many of the children. Their cries were soon stifled in the gurgling water. Colonel Fearon and some of his officers, descending to the gun-deck, to help in opening the ports, found many dead bodies lying here and there of the unhappy wretches already suffocated by the smoke; through the dense wreaths of it they stumbled, and it was with the utmost difficulty they could remain below long enough to carry out Captain Cobb's wishes. In leapt the water, sweeping to and fro, in its resistless haste to the hold, huge heavy bulkheads and seamen's chests. Then knee-deep in water the workers struggled back, cheered by the hope that the waves would hold the fire off the spirit-casks and powder-stores that had been in momentary danger of exploding.

But they had now two enemies to fight, and their dilemma was fearful in the extreme degree. The ship was water-logged, and between the two elements, the crew, preferring always the remote alternative, were at one moment attempting to check the fire by means of water, and, the next, leaving it to rage whilst they endeavoured to exclude the waves. For a languor had seized the vessel—a languor in terrible contrast with her former rolling. They imagined her about to settle down headlong, and lost all hope.

On the upper deck were now huddled more than six hundred men, women, and children, many desperately weak from sickness; crawling, or wildly running about in search for husbands, wives, or parents, praying and groaning, some in a state of absolute nakedness as they had risen from their beds on the first alarm, some stock-still with a vacant stare of hopelessness on their faces, awaiting the end, some on their knees praying, the Roman Catholic soldiers crossing themselves, others tossing their arms and raving, like maniacs, hither and thither; while a number of the veteran sailors and stouter-hearted soldiers sat calmly on the powder magazine, in hope that the explosion, now looked for every moment, might give them a swift ending.

But Captain Cobb kept his head in this awful scene. If, as we must believe, the crown of brave manhood is to rise in intelligent courage as the stress of circumstances makes claim after claim on head and heart, Captain Cobb wore the crown on this fearful night. He now ordered the deck to be scuttled forward, to draw the flames in that direction, as between it and the magazine in that direction were several tiers of water-casks; while he hoped that the wet sails thrown into the after-hold would prevent the fire from spreading to the spirit-room abaft.

Into the after-cabins on the upper deck had fled many of the soldiers' wives with their children, and were now engaged in reading the Bible with some of the lady passengers. These latter for the most part kept a marvellous self-possession, and found strength amid their own fear to speak much consolation to the others. A young man coming to Major M'Gregor asked, "Is there any hope, major?" "We must prepare ourselves," answered the major, "to sleep to-night out in eternity." The lad pressed his hand. "My heart is filled with the peace of God; yet, though I know it is foolish, I dread exceedingly the last struggle."

Here, in the cuddy-cabins, were little children in their cots, smiling in ignorance of the danger, rejoicing that the terrible lurching was over that had so frightened them at first. The elder children, who understood the peril, bravely kept their little brothers and sisters amused with their toys and

"'A SAIL ON THE LEE-BOW!'" (p. 77).

picture-books. Said a senior officer to one of these, "Now is the time to put in practice the lessons you have learnt in the regimental school." "Yes, sir," was the answer; "we are trying to remember them, and we are praying to God."

Men who lived to record their observations tell us that few of the soldiers or sailors seemed to have much fear or hope of another state. There were some indeed who cried out that the hand of God was falling on them for crimes and sins of their youth. But after the first panic, the men faced their fate stoically. One young officer was noticed in the act of removing a lock of hair from his writing-case and folding it in his bosom. Major M'Gregor, scribbling on a scrap of paper a few lines to his father, folded and enclosed them in a bottle; at least it might save his kinsfolk and dear ones from long and terrible doubt as to his fate. He had no sooner done this when some new call on his emotion drove all recollection of the bottle from his head. It was dropped in the cabin, yet by a singular fate ultimately floated off from the wreck and was picked up long afterwards at Barbadoes.

And now the waves sucked higher and higher under their feet, and beat around more furiously, as if angry that the fire should dispute their prey. A voice cried, "What! Is the *Kent's* compass really gone?" It was so: in one of the lurches, the binnacle, torn from its fastenings, was flung across the deck, and the compass dashed to pieces. It was useless, of course, but it seemed a token, sealing their fate and the vessel's, and a bitter cry followed its loss.

It was at this appalling moment that it occurred to the fourth mate, Mr. Thompson, to send a man to the foretop, rather with the ardent wish that some friendly sail might be descried on the face of the waters, than with any expectation that the wish would be realised. Yet all eyes were turned on the man with a flash of expiring hope. Up he climbed and cast his eyes around the horizon. Then came a moment of unutterable suspense; but he made no sign. Then suddenly he threw his head forward, petrified, motionless, his eyes straining upon one spot in the grey waste. Were his lips parting? Surely he was speaking—hush!

'God in heaven! Merciful Father! Yes—he waves his hat. Oh, listen, listen!" Then down upon their tense, still hearts, comes the shout—

"*A sail on the lee bow!*"

Dead silence on deck. Men look at each other's faces and find them livid. Then a cry—a cheer—such a chorus of bursting gladness. Tears—there are plenty now. Hope—it is leaping up, filling the night as with stars. Life—it is full, pulsing, wildly echoing in the shout after shout that goes up from the kneeling multitude; for they are on their knees now. The man springs down upon deck, waving his hat. Over Captain Cobb's face breaks a faint smile: it will not do to rejoice too soon, but even this stern man feels his heart glow within him at the news. To hide his emotion, he shouts his orders prompt and fast. "Hoist the signals—fire the minute guns—down upon the vessel—the help sent from heaven—with all the sail still left us!" Under the three topsails and the foresail the *Kent* moves forward—in her bosom a fiery death, around the tossing grey ocean, and on her decks, friend clasping friend's hand, wife in husband's arms, women showering mad kisses on their babes. Death and life race neck-and-neck. The sailors dash to the guns: load, fire, and reload. Hours—years—of life are pent in each flying, hurrying moment.

The stranger proved to be the *Cambria*, a small brig of two hundred tons burden, commanded by Captain W. Cook, and bound to Vera Cruz, with some twenty or thirty Cornish miners on board, and several agents of the Anglo-Mexican Company. At first she does not observe the signal; or is it that in the raging storm she cannot hear the guns? Surely—surely she cannot have seen, and be leaving these six hundred souls to their doom! The cheers die out. You may hear your neighbour's heart beating.

Two minutes—three—five—of heart-shattering doubt. Then the *Cambria* slowly tacks—hesitates. Then, up fly the British colours. The brig crowds all sail. She bears down on the perishing vessel.

But even now there is small hope when a man comes to think sanely of it. The brig is a very small one, and the *Kent* has been burning for hours. Can the boats rescue six hundred people before the end comes—in small boats, across that terrific sea? It is clearly impossible. The last men would have no chance. In such a juncture the word that now passes has a dreadful significance.

"In what order are the officers to be moved off?" asked Captain Cobb.

Major M'Gregor does not hesitate:—

"Of course *in funeral order*, the juniors first."

Colonel Fearon confirms this: "Most undoubtedly, the juniors first," he says, adding, "and see that any man is cut down who presumes to enter the boats before the women and children."

He raises his voice as he says this, and it is necessary. Already the mad lust of self-preservation is lighting the eyes of the soldiers and sailors as they look at the boats. A moment may disgrace them all; a moment may lift them to heroism. The officers seize this moment. They draw their swords and stand by the starboard cuddy-port where the cutter is lashed.

The ladies and as many of the soldiers' wives as it could safely carry were now bestowed in the cutter. It was half-past two in the afternoon, and the fire had now been raging furiously for four hours and a half, when, hastily wrapped in the first odds and ends of clothing that came to hand, the women in mournful procession advanced from the after-cabins to the starboard cuddy-port, from the outside of which the cutter was suspended. Not a word was spoken—not a cry escaped from their white lips; even the infants ceased to wail, as though conscious of the unspoken anguish that was rending the hearts of their parting parents, or knowingly emulating the fortitude of their elders. In one or two instances ladies begged to be left behind to perish or be saved with their husbands—that was all; and being assured that every moment's delay might—nay, *would*—occasion the sacrifice of human life, they allowed the sailors to tear them from their husbands' arms and without another murmur took their places in the boat, that hung over the raging sea.

To lower a boat in a storm is always a critical task. Twice as the cutter was let down a cry was heard from those on the chains that the boat was swamping. The order was given to "unhook." Captain Cobb, knowing the danger, had stationed a man ready with an axe to cut the tackle if any difficulty occurred in this "unhooking."

And it did occur. The stern tackle was immediately cleared, but the ropes at the bow got foul, and the sailors found it impossible to obey the order. For a while the axe was plied in vain, and the movement became inconceivably critical, as the boat, following the motions of the ship, was gradually rising out of the water. In another instant it would be hanging perpendicularly by the bow, and its passengers flung over into the water. Just then a wave struck the stern and lifted it, enabling the seamen to disentangle the tackle. In a trice the cutter was dexterously cleared, cast off from the ship, and soon was seen battling its way towards the brig—at one instant a speck upon the summit of a billow; the next, deep down, out of sight in the horrid vale beyond, only to reappear and fight its brave way further forward.

The *Cambria* in prudence lay at some distance from the *Kent*, for at any moment the powder might blow up, and so the boats had far to row. To balance the boat and allow the rowers space to ply their labours, the women and children were packed "close as herrings" under the seats and thwarts. Soon, as the drenching spray flew into the boat, they were sitting in water up to their breasts, and it became terrible work to move the boat.

And even when they reached the *Cambria's* side the anxious task was far from over. Someone shouted, "The children first!" and the half-drowned little ones were thrown up or handed to the willing hands above. Then came the women, who with every lift of a wave beneath would spring up and be caught by the Cornishmen hanging over the *Cambria's* bulwarks. One lady alone missed her jump and fell short; she was within an ace of destruction, but as she fell back, managed to clutch at a rope that dangled over the brig's side, and there held on until dragged aboard.

It had been a terrible half-hour for the husbands and fathers that strained their eyes from the deck of the *Kent*. But now as they saw the cutter's crew taken into safety, they seemed to forget their own danger in the storm of joy and gratitude that shook them. Meanwhile the boats from the *Cambria* had drawn near, but found it a hopeless attempt to get alongside in the boiling sea. So Captain Cobb resolved to tie a child to each of the remaining women and lower them by ropes over the stern. As the vessel was tossing, and from the difficulty of seizing the exact moment when the boat was beneath the stern, it was impossible to avoid plunging the poor frightened creatures time after time into the sea. No woman was drowned or lost; but the infant children from cold, exposure, and exhaustion perished almost without exception. As the hurry grew, and the short day began to close, the deaths grew more frequent.

Such agony so long protracted renders the heart callous at last. For twenty-four hours the men had been fighting tempest, and fire, and panic, and it seemed as if nature must give out in mere weariness. Even the women beside the corpses of their babes sat paralysed into stony calm. Yet the story of these later hours is full of episodes of generous gallantry and unselfish devotion. As Death began to deal his blows less sparingly, two or three soldiers, to relieve their wives of a part of their families, sprang into the water with their children and almost instantly perished. One young lady refused to leave her father whilst he stuck to his post, and was only saved by the boats after she had sunk five or six times. Another soldier, placed between the hideous alternatives of losing his wife or his four children, saved his wife and left the little ones to perish in the fire. Another, a fine young fellow, having no wife or children of his own, insisted on having three children lashed to him, with whom he plunged into the water. But he could not reach the boat, and was drawn on board the ship again, not before two of the children were already dead. One man fell down the hatchway into the flames; and another had his back broken and fell overboard quite doubled. Another, again, who fell between the boat and the brig's side had his head literally crushed. Many, in their attempts to clamber on board the *Cambria,* slipped back and were never seen again.

But it grew obvious that to delay with the women alone, was risking the lives of all on board. Captain Cobb and Colonel Fearon, therefore, took counsel together, and ordered that a certain fixed number of soldiers should go in each boat. For a moment again discipline was threatened as the order was issued. Many soldiers in their eagerness instantly leapt overboard. They were drowned to a man. One of these was reaching out his hand to grasp the boat when a wave gave it a sudden toss. The bow descended on the man's skull and he sank. This man's wife, for love of him, had actually hidden herself in the vessel at Deal, preferring to go as a stowaway to being left alone in England. Another man—one of the sailors who had set himself over the powder-magazine, awaiting its explosion—now jumped up in a rage—" Well, if she *won't* blow up, I'll see if I can't get away from her!" And he did.

But the disorder was brief. The moral strength of Captain Cobb and the officers stamped it out; and soon discipline reigned again, though the peril grew and grew. It died out with the death of a number of men who had possessed themselves of one of the three boats remaining to the *Kent,* and filled her with plunder from the cuddy-cabins. This plunder overweighted and sank them.

Lower and lower drooped the red sun, and fiercer spread the flames. Captain Cobb felt that fresh measures must be sought for and discovered. A rope was slung out from the spanker-boom, and the soldiers had to crawl along and then slide down into the boats below. Now in so large a vessel as the *Kent,* the spanker-boom, which projects about sixteen or eighteen feet over the stern, rests on ordinary occasions about twenty feet above the water; but now, from the violence of the sea and pitching of the vessel, it was often lifted to a height of thirty or forty feet above the surface. To reach the rope, therefore, that hung from its extremity, was no easy matter; it needed dexterity of hand and steadiness of head. For it was not only the nervousness of creeping along the boom itself, or the extreme difficulty of afterwards seizing the rope and sliding down it, which lost many lives; but the boat which was at one moment directly below, was the next, by the wind and waves, swept fifteen or twenty yards away. If a man failed, then, to seize the right moment for falling, he was left swinging in mid-air, or dropping the rope, tumbled into the sea, where he sank or was crushed by the returning boat.

Many of the soldiers, unable to face this giddy work, threw themselves out of the stern-windows, and were battered to death or drowned. The wiser ones rigged up rafts out of stray spars and hen-coops, which they flung overboard to help those comrades or to be a last retreat for themselves if the flames drove them from the deck. The men were also bidden to tie ropes about their waists in order to lash themselves to these rafts. Whilst they were doing so, one of the Irish recruits, with a delicacy singular at such a time, being able to find no rope except the cordage belonging to an officer's cot, called out to know if there would be any harm in his appropriating it. There was a group of men, too, on the poop, who, having discovered a box of oranges, refused to slake their almost intolerable thirst before the officers had taken their share.

And now, the greater part of the men having been taken off, the officers began to leave the ship. They left in quiet order, "none appearing to be

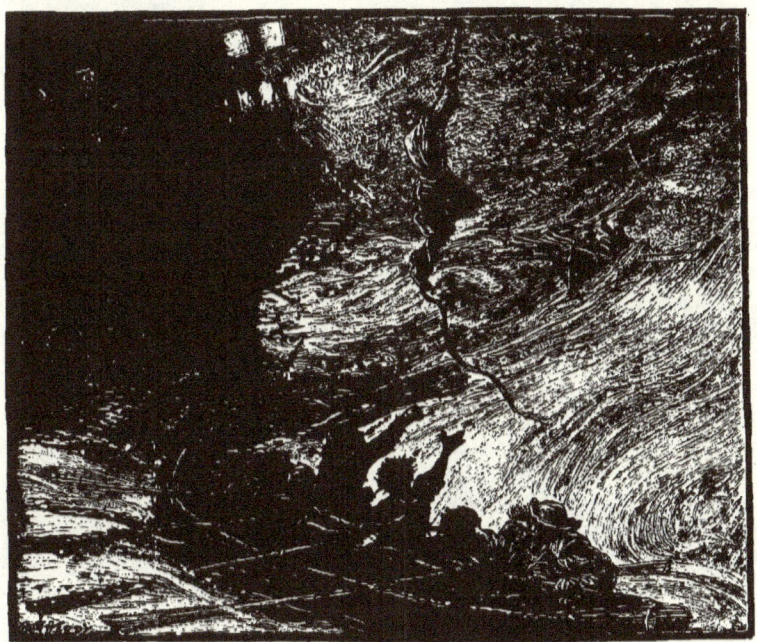

DROPPING INTO THE BOAT (p. 80).

influenced by a vain and ostentatious bravery; nor any betraying an unsoldierlike impatience to quit the ship—those who happened to proceed first, leaving an example of coolness that could not be unprofitable to those who followed. Many, too, who earlier in the day had been overcome by the horrors of the catastrophe, now awoke to play the man in the red light of the setting sun.

For the day was almost done. How must they have thought, as they fixed their eyes on the red ball sinking in the west, of their chances of seeing it rise on the morrow? The cuddy by this time was full of smoke, and strewn with the bodies of those few who had yielded to drunken despair; for there were cowards as well as heroes on board the *Kent*. There were some also whose minds, incredible as it may sound, were set on plunder; and these stalked the safer portions of the wreck like birds of prey. Everywhere the furniture lay strewn and scattered; in one of the cabins was a pig that had broken out from his pen and was snuffing about the rich carpet, and the geese and fowls seem to have got loose on all hands and were cackling with hunger.

The boats were about three-quarters of an hour on each of their journeys. In the intervals many broke down utterly, bursting into tears and lamentations. Almost all the sailors had gone by this time. The remainder of the soldiers, as the darkness thickened around, tied towels and white linen about their heads in order that they might be the more easily recognised by the rescuers.

And soon there were but two classes of men left: on the one hand the indomitable captain and the steady few who insisted on remaining to help rather than seize the opportunity of their own safety; on the other, the cowards whom no threats or entreaties seemed capable of rousing to take the proper steps for their preservation. Captain Cobb used entreaties, then threats: both were equally vain. They refused to journey out along that tossing boom, entreating rather to be lowered as the women had been. But now every moment was precious, and to delay at such work was not to be thought of.

It was getting on for ten o'clock when the boatmen returning for another load shouted out that the *Kent* had sunk two feet since their last trip. The vessel had long lain about ten feet below water-mark; but this was appalling news, for it proved that Death was making ready for his final swoop—had, in fact, begun it. It was now that Colonel Fearon and Major M'Gregor, who had promised to stand by the captain to the last, were induced to leave their posts. There were still three boats to fill. One behind the other, the colonel and the major pulled themselves out over the pitch-black waters on the rocking boom, shaken and pelted by wind and rain. Towards the end the swaying was so violent that Colonel Fearon was drawn down under the boat, and only pulled in by the hair of his head. Major M'Gregor was more fortunate, dropping into the boat without a bruise.

Still Captain Cobb remained and refused to seek the boat until, in his generous desire to save the lives that were entrusted to his charge, he had again endeavoured to urge onward the few who were yet around him. But they were dumb and powerless with dismay. It was only when he found all entreaties useless and heard the guns, whose tackle had been burst asunder by the fast-spreading flames, successively exploding in the hold, into which they had fallen, that this brave man found the moment had come for providing for his own safety. Springing to the boom, therefore, and laying hold of the "topping-lift," or rope which connects the driver-boom with the mizzen-top, he clambered over the heads of the infatuated wretches who still clung there, unable to advance or recede, and dropped into the water, where he was picked up and conveyed with the rest of the party to the *Cambria*.

Yet the boats did not finally leave the blazing vessel until one more appeal was made. For long a boat lay under the *Kent's* stern, while her crew expostulated with the poor cravens. It was only when the flames, bursting from the cabin windows, almost caught their oars on fire that the gallant fellows left the sorry remnant to meet its self-chosen but none the less horrible fate. Already of the *Cambria's* three boats one leaked so that it had to be plugged with sailors' jackets, another was stove in the bows, and the last was so shattered that for the final trip its oars had to lashed to the cutter's ribs. Yet the captain of the *Cambria* would not let the last boat come alongside his brig until satisfied that all hope was over.

The reader must picture for himself the mad alternations of rejoicing and sorrow among the saved. He must imagine the frantic joy with which husband and wife met, or the despair when a wife 'heard of a husband's death. The final scene shall be told him.

The last boat had scarcely returned when the *Kent*, three miles away, showed a sudden rush of flame running along her upper deck and poop, scaling the masts and rigging, till the whole vessel was one blazing pyramid reflecting a crimson glow on the sails of the *Cambria*. Amid the fire waved the signals of distress hoisted that morning in the first flush of hope. They waved till one by one the three masts tottered and fell over the side. At half-past one the flames at last found their way to the magazine. There was a rending uproar; far and high flew the burning timbers, fell headlong, and were quenched; and then the darkness of night descended, lit only by the red ribs of the still floating and still burning wreck.

The fortunes of those few men left on the *Kent* still have to be followed. Driven to the chains, they held these till the masts went overboard, and then clung to them in the water. It would seem as if the last chance of help had gone from them; yet it was not so.

It happened that a Liverpool barque, the *Caroline*, was crossing the Bay of Biscay on her voyage to Alexandria, when her watch observed a bright glow on the horizon, and knew it for the sign of a ship on fire. This was about midnight. The captain, in spite of the fierce sea running, immediately set his maintop-gallant sail, and made for the spot. At one, or soon after, a column of light leapt into the sky; and though too far distant to hear, they guessed it to be the explosion.

Half an hour after, they were near enough to descry the wreck of the *Kent*, lying head to the wind. She was but a skeleton now, yet the ribs and timber-frames revealed the outlines of her double ports and quarter galleries, and proved her to be an Indiaman. The fire had almost reached the water's edge, and above her, as she pitched on the long swell of the Bay of Biscay, floated a long, dark cloud to leeward, dotted with myriads of sparks.

As the *Caroline* came up, her crew noticed the remains of a mast, and some spars, tossing under the weather quarter of the wreck. They thought, as well they might, that no one was left to save. But as the barque came across the bows of the *Kent*, a shout was heard. It seemed to come from the very heart of the fire. The crew strained their eyes, and presently saw a cluster of dark figures clinging about a mast.

In the heavy seas the *Caroline* was hove-to to leeward to be the better situated for intercepting any floating rafts or wreckage. The mate and four seamen pushed off in the jolly-boat through a sea strewn far and wide with heaving timbers, chests, and spars. It was ticklish work to pick their way among these and bring the jolly-boat under the *Kent's* stern.

The first living soul they saw was a man who clung to a spar close under the *Kent's* counter. Through the ports of the gun-room long tongues of flame were lapping around him, and every time the stern heaved up he was caught high in air in the midst of this seeming furnace. Then, as he shrieked, the wreck would dip again, and plunge him deep in water. The rescuers, neglecting their own safety, pulled close and held out their hands. But at the same moment the spar, eaten through by the fire, snapped asunder, and he went down into the sea for ever.

The mate gave orders to back. The jolly-boat was taken round to the floating mast, and six men saved from off it. The party had now to return, as the boat would not safely carry more than eleven persons; but in half an hour they came again and carried off six more.

As they were getting ready for a third venture, came the end. With a last hiss the glowing framework of what was once the stately *Kent* sank and disappeared. The light that so awfully had illumined the sea was blotted out in a moment; the hoarse fury of the flames was hushed, and where they had roared, only the wind whistled.

With admirable forethought Mr. Wallen, the mate of the *Caroline*, had, as the last spark died out, set the spot by a star, and waited for daylight within helping distance, bidding his men shout at intervals to encourage any who might still be afloat and alive on the wreckage. For long there was no answer, and then a feeble "Hallo!" The barque's crew answered it cheerily.

Day broke. On the water still tossed a mast, in the cordage of which four men could be descried. They seemed dead; but as the boat put off, two feebly stretched out their arms. They were rescued. The others were dead: one lay as if sleeping, lashed firmly to the mast, with his head resting on it as if it were a pillow. The other, fixed between the cheeks of the mast, seemed as if rising from a seat to welcome the succour that found him a corpse. His arms were still held out; his eyes fixed in a last stare on the advancing boat. They were left in these same attitudes. Many, no doubt, must have drifted past the *Caroline* in the night, and perished. A boat of the *Kent* was found drifting, but it was empty.

While the *Caroline's* jolly-boat is fighting her way back with the last of the Indiaman's crew, let us turn to the *Cambria*. Unconscious of this completion of her work, she was running for England through the gale. The wind had grown more furious again; her decks were crowded; in her cabin built to accommodate ten people, were now crowded more than eighty. Indeed, there was need to hurry, for pestilence was at their heels. In the tainted atmosphere below deck no light would burn; and the breath of hundreds arising in that close space raised an apprehension at one time that the brig was on fire. In this misery a child—a girl—was born on board. She was christened Cambria, and survived.

Under straining masts, at ten knots an hour, Captain Cook kept on his

RESCUING THE SURVIVORS (p. 84).

course, and on the 3rd of March the cry of "Land!" was heard. That same evening they passed the Scilly Light, and just after noon on the 4th, dropped anchor in Falmouth Harbour.

Of the kindness of the Falmouth people; the thrill which the news carried through England; the testimonials to the crew of the *Cambria;* the measures taken for the relief of the survivors—we have not space to tell. We will leave them as still in the old "funeral order" they disembark in the Cornish harbour—the women first, then the soldiers and sailors, the officers, and last of all the man whose name, to-day half forgotten, deserves to stand high on the roll of British heroes—Captain Henry Cobb.

One woman, twenty-five children, and fifty-four men perished in this catastrophe. There have been deadlier shipwrecks, but scarcely one more tragically full of the details of protracted anguish. Nor should we omit to call attention to one or two circumstances in which the survivors detected the plain hand of Providence. But for the tempest that caused the calamity, Captain Cobb could not have kept the fire at bay by flooding the hold; and the *Kent* would have burnt before the *Cambria* could send a boat to the rescue. The fire too, though it had the ship in its power, was eleven hours in reaching the powder-magazine—an extraordinary length of time. More startling is the fact that the *Cambria* had been unexpectedly kept in port for a month, and had wholly altered her course on the morning of the fire. The *Kent* had sighted no vessel before, nor did the *Cambria* sight one until well in the Channel. And had the *Cambria* been homeward bound, her provisions would not have supplied the sufferers with a single meal; and had she carried a full cargo, not one-half the number could have been rescued without sinking the brig.

Finally, as a monument of heroic obedience to discipline this story deserves to be told many times. Let any reader turn back to the pages that tell of *La Méduse*, and consider what might have been the fate of these six hundred souls, had no spirit of self-sacrifice, no ready acceptance of peril before dishonour, animated the officers of the *Kent*. A stately ship went down: but as her crew stood on the *Cambria's* deck, and, looking back on their fearful track, saw the *Kent* that had passed over the sea like a conqueror, become a pillar of fire in the desert of the waters, they must have felt in their hearts that a better thing had taken her place in the world.

WEXFORD. 1798.

THE SUFFERINGS OF CHARLES JACKSON.

Written by Himself. (Wexford, 1798.)

I WAS born at Sudbury in Suffolk, and at an early period of life went to Ireland. At Cork I married, and received two hundred pounds with my wife. In the beginning of the year 1797, I settled in the town of Wexford as a carver and gilder, where, being the only person in that line of business in that county, I was much employed, and enabled to support my family in a creditable manner, till the breaking out of the late horrid rebellion.

Wexford is a sea-port, borough, market, and corporate town, and rather populous for its size. It is the chief in the county of that name, and the third largest in the province of Leinster. It is governed by a mayor, recorder, and bailiffs. The town is seated on a bay in the Irish Channel, at the mouth of the river Slaney, which is formed by two necks of land with an entrance half a mile broad, and was formerly defended by two forts, one at the extremity of each isthmus: but as this entrance is obstructed by sandbanks, ships drawing more than ten feet of water seldom enter it, but load and unload three miles from the town, near the south side of the haven, where there is sufficient depth of water, but no shelter from the south winds. The town is irregularly built, and the streets are narrow. There is a large and elegant new church in it.

The trade of Wexford is not very extensive; it consists chiefly in barley and malt, of which it exports great quantities, and in beer, beef, hides, tallow, and butter. In 1763 it contained 1,300 houses, of which 650 were slated. In 1788 it had 1,412. But its chief boast and ornament is a magnificent wooden bridge over the river Slaney, which was built by Mr. Cox, an American, with a subscription of £14,000.

On Friday evening, May 25th, 1798, information was first received of the rebels being in force, about twelve miles from Wexford. The troops at that time in the town, consisting of a party of North Cork Militia (between three and four hundred men), and the cavalry and infantry corps of yeomen, were under arms the whole of the night; and on Sunday morning the alarm increased on hearing that the rebels were burning the houses of all the Protestant farmers in the neighbourhood. A party of the North Cork Militia (106 men) were ordered out under the command of Lieutenant-Colonel Foote, and Major Lombard, and marched to a place called Oulard, where they were met by the rebels. The situation of the ground was so unfortunate that the party, after firing three rounds (by which a considerable number of the rebels were killed), was surrounded and cut to pieces, Lieutenant-Colonel Foote, a sergeant, and three privates only escaping.

Lieutenant-Colonel Foote has given the following relation of it in a letter to a friend:—"I marched to a hill called Oulard, where between four and five thousand rebels were posted. From their great superiority of numbers, it was not my intention to have attacked them, unless some unforeseen favourable circumstances would warrant that measure; however, my officers were of a contrary opinion. I met here part of a yeoman cavalry corps, about sixteen; the remainder with their sergeant having that morning joined the rebels. I halted with this corps, while I sent a note by their trumpeter to Wexford, with orders for two officers and forty men to march thence to us to support our detachment, apprehending that the rebels, from their numbers, might intercept our retreat. Afterwards, when I joined the party, I found that they were moved forward by the officer next in command; and the soldiers cried out that they would beat the rebels out of the field. By this movement we were immediately engaged with the rebels, who fired from behind the hedges, without showing any regular front. We beat their advanced party from one hedge to another, killing great numbers of them, till they retreated in much confusion to the main body, which consisted mostly of pikemen. I considered this a favourable opportunity of forming the detachment for the purpose of retreating, or of receiving the enemy in a good position; and I used every exertion to effect it; but, unfortunately, the too great ardour of the men and officers could not be restrained. They rushed forward, were surrounded and overpowered by numbers, they displayed great valour and intrepidity, and killed great numbers of the rebels. Of this detachment none have as yet returned to Wexford but myself, a sergeant, and three privates. I received a wound from a pike in my breast, a slight one in my arm, and several bruises and contusions."

The moment an account of this disaster arrived, the Wexford infantry, which were assembled on the quay, insisted on being allowed to go out to meet the rebels, or revenge the slaughter of their friends. Their officers, to pacify

THE SCENE AT WEXFORD (p. 89).

them, marched them over the bridge of Wexford, and then addressed them, and at last prevailed upon them to return to the town.

The terror of the inhabitants that night can better be imagined than described. To add to it, all the families in the neighbourhood who were able, were seen flying into the town, leaving their property behind them; the women who had lost their husbands in the late engagement, running through the streets with their fatherless children, with all the expressions of distress. Nothing could exceed the anxiety visible in every countenance of the female inhabitants who had husbands, sons, fathers, or brothers belonging to the different loyal corps of volunteers, and the constant apprehension of the arrival of the insurgents

flushed with the recent victory, and now rendered more formidable by having obtained the arms and ammunition of the militia who were slain. It indeed appeared to us, unacquainted with the miseries of civil war, a terrible scene.

GETTING INTO THE BOATS (p. 91).

That night, Sunday, May 27th, the loyal inhabitants were all employed in making preparations for the arrival of our foes, and hourly in hopes of reinforcements from Waterford. The next day, Monday, May 28th, about one o'clock, we saw the smoke of the town of Enniscorthy, then in flames. Enniscorthy is situated on the sea-coast, about eleven miles from Wexford. The loyalists made a most gallant defence, and would have repulsed the rebels had not the Catholic inhabitants treacherously set fire to the town, to smother the troops who were defending it. Thus circumstanced, the troops were obliged to secure their safety in flight, after having cut off about five hundred of the rebels. Here it may not be improper to remark that the manner in which the rebels attacked their opponents was by driving before them a great quantity of horses and cattle in order to disorder their ranks.

At about four o'clock this afternoon, no description can give an adequate idea of the scene presented at Wexford. Such of the Protestant inhabitants as had escaped from Enniscorthy and its neighbourhood, pushed into the town in crowds; persons of the first fortunes in that part of the country, covered with dust and blood, with their infants in their arms, and their wives clinging behind them; and such women as had not been able to procure a horse or seat with their husbands, endeavouring to keep up with the mob of fugitives, with their children in their arms and others hanging to them; women who, but a few hours before, were in possession of every comfort life could afford. The inhabitants of Wexford, still more terrified by the spectacle now before them, were each endeavouring to secure a berth for their wives and children on board some one of the vessels lying in the harbour, every one of which was soon filled as full as it could hold. The gallant husbands and fathers now returned to their respective parades, apparently fortified with a double portion of courage, since the objects of their tenderest care seemed to have been placed in safety. The next morning, Tuesday, May 29th, a party of the Donegal Militia arrived, with two pieces of cannon, and brought news that more assistance was advancing; but about twelve o'clock we received intelligence that a party of the Meath Militia, with three howitzers, had been taken by the rebels. Orders were now given that all fires should be put out, and that such houses as had thatched roofs should be immediately stripped, to prevent the disaffected party from following the example of their associates at Enniscorthy, by setting fire to the town during the time of its being attacked.

On Wednesday, May 30th, in the morning, the troops (the Donegal and Cork Militia, near 600 in all) went out to meet the rebels, who were now supposed to be about 15,000 strong. About three miles from Wexford, at a place called Three Rocks, there was some firing; when the militia, finding them so powerful from numbers, and in possession of the artillery taken the day before, retreated to the town.

There were at this time in the gaol of Wexford, Mr. Beauchamp, Bagenall Harvey, Mr. Edward Fitzgerald, of Newpark, and Mr. J. Colclough, of Bally-toigue, all men of property and of great interest in the county—the two latter were Roman Catholics, but Mr. Harvey was a Protestant—they had been apprehended and committed to gaol by the High Sheriff on Saturday, the 26th of May, in consequence of an order from Government.

A council was called, consisting of the principal officers in the town; and it was resolved that it was impossible to defend the town, as the greater part of the Catholics who had taken up arms had deserted. The proportion of the Catholic inhabitants I believe to have been about three to one Protestant, but only 200 had taken up arms; on the remainder, however, no dependence could be placed. Two gentlemen, Mr. Loftus Richards, a counsellor, and his brother, were appointed to offer to surrender the town to the rebels, and to endeavour to save the lives of the inhabitants; to which conditions the rebels agreed. In the meantime, the troops, accompanied by all the unmarried yeomen, effected their escape to Duncannon Fort, about twenty-three miles off.

I now return to what more immediately relates to myself. On Thursday, May 24th, three days before the breaking out of the rebellion, my wife was brought to bed; and on the Monday following, the day of the battle at Enniscorthy, I thought myself fortunate that I could remove her with her infant, and place them on board one of the vessels, in which we had no doubt of being safely carried to Wales. In this vessel we continued on the open deck, with only a sail to cover us, till Wednesday morning, May 30th, when, about two o'clock, we saw the toll-house and part of the bridge of Wexford on fire.

The town was immediately in an uproar; and, while the cavalry were endeavouring to cut away a part of the bridge, to prevent the flames from communicating to the town, the quays and every avenue leading to the waterside were crowded with women and children, begging in the most pitiable manner to be admitted on board the vessels. But that was impossible; they were already filled in every part. One young lady in particular threw herself into the sea, to get on board a small boat that was near the quay, and would have been drowned, had not some men in a boat taken her up; and they were immediately in great danger of losing their lives owing to the numbers who pressed forward to reach their boat. On seeing the flames, the vessels all weighed and stood towards the mouth of the harbour, where they cast anchor.

About one o'clock a white flag was seen flying in Wexford (a signal that the rebels were in possession of the town), and the captain of our vessel instantly answered it by another. His example was immediately followed by the rest, except two which sailed for Wales. They then again weighed anchor, and stood for the town. We now concluded the die was cast, and that we were to be given up to our enemies. Every entreaty I could urge was strenuously enforced to induce the captain to carry us to Wales, but without effect. With a mind almost distracted, I went into the hold, where my wife and her infant were now lodged, to take what I supposed would be a last farewell, but the horror expressed in her emaciated countenance deterred me from communicating all my apprehensions. At length we arrived at the quay; and, with my charge, I was landed on the beach. Which way to turn me I knew not, and every moment expected that a ball or pike would put an end to my miseries. Towards my own house I was afraid to move, believing that I should be murdered on my way.

While I was in this anxious state of suspense, one of their captains, of the name of Furlong, came up to me, and asked me if I belonged to the town, and whether I had any arms. I told him that at the house where I had lived I had a musket. He bade me follow him and give it up. I requested him to protect us through the town, as we had half a mile to go to my house, which he promised. We passed through crowds of the rebels, who were in the most disorderly state, without the least appearance of discipline. They had no kind of uniform, but were most of them in the dress of labourers, white bands round their hats and green cockades being the only marks by which they were distinguished. They made a most fantastic appearance, many having decorated themselves with parts of the apparel of ladies, found in houses which they had plundered. Some wore ladies' hats and feathers; others, caps, bonnets, and tippets. From the military, which were routed, they had also collected some clothing, which added to the motley show. Their arms consisted chiefly of pikes of an enormous length, the handles of many of them being sixteen or eighteen feet long, scythes, hay-knives, scrapers, currying knives, and old rusty bayonets fixed on poles; some carried rusty muskets. They were accompanied by great numbers of women shouting and huzzaing for the *Croppies*, and crying, "Who now dare say, '*Croppies lie down*'?" alluding to a popular song. It was impossible for a mob to be more wild and frantic; many of the men seemed in a state of intoxication. The houses first attacked were the Custom House, that of Mr. Lee the collector, Captain Boyd's, and the Rev. Mr. Millar's. In a short time nothing remained but the bare walls. The Catholic inhabitants were unmolested, and numbers of them assisted the rebels, and even seized and delivered up their Protestant neighbours, a great number of whom were committed to prison.

Following close the horse of our conductor, I passed safely with my wife and child through this terrible scene to my house. I gave him my musket, and he rode off. My wife lay down on a bed, and I crept under it, thinking to hide myself in case I should be sought for.

I had not been in this situation more than ten minutes when I heard my name called, and a sound of feet on the stairs. Presently the door opened, and one Patrick Murphy, with six others, all armed, came into the room. This Murphy was a near neighbour of mine, and had always professed a great regard for me. My wife, on seeing him, threw herself off the bed with the child in her arms, and fell on her knees, entreating them to spare me. One of them swore, if she did not say where I was, he would blow her brains out. On hearing this, from fear of her being injured, I showed myself, and was immediately seized and dragged downstairs. My wife begged to be allowed to go along with me; but they told her that if she attempted to follow, they would run her through with their pikes. I left my house, suffering the pangs of a man going to an execution, and was conducted to the barracks, near a mile off, through streets filled with creatures who appeared to be more like devils than men.

At the barracks I was put into a room, in which there were about eight others, all expecting soon to be put to death. Every moment some of the rebels, armed with an old bayonet fixed to the end of a long pole, rushed in, asking if there were any bloody Orangemen or informers there. One of the townsmen pointed me out: on which he made a thrust at my throat; but the point was prevented from entering by a thick cushion under my cravat. He then wounded me just below my hip.

At that moment, Counsellor Richards, belonging to the town, who had been obliged to join the rebels to save his own life, came into the room with Mr. Bagenall Harvey—who had been taken out of the gaol, and was made commander-in-chief by the rebels—and seeing the state I was in, requested him to save me, which Mr. Harvey did by taking me out with him. Which way to go I knew not, and entreated Mr. Richards to convey me to a place of safety. He

"THEY MADE A MOST FANTASTIC APPEARANCE" (p. 92).

said he did not know what was best to do with me, but would take me to a Mr. Hughes, at the Foley, a brewery; he accordingly protected me through the midst of the mob, as we had to go almost two hundred yards from the barracks.

Unfortunately, as I entered the house, one of the townsmen saw me, and informed others that an Orangeman had secreted himself in that house. I went up a back staircase, and got into a small room at the top of the house, where was a bed lying upon the ground. Being almost exhausted, I intended to lie down; but had not been above five minutes in the room when I heard persons below searching the house. I opened a window that looked into the garden, and thought to leap out, but fortunately saw the tops of some of the rebel pikes just under me. I should then have crept under the bed, but providentially saw a small door in the inside of the room, belonging to a cupboard which was formed by the eaves of the house. I got in, but was forced to sit almost double.

My pursuers soon afterwards came into the room; and not seeing me, were going out again, when one of them called the others back to examine the cupboard, which he had just observed. I then thought nothing could save me; and if ever living man felt the terrors of death, I did. He opened the door of the cupboard, but providentially, holding his musket slanting, the muzzle, pushed into the cupboard, struck against the roof; on which, supposing it empty, without turning his head he went away. Thus disappointed, I heard them propose to set fire to the house; but that was overruled.

In that situation I continued till ten o'clock at night. I then ventured out, and got over the rocks to a place called Maudlin Town (near a mile from Wexford), to the house of an old woman of the name of Cole, whom I thought I could trust. I found the house empty, and without any furniture, except an old bedstead with some straw upon it. Being fearful I should be seen if I lay on the top, I was forced to get under it and lie the whole night upon nothing but the earthen floor. Having eaten nothing the whole day, and being almost worn out with exertion and agitation of spirits, I endeavoured to sleep; but my terror for fear the rebels should come in and put me to death, prevented me. People came into the cabin several times during the night, but never looked under the bed.

About eight o'clock the next morning, May 31st, the old woman who owned the cabin came home (she was a Roman Catholic), and I made myself known to her, begging in the most earnest manner that she would permit me to remain concealed there till affairs were a little settled. She told me she would as long as she could without endangering herself, and that she would go into town and see how matters went, which she accordingly did; and in about two hours returned with information that the insurgents were searching all the houses for Protestants, and committing them to gaol; and further told me, if I should be found there, that they would kill her, and burn the house; therefore it was necessary I should go to some other place. I thought it prudent to comply. She then gave me some bread and beer, and advised me to try and get among the fields and lie in the hedges by day, and travel by night.

Accordingly now, as every house was shut against me, I had no friends to fly to for refuge. I got out at her back-door and went about two miles across the country, when I met an old woman, and requested her to show me what road I had better take to effect my escape. She told me it was in vain to attempt it; for that, if I did not belong to the rebels, my own brother would betray me. I left her, and went on; but soon heard voices behind me, calling on me to stop, and I should have mercy. I turned round, and saw six men advancing with pikes in their hands. They seized me, and conducted me back to town, and then put me into gaol, in which I found about two hundred and twenty Protestants.

The gaol is a very strong building situated at a short distance from the barracks, and so built round with walls that you can see no person whatever pass or repass.

Towards the evening of this day (May 31st) a fellow of the name of Dick Monk, one who had formerly been a shoe-black in the town, but now was raised by the rebels to the rank of a captain, came into the gaol, and bade us prepare our souls for death, for that all of us, except such as upon examination he should release, would be put to death at twelve o'clock that night. The manner of his examining was twofold: first politically, and then religiously. The form of his political examination was this:—

Question. Are you straight?
Answer. I am.
Question. How straight?
Answer. As straight as a **rush.**
Question. Go on then.
Answer. In truth, in trust, in unity, and in liber**ty.**
Question. What have you got in your hand?
Answer. A green bough.
Question. Where did it first grow?
Answer. In America.
Question. Where did it bud?
Answer. In France.
Question. Where are you going to plant it?
Answer. In the Crown of Great Britain.

They then gave each other the hand, but in a way I did not understand. The preceding questions and answers, however, appear to be a part of the "United Irishmen's Catechism," by which they know each other.

The religious examination was this:—

Question. Are you a Christian?

If the person answered "Yes," he was requested to cross himself, and say the Ave Maria. If he could do this in the Roman Catholic manner, and go through the other form, then he was acquitted.

I believe Monk, after having gone through this twofold examination with several persons, selected six to be saved, and took them with him out of the prison. The situation of us that remained can better be imagined than described. We all went directly to prayer, and spent the night in the most horrid suspense. No one, however, came near us that night. The next morning,

June 1st, some potatoes and water were brought us, which proved a very seasonable relief.

On the Sunday following, June 3rd, a man of the name of Murphy, by trade a labourer, but who had been an evidence against some of the United Irishmen at the preceding assizes (though none of them suffered), was taken up by the rebels, and condemned to die.

On Monday morning, June 4th, about nine o'clock, John Gurly, one of the prisoners, came to me; "Jackson," said he, "the Lord have mercy upon you! You are called to go into the yard with my brother Jonas and Kinneith Mathews." The words had such an effect on me, that my tongue cleaved to the roof of my mouth; for I thought I was called to be executed. The gaoler came in, and took us into the yard, where was one Edward Fraine, a tanner, who lived in John Street, and was supposed to make by his trade £300 a year. There were also many other persons belonging to the town. Fraine was captain of the rebel guard for the day. As soon as I came out, he said, "Mr. Jackson, I believe you know what we want of you." I answered. "Yes, I suppose I am going to die." I then fell upon my knees, and begged that, if this was the case, I might be allowed to see my wife and child.

He swore that I should not; that I was not then going to die, but that a man was to die at six o'clock that evening, and that he did not know more proper persons to execute him than me and the two others. He added, "I suppose you can have no objection, as he is a Roman Catholic?" "Why sir," said I, "should I have no objection to commit murder?" "You need not talk," replied he, "about murder. If you make any objections, you shall be put to death in ten minutes; but if you do your business properly, perhaps you may live two or three days longer. So I expect you three will be ready at six o'clock this evening." Another then came up and said, "Mr. Jackson, if you could procure a few orange ribbons, to tie about your neck at the time of the execution, it would, I think, have a very pretty appearance; and, at the same time, I have a couple of balls much at your service, when it is over; as I think it is a pity you should get no return for the favour you confer."

After these taunts we were carried back to our cells, and spent the day in prayer till six o'clock; at which time, being brought to the great door, we found the prisoner Murphy with nearly a thousand men about him. The procession went in the following order:—A large body of pikemen, who were formed into a hollow square. A black flag. Then the drums and fifes. Murphy, the condemned man, came next, followed by me, with Gurly and Mathows behind me. As soon as this arrangement was made, the Dead March was struck up and beaten from the gaol to the place of execution, which was about a mile and a half off, on the other side of the bridge, on a wide strand. The procession passed by my house. When I came opposite to it, I was so much affected as almost to faint; some water was brought me, and I proceeded.

"I WAS NEXT CALLED UPON" (p. 98).

As soon as we reached the destined spot, all the rebels, with their arms in their hands, knelt down and prayed for about five minutes. This I understood was because the victim was a Roman Catholic. An order was then given to form a half-circle with an opening to the water. The poor man was directed to kneel down, with his back to the water, and his face towards us; which he did, with his hands clasped. I requested to be allowed to tie my cravat round his eyes. They told me not to be too nice about the matter, for in a few minutes it would be my own case.

The muskets were then called for, but it was suggested, if they gave us three muskets, we might turn and fire at them; on which it was settled that we should fire one at a time. The first appointed to fire was Mathews, and it was remarkable the piece missed fire three times.

During this time, the countenance of the condemned man exhibited such an appearance of inexpressible terror as will never be effaced from my memory. The man who owned the musket was "damned," and asked what sort of piece was that to carry to a field of battle? A common sporting gun was then brought, and fired by Mathews, and the ball hit the poor fellow in the arm.

I was next called upon, and, suspecting that I should not fire at their object, but turn upon them, two men advanced, one on each side of me, and held cocked pistols at my head; two also stood behind me with cavalry swords, threatening me with instant death if I missed the mark. I fired, and the poor man fell dead; after which, Gurly was obliged to fire at the prostrate body. When it was over, a proposal was made that I should wash my hands in his blood, but this was overruled; they said, as I had done my business well, I should go back. A ring was now formed round us, and a song in honour of the Irish Republic was sung to the tune of "God save the King!" This dreadful business had taken up about three hours, when we were marched back to the gaol.

Two days passed without my being particularly noticed; but during that period many prisoners were taken out, a few at a time, and, being carried to the camp, were piked to death. On Wednesday, June 6th, information having been received that the rebels were defeated at Ross, to revenge the loss, fifteen of the Wexford, and ten of the Enniscorthy people, were ordered out of the gaol for execution.

When this notice was given, I ran into my cell, got upon my knees in a dark corner, and pulled some straw over me; but a man of the name of Prendergast came in and drew me out, uttering shocking threats against me. He dragged me into the yard, where I found my unhappy comrades upon their knees. One of them, who had been bred a Protestant, but had become a Catholic, and who was now imprisoned on a charge of being an Orangeman, requested to have the priest with him before he died. This was immediately granted; and a messenger was sent to Father Curran, the Roman Catholic parish priest of Wexford; he presently came, and, to give effect to his admonition and intercession, had dressed himself in his cowl, and bore a crucifix in his hand; he held up the crucifix, and all present fell on their knees; he exhorted them in the most earnest manner; he conjured them, as they hoped for mercy, to show it; he made every possible exertion to save the lives of all the prisoners, but it was in vain. He said he could witness that the Wexford people had never fired upon them or done them any injury; and that he could not again say mass to them if they persisted in their cruel resolutions. At last, he influenced them so far as to prevail upon them to return into the gaol the fifteen Wexford men; but for those from Enniscorthy he could obtain no remission; accordingly these ten unfortunate persons were murdered.

We then were taken back to our confinement, and in that state remained for a fortnight, every day seeing more prisoners brought in, and others taken out to be massacred, each of us apprehending it would next be his lot. On June 20th, about eight o'clock in the morning, we heard the drums beat to arms and the town bell ring, which was a sure sign to us of our friends being near; but, at the same time, we expected we should be cut off before they could arrive and release us.

In this terrible state of suspense we remained till four o'clock in the afternoon, when we heard a horrid noise at the gate, and a demand for all the prisoners. Eighteen or twenty were immediately taken out to the bridge of Wexford, and there piked to death, and in about half an hour the rebels returned for more victims. In the whole, they took out ninety-eight. Those who were last called out were seventeen in number. Mr. Daniell and Mr. Robinson, both gaugers; Mr. Atkins, a tide-waiter; Mathews and Gurly, who were with me at the execution of Murphy, were included in this lot. When we were turned out of the ward in which we had been confined, into the gaol-yard, we all fell upon our knees, and (wonderful inconsistency of man!) several of the rebels who were to attend us to execution, and perhaps to be our murderers, knelt down with us and began to pray.

It happened that I was so placed in the group as to be surrounded by persons much taller than myself, which either caused me to be unnoticed, or the rebels who came into the gaol to demand us did not personally know me; but while I was in that situation on my knees, my name was repeatedly called, and the ward was searched for me. This was owing to the mob having particularly called me by name, and demanded that I should be brought out of the gaol. I was so overcome with terror and agitation that I did not answer the frequent repetitions of my name. During this time there was indeed a man among the rebels, who saw and knew me, and made signs to me to be silent. This man was a black, and had been servant to a gentleman in the town of Wexford. To the delay occasioned by their not discovering me, it will hereafter appear that I and probably many others owed our lives, as a considerable time was spent in searching for me, before it was known that I was on my knees among the prisoners; who were then ordered to rise and go forward. The mob at the outside, at the head of whom was Dixon, a publican (who had been made a captain by the rebels), and his wife, were very clamorous on account of the delay. The moment Mathews put his head out of the gaol, he was shot dead; which would probably have been the fate of us all, had not Mrs. Dixon, when Mathews fell, immediately advanced, and desired they would desist, as they ought to allow the people on the bridge *the pleasure of seeing us.*

We were accordingly marched to the bridge, and, when we came in sight of the people assembled there to witness the execution, they almost rent the air with shouts and exultations, which, with a violent storm of wind that had

"THEY LEFT US ON OUR KNEES" (p. 101).

suddenly risen, a sky that appeared of the blackest colour, and a continual firing of guns by the undisciplined mob, all together produced an effect the most horrible that the imagination can form. I felt as if cold lead was in my veins; a benumbing kind of stupor deadened all my faculties. My mind urged me to implore mercy of Heaven, but I could scarcely articulate a word of prayer. It was a condition that cannot be described.

When we arrived at the fatal spot on the bridge, I and my sixteen fellow-prisoners knelt down in a row. The blood of those who had been already executed on this spot (eighty-one in number) had more than stained, it streamed upon the ground about us.

They first began the bloody tragedy by taking out Mr. Daniell, who, the moment he was touched with their pikes, sprang over the battlements of the bridge into the water, where he was instantly shot. Mr. Robinson was the next; he was piked to death. The manner of piking was by two of the rebels pushing their pikes into the front of the victim, while two others pushed pikes into his back, and in this state, writhing with torture, he was suspended aloft on the pikes till dead. He was then thrown over the bridge into the water. They ripped open the belly of poor Mr. Atkins, and, in that condition, he ran several yards, when, falling on the side of the bridge, he was piked. Thus they proceeded till they came to Gurly, who was next to me.

At that moment one of them came up to me, and asked me if I would have a priest. I felt my death to be certain, and I answered, " No." He then pulled me by the collar; but was desired to wait till Gurly was finished. While they were torturing him, General Roche rode up in great haste, and bade them beat to arms, informing them that Vinegar Hill camp was beset, and that reinforcements were wanting. This operated like lightning upon them; they all instantly quitted the bridge, and left Mr. O'Connor, an organist; Mr. William Hamilton, the bailiff of the town; and myself, on our knees. The mob (consisting of more women than men) which had been spectators of this dreadful scene, also instantly dispersed in every direction, supposing the King's troops were at hand.

We were so stupefied by terror that we remained for some time on our knees, without making the least effort to escape. The rebel guard soon came to us and took us back to the gaol, telling us that we should not escape longer than the next day, when neither man, woman, nor child of the Protestants should be left alive. But it pleased God to prevent their dreadful intentions from being carried into effect, by giving success to His Majesty's arms.

We entered the gaol with hearts overflowing with gratitude to the Almighty for our late wonderful preservation. For the arrival of the troops we looked with some hope and extreme anxiety the whole night, till about five o'clock in the morning, when we heard the joyful sound of cannon. Our agitation increased; one moment expecting the troops to arrive, and the next that we might on the instant be put to death; when, about eleven o'clock, June 21st, the turnkey came to us to inform us that we might walk out into the large yard. He addressed us by the title of " Gentlemen," from which we were assured that some great alteration had taken place; but we suppressed our feelings, lest the news which influenced them might not be true. About three o'clock, the captain of the rebel guard, a Mr. Murphy, came in and addressed Major Savage, one of the prisoners, offering him the keys of the gaol, and arms for us all, if he would admit some of the rebels into the gaol, and strive to save them from that fate their own consciences told them they so richly deserved. This Murphy kept an earthenware shop on the quay at Wexford. His offer was instantly accepted by all, and accordingly we obtained the arms of those who a few minutes ago were guarding us.

The rebels now changed situations with us, and, as agreed upon, were locked up by Major Savage, who brought all of us who had muskets to the iron rails on each side of the great prison door. Here we stood determined to conquer or die, if attacked. About five o'clock we had the heartfelt gratification of seeing the gallant Captain Boyd, accompanied by the following persons, who with great magnanimity volunteered in that perilous service, and ran a risk of devoting their own lives to save the property and lives of the Protestant inhabitants who remained in the town: they were all members of the Wexford cavalry corps but one: Captain James Boyd, member of Parliament; Lieutenant Perceval, High Sheriff for the county; Corporal John Stetham, Corporal William Hughes, A. H. Jacob, of the Enniscorthy corps; and the following privates—John Tench, Joseph Sutton, Archer Bayly, Marcus Doyle, Abraham Howlin, John Byrne, and William M'Cabe. Mr. Boyd's servant, Christopher Irwine, permanent sergeant of the troop, followed them rapidly on foot, his horse having been shot. They dashed into the town with a degree of valour bordering on despair, and announced with a loud voice that the army was at their heels. This gave the rebels such an electric shock that, panic-struck, they fled in all directions; some over the bridge, others to the Barony of Forth. Their consternation was so great that very few of them attempted on their flight to injure the inhabitants of the town. One rebel fired at Messrs. Rudd and Jacob, but the former soon despatched him. A rebel fired at Lord Kingsborough in the street, for which another person, a loyalist, instantly shot him. Captain Boyd, as he passed the gaol, called out to us not to leave the gaol at present, as the troops expected in town might suppose us enemies. This precaution proved not to be necessary, for the troops were encamped a mile short of the town, and orders issued by the generals that no man should be put to death unless he had been tried and condemned by a "court-martial."

In about an hour after Captain Boyd left us, two companies of the Queen's Royals arrived, and, giving three cheers, set us at liberty. All the green boughs were immediately torn from the windows; and "LIBERTY AND EQUALITY," which before were conspicuous on every door, were now nowhere to be seen. Reprieved criminals only can have experienced such feelings as ours on being released. The scene that followed no pen can describe. Women running in every direction towards the gaol, trembling for the fate of their relatives who had been imprisoned: wives seeking for their husbands, mothers for their sons, sisters for their brothers, and children for their fathers. The ecstasy of those who discovered their friends, and the distraction of others who had lost their dearest connections, cannot be imagined. The gallant soldiers, who were witnesses of what passed, though now accustomed to distressing spectacles, could not refrain from shedding tears, or joining in the exultations. In some instances, the wife, seeing her husband, would rush into his arms, and overwhelm him with caresses, but, on inquiring for a brother, learnt he was no more! . . . But to relate the particulars of that never-to-be-forgotten day, would fill a volume. Of myself I will not say more than that, in the midst of the scene I have attempted to describe, my wife with her infant appeared before me! The sensations of both left us no power of utterance. She saw me, as it were, restored to life; and till then I was ignorant of her fate. We had been separated three weeks and two days, during which I was in constant expectation of death; and she had lingered with scarcely a gleam of hope that I should escape. My infant I had scarcely contemplated a moment in peace from the hour of its birth.

We quitted a spot become horrid to me, and went to the place where I once had a comfortable home. The house was standing uninjured; but everything belonging to me had been destroyed, even to my working tools, within half an hour after the time I was first taken to gaol. A lady in the neighbourhood humanely afforded us an asylum, and once more we sat down in security.

THE LOG-HUT.

I WAS travelling along a road altogether new to me: in fact it was a road that had been opened only the preceding year. Two friends of mine, who had essayed to travel it the past autumn, had supplied me with a sketch of the route, containing the names of the few settlers found along it and the computed distance between the respective houses. I therefore, as a matter of course, marked off the different places where I was to halt; and if anything occurred to prevent me from stopping at the destined places, my whole plan would become disarranged.

So far I had been able to keep to my previously arranged plan; and just as the shades of evening were beginning to enshroud the valley that reposes at the foot of the wild and lofty Pachono mountain, I approached the lone cottage which was marked out on my travelling-chart as the place for me to pass the night in. Although I had never been in that part of the country, yet the building of square logs or "blocks" that now presented itself was in some measure an old acquaintance, since, poor and lonely and cheerless as it seemed, it had acquired a name in the history of that part of the country with which it was connected. Its wooden walls were blackened with the tempests of half a century, and the traditionary tales connected with it were familiar to every child in the distant settlement.

A person of the name of Larner had been induced to settle here, long before any of the valleys in the southern district of the country (now full of people) contained one white inhabitant. What induced this hardy man to bury himself and a young family in the wilderness, so far from all the pale-faces, as the Indians called the white people in those days, is difficult to conceive. On his way to this secluded dell, he must have passed through many a valley which presented a fertile soil, and a more serene climate; but induced by some feeling which must now remain a secret, Larner, with a wife and four or five children, accompanied by a younger brother, took possession of the extreme head of a mountain valley, and there built the sombre-looking building now before me. It has been surmised by many that the contiguity to the adjoining mountain was his chief inducement to settle here, for he was a remarkably keen hunter. There certainly were more wolves and panthers in that vicinity

"THE YOUNG FELLOW . . . SHOT HIM THROUGH THE BRAIN" (p. 107).

than in any other part of the state, besides an abundance of elk and deer, with a great variety of game of smaller note. They did not devote their time exclusively to hunting; for when they had resided here some half-score of years, they had managed to clear away the forest trees from a few acres of land, sufficient to grow more grain than the family would consume.

About this period the Larners were waited on by two Indian warriors of the Six Nations, who informed them that, if they valued their own safety, they must immediately fly from the abode they had so long inhabited. This piece of intelligence, which was delivered with much apparent sincerity, was at the time but little heeded; for although they had never before been actually threatened by the Indians who had occasionally visited them, they had sometimes used a little caution when they suspected a party of Indians were anywhere in the vicinity.

One day, shortly after the visit of the two warriors, the younger of the brothers returned from an excursion on the mountain, with the somewhat startling intelligence that he had crossed, on his way down, the trail of an Indian party, and he should judge from its appearance that the number was something considerable. He further stated that he had, from the summit of an adjoining hill, carefully surveyed the forests all around, but no curling smoke rose above the green foliage (for it was summer) to denote their hunting-fires, neither had he heard the report of fire-arms during the whole day.

To those acquainted with the subtlety of the Indian character, this report was somewhat alarming, and the lone family determined to be circumspect in all their movements. Their arms consisted of three rifles, one used by each of the brothers, and the remaining one by the oldest son, a stout youth of nineteen. It was agreed that they should keep watch during the night, the brothers and the son taking it by turns; and the fire was extinguished before it became quite dark.

Some hours after midnight, and while the father of the family was keeping watch, he thought he perceived a bright spark of fire advancing slowly across the small piece of meadow in the direction of the house; and, as it came nearer, he distinctly saw part of the body of a naked Indian. There was no mistaking the intention of the incendiary; and as all was parched and dry with the scorching sun of July, a fire once kindled against the time-seasoned log-walls of their dwelling, the whole building would be in a blaze in a few minutes.

Larner was in the upper storey, at an opening in one end of the building; but as the Indian came nearer, he changed his course a little, as if he intended to make his fire in the rear of the house.

It was a moment of extreme anxiety. If Larner permitted the villain to pass the rear of the building, they were all in a short time to be burnt out, and most probably massacred by the merciless beings no doubt in ambush close by. If he fired and shot him, retribution would certainly await them all, and in either case he considered them a doomed family. But he did fire; and long before the reverberations were silent in the adjoining mountains, the Indian had given one lofty bound and shrieked the shriek of death.

The report of his rifle brought the whole family to his side, and he related to them all that had taken place; and it seemed a matter of uncertainty whether the Indians would attack them under cover of the yet remaining darkness or postpone their onset until the return of day.

It seems they *did* wait for daylight; and when it returned they commenced firing at the different windows or openings, wherever they imagined they might reach the inmates. This plan, however, had not much effect. One of the younger children received its death-wound; but the rest escaped unharmed for the present.

As I before stated, in the back part of the building there was no opening. The Indians, finding the plan of firing at the windows not likely to produce much effect, determined upon making a circuit through the neighbouring woods, and thereby gaining the defenceless rear of the dwelling. This plan, however, was anticipated by the besieged; for when the firing ceased, the Larners suspected they would be making this movement. The two brothers therefore, without much difficulty, contrived to make two small openings in the shingled roof; and when the assailants emerged from the woods behind the building, the two leaders were instantly shot down.

The rest, unappalled, rushed forward; and before the brothers could reload their pieces, there were a score of savages under the shelter of the building. The son, too, had not been idle; for by thrusting one half of his person through the end window, he had been enabled to fire upon them as they rushed for the house, and had made one of them bite the dust.

Yet, after all, what availed it? Should the Indians instantly set fire to the house, they would all be burnt alive. The brothers, therefore, immediately resolved upon the family quitting the premises and making for the woods.

But this plan was nearly fatal to the whole party; for before they had crossed the slight hollow in front of the woods, the two brothers and three children fell to rise no more. The eldest son was singled out by a tall powerful Indian who pursued him across a field of growing rye. They were each armed with a rifle, yet neither of them stopped to fire. Young Larner, perceiving that the Indian gained rapidly upon him, for his knee had been slightly injured by a ball, bethought himself of a stratagem which ultimately saved him. Some of the party near the house were yet occasionally firing at the fugitives that made for the woods; so young Larner, as if he had received a death-wound, fell amongst the tall grain. The Indian instantly squatted in the rye also, being apparently suspicious of some trick in his intended victim; but in a short time he raised himself upon his knees, in order to scrutinise the place where young Larner lay, when the young fellow, who had been arranging his piece for such an occasion, fired at the Indian, and shot him through the brain.

He did not wait to reload; but in spite of the soreness of his knee, pushed for the woods, which were but a short distance off.

Once behind a sheltering tree, he reloaded his rifle, and having done so, had the satisfaction to find that none of the surviving Indians pursued him. They were many of them engaged in scalping his father and uncle, and a younger brother and two sisters, while others were in pursuit of his mother and elder sister, who had succeeded in reaching the woods.

For two nights he continued to wander in the forest; but during the day he remained in some hollow tree. At last, hungry and weary, he reached a distant settlement on the river Delaware, the inhabitants of which immediately formed themselves into an armed party, and set off for the scene of slaughter. On reaching the place, they presently discovered the dead bodies of nine Indians, and two Larners, and the remainder of the family, except the eldest daughter and the mother. The two last mentioned, it was evident, had been carried off by the surviving Indians, for their bodies were nowhere to be found.

This party remained three or four days in the vicinity of these late scenes of blood; but the mother and daughter returned not. From this period the place was deserted for some years; but the surviving young Larner marrying, he and his wife took possession of the lone and blood-stained building. The tribe of Indians had removed far away to the vicinity of the Seneca and Ciaaga lakes, so that there was no longer any danger to be apprehended from such rude and barbarous neighbours.

Years rolled on, and brought with them a new generation of that devoted family; but more than twenty years passed away without any tidings of the missing females. About this period, some settlers from the part of the country where the Larners originally resided, located themselves in the vicinity of the above-mentioned lakes, where they lived in peace and goodwill with the Indians, from whom they learned the fate of the missing mother and daughter.

They stated that they were pursued and soon captured in the woods; and although they would only submit to be dragged along by force, in that manner they proceeded for a portion of two days. But this mode of proceeding was found so inconvenient to the party, that when they reached the caves in the Moose Mountain, a council was held on the prisoners, when they were adjudged to die. They were then tomahawked, according to the custom of those barbarians; and they had no doubt but their skeletons might be found there still.

This information was some time after imparted to the son and brother of the deceased, who, embracing the first opportunity, accompanied by three friends, repaired to Moose Mountain, sought out the caves, that were almost entirely unknown to the white men, and found the two skeletons in the very position they had fallen beneath the tomahawks of their murderers. They were then removed with much care and labour to the residence of the son, who, with true filial affection, interred them in the same grave with the mouldering bodies of their departed kindred.

. At the time I visited this lone dwelling, the son, who had escaped the family massacre, was still occupying it. He was now old and grey-headed; but he still occasionally took his rifle into the woods in pursuit of game. He too had been the father of a family of sons and daughters, now all grown up, and all except one, I believe, married and settled, one or two in his own district; but the others had been induced to wander away to the Far West. He is still looked upon with a sort of veneration; and scarce a lonely traveller ever visits him to whom he does not relate the lamentable fate of his family.

MISSING!

VERY reader of romance has his pet taste — ranging from the love-affairs of American girls, to the slaughter of African savages. One will love a highwayman, another a Puritan maiden, a third will travel anywhere, so it be in the company of a detective; and I know an old gentleman with a back-garden which he cultivates with tender care, who, among his pansies and carnations, will sit and read of pirates by the hour. Even in pirates he has a crude taste, for his favourite is Captain Blackbeard (who at the best was a stagey villain), and the scene over which he gloats with keenest relish is that of Blackbeard and his mates lighting a brimstone fire in the hold and sitting over it to find who among them could endure it longest.

The present writer confesses to a taste for " Mysterious Disappearances." He regrets that it is not so hearty, quite, as it was some years back. But to this hour a placard on a hoarding if headed " *Missing !* " has a subtle power that will hold him fascinated for minute after minute, to read of the gentleman of sandy exterior who " left his home," and has not, up to date, returned ; of his diamond breast-pin (he always has a diamond breast-pin), his moles, his dark tweed suit, and habit of stooping, &c. &c. And the taste is of a high order. For, first, conceive the situation with which the romance opens. A respectable man —say, a chartered accountant—with tall hat, watch-chain, and all the outward signs of decent living, steps from his varnished front-door down into a busy thoroughfare (or deserted suburban road, according to taste) and—disappears for ever, melts, vanishes into air ! How it ennobles the man ; how it wreathes his black hat with a halo ! From a plain chartered accountant he has become something weird, indefinite, out of nature. A goblin might envy him.

But—and this is more important—reflect also on the imaginative forces that such an act sets to work. There is not a servant-girl in the neighbouring streets that is not lifted at once to the heights of creative fiction—that does not in fancy pursue this irresponsible body in space, tracking with the mind's eye its airy jauntings. And consider finally that there is practically no limit to the possible hypotheses. A man is adrift among the millions of his fellow-men and women—no more is known. He may be dancing, marrying, murdering, or being murdered. It is understood that large numbers of intelligent people find pleasure in reading the " love-passages " in novels. But what a poor narrow pursuit it is ! If a man is in love with a woman, and tells her so, he will either be accepted or dismissed. But if a man be missing, *anything* may happen to him.

Everyone has read of Ginevra, and heard the ditty of the " Mistletoe Bough'';

and most men have followed in imagination (since Matthew Arnold revived old Glanville's narrative) the dim figure of that scholar in ancient Oxford who threw up his dull studies to join the gipsies, whereby his college rooms knew him no more. But for vague grandeur listen to the story of another youth.

He also was an Oxford student—one, as tradition says, marked out for eminence in the Church, and distinction as a theologian. One day he vanished utterly from amongst his friends; nor could search nor speculation yield a hint as to the course he had taken. Almost simultaneously with his departure, men heard of the advent, on the blue Mediterranean, of a daring corsair, who swept the sea like a bird of prey, always daring, and always successful. Ships of all nations were his victims; and the spoils were carried off to a small barren island, which he made his stronghold. Report spoke also of an extremely beautiful and accomplished lady whom he had made the partner of his wild life; and it was said that to her influence his choice of profession was due. At any rate, when the lady died, he distributed the immense booty he had accumulated, the pirates dispersed, and the rock was left without a tenant. Almost immediately after, the student reappeared at Oxford, and quietly resumed his interrupted studies. Of his absence no man could induce him to speak. He took holy orders, rose from step to step in the clerical profession, and died Archbishop of York!

There is an Oriental flavour in this tradition, and the sober-minded reader is free to disbelieve it. But here is one that rests on stronger authority.

Dr. Everhard Feith, author of the learned tract "Antiquitates Homericæ," was a native of Flanders; but from his own country, then distracted by civil dissensions, he passed over to France, where he won considerable respect and distinction as professor of Greek in the University of Liège. Nor was he content with the classical learning that France could afford, but made frequent journeys to Rome, to study the inestimable manuscripts in the Vatican, and also to Greece and the German universities. In fact we are told there was no remarkable seat of learning or school of philosophy that he did not visit, winning everywhere golden opinions as a distinguished scholar.

The professor had returned to Liège after one of these periodical absences, and was engaged in delivering his yearly course of lectures, when walking out one day into the streets of the town, which were full of people, he was beckoned to by a stranger who stood on the opposite side of the road.

Many passers-by (for the thoroughfare was a busy and populous one) saw the professor cross the road and with the stranger enter a house on the other side. From that moment he was never seen again dead or alive.

Hypothesis is just as open to us to-day as to his fellow-townsmen then. Was he murdered in the house? and if so, for what reason? Had he in his many travels joined a secret society and become suspected of betraying it? Had he simply made a deadly foe of some private individual? Was he weary of the dry bones of learning and inclined to sport with public curiosity? or had he committed a secret crime, the detection of which he feared? Did he, tired of the world, enter a monastery? We all know that in the great ice accident on the Serpentine many disappeared whose bodies were never found at the bottom. It would seem as if a man's personality became to him at times, even in prosperity, an insupportable garment. However, conjecture beats an idle wing. All we know is that Dr. Everhard Feith crossed a crowded street at noonday, walked into a house in the sight of many who knew him,. and thereafter became a phantom, a nothing, or, at the most, a name to set on the title-page of the "Antiquitates Homericæ."

Let us take a case in which the mystery was partially, but only partially, solved. At Margate, in the year 1812, there lived an officer in the Coastguard or, as it then was, the Preventive Service. He was a steady, reputable man ; married, and with a family; and was pretty well known to the whole town.

One dim afternoon he went out, as his duty was, to patrol the cliffs as well to look out for any signs of smuggling as to discern, and carry news about, any vessel that might be in difficulties off the coast. The month was November, the hour about four in the afternoon ; the weather squally, with slanting gusts of rain. He was a man in the prime of strength, healthy in mind and body; had a red, hearty face, and bushy black beard. His manner was hearty and frank. In short, he was a commonplace man who knew his business and had a cheery word for his neighbours.

A little imagination will serve to call him up, as with pea-jacket buttoned up to the chin, spy-glass under arm, black beard beaded with drops of rain, and head stooped to the wind to keep his glazed hat from blowing away, he moved westwards along the downs.

There were not many people abroad on this raw afternoon ; but one or two met and stopped to exchange a word with him. All agreed afterwards that his manner was perfectly steady and natural. The last who met him looked back after passing, and saw his figure still sauntering quietly westward along his beat, and vanishing into the drizzle and darkness of the approaching night.

Out of that drizzle and darkness he never appeared. "Quite a simple explanation," the reader will say; "the man tumbled over a cliff in the dark and was washed out to sea."

So people thought when on the following morning he was missed. The night had been pitchy black, with gusts from the south severe enough to be a considerable danger to a man who had made a false step near the cliff's edge. Search was made for the man's body, but without effect; his wife and children mourned for him; another took his place in the Preventive Service; his disappearance ceased to be talked of and was forgotten.

"Thirty years later," says the narrator of this story, "that is, in the summer of 1842, walking with one of my children along the downs, I saw a farmer ploughing at a short distance beyond the flag-staff, and stopped to talk with him on the subject of seaweed manure. While we were conversing, the man observed something glitter in the furrow he had just made. It was the button of a naval officer.

"This led to further examination. The earth was removed, and little more than a foot beneath the surface, the skeleton of a man, with several fragments of his dress, was discovered. It was ascertained that the uniform he had worn was that of the Preventive officers; and it seems probable from various circumstances that we had discovered the skeleton of the man who disappeared in 1812."

Here, of course, the suspicion is that of foul play; for a man may kill himself, but can hardly dispose of his own body. Let us follow this story up with another that has a happier ending.

In the woods to the east of Cromarty, and occupying the summit of a green insulated eminence, is the ancient burying-ground and chapel of St. Regulus. Bounding the south there is a deep narrow ravine, through which there runs a small trickling streamlet, whose voice, scarcely heard during the droughts of summer, becomes hoarser and louder towards the close of autumn. The sides of the eminence are covered with wood, which, overtopping the summit, forms a wall of foliage that encloses the burying-ground except on the east, where a little opening affords a view of the northern Sutor over the tops of trees which have not climbed high enough to complete the fence. In this burying-ground the dead of a few of the more ancient families in the town and parish are still interred; but by far the greater part of it is occupied by nameless tenants, whose descendants are unknown, and whose bones have mouldered undisturbed for centuries. The surface is covered by a short yellow moss, which is gradually encroaching on the low flat stones of the dead, blotting out the unheeded memorials which tell us that the inhabitants of this solitary spot were once men, and that they are now dead—that they lived, and that they died, and that they shall live again.

Nearly about the middle of the burying-ground there is a low flat stone, over which time is silently drawing the green veil of oblivion. It bears date 1690, and testifies in a rude inscription that it covers the remains of Paul Feddes and his son John, with those of their respective wives. Concerning Paul tradition is silent; of John Feddes, his son, an interesting anecdote is still preserved. Some time early in the eighteenth century, or rather perhaps towards the close of the seventeenth, he became enamoured of Jean Gallie, one of the wealthiest and most beautiful young women of her day in this part of the country. The attachment was not mutual, for Jean's affections were already fixed on a young man who, both in fortune and elegance of manners, was superior, beyond comparison, to the tall red-haired boatman, whose chief merit lay in a kind, brave heart, a clear head, and a strong arm. John, though by no means a dissipated character, had been accustomed to regard money as merely the price of independence, and he had sacrificed but little to the Graces.

His love-suit succeeded as might have been expected; the advances he made were treated with contempt, and the day was fixed when his mistress was to be married to a rival. He became sad and melancholy, and late in the evening which preceded the marriage-day he was seen traversing the woods which surrounded the old castle; frequently stopping as he went, and by wild and singular gestures giving evidence of an unsettled mind. In the morning after he was nowhere to be found.

His disappearance, with the frightful conjectures to which it gave rise, threw a gloom over the spirits of the townsfolk, and affected the gaiety of the

"'YOU COME FROM CROMARTY, DO YOU NOT?'" (p. 114).

marriage-party. It was remembered, even amid the festivities of the bridal, that John Feddes had had a kind, warm heart; and it was in no enviable frame of mind that the bride, as her maidens conducted her to her chamber, caught a glimpse of several twinkling lights that were moving beneath the brow of the distant Sutor. She could not ask the cause of a feeling so unusual; her fears too surely suggested that her unfortunate lover had destroyed himself, and that his friends and kinsfolk kept that night a painful vigil in searching after the body. But the search was in vain, though every copse and cavern, and the base of every precipice within several miles of the town were visited, and though during the succeeding winter every wreath of sea-weed which the night-storms had rolled upon the beach, was approached with a fearful yet solicitous feeling. Years passed away, and, except by a few friends, the kind, enterprising boatman was forgotten.

In the meantime, it was discovered, both by herself and the neighbours' that Jean Gallie was unfortunate in her husband. He had, prior to his marriage, when one of the gayest and most dashing young fellows in the village, formed habits of idleness and intemperance, which he could not or would not shake off; and Jean had to learn that a very gallant lover may prove a very indifferent husband, and that a very fine fellow may care for no one but himself. He was selfish and careless in the last degree; and unfortunately, as his selfishness was of the active kind, he engaged in extensive business, to the details of which he paid no attention, but amused himself with wild vague speculations, which, joined to his habits of intemperance, in the course of a few years, stripped him of all the property which had belonged to himself and his wife. In proportion as his means decreased, he became more worthless, and more selfishly bent on the gratification of his appetites; and had squandered almost his last shilling when, after a violent fit of intemperance, he was seized by a fever, which in a few days terminated in his death; and thus, five years after the disappearance of John Feddes, Jean Gallie found herself a poor widow, with scarcely any means of subsistence, and without one pleasing thought connected with the memory of her husband.

A few days after the interment, a Cromarty vessel was lying before sunrise near the mouth of the Spey. The master, who had been one of Feddes' most intimate friends, was seated near the stern, employed in angling for cod and ling. Between his vessel and the shore a boat appeared, in the grey light of morning, stretching along the beach under a light and well-trimmed sail. She had passed him nearly half a mile when the helmsman slackened the sheet, which had been close-hauled, and suddenly changing the tack, bore away right before the wind. In a few minutes the boat dashed alongside. All the crew except the helmsman had been lying asleep upon the beams, and now started up, alarmed by the shock.

"How, skipper," said one of them, rubbing his eyes, "how in the name of wonder have we gone so far out of the course? What brings us here?"

"You come from Cromarty, do you not?" said the skipper, directing his speech to the master, who, starting from his seat at the sound, flung himself half over the gunwale to catch a glimpse of the speaker.

"John Feddes—by all that's miraculous!" he exclaimed.

"You come from Cromarty, do you not?" reiterated the skipper. "Ah, Willie Mouat! Is that you?"

The friends were soon seated in the snug little cabin of the vessel; and John, apparently the less curious of the two, entered, at the other's request, into a detail of the particulars of his life for the five preceding years:—

"You must know, Mouat," he said, "how I felt and what I suffered for the last six months I was at Cromarty. Early in that period I had formed the determination of quitting my country for ever; but I was a weak, foolish fellow, and so I continued to linger like an unhappy ghost, week after week, and month after month, hoping against hope, until the night which preceded Jean Gallie's wedding-day. Captain Robinson was then on the coast, unloading a cargo of Hollands. I made it my business to see him; and after some little conversation, for we were old acquaintances, I broached to him my intention of leaving Scotland. 'It is well,' said he; 'for friendship's sake, I will give you a passage to Flushing, and, if it fits your inclination, a berth in a privateer I am now fitting out for cruising along the coast of Spanish America. I find the 'free-trade' does not suit me; it has no scope.' I considered his proposals, and liked them hugely. There was, indeed, some risk of being knocked on the head in the cruising affair, but that weighed little with me; I really believe that, at the time, I would as lief have run to a blow as have avoided one. So I closed with him, and the night and hour were fixed when he would land his boat for me in the *hope* of the Sutors. The evening of that night came, and I felt impatient to be gone. You wonder how I could leave so many excellent friends without so much as bidding them farewell. I have since wondered at it myself; but my mind was filled at the time with one engrossing object, and I could think of nothing else. Positively I was mad. I remember passing Jean's house on that evening, and catching a glimpse of her through the window. She was so engaged in preparing a piece of dress, which I suppose was to be worn on the ensuing day, that she did not observe me. I cannot tell you how I felt—indeed, I do not know; for I have scarcely any recollection of what I did or thought until a few hours after, when I found myself aboard of Robinson's lugger, spanking down the firth. It is now five years since, and in that time I have both given and received some hard blows, and have been both rich and poor. Little more than a month ago I left Flushing for Banff, where I intend taking up my abode, and where I am now on the eve of purchasing a snug little property."

"Nay," said Mouat, "you must come to Cromarty."

"To Cromarty; no, no, that will scarcely do."

"But hear me, Feddes;—Jean Gallie is a widow."

There was a long pause. "Well, poor young thing," said John at length with a sigh; "I should feel sorry for that; I trust she is in easy circumstances."

"You shall hear."

The reader has already anticipated Mouat's narrative. During the recital of the first part of it, John, who had thrown himself on the back of his chair, continued rocking backwards and forwards with the best-counterfeited indifference in the world. It was evident that Jean Gallie was nothing to him. As the story proceeded, he drew himself up leisurely and with firmness, until he sat bolt upright, and the motion ceased. Mouat described the selfishness of Jean's husband, and his disgusting intemperance. He spoke of the confusion of his affairs. He hinted at his cruelty to Jean when he had squandered all. John could act no longer—he clenched his fist, and sprang from his seat.

"Sit down, man!" said Mouat, "and hear me out; the fellow is dead."

"And the poor widow?" said John.

"Is, I believe, nearly destitute. You have heard of the box of broad pieces left her by her father? She has few of them now."

"Well, if she hasn't, I have; that's all. When do you sail for Cromarty?"

"HE WAS ARRESTED" (p. 117).

"To-morrow, my dear fellow, and you go along with me; do you not?"

Almost anyone could supply the conclusion of this narrative. Soon after John had arrived at his native town, Jean Gallie became the wife of one who, in almost every point of character, was the reverse of her first husband; and she lived long and happily with him.

In the year 1723 a young man who was serving his apprenticeship in London to a master sailmaker, obtained leave to spend his Christmas holidays with his mother, who lived not very far from Deal, in Kent. Being an apprentice only, he was poor; and being poor, he determined to walk the journey. He arrived in Deal late one evening, and as he was not only fatigued but suffering considerably from sickness which had overtaken him during the last few miles, he determined to get a lodging for the night in that town. He therefore made his way to an inn, the landlady of which knew his mother, and asked her to put him up. The landlady replied that her house was full—every bed occupied. Still she did not wish to disoblige the son of her acquaintance, so told him that if he did not object to sleep with her uncle, a seafaring man, or, to speak more particularly, the boatswain of an Indiaman, he was welcome. He readily accepted this offer; and the boatswain, on being appealed to, did not object in the least. So, after spending the evening together, the two men retired to bed.

The young sailmaker, however, had not been in bed for more than an hour or two, when he was attacked again with the feeling of sickness which had pursued him throughout the day. He woke his bedfellow and asked the way to the garden. The boatswain sleepily told him that the way lay through the kitchen; "but," said he, "the door into the yard is rather difficult to open, you will find, for the latch is out of order. You had better take my knife—you will find it in my pocket—to raise the latch with."

The young man thanked him, searched for the knife, found it, and made his way to the garden. He was absent about half an hour, and, on returning to his room, was considerably surprised to find the bed empty. His companion had gone.

However, the young sailmaker did not think much of it; and being naturally impatient to see his mother and his native place, rose before daybreak and pursued his journey. He reached home before noon.

The landlady had been told of his intention to leave early, and so was not surprised that he did not appear in the morning. What *did* surprise her, though, was that her uncle did not come down to breakfast. "Curious hours," she thought, "for a seafaring man who is not accustomed to sleep heavily." But as hour after hour passed, and still he did not appear, she entered the room to call him. Her horror may be guessed when she found the bed soaked in blood, and untenanted.

Of course the hue and cry was raised at once; but no trace of the boatswain appeared. Further and closer examination, however, revealed a trail of blood from the bedroom downstairs to the street, and then at intervals to the edge of the pier-head. Of course suspicion at once fell on the young man who had slept with him. Everybody thought, though the motive was hidden, that he had murdered the older man and thrown his body into the sea from the edge of the pier. A warrant was made out; and he was arrested that very evening as he was quietly sitting in his mother's house.

On being examined and searched, the young man's shirt and trousers revealed stains of blood; and in his pocket was of course the knife, as well as a curious silver coin which the landlady swore upon oath belonged to the missing man. She had seen it in his possession on the evening of the supposed murder. Under these circumstances, the young man was sent up to take his trial at the assizes.

It seems extraordinary that any judge should have directed the grand jury to find a true bill of murder, in a case where the body of the murdered man was not forthcoming; but such would appear to have been the case. The prisoner in his defence told the simple story as we have given it above; but he was forced to confess that he could not account for the blood-stains, unless he got them after he returned to bed; and as for the silver coin he could give no explanation whatever about it. Naturally his tale was not believed. Against it were to be set the plain evidence of the blood-stains and the certainty of the boatswain's disappearance. The youth was found guilty, and condemned to death. So convinced was the judge of his guilt that he ordered the execution to take place in three days' time. The young man was led to the gallows, still protesting his innocence with an earnestness that caused many to pity although none believed him.

Hanging was a clumsy business in those days. The young man was tall; his feet now and then touched the ground; his friends pressed around the gallows (how strange this sounds in our days!) and managed to give the body a certain amount of support as long as it was suspended. When the apparently inanimate corpse was cut down, they carried it away, and applied every effort to restore life. Their endeavours were successful. The youth recovered; was spirited away by night to Portsmouth, where he changed his name and enlisted on board a man-of-war. The vessel sailed in a day or two; and so justice was cheated of an innocent victim.

Five years' service found the young sailmaker elevated, by steady conduct, to the post of master's mate. It chanced at the same time that his ship was paid off in the West Indies, and he, with some others of the crew, were transferred to another man-of-war that had just come into port, short of hands, from a different station. Imagine his emotion when, in the first person he saw on his new ship, he found the very man for whose murder he had been tried, condemned, and hanged five years before!

It was true. And it would be hard to say which of the two was the more surprised at the other's story. For thus the mystery was explained by the boatswain:—

Unknown to the landlady, his niece, he had been, on the day of the young man's arrival at Deal, bled by a barber for a pain in his side. When in the middle of the night he was awakened, as has been told, he found that the bandage around his arm had slipped, and that he was bleeding freely.

Being somewhat alarmed at this, he left his bed, dressed, and stole out of the house to knock up the barber, who lived just across the street. But it happened that at the time a press-gang was returning through the streets of Deal from its nocturnal raid on some of the less reputable taverns. The men had met with ill-success and were out of temper. Coming on the unfortunate boatswain just as he left the public-house, they laid hands on him and haled him off to the pier, where their boat was waiting. In a few minutes they were on board a frigate then under weigh for the East Indies. The poor man was so dejected by this untoward turn of fate, that he omitted even to write home to account for his sudden disappearance.

The matter of the silver coin alone remained without explanation; and this could only be supplied by conjecture. The hypothesis, however, was likely enough true that when the young sailmaker took the knife out of the boatswain's pocket and transferred it to his own, *the coin had stuck between the blades of the knife*

AMONG THE SHARKS.

I.—THE "MAGPIE" SCHOONER.

IT was in the month of August, 1826, that a little schooner, the *Magpie*, was cruising in the Caribbean Sea, between the Island of Cuba and Havannah, on the look-out for a pirate vessel that for some time had been the scourge of the neighbouring islands. The schooner was commanded by a Lieutenant Smith.

The 26th had been a hot and sultry day; and as it advanced the wind grew lighter and lighter, until at length, towards evening, it fell a dead calm. The *Magpie* lay becalmed off the Colorados Rock, her head pointed shorewards, as if she slept upon the still waters. The crew hung listlessly about the deck, as they always do in such weather. Seamen do not like a calm; in some way or other it always seems to impress them with a notion of coming trouble. But at length they were all gathered together under an awning in the forward part of the schooner, spinning yarns to while away the time. Lieutenant Smith with his telescope kept a good look-out for any sign of the pirate vessel that might chance to appear. But at length, as twilight drew on, his glass became of no further service, so he laid it down and went below to his cabin.

From this till about eight o'clock in the evening absolute silence reigned on board the schooner. At that hour the mate, who was on deck, noticed a small black cloud of vapour resting under the moon. At the same time a light breeze arose from the south.

This was a nasty sign. The dark cloud began to increase rapidly, and the mate, though he saw no reason to anticipate any great danger, thought it right to tell Lieutenant Smith what he saw.

Lieutenant Smith was at once on the alert, went upon deck, and finding the land breeze increasing with every moment, ordered the sails to be furled without delay.

But he was too late. While he was speaking, the cloud, still gathering volume, was drawing nearer and nearer with every second. A horrible sigh preceded it, a sigh that grew to a wild roar, as, with growing violence, the landward sea rose and rose in the shape of a steel-black wall, sweeping towards the *Magpie*. All around the sea was still as a pond; here alone it was one sheet of curded foam as it flew up and blew from the crest of the fatal wave.

For one moment the lieutenant's voice was heard shrieking to his men to cut away the masts; the next the hurricane was on them. Down swooped the black wall of water; the black cloud at the same instant enwrapped them, shutting out the day. The wave caught the schooner, flung her upon her side—and in an instant almost she was gone for ever.

Two of the crew only were below, and these went down with her. Of the rest, who were on deck, Meldrum, the gunner's mate, says that by the glare of a vivid flash of lightning he saw the faces of his comrades lit up as they struggled in the water around him. The flash passed in a moment. In the pitchy darkness that followed he struck out lustily, managed to get clear of the eddy of the sinking ship, and, to his surprise, found that already night was beginning to give way to radiant daylight again.

Almost at the same moment he perceived something floating, just within his grasp. He clutched at it. It was an oar. In a second or two another drifted towards him. He caught this too, and floating easily by means of them, managed to get a good look around.

Even before the darkness had cleared away, during the breathless seconds that followed the sinking of the schooner, he had heard a voice, which he recognised for Mr. Smith's, calling out to know if anyone were near. And now he saw the lieutenant and six others of his comrades clinging to a boat that providentially had parted from the vessel and floated clear of her. The squall had passed; the sea was tranquil again, the sky serene. It seemed impossible to believe in the hideous tragedy that had just been so swiftly enacted.

The rest of the crew, now struggling in the water, made a rush towards the boat. Several men attempted to get into her at once. In the struggle she of course capsized, rolled over and over, and at length rested, keel upwards. Henceforward she was useless, except as a float. Some of the men flung themselves across the keel, others gained a hold with their hands; and so all rested for a minute to take breath.

But, as Lieutenant Smith reminded them, they could not hang on in this way for ever. He therefore ordered them to let go their hold and allow her to be righted. He was obeyed. The men on the keel slipped off; the others managed to turn the boat over, and two men were ordered into her to bale out the water with their hats. The rest had to hold on by the gunwale, while this was being done, and keep themselves above water as they best could, until the boat should be light enough to take them in, in safety.

The two men in the boat worked their hardest; and there seemed every prospect of their being successful, when one of them, glancing up for a moment from his task, suddenly cried out—

"A shark! a shark! I see his fin!"

Instantly all was confusion and terror. The men forgot all but their fear of the shark; they struggled to clamber into the boat, and upset her again.

Lieutenant Smith was not daunted. He shouted and shouted, until at length he managed to make his voice heard and to reassert his authority. The boat was righted once more; the baling began again; and the men were ordered to splash about with their legs in the water, to frighten off the sharks.

By this time darkness had come down; and all through the night the men were struggling to get the boat clear of water. This was a labour of Hercules, for at first, until the gunwale was well above the surface, the water poured in pretty well as fast as it was poured out; and it was next to impossible to prevent the men from occasionally giving a lurch that upset the work of an hour. But at length perseverance seemed to be winning. As morning broke the boat would hold four men, and these were rapidly getting the water out.

"'A SHARK! A SHARK!'" (p. 120).

But, alas! at this moment, the dreadful cry was again heard—"A shark! a shark!"

It was true this time. Within a minute no less than fifteen of the monsters were among them! In the panic that at once arose the boat was overturned again, and all the crew lay at the mercy of the brutes. At first the sharks did no mischief, but played about, every now and then passing over the boat or rubbing against the men. But at length a terrible shriek went up. One of the men had his leg bitten off.

Blood being once tasted, the sharks were no longer playful. Soon another cry was heard, then another. The carnage had begun. Some were bitten in two, some torn from the boat, others in sheer fright flung up their hands and sunk beneath the waters.

Nevertheless Lieutenant Smith did not lose his presence of mind. He still gave orders, and the crew—or what was left of them—still obeyed. The waters by this time were red with blood. At length but six men were left. Yet the boat was again righted, and the baling was resumed.

The lieutenant was holding on by the stern and cheering the balers at their work. It was while in this position that he ceased splashing for a moment while he looked into the boat to see how the men were getting on; and at that moment a shark bit off one of his legs above the knee.

It is hardly possible to credit it, but it is true nevertheless, that he bore the agony without uttering a cry or a groan, in order that he might conceal his situation from the remainder of his crew. But when the shark's teeth closed on his other leg, he could not for all his heroism prevent a low moan escaping him. His hands quitted their hold on the stern; and he was about to sink, when two of his men, hearing the sound, rushed forward, managed to seize and lift him into the boat, and set him, all torn and agonised as he was, down in the stern-sheets.

And yet as he lay there, writhing in anguish, through a long summer's day, in the heat of a burning climate, he could still manage to keep his faculties alive, and exert them for the saving of his crew. Himself without food or drink, he could yet express sorrow for his comrades' condition. He called one of the survivors to his side—a lad named Wilson—and said to him calmly—

"You are young, and I think the most likely to survive. Should it be possible for you to hold out and return to Jamaica, tell Admiral Sir Lawrence Halstead that I was bound for Cape Ontario when this fatal disaster occurred; tell him that my men have always done their duty, and that I hope I have done the same. No blame, at any rate, should attach to them. I have one last favour to ask him— that he will promote Meldrum to be a gunner."

After uttering these words he shook each of the men by the hand and said good-bye; and as long as speech yet remained to him, had always a word of comfort to say. The long day, insufferably hot, dragged by; and towards sunset speech failed him. He lay in the stern-sheets, scarcely breathing, until evening, when, on another alarm of the sharks, some of the men pressed down one side of the boat. It upset. Lieutenant Smith rolled overboard, and sank for ever.

There were now but four left alive, for of the bleeding seamen all but these had dropped into the deep. They were the young mate, Maclean; Meldrum, the gunner's mate; the boy Wilson; and another seaman. Maclean, catching the spirit of his dead superior, persuaded them to right the boat again. They did it at last; and it was now able to hold them all. They began baling again as fast as they could, and continued till they were worn out. And all this time the sharks swam round and round them, endeavouring sometimes to upset the boat. Their efforts however were unsuccessful, and at length, being perhaps gorged, they made off.

But twenty hours of this awful battle may well have been too much for man's intellect to bear. The sun had beaten pitilessly down on their heads all day. Of food and water there was not a bite or sip to be had. The oars were lost; and even the cool of the night was a horror, for while it lasted they had no chance to espy a passing vessel. At about three in the morning, Wilson and the seaman fell raving mad, and in their paroxysms jumped overboard. Both perished.

The two survivors, Maclean and Meldrum, worked on at intervals through most of the night; and having at last baled the boat dry, lay down and slept. When they awoke again, so utterly worn out were they, day had long dawned. Again a fierce sun beat down on them. They looked in each other's faces and shuddered. Around them stretched a silent, unbroken sea. They were without drink. Food they did not somehow desire; but a burning thirst consumed them. Their tongues were swollen so as to fill their mouths; and yet they had strength to refrain from drinking the sea-water, knowing the sufferings, and perhaps madness, that would follow.

As the day wore on, a horrible thought took possession of them. Would it come to this—that the stronger must in the end be driven to kill his comrade and drink his blood? They trod the thought down, but it recurred. Both were strong men: both had knives. Each read the hideous temptation in the other's face. They did not dare to speak, but sat down, one in the bows and one in the stern, waiting—waiting for death.

In silence the minutes dragged by. One man was praying; the other fell on his knees and followed his example. But when they arose they did not dare to speak. They sat with bowed heads, fighting down the passion that set their fingers itching to be at their knives, and waited.

A sound in the bows made Meldrum look up. It was no sound of human voice, but rather of wild excitement working in the throat and stifling speech. Opposite him Maclean stood gasping, his eyeballs starting, his hand pointing forward. At first Meldrum thought the finger pointed at him; but no, it pointed further, over his shoulder, out over the ocean.

He turned. God be praised! There shone a white speck on the horizon, flashing against the sun. It was a sail.

"A brig! a brig!"

The two men found their voices at last. The brig was making towards them. As her hull at length came into view, Meldrum flung his jacket into the air for joy. The two rushed together, and shook hands in the middle of the boat. Tears choked their utterance. But at length Maclean found voice to hail again and again. He shouted with all his lungs, although the distance was too great for his voice to reach by any possibility.

Nearer and nearer drew the brig. Hunger and thirst were forgotten now. There was no room in their hearts for anything but hope. Nearer she came. The two men were beginning to feel sure that they had been spied, when—

Another sail went up on the brig. In another moment she had shifted her course.

Imagine the feelings of these two men as they looked. The hope faded out of their eyes; but still they shouted and waved their jackets. They even endeavoured by paddling with their hands to propel the boat towards the brig. It was no good. They were not seen by the brig's crew; their voices could not reach; the ship was fading further and further from them; and they were being left to perish.

And now Meldrum rose up and stood on his feet, looking Maclean in the eyes. "I am going to swim to the brig," said he.

Maclean thought that he was mad. The distance was more than two miles, and Meldrum, though naturally a very strong man, was by this time weak with hunger and suffering. But Maclean did not chiefly consider these reasons against the attempt; instead, he pointed with his finger over the deep blue waters, where every now and then a shark's fin would glisten in the sun.

"It's our last chance," said Meldrum; and as Maclean was silent, added a word or two to be taken to his wife in case his comrade should by any providential means be saved. "And if you spy a shark after me, don't let me know, that's all. Let me die quickly, if I must. I shall splash, but I won't look behind me."

"Don't do this, Meldrum; it's throwing away your life."

For answer the gunner's mate dropped on his knees, said a short prayer, and jumped overboard.

His splash scared away the sharks that were hanging round the boat. At any rate they disappeared for a moment or two, and then Maclean, as he cheered on his comrade, saw three of them pass the boat in pursuit of him.

Meldrum swam well and strong, splashing all the while with his legs, and lifting his body high every now and then while he shouted. Maclean shouted too, doing his utmost to cheer the swimmer, though every moment he expected to see him throw up his hands and disappear for ever. Meldrum himself at one moment saw the fin of a shark quite close, but he only swam the faster; and still no one appeared on the brig's deck.

He swam on, followed by his comrade's eyes. But his strength was giving out at last. The wind too had freshened, and the brig began to move more quickly. He felt that all was done. He had accomplished but two-thirds of the way, and already his arms were heavy as lead. He was on the point of giving up the fight, of turning on his back and floating motionless until such time as the sharks might be pleased to eat him.

A head appeared on the vessel's deck. A man was looking over the bulwarks.

Meldrum raised his arms, jumped up in the water, and with a ringing shout—a last desperate cry—fell prone and helpless on the waves.

But he was seen! The man leaning by the bulwarks started, rubbed his eyes, looked again, and ran to summon the officers with their glasses. In five minutes' time the brig was hove-to, a boat was put off, and Meldrum hauled on board, more dead than alive. But he was still able to lift himself off the thwart and point towards his comrade.

"HE SHOT HIGH OUT OF THE WATER" (p. 128).

So in a few minutes more Maclean was also saved, and the sharks cheated after all.

The brig proved to be an American; and at first the story told by the survivors was held to be incredible by all on board. They were taken for pirates. But at length they were landed at Havannah, conveyed thence to

Port Royal by the first man-of-war that touched there, and at a court-martial, held by Sir Lawrence Halstead, the truth came out.

For a long time Meldrum could not be prevailed upon to tell his story. Maclean did so instead; and when the young mate had finished his tale of gallantry, the two men,' forgetting all an Englishman's reserve, burst into tears and fell into each other's arms. It was a strange scene for a court-martial. The officers who sat as their judges were almost as deeply affected. And the result was that Meldrum was at once promoted, according to the last-expressed wish of his brave lieutenant.

II.—VOLNEY BECKNER.

THE young hero whose name is written above this story was born at London-derry in 1748. His father was a fisherman of that place, a poor man, and unable to afford the boy a regular education; he made up for this, however, in some degree by instructing him at home, and training him rigidly for the seafaring life he was in time to lead. While still a baby he was taught by his father to be absolutely fearless in the water, to move and guide himself with confidence even when the waves were rough. He was often thrown from the stern of the boat and encouraged to sustain himself by swimming; and not till the boy's strength gave signs of failing would his father plunge in to help him. It was a rough training, but a successful. At the age of four young Volney was able, it is asserted, to swim three or four miles in the wake of his father's vessel; and only when exhausted would he take the rope that was thrown out astern, and suffer himself to be pulled on board in safety.

When the boy was nine years old he was entered as an apprentice on board a merchant ship in which his father occasionally sailed, and he quickly distinguished himself by the confidence with which he would climb to the mast-head in the most furious weather, and hang there as calmly as if lying in his hammock. His fare was rough enough in all conscience—biscuits that had to be broken with a hatchet, and were then found to be full of weevils; water full of worms, and muddy to boot; such appears to have been his ordinary diet. His bed was a bare plank. And yet he was healthy.

In his twelfth year, so highly had this boy distinguished himself in danger that he was promoted in the vessel and received double his usual pay. " I do not doubt," said his captain once, in presence of the whole crew, "that if this little man continues to display so much valour and prudence, he will obtain a place very far above that which I now occupy."

And this is the sequel:—

The vessel to which Volney belonged was bound for Port-au-Prince, in France. His father was on board for this voyage; and the ship, too, carried a number of passengers. Among these was a little girl, the daughter of a rich American merchant.

It happened that one day the little girl had slipped away from the nurse, who was ill and lying down in the cabin, and ran upon deck. She was not used to this liberty, and while she climbed up on the bulwarks, to take a look at the broad plain of waters all around, the ship gave a sudden lurch. It turned the little girl dizzy. She missed her hold, toppled a moment, and then plunged over the vessel's side with a scream, down into the waves.

Volney's father happened to be splicing a rope upon deck. His back had been turned towards the little girl, so he did not see the first stages of the accident that he certainly would have prevented. But he heard the shrill cry and turned round. In an instant he had leapt to the vessel's side and was looking down into the waters.

He saw a little face rise out of the waves, and a tiny pair of hands stretched out to him. He slipped off his boots and, with a shout to his comrades to put the ship about, he dived off to the rescue.

Six strokes enabled him to catch the little girl's frock as she sank for the second time. He drew her close to his breast, and holding her head well above the water, struck out with one hand for the vessel.

Beckner was a strong swimmer, and a rescue such as this was the merest trifle to him. But just at this moment he lifted his head and saw a shark advancing directly towards him!

Those on board had also seen the shark at the same moment, and now the bulwarks were crowded with frightened faces. But no one dared to dive into the sea. Instead, the crew contented themselves with firing off several muskets. They had no effect. The shark drew closer and closer, lashing the sea with his tail. His jaws were opened to seize his prey.

At this moment, however, another splash was heard. It came from little Volney who, seeing his father's peril, had caught up a broad and pointed sabre, and, armed with this, had sprung into the sea.

He struck the water, diving far and true, and came up under the shark. Next instant, the sabre was driven up to the hilt in the monster's belly. Thus swiftly assailed and deeply wounded, the shark turned, quitted the track of his prey, and now attempted to get at young Volney who never ceased to stab and hack at his foe. The water was crimson with blood.

It was a terrible sight. On the ship stood the American trembling for his child, the crew with their muskets uncertain where to aim, not knowing even *whose* blood it was that thus stained the waves. In the sea struggled the sailor, the child, and the brave boy who, to save his father, had flung himself into the jaws of death.

By this time all three were close under the ship's side. A number of ropes were instantly thrown out to father and son, and each succeeded in grasping one. A score of stout hands were hauling them up. Already the breathless anxiety of the last few moments was giving way to cries of joy. " Here they are—here they are!" "They are out of danger!" "They are saved!"

But no—they were not saved. Already they were dangling a foot or two above the water, when the shark, maddened with his wounds, and enraged to see his prey escaping, plunged deep in the sea for a spring.

The next instant he shot high out of the water, like a rising salmon. A hideous snap of teeth was heard. The boy was bitten asunder.

Part of his poor lifeless body was dragged on board. The father and the fainting child were saved: and when we reflect that the generous action that saved them was performed by a boy of twelve years and a few months, we may surely rank it in the very first class of noble deeds.

"DICK CAME TEARING ON DECK"

A RACE HOME.

OME men are born lucky, they say (it was the second mate that spoke), and some say there's no such thing as luck. Well, in matters of sailing, all I know is that I've seen captains who'll toil and sweat and be up early and late to make a quick passage; and as often as not, along comes a fellow who has left the same port, maybe, a week later, and sails past with his hands in his pockets, and gets home a week ahead. Luck or no luck, it's something I never had explained.

Take the case of Dick Swift. He was master of a trader between London and Hamburg; and in the way of fast sailing was reckoned not to have his equal. When he once got accustomed to a vessel he never liked to part from her; for he would find out her trim to an inch of canvas, and he was not a man to spare a sail or a ship either. Let the wind blow how it would, he despised to take in a reef. If such advice were offered, he'd always answer, "It loses too much time," or "What's the use of having canvas on board if you don't use it?" He could never bear the thoughts of reefing, and if the wind didn't serve, he'd say, "Then it must blow us back, that's all. I've promised to sail at such-and-such an hour, and sail I will."

Well, in the year 1802, war between England and France was broken off for a time, and of course the peace was taken advantage of. In particular, a large number of vessels was freighted at once for Hamburg, Amsterdam, and

73

such-like Eastern ports. One of these was the *Good Intent*, Captain Dixon, and he told me what I am going to tell you.

One morning, as the sky cleared a bit, so that you could see a good distance, the *Good Intent* was running along at a good six knots an hour, with a fine breeze aft. Dixon was a careful man, and as the weather was squally, he didn't care to carry too much canvas. His motto was: "Better be a few hours late than come into port with a shivered topsail."

He had taken up his telescope, and was looking out astern to see what other vessels were on the same course, when suddenly he saw a trader coming in sight, with sky-scrapers and every inch of canvas set, as if there was not a cap-full of wind stirring. "I'll be bound it's Dick," said Dixon: "and I know for certain we sailed a tide before him."

Well, it was Dick. Presently his vessel overhauls the *Good Intent*, and he sings out—

"How d'ye do? How d'ye do, Dixon? Fine breeze, eh?"

"Where in the world are you bound for in all this hurry?" answers Dixon. "You carry canvas enough for a seventy-four."

"Oh, I'm on hasty business. Owners tell me to look sharp, and I like to obey orders. I've done so ever since I was mate aboard a man-o'-war; and the resolution being good and lawful, I don't like to break it. By-the-by, that's a tidy craft of yours, but she don't seem to sail as well as mine. Ta-ta, mate! My craft's getting impatient. I shall see yon in Hamburg; I'll tell the agents you're coming!"

His vessel shot ahead of Dixon's, and in a few hours was very near out of sight. Dixon didn't care for this chaff more than any other man; but he wasn't going to be fooled into running a race and risking his cargo, more especially as he saw there was a squall coming. He saw it running along the water's edge; so he took down his royals and made everything snug, making up his mind, not without a chuckle, that Master Dick would have some of his tackle overboard before very long.

Down came the squall. The *Good Intent* weathered it easily, though it was a pretty stiff one. And soon, the weather clearing, Dixon had his royals hoisted again. The breeze was still aft, and he cut along at eight knots an hour. This was what the boys used to call "one of Dixon's gallops," and it used to make the old man a bit angry. He couldn't abide sarcasm.

Well, as soon as the weather cleared he picked up his glass and saw that Dick had lost his top-sail. It had happened in this way:—

Dick was within ten leagues of Cuxhaven when the squall caught him. He was down below at the time, and the mate, who was on deck, seeing it coming, gave orders to strike the royals and reef the try-sails. But the words were scarcely out when Dick came tearing on deck, shouting with all his lungs—

"Top-men, let those sails alone! Who told you to reef and strike?" he added, turning on the mate.

"A squall coming on, sir."

"What's that to do with me? I reckon it ain't going to blow us out of the water."

"Shall we hoist the royals again, sir?" called one of the top-men.

"No, never mind. As they're down let 'em stay."

It was just as well that they were struck; for when the squall came it took the vessel with such violence that, in spite of all Dick's manœuvring, it carried away his top-mast, and split his main-sail to ribbons. However, he got to Cuxhaven without any more damage, and soon reached the Bourse at Hamburg, where he did not forget to speak of his quick passage, and the number of vessels he had given the go-by to.

Dixon came in next morning with not a stitch of sail damaged. Dick met him on the Bourse.

"Hulloa, in at last! Slow work—slow work, my boy."

"If it's slow, it's sure," answered Dixon. "When I come into port I bring in my vessel with me—every stick of it. I don't come towing into port without a top-sail, or with my main-sail cut to ribbons."

"Oh, hang the top-mast! It was old and good for nothing, and now I shall get a new one; so the loss looked at in a proper light is all gain. As for the main-sail, it's only a few yards of canvas spoiled. The owners don't mind that, provided I make a quick passage."

"Well, well," said Dixon. "I haven't time for talk, anyway. I must get out my cargo and be off again in three days."

"Why, what's all this bustle about?"

"That's more than I know. All I can tell you is that the ship is taken by three English families, who leave for London immediately, so I am bound to sail, with or without a cargo."

"Well," said Dick, "I'll walk with you to the quay. But in spite of all your bustle and hurry I don't mind betting that I see the Thames as soon as you."

"Time will show, time will show. But don't loom too large lest you should be mistaken. You can't serve me as you served the Hull traders."

I may as well explain here that Dick had once been master of a Hull trader, and one day a fleet of them had dropped down to Grimsby, and thence to Spurn, where, finding the wind blowing stiff from the south-east, and fearing to be thrown on the stony binks, they hove-to, and waited for better weather. Dick started a day after them, got his cargo aboard, and dropped down to Grimsby with the tide, where he anchored and got everything in good sailing trim, not meaning to bring up at Spurn Light if the tide would last him long enough. Next tide, away he went with all the sail he could muster, and when he arrived at Spurn he found all the others, that had started two days before him, lying at anchor. He lay-to for a short time. "What are you all doing here at anchor," he asked, "when you ought

to be out at sea?"   "Why, you wouldn't have us go to sea in this gale?"
replied the master of a vessel alongside.   "To be sure I would.   I'm not
going to waste time here.   I'm off to sea, blow high or blow low.   So good-bye
to you all!   I mean to see London the day after to-morrow."

Dick kept his word.   He sailed off straight, and reached London safe and
sound in forty hours.   Many of the shipmasters felt ashamed at being left behind,
and made up their minds to sail after him; but by this time they had lost

"A SHOT WAS FIRED AT HIM"

their tide, and when it ebbed again, the wind had chopped right in their
teeth, and held them a day longer; and when they got to sea at last, why, the
gale had dropped to a calm, or something like it, so they made but slow
work of it.

Dick got his cargo landed, and was soon freighted and ready for sea again.
He was asked a good many questions about the other ships, to all of which
he just answered that "he supposed they were at Spurn waiting for him to
return and tell them what news was stirring in London."

He got his clearance, and set off back to Hull.   When he reached the Nore,
he found half a dozen of the Hull traders there at anchor, and of course did
not forget to congratulate them on their swift passage.   His jeers made them

rather sore, but there was no help for it. At the Spurn he found the rest
of them, and saluted them all as he passed. There was one vessel commanded
by Joseph Benton. Joseph was no friend of Dick's, and often spoke against
him. So Dick made a point of passing very close alongside.

"Good day, Mr. Benton! Any news at sea? All well at Spurn Point?"

"I don't know," answered Joseph, pretty sulkily. "What's the news in
London, if you come to that?"

"The news in London? Why, I don't know that there's any except that
the King and Lord Mayor are both getting anxious about you, and fretting
themselves to a shadow. However, you'll have a chance of getting to the Nore
to-night, and to London some time or another; though, to be sure, a west
wind is not altogether the sort of thing to work up the Thames. Good-bye!
I'll tell the folks in Hull that you're moving!"

And with this Dick put his vessel to the wind, and was soon out of sight.

But to return to the yarn. Captain Dixon made the best haste he could to
get his ship cleared of her cargo, and made everything ready for the passengers.

Dick also discharged his cargo, and was waiting for a freight to take
back to England, while his top-mast and main-sail were being prepared.

'Twas just about this time that Bonaparte was marching into Germany, and
had passed what they called the "Decree of Non-intercourse." The two captains
happened to be at the Bourse one afternoon, when one of the merchants called
them aside, and told them that from private information he had learnt that
an order had arrived from the French authorities to seize all English shipping
in the Elbe.

"They will, will they?" said Dick; "they must look sharp to catch me,
then."

"What do you mean to do?" asked Dixon.

"Why, to cut cable and run, to be sure. It'll soon be dark. There's a
night tide, and it shall take me out to sea before ever a mounseer knows that
my anchor is weighed."

"But how are you to get to sea without a top-mast, and with your main-
sail in ribbons?"

"Why, things being as they are, I'd go to sea with an old blanket for trysail. And what's more, I don't mind betting you a glass of grog that I reach
the Thames before you."

"Done," said Dixon. "You're lucky enough, in all conscience; but I think
I'm going to win this time."

"We'll see. I'm off now to see about putting a few stitches in the sail,
and to rig up something in place of a top-mast."

"And I must be down to the quay to see about my passengers. For
unless these Frenchmen are to get to wind'ard of us, there's a plenty of work
on hand."

"Well, don't forget the glass of grog."

The two captains parted. Dick was not idle. In ten minutes all hands were at work repairing damages for dear life in order to catch the next tide.

Night came, and Dixon, who had warped out quietly, got to sea unobserved. Dick had bigger difficulties to get over. He was obliged to have his work done quietly, for fear of putting the authorities on the alert. However, from the tattered state of the vessel they hadn't a notion that he meant to slip off. Dick kept a sharp look-out, and the moment an opportunity came, cut his cable and silently dropped down with the tide. And as soon as ever he was clear of the other shipping, up went every stitch of canvas.

Luckily a stiffish breeze was blowing from the eastward. He was hailed by several vessels, but gave no answer. A shot was fired at him; but Dick was born, as I said, under a lucky star. He dashed by and got out to sea. The armed corvette that had fired at him went in pursuit.

Dick knew every inch of the coast. He shaved every sand and shoal so close, that the corvette fell into the trap. Getting a trifle too much to the larboard of Dick's course, she stuck fast aground, and had the pleasure of seeing the little vessel fade away in the distance, with three British cheers for an adieu.

Dick was now safe in the German Ocean. He had plenty of sea-room, and a stiff breeze behind him. His sail was rather the worse for wear, and the bit of spar he had rigged up for a top-mast was a queer-looking object. But all the same he made good way. When daylight broke, he looked about for Dixon's ship. She was just visible, far ahead. "I begin to think," said Dick, "that my glass of grog is lost this time."

Pretty soon a fog began to come on. It thickened and thickened, and finally hid all the other vessels from view. Dick wouldn't lay-to. Instead, he set his bells going and stuck to his course as well as he could.

In twenty-four hours the fog cleared off, and the English coast lay ahead like a black streak on the sea. The wind had been pretty stiff, and Dick's vessel was a curious sight. He had fallen foul of a large ship in the fog, and his jibboom was nowhere to be seen.

Well, he didn't care if only he could get the weather-gauge of Dixon; and, to shorten the yarn, by one dodge and another he managed to reach the Thames without any further damage. As usual, he was the first in.

A few hours later he saw Dixon coming up.

"Holloa, Dixon!" he called out; "where on earth have you been loitering? Why, you were twenty miles ahead of me before the fog came on."

"Where's your jibboom?" asked Dixon.

"Why, as to that, I can't exactly say *where* it is. All I know is that it went overboard in the fog; and as I was hurried, I couldn't stay to look after it."

"A pretty sailor, you, to come into port without a jibboom."

"Oh, aye. I've lost that. But—I've won my grog!"

AN ELEPHANT-HUNT.

E had ridden nearly thirty miles, having seen large quantities of game, including antelopes, buffaloes, giraffes, and rhinoceroses, none of which we had hunted, as we were in search of elephants. This was the country where the *aggageers* had expected without fail to find their game.

They now turned and descended a sandy valley at the foot of the mountains, the bottom of which appeared to have been overflowed during the wet season. Here were large strips of forest and numerous sandy watercourses, along the dry bed of which we quickly discovered the deep tracks of elephants. They had been digging fresh holes in the sand in search of water, in which welcome basins we found a good supply. We dismounted and rested the horses for half an hour, while the hunters followed up the tracks on the bed of the stream. Upon their return they reported the elephants as having wandered off upon the rocky ground that rendered further tracking impossible. We accordingly remounted, and upon arriving at the spot where they had lost the tracks, we continued along the bed of the stream. We had ridden about a mile, and were beginning to despair, when suddenly we turned a sharp angle in the watercourse, and Taher Sheriff, who was leading, immediately reined in his horse and backed him towards the party. I followed his example, and we were at once concealed by the sharp bend of the river.

He now whispered that a bull elephant was drinking from a hole it had scooped in the sand, not far round the corner. Without the slightest confusion, the hunters at once fell quietly into their respective places, Taher Sheriff leading, while I followed close in the line, with my Tokroories bringing up the rear; we were a party of seven horses.

Upon turning the corner, we at once perceived the elephant, that was still drinking. It was a fine bull; the enormous ears were thrown forward as the head was lowered in the act of drawing up the water through the trunk; these shaded the eyes, and, with the wind favourable, we advanced noiselessly upon the sand to within twenty yards before we were perceived.

The elephant then threw up its head, and, with ears flapping forward, it raised its trunk for an instant, and then slowly but easily ascended the steep bank and retreated. The aggageers now halted about a minute to confer together, and then followed in their original order up the crumbled bank. We were now on most unfavourable ground; the fire that had cleared the country we had hitherto traversed had been stopped by the bed of the torrent. We were thus plunged at once into withered grass above our heads, unless we stood in the stirrups; the ground was strewn with fragments of rock, and altogether it was ill-adapted for riding.

However, Taher Sheriff broke into a trot, followed by the entire party, as the elephant was not in sight. We ascended a hill, and when near the summit, we perceived the elephant about eighty yards ahead. It was looking behind during its retreat, by swinging its huge head from side to side, and upon seeing us approach, it turned suddenly round and halted.

"Be ready and take care of the rocks!" said Taher Sheriff, as I rode forward by his side. Hardly had he uttered these words of caution, when the bull gave a vicious jerk with its head, and with a shrill scream it charged down upon us with the greatest fury.

Away we all went, helter-skelter, through the dry grass, which whistled in my ears, over the hidden rocks, at full gallop, with the elephant tearing after us for about a hundred and eighty yards at a tremendous pace. "Tétel" was a sure-footed horse, and being unshod, he never slipped upon the stones. Thus, as we all scattered in different directions, the elephant became confused and relinquished the chase; it had been very near me at one time, and in such ground I was not sorry when it gave up the hunt. We now quickly united, and again followed the elephant, that had once more retreated. Advancing at a canter, we shortly came in view. Upon seeing the horses, the bull deliberately entered a stronghold composed of rocky and uneven ground, in the clefts of which grew thinly a few leafless trees the thickness of a man's leg. It then turned boldly towards us, and stood determinedly at bay.

Now came the tug of war! Taher Sheriff came close to me and said, "You had better shoot the elephant, as we shall have great difficulty in this rocky ground." This I declined, as I wished to end the fight as it had been commenced, with the sword; and I proposed that he should endeavour to drive the animal to more favourable ground. "Never mind," replied Taher, "Inshallah (please God) he shall not beat us." He now advised me to keep as close to him as possible, and to look sharp for a charge.

The elephant stood facing us like a statue; it did not move a muscle beyond a quick and restless action of the eyes, that were watching all sides. Taher Sheriff and his youngest brother Ibrahim now separated, and each took opposite sides of the elephant, and then joined each other about twenty yards behind it; I accompanied them, until Taher advised me to keep about the same distance upon the left flank. My Tokroories kept apart from the scene, as they were not required. In front of the elephant were two aggageers, one of whom was the renowned Roder Sheriff, with the withered arm.

All being ready for action, Roder now rode slowly towards the head of the cunning old bull, who was quietly awaiting an opportunity to make certain of someone who might give him a good chance.

Roder Sheriff rode a bay mare, that, having been thoroughly trained to these encounters, was perfect at her work. Slowly and coolly she advanced towards

"AWAY WE ALL WENT", (p. 196).

her wary antagonist, until within about eight or nine yards of the elephant's head.

The creature never moved, and the *mise-en-scène* was beautiful; not a word was spoken, and we kept our places amidst utter stillness, which was at length broken by a snort from the mare, who gazed intently at the elephant, as though watching for the moment of attack.

One more pace forward, and Roder sat coolly upon his mare, with his eyes fixed upon those of the elephant.

For an instant I saw the white of the eye nearest to me.

"Look out, Roder! he's coming!" I exclaimed. With a shrill scream, the elephant dashed upon him like an avalanche!

Round went the mare as though upon a pivot, and away over rocks and stones flying like a gazelle, with the monkey-like form of little Roder Sheriff leaning forward, and looking over his left shoulder as the elephant rushed after him.

For a moment I thought she must be caught. Had the mare stumbled, all were lost; but she gained in the race after a few quick bounding strides, and Roder, still looking behind him, kept his distance so close to the elephant, that its outstretched trunk was within a few feet of the mare's tail.

Taher Sheriff and his brother Ibrahim swept down like falcons in the rear. In full speed they dexterously avoided the trees, until they arrived upon open ground, when they dashed up close to the hind-quarters of the furious elephant, who, maddened with excitement, heeded nothing but Roder and his mare, that were almost within its grasp.

When close to the tail of the elephant, Taher Sheriff's sword flashed from its sheath, as grasping his trusty blade he leapt nimbly to the ground, while Ibrahim caught the reins of his horse. Two or three bounds on foot, with the sword clutched in both hands, and he was close behind the elephant. A bright glance shone like lightning, as the sun struck upon the descending steel. This was followed by a dull crack, as the sword cut through skin and sinews, and settled deep in the bone, about twelve inches above the foot. At the next stride the elephant halted dead short in the midst of its tremendous charge. Taher had jumped quickly on one side and had vaulted into the saddle with his naked sword in hand. At the same moment, Roder, who had led the chase, turned sharp round, and again faced the elephant as before; stooping quickly from the saddle, he picked up from the ground a handful of dirt, which he threw into the face of the vicious-looking animal, that once more attempted to rush upon him. It was impossible! The foot was dislocated, and turned up in front like an old shoe.

In an instant Taher was once more on foot, and again the sharp sword slashed the remaining leg. The great bull elephant could not move! The first cut had already disabled it: the second was its death-blow; the arteries of the leg were divided, and the blood spouted in jets from the wounds.

I wished to terminate its misery by a bullet behind the ear, but Taher Sheriff begged me not to fire, as the elephant would quickly bleed to death without pain, and an unnecessary shot might attract the Basé, who would steal the flesh and ivory during our absence. We were obliged to return immediately to our far-distant camp, and the hunters resolved to accompany their camels to the spot upon the following day. We turned our horses' heads and rode direct towards home, which we did not reach until nearly midnight, having ridden upwards of sixty miles during the day.*

* For leave to insert the above, which is taken from Sir Samuel Baker's "Nile Tributaries of Abyssinia," we have to thank Messrs. Macmillan and Co.

THE RUSSIAN SUPERCARGO.

UR ship was bound for the coast of New Albion. On the 29th of September, 1808, we were opposite Vancouver's Cape Flattery, in 48° 25′ N. latitude. We then followed the coast during several days for the purpose of sketching it. The natives came out in great numbers, and sometimes we were surrounded by more than one hundred of their boats, which, although small, generally held from three or four to ten people. We never allowed more than three at a time to come on board, a caution which seemed the more necessary as they were all well armed. Several of them had muskets; others had arrows pointed with stag's antlers, iron lances without handles, and bone forks fixed on long poles. Moreover, they had a species of arms made of whale-ribs, of the shape of a Turkish sabre, two inches and a half long, a quarter of an inch thick, and blunt on both edges; this weapon we understood they used in their night attacks, so common among these savages, killing their foes while asleep. They offered us sea-otters, reindeer-skins, and fish for sale. For a large fish we paid them a string of blue beads a quarter of a yard long and a few loose glass beads; but for beaver-skins they would take nothing less valuable than broad-cloth.

A few days after this we had a violent storm, which lasted for three days, the wind blowing from the south; at length a sudden calm ensued, but the motion of the waves continued very high. At daybreak the fog, which had till then surrounded us, disappeared, and we saw the shore at the distance of about ten or twelve miles. The calm rendered the sails useless, and the high waves would not allow us to have recourse to the oars; the current, therefore, carried us rapidly towards the shore.

We thought ourselves lost, when happily a north-westerly breeze sprang up, by the help of which we got out of our perilous fix. Soon, however, a new storm arose, which was again interrupted by a calm; and at last, on the 1st of November, after much anxiety, and still more unavailing labour, our ship was cast on shore in 47° 66′ N. latitude, nearly opposite the Island of Destruction.

Happily the ship had run on soft ground, and during high water. When the tide, therefore, had receded, we found her still entire, although she had been terribly shaken, and was half full of water. There was, however, no possibility of saving her; we therefore went on shore, taking with us the guns, muskets, ammunition, and every other article which we thought we might find useful in our desolate state.

Our first care, when landed, was to clean and load our fire-arms, as we had every moment reason to expect a visit from the natives, against whose cupidity and savage fury we had no other security than our resolution.   This being done, we made two tents with our sails, and had scarcely finished, when we saw a host of savages bearing down upon us.   The mate, accompanied by four hunters, had gone on board for the purpose of taking down the tackling from

"HE HELD A LANCE IN ONE HAND, AND IN THE OTHER HE HAD A STONE" (p. 142).

the ship.   They had taken a burning match with them, there being still a few guns left in the brig.   The captain, standing near her, gave the necessary orders, while I had the charge of watching the motions of the enemy and guarding our little camp.

Our tent was occupied by Mrs. Bulugin (the captain's wife), an Aleootskian from Kadjak, a woman of the same nation, myself, and two natives, who had joined us without any invitation.   One of them, an elder, invited me to his hut, which he said was not far off; but prudence restrained me from accepting this invitation.   I endeavoured to inspire him with a friendly feeling towards us, and he promised that he would not injure us, and would also endeavour to prevent his countrymen from doing so.   In the meantime, however, I was informed that the Koljushes were carrying off our stores. I entreated our people to bear with them as much as possible before they proceeded to hostilities, and represented to the elder the impropriety of the conduct of his party, and begged him to induce them to desist. But, as we could not converse freely, it took me some time to convey my sentiments to him, and in the meanwhile the question was decided without our interference.

Our people began to drive the savages away, and they in turn began to pelt us with stones. As soon as I was informed of this I rushed out of the tent, but at the same moment our hunters fired, and I was pierced in the chest with a lance.

I ran back for a musket, and on coming out again saw the man who had wounded me; he held a lance in one hand, and in the other he had a stone which he hurled at my head with such violence as to make me stagger to the ground. I fired, however, and he fell down dead. The savages soon took to flight, leaving two dead behind, and carrying one dead and a great many wounded with them. On our side there were few who had not received some hurt or other, with the exception of those who had been on board. Our captain had been stabbed in the back. A great many lances, cloaks and hats, which strewed the field of battle, formed our trophies of this sad victory.

We spent a comfortless night, and in the morning went to examine the country, with a view of finding a spot where we might winter in safety; but we found the whole coast thickly covered with forest, and so low that at high water it would be overflowed. It was consequently in no way adapted for our purpose. The captain, therefore, collected us all together and informed us that by next spring the Company's ship, *Kadjak*, would touch upon this coast, in a harbour not more than sixty-five miles distant from the spot where we were; to which harbour he proposed we should immediately proceed. As there was neither bay nor river marked on the chart which could impede our journey, he thought it might be very speedily accomplished; and that while the savages were engaged in plundering the vessel we should have nothing to fear from them, since they could derive no advantage from annoying us. We all, therefore, unanimously replied, "Be it as you propose; we shall not disobey you."

Thus we entered upon our march, each of us armed with two muskets, one pistol, a quantity of ammunition, besides three barrels of powder, and some provisions which we carried with us. Previously to our departure, however, we took care to spike the guns, destroy the muskets, and throw them, together with the remaining gunpowder, pikes, hatchets, and other iron tools, into the sea. We crossed a river in our boat, and after advancing about twelve miles through the forest, we stopped for the night, and having set our watches, passed it without being disturbed.

In the morning we continued our route, left the forest, and again approached the coast, when we halted in order to clean our fire-arms. About two o'clock p.m.

we were overtaken by two savages, one of whom was the elder who had visited us on our first landing. They gave us to understand that by following the coast we should meet with many impediments, both from its sinuous windings and from the rocks, of which latter they reported that some were impassable. They also showed us a beaten track through the forest, which they advised us to follow, after which they prepared to leave us.

Before their departure, however, I endeavoured to give them a more formidable idea of the power of our fire-arms, by firing with a rifle at a small ring marked upon a board at a distance of 120 feet. The ball pierced the board where I had marked it, and the savages, after having examined the aperture, and measured the distance, departed.

During the night a violent storm arose, accompanied by rain and snow; and, the bad weather continuing through the following day, we were obliged to wait in a cave till it was over. During all this time we were beset by the savages, who frequently rolled stones upon us from the top of the hill.

The weather clearing up the next morning, we pursued our journey till we reached a stream of some depth, which we followed on a beaten path, in the hope of meeting with a shallow part where we might ford it. Towards evening we arrived at a large hut. The inhabitants had left, but a fire was still burning near it, and it contained a large supply of dried kishutchos (a species of salmon), and opposite to it, poles were fixed in the water for the purposes of fishing. We took twenty-five of the fish, for which we left six yards of beads by way of payment; after which we encamped for the night about 200 yards from the hut, in the forest.

In the morning we perceived that we were surrounded by a troop of savages, armed with lances, forks, and arrows. I went forward and fired my piece over their heads, which had the desired effect; for they immediately dispersed and hid themselves amongst the trees, and allowed us to proceed. In this manner we had continually to contend against the savages, whom we endeavoured to avoid. But they were constantly besetting our camp, watching for a favourable moment to annihilate us.

On the 7th of November we met three men and a woman, who gave us some dried fish, speaking at the same time very ill of the tribe among whom we had hitherto suffered so much, and extolling their own. They followed us till the evening, when we reached the mouth of a small river, on the opposite side of which stood a village consisting of six huts. Here they advised us to wait till high tide, which would occur about the middle of the night; and promised to get us boats in which to cross over. They added that it would not be safe to cross at low water.

We felt, however, no inclination to trust ourselves in their hands during the night, and therefore retired to some distance, where we encamped till the next morning.

When we came again to the mouth of the river, we saw nearly two hundred savages near the huts, but as we could obtain no answer to any of our questions respecting a passage, we proceeded upwards in search of a ford.

As soon as the natives perceived our intention, they sent us a boat rowed by two men, who were completely naked. As this boat could not have held above ten people at a time, we begged them to send us another, that we might all cross at the same time. They complied with our request in sending a second boat, but so small a one that not more than four persons could sit in it. It was attended by the woman whom we had met the day previous. The small boat was assigned to Mrs. Bulugin, a male and a female Aleootskian, and a youth who had been apprenticed on board the ship, whilst nine of the boldest hunters embarked in the other, the others remaining on the bank.

"WE FOUND THE HUTS DESERTED" (p. 145).

As soon as the great boat had reached the middle of the stream, the savages who pulled it drew out a piece of wood which closed a hole that had been purposely made at the bottom of it, threw themselves into the water, and swam ashore. The boat was carried along by the current and came at one period so near the opposite shore, that all our people in it were wounded by the darts and arrows which the savages threw at them.

But fortunately the current took an opposite direction, and they succeeded in landing on our side at the moment when the boat began to sink. Those in the small boat, however, all fell into the hands of those treacherous barbarians, who, justly supposing that the muskets which had been in the boat must have become useless by the wet, now crossed over in order to attack us.

We, on our part, entrenched ourselves as well as circumstances would admit. After they had placed themselves in a line opposite to our position, they began shooting their arrows at us, and once even fired a musket. Luckily, however, we had a few muskets still left dry, with which we ultimately succeeded in driving off our enemies, after having wounded several of them and killed two. We, on our side, had one man mortally wounded; and as we would not allow him to fall a victim to these barbarians, we carried him along with us; but before we had advanced one mile, his sufferings became so great that he begged us to leave him to die in the forest, since our carrying him with us could not save him, and would only impede our flight. We therefore took leave of our dying companion, and proceeded onwards for some distance. At length we encamped in a convenient spot in a hilly part of the forest.

Now that our immediate danger was over, we began to reflect on our horrible situation. Our poor captain, in particular, who had lost a wife whom he had loved more than himself, suffered an anguish beyond description. We could not conceive whence all the savages we had seen could have come, and how they could possibly be the inhabitants of those few huts. But we afterwards learnt that they had assembled from all parts of the coast for the purpose of intercepting us, and that there were amongst them above fifty of those who had made the first attack upon us on our being cast on shore. Some had come even from Cape Greville.

During the 9th, 10th, and 11th it rained incessantly, and we wandered about the hills, scarcely knowing where, but only anxious to hide ourselves from the natives, whom we dared not meet in such unfavourable weather, our fire-arms having become perfectly useless. We suffered dreadfully from hunger, and were compelled to feed upon sponges, the soles of our boots, our furs, and musket-covers.

At last, however, even these wretched means failed us, and we again approached the last-mentioned river; but discovering two huts, and fearing to encounter the savages (for the weather was still wet), we again retreated into the forest, where we passed the night. On the 12th, the last morsel of bread being consumed, and the quantity of sponges found not proving sufficient for sixteen men, we killed our faithful companion, a dog, and shared his flesh amongst us. Our distress had now arrived at such a pitch, that our captain resigned his command into my hands with the approbation of the whole crew, declaring himself unable to conduct us any longer.

On the 13th the rain continued. On the 14th the weather cleared up, and we resolved to attack the two huts which we had noticed. We found them deserted by all the inmates, except a lad about thirteen years of age, who was a prisoner. This lad informed us that the owners of these huts had hastily crossed the river on noticing our foot-marks. After taking twenty-five dried fish for each man, we retreated to the woods.

We had not proceeded far, when we saw one of the natives running after us, apparently with the intention of making some communication; but as we were apprehensive lest he should discover our retreat, we aimed at him with our muskets and so forced him to withdraw. We advanced till we reached the head of a rivulet, where our party halted. I then went with one of the hunters and an Aleootskian to a neighbouring hill, for the purpose of re-connoitring.

The hunter led the way, but scarcely had he reached the summit when I saw an arrow pierce his back. I immediately shouted to the Aleootskian to draw the arrow out of his wound; but at the same moment he was also wounded. I looked round, and perceived a number of savages on a hill opposite, and about twenty others running towards us with the intention of cutting us off from our comrades. The arrows fell about us like hail. I fired my rifle and wounded one of the savages in the leg, which induced the whole party to take to their heels, carrying the wounded man with them on their shoulders.

The wounds of my two companions proved slight; and we remained on this spot for two days in order to recruit our strength. Finding it impracticable to reach the harbour this season, having no means of crossing the river, we resolved to follow the stream upwards, till we should reach a convenient spot for fishing, where we intended to entrench ourselves for the winter, after which we might act according to circumstances.

This march was a very laborious one, for we were frequently compelled to leave the banks of the river on account of the thick underwood and rugged precipices with which they were lined. The rain moreover was incessant. After several days' journey, our progress in a straight line did not exceed twenty knots. We were fortunate enough, however, to meet occasionally with some of the natives fishing in their boats on the river, who consented to sell us a few fish for beads and other trifles. At last, worn out with fatigue and hunger, we reached two huts; and necessity again compelled us to make a forced purchase of fish, as the inhabitants were at first unwilling to sell us any, alleging that the high water allowed the fish to pass over the framework which they had laid across the river, and had rendered them scarce.

We encamped at a short distance, and on the following morning were sur-prised by the arrival of two of the natives, who, after some general conversation, desired to know if we were inclined to ransom Mrs. Bulugin. The captain instantly offered his last cloak, and every one of us added some part of his clothes; so that we soon formed a considerable heap, which we cheerfully offered for the ransom of the unfortunate captive. But the savages insisted on having four muskets in addition, declaring that their countrymen would not part with her for a lower price. Not wishing to give them an absolute denial, we demanded that we should be allowed to see the lady before we took further steps. The savages consented, and she soon appeared, attended by a great number of them, on the opposite shore. At our request, two men accompanied her in a boat till within fifteen or twenty fathoms of us, where we again began bargaining for her.

It would be in vain to attempt a description of the ensuing scene. The unfortunate couple were melted into tears, and their convulsive sobs almost deprived them of utterance. We also wept; and none but the unfeeling natives remained unmoved. The lady told her husband that she had been humanely and kindly treated, that the other prisoners were also alive, and now at the mouth of the river. In the meantime the natives persisted in their demand for four muskets; and finding us unyielding on this point, they at length carried their prisoner back to the opposite shore.

Mr. Bulugin, upon this, assuming the air of a commander, ordered me peremptorily to deliver up the muskets. In vain did I urge the impolicy of such an act, representing that having but one serviceable musket for each man left, the giving up of so many, which would be immediately employed against us, would lead to our certain destruction. He persisted in his demand, till the men all declared they would not separate themselves from their muskets at any price. In thus determining, we all felt deeply for the distress of the poor man; but when it is considered that our lives or liberty were at stake, our conduct will be judged leniently.

After this sad event we pursued our journey for several days, till we were suddenly stopped by a heavy fall of snow; and as there was no appearance of its melting speedily, we began to clear a spot and collect materials to build a house, residing in the meantime in temporary huts. We constantly saw boats with natives on the river; and one day a youth, the son of an elder, with two other men, landed with his canoe and paid us a visit. He told us that their hut was not far off; and on our offering to send one of our men with them for the purpose of purchasing provisions, they seemed highly pleased, expecting, no doubt, to obtain another prisoner. But in this they were disappointed. The man went with them, but the young savage was detained as a hostage till his return.

He soon came back empty-handed; for the savages, whom he had found to the number of six men and two women, would not sell him anything. Having thus been cheated by these savages, we now detained them all, and despatched six of our men, armed with muskets, in their boat to the hut, whence they soon returned with all the fish they could find in it. We then made some presents to our prisoners, and dismissed them. Soon after, an old man brought us ninety salmon, for which we paid him with copper buttons.

A few days after this, we entered upon our new habitation. It was a square hut, with sentry-boxes at the angles. Soon after, we were again visited by the elder's son, our neighbour. We asked him to sell us some fish; but receiving a rude answer, we put him under arrest, declaring that he should not be released till he had furnished us with our winter store, viz., four hundred salmon and four bladders of caviar. He immediately despatched his companions, who returned to him twice in the course of a week, holding secret conferences with him. At last he asked us for a passage for his boats, which being granted, we soon saw thirteen boats, containing about seventy persons of both sexes, going down the river. These people soon returned to us with the articles required. We also obtained from them a boat sufficiently large to carry six persons. We then dismissed the young man, after presenting him with a spoiled musket and a few clothes.

We frequently sent our boat up the river, and wherever we found any fish in the huts, seized upon them as lawful prizes. One day, when our boat was absent on one of these excursions, we had occasion to stop several boats full of savages who were rowing in the same direction. As soon as our boat returned, we allowed them to proceed. They declined, however, saying that as our boat had taken away their fish, they had no further business. I endeavoured to make them understand that, having been driven into this spot by their cruelty, we had no other resource for the preservation of our lives than seizing upon their stores. I assured them, however, that we would content ourselves with what we ôould find up the river, if they would leave us unmolested for the winter, nor would we ever, in such case, send our boat downwards. This diplomatic point having been agreed to, we remained undisturbed during the winter, and in possession of abundance of food.

Being informed that the savages were gathering in large numbers at the mouth of the river, and preparing to obstruct our progress along the coast in every possible manner, we resolved to build another boat, with which we might in the ensuing spring ascend the river as high as possible, and then, turning towards the south, endeavour to reach the river Columbia, about which the natives are less barbarous. The task was difficult, but it was executed; and we only waited for mild weather to enter upon our hazardous expedition, when an event occurred which frustrated the whole of our plan. Mr. Bulugin resumed his command; and having embarked in our boats, we left our barrack on the 8th of February, 1809, and sailed down the river. We stopped at the same spot where, the year before, Mrs. Bulugin had been produced to us. We now clearly perceived the object of our captain; but so great was our compassion for his sufferings, that we silently resigned ourselves to the dangers to which he was about to expose us.

Here we were visited by an old man, with a water-tight basket made of branches, full of a species of root of which mariners brew a kind of acid liquor. He showed himself very attentive, and offered to pilot us down the river, the navigation of which was rather intricate, on account of the many trees that were floating in it. We accepted his offer and he acquitted himself honourably.

Having reached a small island, he ordered us to lie-to, and went on shore. He returned soon after, informing us that there were many people on the island, who would shoot us if we attempted to pass. He offered, therefore, to take us through a narrow channel, where we should be safe. We had nothing left but to trust to his honour, and we were not disappointed. We reached the mouth of the river in safety, and landed on a spot opposite an Indian village.

Here our guide left us after we had presented him with a shirt, a neckcloth, and a tin medal, cast for the occasion, which we requested him to wear suspended round his neck.

Next morning we were visited by a great many natives, and among them we recognised the woman who had deceived us, and drawn Mrs. Bulugin and her companions into captivity. We immediately seized her, together with a young man, and having fastened logs of wood to their feet, we declared that they should remain our prisoners till our people were restored to us.

"WE AGAIN BEGAN BARGAINING FOR HER" (p. 146).

Soon after, the woman's husband made his appearance, and assured us that they were not among them, having been allotted to another tribe; but that he would go in search of them, and bring them to us in four days if we would promise not to kill his wife in the interval.

We now entrenched ourselves on a neighbouring hill; and about a week after, a number of savages appeared on the opposite shore of the river, expressing a wish to enter into a treaty with us. I immediately went down to the water's edge, attended by several of our people. An elderly man, dressed in the European style, appeared as leader of the opposite party, amongst whom was Mrs. Bulugin.

She immediately told us that our female prisoner was the sister of the chief, that they were both kind people, to whom she owed the greatest obligations, and demanded that we should instantly set our prisoner at liberty.

On our telling her, however, that her husband would not liberate the woman unless she herself was first restored to him, she replied, to our horror and consternation, that she was very well contented to stay where she was! At the same time she advised us to deliver ourselves also to her present protectors. Their chief, she said, was a candid and honourable man, well known on this coast, who would, without the least doubt, liberate and send us on board two vessels now lying in the Bay of St. Juan de Fuca. As to the other prisoners, she said they were dispersed among the tribes in the vicinity.

I tried for some time to persuade her to a different determination; but finding her immovable in her resolution, I returned and reported her answer to her husband.

The poor man thought at first that I was joking, and would not believe me. But after a little consideration, he fell into a complete fury, took up his musket, and swore he would shoot her. But he had not gone many steps when he relented. He stopped, and bursting into tears, begged me to go by myself and try to bring her to reason, and even to threaten that he would shoot her.

I went and did as he bade me; but the woman resolutely replied, "As to death, I fear it not. I would rather die than wander with you again through the forests, where we may fall at last into the hands of some cruel tribe, whilst now I live among kind and humane people. Tell my husband that I despise his threats."

This cruel answer almost deprived the unfortunate and doting husband of his senses. He leant against a tree and wept bitterly. In the meantime I reflected upon his wife's words, and ultimately determined to follow her advice. I communicated my resolution to my companions, who at first unanimously declared against it; but on the captain's declaration that he would follow my example, they begged to be allowed to consider till the next morning.

The morning came, and the savages appeared again, renewing their demand for the restoration of the captives. This was immediately agreed to, and at the same time with Mr. Bulugin, and three others of our party, I surrendered myself to their discretion. The remainder of our comrades, however, obstinately refused to follow. Having taken, therefore, a hearty farewell of them, we departed with the tribe to which we now belonged.

The next day we reached the village of the Koonishtshati (a tribe in the neighbourhood of Cape Flattery), where my host, the chief, Yootramaki, had his winter residence. Mr. Bulugin went to the master of his wife, whilst the three others fell into various hands. The remainder of our companions attempted to reach the Island of Destruction, but foundered upon a rock; and after losing all their gunpowder, had some difficulty in escaping with their lives. They tried, therefore, to overtake us; but being intercepted by another tribe, they were all taken prisoners and dispersed along the coast.

At the end of about a month my master returned to his village near Cape Flattery, taking with him the captain and me. For he had purchased Mr. Bulugin from his master, with a promise of purchasing the wife also. We lived some time very comfortably; but afterwards our situation frequently changed, the savages sometimes selling, sometimes giving us, among themselves.

The fate of the husband and wife, who had become reconciled to each other, was truly cruel. Sometimes they were united; sometimes they were separated, and lived in constant fear of being torn apart for ever. At last death kindly released them. The lady died in the August of 1809, and in February in the following year her disconsolate husband followed her—but not to her grave, for his wife had been at the time of her death in the hands of such a barbarian that he would not even allow her a burial, but had her exposed in the forest.

In the meantime I had passed the greater part of my captivity with the good Yootramaki, who treated me like a friend. These people are like children, and pleased with every trifle. I found, therefore, no difficulty in ingratiating myself with them; and the construction of a paper kite and a watchman's rattle spread my reputation, as well as that of the Russian nation in general, far among them.

At last their veneration for my abilities was carried so far, that in one of the general assemblies of the elders, it was resolved that they would henceforward consider me as one of their equals, and from that time forward I always enjoyed the same honours as my master or any other chief, which made my life much more endurable.

They often wondered how Bulugin, who could neither shoot birds flying nor use the hatchet, could have been chosen as our chief. During the ensuing winter, so great a dearth of provisions ensued that one beaver was paid for ten salmon. With some chiefs, indeed, the want was so great that three of our countrymen took refuge with me, their masters not being able to keep them, and Yootramaki was kind enough to support them till the next spring, when they were demanded back by their owners, and I had influence enough to ensure them immunity for their flight.

In the month of March, we again removed to our summer village, where I built for myself a hut, with embrasures for defence, and of so novel a construction that the chiefs came from great distances in order to see and admire it. But this state of things was not to last long, for in the meantime, God had heard our prayers, and provided for our deliverance, and our troubles were coming to an end.

On the 6th of May, an American brig, the *Lydia*, under the command of Captain Brown, visited the coast. I went on board, and was overjoyed to find one of our companions, whom the captain had released from his captivity near the river Columbia. This honest tar immediately offered to ransom the whole of us. The savages, however. who thought this a good opportunity for obtaining large quantities of European goods, made such exorbitant demands, that Captain Brown, to cut the matter short, took one of the chiefs into custody, and declared that he would detain him till all were delivered up to him for a moderate price, for which several of us had already been ransomed.

This proceeding had the desired effect. ·In less than two days he liberated thirteen of us. Seven had died during our captivity; one had been sold to a distant nation, where he remained; and one was ransomed in 1809, by another American vessel near the river Columbia. On the 10th of May our vessel weighed anchor; and after touching at several points of the coast for the purpose of barter, we were safely landed on the 9th of June at New Archangel.

THE MARCHIONESS DE GANGES.

THIS lady, whose misfortunes have been the subject of romances, poems, and melodramas, was born at Avignon in the year 1636. Nature and fortune seemed to have united to load her with their favours in early life, only that she might feel more acutely the horrors of her subsequent fate. When she was little more than thirteen she was married to the Marquis de Castellane, a grandson of the Duke of Villars. On her being introduced at Versailles, Louis XIV., who was then very young, distinguished her amidst the crowd of beauties which embellished the most brilliant Court in Europe. The exquisite loveliness of the Marchioness, the illustrious family of her husband, the immense fortune which she had brought him, and the kind attention with which she had been honoured by the King, all conspired to render her the fashion, and she was soon known in Paris by no other appellation than that of the beautiful Provençal. Her first ties were soon broken. The Marquis de Castellane, who was in the naval service, perished by shipwreck on the coast of Sicily. The Marchioness, a blooming widow, rich, and without children, quickly saw all the most splendid youths of the Court flocking around her, and suing for her hand. Her unpropitious star destined her to give the preference to the youthful Lanede, Marquis de Ganges. She was united to him in the month of July, 1658. Two months after the celebration of the marriage the Marquis took his wife to Avignon. Their bliss during the first year of their union was uninterrupted.

The Marquis de Ganges had two brothers, the Abbé and the Chevalier de Ganges. Both were so deeply smitten with the charms of their sister-in-law that they instantly became enamoured of her. At the expiration of two or three years some differences arose between the married couple: too strong a tendency to dissipation on the one side, and on the other a little coquetry, which no doubt was entirely innocent, occasioned this slight disagreement. The Abbé, who was naturally of an intriguing disposition, exasperated and reconciled the husband and wife just as it suited his purposes. As his sister-in-law made him her confidante, he hoped that he should ultimately render her favourable to his passion; but as soon as he disclosed it his love was disdainfully rejected. With the same pretensions the Chevalier made the same attempt, and was just as badly received.

Not being able to succeed, the two brothers mutually confided to each other their criminal wishes, and blending together both their resentments they agreed to take joint vengeance. From that period they sought the means of getting rid of their sister-in-law. Poison was administered to the Marchioness in milk-chocolate; but whether it was that the poison being put in with a trembling hand was not sufficient in quantity, or that the milk blunted the effect of it, she sustained but little injury from it. The crime, however, did not pass undiscovered.

To put a stop to the rumours on this subject which were current in the city, the Marquis proposed to his wife to spend the autumn on his estate of Ganges. The Marchioness consented, which seems rather extraordinary; but in human events there are always some circumstances which are inexplicable. It appears that the Marchioness had forebodings of her fate; for in a letter to her mother, dated from the castle of Ganges, she declared that she could not traverse the gloomy avenues of that melancholy residence without a feeling of terror.

Her husband, who had accompanied her thither, left her with his two brothers, and returned to Avignon. Not long before her quitting that city the Marchioness had come into possession of a considerable inheritance; and it is a fact that proves that she suspected the family into which she had entered, and perhaps even her husband, that she made a will at Avignon, by which in case of her death she confided her property, till her children were of age, to Madame de Rossau, her mother. This will became the pretext of an inveterate persecution of the Marchioness by her brothers-in-law. They so strongly and perseveringly pressed her to revoke it that she was at last weak enough to consent. They had no sooner carried their point than they made a second attempt to poison her, but with no better success than before.

The monsters had, however, gone too far to allow of their receding. Being one day obliged to keep her bed by indisposition, the Marchioness saw her brothers-in-law enter the room. In one hand the Abbé had a pistol, and in the other a glass of poison; the Chevalier had a drawn sword under his arm.

"You must die, Madame," said the Abbé; "choose whether by pistol, sword, or poison." The Marchioness, in a state bordering on distraction, could not believe her senses. She sprang out of bed, threw herself at the feet of her brothers, and asked what crime she had committed.

"Choose!" was the only answer the assassins made.

Seeing that there was no hope of assistance, the unfortunate lady took the glass which the Abbé presented to her, and swallowed the contents while he held the pistol to her breast. This horrible scene being finished, the monsters retired, and locked the victim into the room, promising to send to her a confessor, the spiritual aid of whom she had requested as a last favour.

She was now alone; her first thought was how to escape; her next was to try various means of removing from her stomach the poison which she had been forced to take. In the latter she partly succeeded by putting one of the locks of her hair down her throat. Then, half naked, she threw herself into the courtyard, though the window was nearly eight yards from the ground. But

"'YOU MUST DIE, MADAME'" (p. 154).

how was she to escape from her murderers, who would speedily be aware of her flight, and were masters of all the outlets from the castle?

The unfortunate Marchioness implored the compassion of one of the servants, who let her out into the fields through a stable-door. She was quickly pursued by the Abbé and the Chevalier, who represented her as a mad woman to a farmer in whose house she had taken refuge. It was here that the crime was to be consummated. The Chevalier, who hitherto had appeared less ferocious than his brother, followed her from room to room, and having come up to her in a remote apartment, the villain gave her two stabs in the breast and five in the back, at the moment that she was trying to get away.

The blows were so violent that the sword was broken, and part of it remained in the shoulder. The cries of the miserable lady brought the neighbours to the place, and the Abbé, who had stayed at the door to prevent any help coming to her, entered the house with the crowd. Enraged to see that the Marchioness was not yet dead, he presented his pistol to her breast, but it missed fire.

The spectators, who had hitherto been terrified, now rushed to seize the Abbé, but by dint of hard struggles he effected his escape.

Madame de Ganges lived nineteen days after this event, and did not expire till she had publicly implored the Divine mercy for her assassins. On her body being opened, the bowels were found to be corroded by the effect of the poison. Her husband was present during her last moments. There were very strong presumptions against him; but the Marchioness, still compassionate amidst the severest sufferings, did all that lay in her power to clear him from suspicion.

The parliament of Toulouse lost no time in instituting judicial proceedings against the criminals, and by a decree which was issued on the 21st of August, 1667, the Abbé and the Chevalier de Ganges were outlawed and sentenced to be broken on the wheel. After having his property confiscated, and been degraded from the rank of nobility, the Marquis was condemned to perpetual banishment by the same decree.

The Chevalier found shelter in Malta, and was subsequently killed in an engagement with the Turks. As to the Abbé, he sought an asylum in Holland, and there under a fictitious name he passed through a variety of adventures, which might furnish the subject of a romance. It is much to be regretted that two such execrable wretches should have escaped the punishment which was so justly awarded to them by the parliament of Toulouse.

THE EXECUTION OF EARL FERRERS.

FROM HORACE WALPOLE'S LETTERS.

WHAT will your Italians say to a peer of England, of one of the best families, tried for murdering his servant, with the utmost dignity and solemnity, and then hanged at the common place of execution for highwaymen,

"HE PLAYED AT PIQUET WITH THE WARDERS" (p. 158).

and afterwards anatomised? This must seem a little odd to them, especially as they have not lately had a Sixtus Quintus.

I have hitherto spoken of Lord Ferrers to you as a wild beast, a mad assassin, a low wretch, about whom I had no curiosity. If I now am going to give you a minute account of him, don't think me so far part of an

English mob as to fall in love with a criminal merely because I have had the pleasure of his execution. I certainly did not see it, nor should have been struck with mere intrepidity. I never adored criminals, whether in a cart or a triumphal car; but there has been such wonderful coolness and sense in all this man's last behaviour that it has made me quite inquisitive about him, not at all pity him. I only reflect what I have often thought, how little connection there is between any man's sense and his sensibility, so much so, that instead of Lord Ferrers having any ascendant over his passions, I am disposed to think that his drunkenness, which was supposed to heighten his ferocity, has rather been a lucky circumstance. What might not a creature of such capacity, and who stuck at nothing, have done, if his abilities had not been drowned in brandy?

I will go back a little into his history. His misfortunes, as he called them, were dated from his marriage, though he had been guilty of horrid excesses unconnected with matrimony, and is even believed to have killed a groom, who died a year after receiving a cruel beating from him.

His wife, a very pretty woman, was sister of Sir William Meredith, had no fortune, and, he says, trepanned him into marriage, having met him drunk at an assembly in the country, and kept him so till the ceremony was over. As he always kept himself so afterwards, one need not impute it to her. In every other respect—and one scarce knows how to blame her for wishing to be a countess—her behaviour was unexceptionable. He had a mistress before, and two or three children, and her he took again after the separation from his wife. He was fond of both, and used both ill; his wife so ill—always carrying pistols to bed, and threatening to kill her before morning, beating her, and jealous without provocation—that she got separated from him by Act of Parliament, which appointed receivers of his estate in order to secure her allowance. This he could not bear. However, he named his steward for one, but afterwards finding out that this Johnson had paid her fifty pounds without his knowledge, and suspecting him of being in the confederacy against him, he determined, when he failed of opportunities of murdering his wife, to kill the steward, which he effected, as you have heard.

The shocking circumstances attending the murder I did not tell you: indeed, while he was alive, I scarce liked to speak my opinion even to you, for though I felt nothing for him, I thought it wrong to propagate any notions that might interfere with mercy—if he could be thought deserving it—and not knowing into what hands my letter might pass before it reached yours, I chose to be silent, though nobody could conceive greater horror than I did for him at his trial. Having shot the steward at three in the afternoon, he persecuted him till one in the morning, threatening again to murder him, attempting to tear off his bandages, and terrifying him till in that misery he was glad to obtain leave to be removed to his own house; and when the earl heard that the poor creature was dead, he said he gloried in having killed him. You cannot conceive the shock this evidence gave the court. Many of the lords were standing to look at him; at once they turned from him in detestation.

I have heard that on the former affair in the House of Lords he had behaved with great shrewdness; no such thing appeared at his trial. It is now pretended that his being forced by his family against his inclination to plead madness prevented his exerting his parts; but he has not acted in anything as if his family had influence over him, consequently his reverting to much good sense leaves the whole inexplicable. The very night he received sentence he played at piquet with the warders, and would play for money, and would have continued to play every evening, but they refused.

Lord Cornwallis, Governor of the Tower, shortened his allowance of wine after his conviction, agreeably to the late strict Acts on murder. This he much disliked, and at last pressed his brother the clergyman to intercede, that at least he might have more porter, "For," said he, "what I have is not a draught." His brother represented against it, but at last consenting (and he did obtain it), then said the Earl, "Now is as good a time as any to take leave of you—adieu!"

A minute journal of his whole behaviour has been kept, to see if there was any madness in it. Dr. Munro, since the trial, has made an affidavit of his lunacy. The Washingtons were certainly a very frantic race, and I have no doubt of madness in him, but not of a pardonable sort. Two petitions from his mother and all his family were presented to the King, who said, as the House of Lords had unanimously found him guilty, he would not interfere. Last week, my Lord Keeper very good-naturedly got out of a gouty bed to present another. The King would not hear him. "Sir," said the Keeper, "I don't come to petition for mercy or respite, but that the £4,000 which Lord Ferrers has in India Bonds may be permitted to go according to his disposition of it to his mistress' children, and the family of the murdered man." "With all my heart," said the King, "I have no objection; but I will have no message carried to him from me."

However, this grace was notified to him and gave him great satisfaction; but, unfortunately, it now appears to be law that it is forfeited to the sheriff of the county where the fact was committed; though when my Lord Hardwicke was told that he had disposed of it, he said, "To be sure he may, before conviction."

Dr. Pearce, Bishop of Rochester, offered his services to him: he thanked the bishop, but said, as his own brother was a clergyman, he chose to have him. Yet he had another relation who has been much more busy about his repentance. I don't know whether you have ever heard that one of the singular characters here is a Countess of Huntingdon, aunt of Lord Ferrers. She is the Saint Theresa of the Methodists. Judge how violent bigotry must be in such mad blood! The Earl, by no means disposed to be a convert, let her visit him, and often sent for her, as it was more company; but he grew sick of her, and complained that she was enough to provoke anybody. She made her suffragan,

Whitfield, pray for and preach about him; and that impertinent fellow told his enthusiasts, in his sermon, that my lord's heart was stone.

The Earl wanted much to see his mistress: my Lord Cornwallis, as simple an old woman as Lady Huntingdon herself, consulted whether he should permit it. "Oh! by no means; it would be letting him die in adultery!" In one thing she was more sensible. He resolved not to take leave of his children, four girls, but on the scaffold, and then to read to them a paper he had drawn up, very bitter on the family of Meredith, and on the House of Lords for the first transaction. This my Lady Huntingdon persuaded him to drop; and he took leave of his children the day before. He wrote two letters in the preceding week to Lord Cornwallis on some of these requests; they were cool and rational, and concluded with desiring him not to mind the absurd requests of his (Lord Ferrers's) family in his behalf.

On the last morning he dressed himself in his wedding clothes, and said, "He thought this at least as good an occasion of putting them on, as that for which they were first made." He wore them to Tyburn. This marked the strong impression on his mind. His mother wrote to his wife in a weak, angry style, telling her to intercede for him as her duty, and to swear to his madness. But this was not so easy; in all her cause before the Lords she had persisted that he was not mad.

Sir William Meredith, and even Lady Huntingdon, had prophesied that his courage would fail him at last, and had so much foundation, that it is certain Lord Ferrers had often been beat: but the Methodists were to get no honour by him. His courage rose where it was most likely to fail—an unlucky circumstance to prophets, especially when they have had the prudence to have all kind of probability on their side. Even an awful procession of above two hours, with that mixture of pageantry, shame, and ignominy, nay, and of delay, could not dismount his resolution. He set out from the Tower at nine amidst crowds—thousands. First went a string of constables; then one of the sheriffs, in his chariot-and-six, the horses dressed with ribbons; next Lord Ferrers in his landau-and-six, his coachman crying all the way; guards on each side; the other sheriff's carriage followed empty, with a mourning coach-and-six, a hearse, and the Horse Guards. Observe that the empty chariot was that of the other sheriff, who was in the coach with the prisoner, and who was Vaillant, the French bookseller in the Strand.

How will you decipher all these strange circumstances to Florentines? A bookseller in robes and in mourning, sitting as a magistrate by the side of the Earl; and in the evening everybody going to Vaillant's shop to hear the particulars. I wrote to him, as he serves me, for the account; but he intends to print it, and I will send it you with some other things, and the trial.

Lord Ferrers first talked on indifferent matters, and observing the prodigious confluence of people (the blind was drawn up on his side), he said, "But they never saw a lord hanged, and perhaps will never see another."

One of the dragoons was thrown by his horse's leg entangling in the hind wheel; Lord Ferrers expressed much concern, and said, "I hope there will be no death to-day but mine;" and was pleased when Vaillant made excuses to him on his office. "On the contrary," said the Earl, "I am much obliged to you. I feared the disagreeableness of the duty might make you depute your under-sheriff. As you are so good as to execute it yourself, I am persuaded the dreadful apparatus will be conducted with more expedition."

The chaplain of the Tower, who sat backwards, then thought it his turn to speak, and began to talk on religion, but Lord Ferrers received it impatiently. However, the chaplain persevered, and said he wished to bring his lordship to some confession or acknowledgment of contrition for a crime so repugnant to the laws of God and man, and wished him to endeavour to do whatever could be done in so short a time. The Earl replied, "He had done everything he proposed to do with regard to God and man; and as to discourses on religion, "you and I, sir," said he to the clergyman, "shall probably not agree on that subject. The passage is very short; you will not have time to convince me, nor I to refute you; it cannot be ended before we arrive." The clergyman still insisted, and urged that at least the world would expect some satisfaction. Lord Ferrers replied with some impatience, "Sir, what have I to do with the world? I am going to pay a forfeit life, which my country has thought proper to take from me. What do I care now what the world thinks of me? But, sir, since you desire some confession, I will confess one thing to you; I do believe there is a God. As to modes of worship we had better not talk on them. I always thought Lord Bolingbroke in the wrong to publish his notions on religion. I will not fall into the same error."

The chaplain, seeing it was in vain to make any more attempts, contented himself with representing to him that it would be expected from one of his calling, and that even decency required, that some prayer should be used on the scaffold, and asked his leave at least to repeat the Lord's Prayer there. Lord Ferrers replied, "I always thought it a good prayer; you may use it if you please."

Whilst these discourses were passing, the procession was stopped by the crowd. The Earl said he was dry, and wished for some wine and water. The sheriff said he was sorry to be obliged to refuse him. By late regulations they were enjoined not to let prisoners drink from the place of imprisonment to that of execution, as great indecencies had formerly been committed by the lower species of criminals getting drunk. "And though," said he, "my lord, I might think myself excusable in overlooking this order out of regard to a person of your lordship's rank, yet there is another reason which I am sure will weigh with you. Your lordship is sensible of the greatness of the crowd; we must draw up to some tavern; the confluence would be so great that it would delay the expedition which your lordship seems so much to desire." He replied he was satisfied, adding, "Then I must be content with this," and took some pig-tail tobacco out of his pocket. As they went on, a letter was thrown into

"HE MOUNTED THE SCAFFOLD" (p. 162).

his coach; it was from his mistress to tell him it was impossible, from the crowd, to get her up to the spot where he had appointed her to meet and take leave of him, but that she was in a hackney-coach of such a number. He begged Vaillant to order his officers to try to get the hackney-coach up to his. "My lord," said Vaillant, "you have behaved so well hitherto that I think 'tis pity to venture unmanning yourself." He was struck, and was satisfied with seeing her.

As they drew nigh he said, "I perceive we are almost arrived; it is time to do what little more I have to do," and then, taking out his watch, gave it to Vaillant, desiring him to accept it as a mark of his gratitude for his kind behaviour, adding, "It is scarce worth your acceptance, but I have nothing else; it is a stop-watch, and a pretty accurate one." He gave five guineas to the chaplain, and took out as much for the executioner. Then giving Vaillant a pocket-book, he begged him to deliver it to Mrs. Clifford, his mistress, with what it contained, and with his most tender regard, saying, "The key of it is to the watch, but I am persuaded you are too much of a gentleman to open it." He destined the remainder of the money in his purse to the same person, and with the same tender regards.

When they came to Tyburn his coach was detained some minutes by the conflux of people, but as soon as the door was opened he stepped out readily and mounted the scaffold; it was hung with black by the undertaker, and at the expense of his family.

Under the gallows was a new-invented stage, to be struck from under him. He showed no kind of fear or discomposure, only just looking at the gallows with a slight motion of dissatisfaction. He said little, kneeled for a moment in prayer, said, "Lord, have mercy upon me, and forgive me my errors," and immediately mounted the upper stage. He had come pinioned with a black sash, and was unwilling to have his hands tied or his face covered, but was persuaded to both. When the rope was put round his neck he turned pale, but recovered his countenance instantly, and was but seven minutes from leaving the coach to the signal given for striking the stage. As the machine was new, they were not ready at it; his toes touched it, and he suffered a little, having had time by their bungling to raise his cap, but the executioner pulled it down again, and they pulled his legs, so that he was soon out of pain, and quite dead in four minutes.

He desired not to be stripped and exposed, and Vaillant promised him, though his clothes must be taken off, that his shirt should not. This decency ended with him; the sheriffs fell to eating and drinking on the scaffold, and helped up one of their friends to drink with them, as he was still hanging, which he did for above an hour, and then was conveyed back with the same pomp to Surgeons' Hall to be dissected.

The executioners fought for the rope, and the one who lost it cried. The mob tore off the black cloth as relics, but the universal crowd behaved with great decency and admiration, as they well might, for sure no exit was ever made with more sensible resolution, and with less ostentation.

If I have tired you by this long narrative, you feel differently from me; the man, the manners of the country, the justice of so great and curious a nation, all to me seem striking, and must, I believe, be more so to you, who have been absent long enough to read of your own country as history.

*   *   *   *   *   *   *

In a subsequent letter Walpole says:—"That wonderful creature Lord Ferrers, of whom I told you so much in my last, and with whom I am not going to plague you much more, made one of his keepers read *Hamlet* to him the night before his death, after he was in bed; paid all his bills before morning, as if leaving an inn; and half an hour before the sheriffs fetched him, corrected some verses he had written in the Tower, in imitation of the Duke of Buckingham's epitaph, *Dubius sed non improbus vixi.* What a noble author have I here to add to my catalogue!"

A CRIMINAL GOING TO EXECUTION.

"I PUT 'PUNCH' ON MY SHOULDERS" (p. 100).

STRUGGLES WITH THE SEA.

I.—AN ONLY SURVIVOR.

I WAS master of the brigantine *Glencoe*, 125 tons register. The crew consisted of myself, four men, and a boy—six hands all told. On Sunday, October 22, 1882, I sailed from Hartlepool, bound to Hull Bridge, with a cargo of coal. In the afternoon of the following day I passed through Yarmouth Roads, weather moderate, and wind varying from S. to S.E. At midnight and until 1 a.m. on the Tuesday, the vessel was under all plain sail. The weather then became squally; the barometer was at 28·90, and still falling; so I called the watch to shorten canvas. My intention was to get Harwich, or, if the wind kept S.E., to get Burnham River. At 2.30 the wind came from S., sometimes blowing a gale, succeeded by dead calm. Sometimes we were wallowing about in the sea in a calm, and the next minute the wind would come in a tremendous puff. This continued till 8 a.m., when it became a strong gale from the S.E. I sighted the Shipwash Light-vessel at 10 o'clock, the wind blowing a hurricane. The vessel was now under double-reefed mainsail, main and middle staysail, lower topsail, fore staysail, and foretopmast staysail.

On sighting the Shipwash all hearts were glad that we had made such a good land-fall. About a mile from the Shipwash the weather was again speechless calm, and continued so till mid-day, when it came a smart breeze from the S.S.W. I then made canvas to get port; put on her jib, maintopmast staysail, and upper topsail. At 2 p.m. it came a strong gale from S.E., and I had to reduce canvas. The sea was very heavy; the whole of the bulwark on the lee side, and part of that on the weather side, was washed away. It was with joy that at 2.30 I made the Cork Light-ship; wind still from the S.E., a hurricane; but I thought I was all right, and I sang out, "Now, boys, for Harwich!" I ordered the mate to see the range of cable was all right to bring up in Harwich Harbour. When he went forward he found all the chain cable overboard to leeward, some forty-five fathoms in the bight. While he was reporting this to me I could see a brig going into Harwich Harbour. I saw her brail the main trysail up and immediately sheet it home again. One of my men said, "Buoy off the lee bow, master." It was the Platters, a short distance from Harwich Harbour. The wind had suddenly shifted from S.E. to W., caught the vessel aback, and put her about. I would have brought up then had not the cable been overboard; but that being impossible, I hove her to and let her drive, while we attempted to get the cable on board. We had to use a tackle, and it was very slow work; but ultimately we succeeded and it was lashed. I went to lend a hand, and sent the boy to keep a look-out. He reported Bawdsey Buoy on the weather bow. I then said, "Now, boys, we will wear ship," and at the same time ordered the mainsail to be lowered, and up foretopmast staysail and foresail. When I tried to wear her I found she had water in her, because she would not alter her course more than two points by fall down into the sea; a second ratline immersed.

During all this, the sea was breaking clean over us. We hoisted the jib, and away went the jib-boom. My idea then was to get the anchor ready to let go, to cant her head to westward, and, when the topsail came aback, to slip the cable, and sail her to land, to save life. But, to my great surprise, the cable had broken the lashings, and gone overboard again. I resolved to try and get the cable (the inboard part) up from below, and, if we could get the shackle, to bend it on to the anchor. There was not time to get the lee chain in. I could see the breakers on the Shipwash, and I knew that was where I must go if I could not get her head round. It was of no use; before we could get the cable up, we drove broadside on to the Sand, being perfectly powerless to avoid it. She lay port side on the Sand. We first tried to launch the boat, but a sea breaking over us fell into the boat, and smashed her from stem to stern. We then had to take to the rigging. We got into the fore-top; but, as the ship was breaking up, the masts gradually gave way, until they were lying flush with the water. The sea was making a clean breach over us.

Being an American-built ship, the upper portion of the cabin formed a sort of deck-house, and, as the vessel lay, was the most prominent part of her. We soon saw that was the safest place, and we crawled along the rigging to the deck. My brother-in-law being the lowest in the rigging was the first man to reach the deck; but he had barely done so when it blew up, and he was pitched head-foremost into the hold. I was the next to follow, and seeing what had happened, I seized the fore-brace, made a hitch round my waist, and jumped into the hold after him. I fully expected to fall on the cargo, but the cargo was gone, her bottom was out, and nothing but the sea in her. I hauled myself up by the brace, the deck planks affording me foothold. On reaching the deck, I saw the rest of the hands on the house, with the exception of the boy, who was against the fore-rigging, holding on by the starboard rail. I went to him, and assisted him to the house. I then asked the mate, "Where's old 'Punch'?" and he replied, "In the cabin." "Punch" was a Bedlington terrier, a present from Mr. Purdy, a ship-chandler at Seaham Harbour. I went to the door of the cabin (now full of water), and found poor "Punch" clinging to the steps. I took him under my arm, and joined my shipmates on the house-top, making five of us. They had each got their legs down the skylight, and had hold of some mainsail tires which were rove through a glass rack inside the skylight. (For the benefit of the uninitiated, I may explain that mainsail tires are small ropes used in stowing the mainsail.) There was not room for me to get into the skylight like the rest, and I said to the mate, "Let me have one leg down, Dick." In another second, before Dick had time to reply, or I to get secured, a huge sea swept both house and us overboard.

I had no idea how long I was in the water, but when I recovered my senses I was scratching at something, which I thought was the ship's side. I then saw a glimmering of light above and ahead of me. I was fully dressed, and had both sea-boots and oilskins on, and it was a desperate struggle, through wreckage, to reach that light; but reach it I did, and found it was the cabin-top or house upside-down. I saw nothing of my shipmates; I was alone. I seated myself on the edge, with my arm down the funnel-hole, and held on. I became unconscious, and how I went through the breakers, and off the Sand, I never knew; but when I regained consciousness I was in comparatively smooth water, on the lee side. The dog was licking my face. Poor "Punch" seemed delighted to have found me.

I surveyed my position. I knew that I must soon drift into heavy seas again and, therefore, must secure myself. I had three mainsail tires and there were the projecting bolts which had fastened the house to the ship's deck. If I had had another tire I could have lashed myself all-fours. I took off my silk neckerchief and tied it round my waist, and then made the tires fast to the bolts and my silk waistband.

My frail raft was whirled about, by wind and water, like a spinning-top. I put "Punch" on my shoulders, with his fore-paws round my neck and resting on my chest. I held on to the dog with my left hand, and to the raft with my right. Every sea that broke against my raft, and buried me in water, caused "Punch" to bark with anger. During the dark hours of that awful night the dog was wonderful comfort to me. In my fearful loneliness he was company, something living, and he gave me a little warmth. At length his bark ceased, he grew cold, and I found he was dead. I pulled him down on to my knee, kept him there for a time, and then threw him overboard. While he was on my shoulders his claws had penetrated my oilskin and clothing, and entered my flesh, causing a wound which afterwards festered.

As I expected, the sea grew heavier as I left the Sand. During the night I saw a steamer's lights; she approached within a very short distance from me, and passed on. I shouted as hard as I could, but with the noise of wind and sea it was impossible they could hear me. After that I became unconscious, I know not for how long. On recovering consciousness, I found the wind had lulled, and the sea was less. Daybreak that morning was the happiest experience of my life. At sunrise, I saw a barque steering right for me; but, when within about three miles of me, he altered his course, and I was again without hope. I dreaded another night in the water, and was determined, rather than endure it, to cut my lashing and go overboard.

In the afternoon of that day, after I had been twenty-seven or twenty-eight hours in the water, I saw a vessel standing in. I had neither hat nor anything else I could use as a signal, but I stripped some pieces of lining from the cabin-top, and waved them. Those on the vessel saw me, and rescued me. She was the smack *Forager*, Captain Pudney. I learnt afterwards that they had at first taken my signal to be the Outer Garbard Buoy; but, on taking a look through the glass, the mate exclaimed, "No! by Heaven, that's a man on a piece of wood. Call the captain!" The captain ordered the boat to be got ready, and go to the object; and it was done, at very great risk. When the boat reached me, I had just strength to jump on board, and then sank exhausted. Every kindness was shown me on board the *Forager*, and under great difficulties they landed me at Lowestoft.

It was three months before I could do anything, and two years before I was able to go to sea again.

II.—CAPTAIN WEBB'S CHANNEL SWIM.

THE reader who turns to the first volume of THE WORLD OF ADVENTURE will find in the chapter headed "Tales of Niagara" the tragedy that closed the life of Captain Webb. But the story of the great feat which won him renown has a far higher claim to be included in any collection of brave deeds. For the catastrophe at Niagara was but the event of a foolhardy enterprise; while the exploit of swimming from Dover to Calais owed its success to calculated pluck and endurance.

Early in the afternoon of Tuesday, August 24th, 1875, the Admiralty Pier at Dover was crowded. The air was still, the sea calm as a mirror, and the white cliffs of the coast reflected the sunshine with dazzling brightness. No more favourable day could have been chosen by the man who now, at four minutes to one, dressed in a pair of red silk swimming-drawers, stepped briskly through the throng, and almost before a cheer arose, had reached the end of the pier and dived off the steps.

He was a fair, handsome, resolute-looking man, twenty-seven years of age ; in height, 5 feet 8 inches only, but otherwise a giant. His chest measured a full 43 inches, and his weight fell scarcely under 14 stone. For the rest, the clear tint of his skin proved him in perfect condition, and the firm resolution on his face showed him full of hope.

He had been some time in training for this attempt to swim the Channel. On July 3rd he had swum twenty miles from Blackwall to Gravesend in four hours and fifty-two minutes. A fortnight later he had traversed the distance between Dover and Ramsgate in eight hours and forty minutes. And on August 12th, just twelve days ago, he had made a gallant essay to perform the feat he is now attempting. Though unsuccessful then, he was beaten rather by the weather than by any lack of endurance, and had thrown into the shade the previous exploit of J. B. Johnson, a famous ex-champion swimmer, whose attempt to cross the Channel had been made on August 24th, 1872—exactly three years before. Johnson swam down Channel towards Folkestone for about sixty-five minutes, and then was forced to give in, when he had covered only some seven miles. Webb, on the other hand, though met at the outset with a nasty chopping sea and a difficult wind, yet fought the waves for six hours and forty-nine minutes, and left the sea about midnight, quite fresh and hearty, and fully resolved to make a second attempt, and win.

And to-day, as he dives off the Admiralty Pier, he has all in his favour for success, if indeed the feat be possible. The day is warm, as we have said, and the water calm. But as it is sure to be chilly at nightfall, the swimmer has anointed his body with a thick coating of porpoise-grease to resist the cold. A small lugger, the *Anne*, is waiting to escort him ; and also a couple of stout rowing-skiffs, the one containing his cousin, Mr. G. H. Ward, who is to supply him with refreshment and generally look after him, and one or the other of the two referees (Mr. A. G. Payne and Mr. H. F. Wilkinson, of the *Field* newspaper), who had come at the Captain's own request to see fair play. The other skiff is used to take messages backwards and forwards to the lugger.

Captain Toms, on board the *Anne*, advises Webb to steer S.E. by S. half S. —a line that will take him direct for the French coast ; and, cheered on his way by shout after shout from the little fleet of boats that are accompanying him for some way to wish him "good speed," the swimmer, with long steady breast-strokes of about twenty to the minute, shoots out to sea from Dover Harbour, on the back of the ebb tide that is still running down Channel.

Captain Toms had not given his advice without much calculation. The course mapped out for Webb was this: to keep his face fronting the opposite shore and swim athwart the tides, that would, as far as could be predicted, carry him down Channel some way upon the off side of the South Sand Head Light, down towards Cape Grisnez with the next ebb, and with the return flood wash him up towards his goal on the French coast. How excellent was Captain Toms' reckoning will be seen in the sequel.

Meanwhile, though the distance seems traversed but slowly, the swimmer forges ahead with his slow breast-stroke till about a quarter to three, when he pauses to drink a cup of good ale that is handed him by his cousin, and again cuts across the ebb. At three o'clock the tide begins to run up Channel. By this time Webb is well clear of the white cliffs and seems almost motionless on the billows, about three and a half miles out at sea, for the absence of any object to mark his progress makes it appear slow indeed.

"THEY HELP HIM ASHORE" (p. 171).

After another hour and a half he pulls up to drink another mug of ale. As he swims past Dover, being now more than four miles distant from the land, he is going fresh and strong, and calls out "All right!" to his friends in the skiff who are inquiring about his condition. He certainly looks all right, and at half-past six takes a cup of beef-tea before settling down to his evening's work. At this point he is inspirited by the companionship of Mr. Chambers, a staunch friend and supporter, who having rowed out from Dover, now plunges off his boat into the sea to swim alongside the Captain for a time.

The afternoon drops into twilight and still the calm continues, and still Webb, without sign of flagging, is breasting his way up Channel on the flood, taking no solid food, but now and then breaking the monotony of his work with a cup of beef-tea or hot coffee. At half-past nine he calls out that a jelly-fish has stung him, and asks for a little brandy.

It is night by this time, and a placid moon lights up the swimmer so that his friends can see him plainly all the while. At 10.30 he is visited by a steam-tug that has put out from Dover for the purpose, yet, strange to say, leaves the man, who has now been ploughing through the waves for more than nine hours, without even the encouragement of a parting cheer. But at 11.45 the mail-boat, passing on her way to Calais, burns a red light, casting its glow on the spot where Webb is swimming and on the face of the Captain himself. The passengers and crew catching sight of him raise shout after shout, that, as he afterwards said, raised the heart within him to fight the struggle out.

The tide has turned again and carries him south-west, once more under the moon. It is in the very best direction—for he now lies about a dozen miles from the South Foreland Lights, and eight or nine from Cape Grisnez and Calais. Throughout the night at intervals the friend and reporters call out and cheer him from the boats.

It is still the breast-stroke, as they can see in the moonlight. On board the pilot boat, young Baker stands ready all the time to spring to Webb's aid if cramp should take him or exhaustion prove too much for him; and several times he dives to hand the Captain his refreshments. Yet, oddly enough, as the battle begins to tell on the intrepid swimmer he takes less and less sustenance.

And now his friends begin to fear indeed for his success. The night luckily continues calm, but as the morning breaks and they see him more clearly, they see also that the long exposure has told on him sorely. Yet that part of the task which he has already accomplished is as nothing compared to the fight in store for him.

With the first paling of dawn the chalk cliffs of Cape Grisnez are distinctly visible, but the distance cannot be gauged by the eye. They seem like phantoms on the horizon. As the day grows, however, and the sun gets up, the promontory seems close at hand and almost within the swimmer's grasp.

But now, at five o'clock, the flood tide sets in and drifts him eastward towards Calais. And in an hour or so a breeze comes with it, ruffling the waves and dashing them in the swimmer's face. For a while he battles on without sign; then faintly calls out that the wind "is killing him by inches." His motion is but languid. His face appears grey and aged. His friends fear indeed that his strength is giving out and that he will miss success almost within grasp of it. Young Baker, the diver, sits ready with a life-line, for the Captain may sink almost without a moment's warning.

Certainly it is bitter to watch his strength failing, and think it more than probable that all the pluck and hardihood of this man must go for nothing. It is true that his swim is already the finest recorded; but what is this, if the end be not attained? To the eyes of those on board the lugger it is evident that the crisis is close. Success or failure will hang on the next few minutes; and looking at the waves that were running higher and higher, they saw failure written on the face of them.

After all, it is moral endurance that usually wins the day. Baker has plunged in beside the swimmer, encouraging him by every effort, in the way of advice and example, to continue. And now over the waves there rings out a lusty British cheer. It comes from a boat's crew of the *Maid of Kent* (the mail-packet that had passed and cheered him last night) who now have rowed out from Calais to watch the event and help if possible.

And they can help. The shore is now, at 9.45, only half a mile distant. The sea is covered with crested waves that even break over the little boats around. The new-comers perceive the face of the exhausted man and hit on an expedient. Pulling to windward they keep between the waves and Webb, turning their boat into an extempore breakwater, and cheering in a way that it does the heart good to hear.

It rouses Webb to a last effort. A little more vigour creeps into the slack arms. Inch by inch, foot by foot he draws closer to the shore. With "heat of controversy" he disputes the right of the wind to beat him in these last few moments — until at length there are but a few yards more. Then to the joy of the spectators he touches ground !—but, being too weak to stand, sinks down in the water. It is no matter. The feat has been performed; the Channel has been swum. A couple of men instantly rush towards him, and help him ashore in kindly arms. By the watches it is forty-one minutes past ten; and Webb has been swimming for *twenty-one hours and three-quarters.* It is a big action, and men's hearts grow hot as they lift him up and help him to walk to the carriage that is waiting for him.

The spot where Webb landed is about two hundred yards to the west of Calais pier. Arm-in-arm with the men who had sprung to his aid, he walked modestly up the beach, and was driven to the Paris Hotel, where his friends put him to bed. For a short while he was delirious, but soon sank into a sound sleep. And the mid-day mail-boat carried back to Dover the news of his success and reported him as doing well, with a medical man in attendance.

He awoke almost himself again; and on the afternoon of Thursday arrived at Dover in the steamship *Castalia*, which was flying all her colours in his honour. It is needless to say that he was cordially welcomed, or to dwell on the recognition that his prowess received throughout England. His name has become a household word.

On landing he said he was "All right;" nor did he appear to suffer at all from the effects of his exertions on the previous days, but walked up the pier unaided. At the top he was greeted by his pilot and crew with flying flags and banners, and amid more cheering drove off to his hotel.

A PLUCKY WHALE.

ON the 1st of June, 1850, the whale-ship *Ann Alexander*, Captain John S. Deblois, sailed from New Bedford, Massachusetts, for a cruise in the South Pacific. On the 20th of August, 1851, she was lying in a favourable spot for her fishing, in lat. 5° 50' S. and long. 102° W., and at about nine in the morning sighted several whales.

"HE OPENED HIS JAWS AND TOOK THE BOAT IN" (*p.* 172).

By noon on the same day they had succeeded in making fast to one. Two boats—one commanded by Captain Deblois himself, the other by his first mate —had gone after the whales. The whale which they had struck had been harpooned by the larboard (the mate's) boat and did not relish it. Rushing at it with terrific violence, he opened his enormous jaws and took the boat in, crushing it in bits as small as a common-sized chair.

Fortunately the crew had already flung themselves into the water; and Captain Deblois, making all speed towards them with the starboard boat, succeeded in rescuing the whole crew, nine in number. Apparently, to have a boat eaten in this manner afforded no excessive surprise to Captain Deblois, but he afterwards confessed himself unable to understand how his men escaped deglutition.

There were now eighteen men in the starboard boat—the captain, the first mate, and the two crews. The men who had been left on board the *Ann Alexander* had, of course, witnessed the catastrophe, and now getting out the waist-boat, despatched her to their captain's relief. The distance from the ship was about six miles.

As soon as the waist-boat arrived, the crews were divided, and it was resolved to pursue the whale and make another attempt upon him. They separated, therefore, and (as is usual on such occasions) proceeded after the whale at some little distance from each other, with the result that in a short time they caught him up and prepared to give battle.

The waist-boat, commanded by the first mate, was in advance. As soon as ever the whale grew aware of the contemplated attack, he turned his course suddenly and made a tremendous dash for this boat, seized it in his extended jaws, and crushed it into small atoms. The men again flung themselves into the waves, and again were lucky enough to escape without loss of life.

Again the captain was equal to the occasion. Seeing the perilous fix of his men, and at the risk of meeting the same fate, he steered to their rescue, and in a short while succeeded in pulling them, one by one, on board. He then ordered the boat to put for the ship as speedily as possible, for it was laden pretty well to the water's edge, and half of its occupants were completely exhausted. They were by this about seven miles from their ship.

Consequently their dismay may be guessed when, looking round, they discovered the whale again making towards them with his jaws widely extended! Escape from death seemed now out of the question. For even were they not so far from the ship, there was no possibility of aid from that quarter. On came the monster, maddened by the wounds of harpoons and lances. He came within a few cables' length—then, for some unaccountable reason, swerved suddenly and passed them by, a short distance to the right. The men gave each a gulp, partly of relief, partly of amazement; they caught up the oars and pulled with all speed to the ship, where they climbed on board in safety.

Captain Deblois by this time had enough of conducting the attack in boats. So shortly after reaching the *Ann Alexander* he despatched the remaining boat to pick up the oars and timbers of its demolished fellows, and determined to pursue the whale with the ship.

Accordingly, as soon as the boat returned with the salvage, sail was set, and the *Ann Alexander* proceeded after the whale. In a short time she overtook him, and a lance was thrown into his head.

The ship was passing him by, before tacking about, when one of the crew gave a shout of astonishment. Captain Deblois rubbed his eyes.

"Well, I'm jiggered!" he said.

Sure enough, the whale was rushing at the ship!

The captain shouted to his men to haul the vessel close up to the wind. The monster made a blind rush, missed them by a cable's length, and passed on, as one of the men remarked, "for all the world as if he'd forgot some important business." The blood of Captain Deblois was up. He ordered further pursuit. On went the whale, and on after him flew the *Ann Alexander*. This lasted for two or three miles. The ship was gaining—she was within fifty rods of her prey—the men were getting their harpoons ready—

And then the whale disappeared: quietly settled down deep beneath the surface of the water, and "lay low," like Br'er Fox in the fable.

Captain Deblois allowed that he was accustomed to the ways of whales, but this one knocked a hole in his theories. "There's suthin' about this here beast that lays over *me*," he observed, and scratched his head; "he's a notion of sport, though, and that there's no gainsaying."

Night drew on, and found the *Ann Alexander* still hovering round the spot, and the captain still scratching his head and muttering. The whale continued to lie low, however, and, as darkness came down, Captain Deblois was just about to pronounce the pursuit at an end, when he found himself no longer in a position to decide. In fact, the game had passed out of his hands.

The whale, apparently, had determined on a little sport of his own. It is told of a certain English regiment quartered in Montreal not many years ago, that some of its officers formed a laudable resolution to introduce the noble sport of fox-hunting into Canada. The country teemed with foxes, they argued, and nothing remained but to organise a pack of hounds. Accordingly they collected together every dog in the district that had the least sporting strain in its pedigree, formed a pack, and posted a list of hunting appointments. The first meet was a pronounced success. Montreal society took up the idea with fervour, and everyone turned out to see. There were carriages by fifties, and riders in their hundreds, not to speak of a vast expectant throng of pedestrians, washed and unwashed. Nor was all this enthusiasm thrown away. Almost at once a fox was found, and away after him streamed the ill-assorted pack, the gallant officers in their scarlet, the civilian riders of both sexes, and the pedestrian crowd. For a while all went well. In a ten minutes' burst the fox went well and took them straight, and then all of a sudden in the open he stopped, and appeared to be reflecting. On came the pack, and the fox turned leisurely round. He waited for the pack, and quietly killed the leader, a sort of mongrel, half terrier, half lap-dog, adorned with a blue ribbon about the neck. The pack stood round and hesitated; then the fox began to pursue them. Forthwith arose the shrieks of ladies, trembling for their pets' safety. The officers dismounted and went to the rescue. Right and left the pack scattered and the fox "had a good time," until inconsiderately felled by the but-end of a hunting-crop. But he died not in vain, having vindicated his country henceforward from the importation of exotic sport. He saved his race, and fox-hunting in Montreal that day received its death-blow.

We give the anecdote as it was told us; for, true or not, it illustrates the position of Captain Deblois at the moment when he determined to abandon the pursuit of his whale. As he turned to give the order, he saw, for one brief instant, a dark form on the port bow of the *Ann Alexander*, and then— was lying flat on deck, seeing innumerable stars, and feeling very uncomfortable at the back of his head.

The whale had charged the ship, ramming her this time with a precision and violence that set her quivering from stem to stern. The captain staggered up to his feet, the crew picked themselves out of the scuppers, and all gazed about in blank astonishment. One sailor, ignorant of the cause, but dismally aware of the effect, ran about screaming that they were on a rock.

Captain Deblois scratched his head again, and descended into the forecastle, only to return the next minute with a long face. To his horror he found that the whale had struck the ship about two feet from the keel, abreast the foremast, knocking a large hole completely through her bottom. The water was roaring and rushing impetuously into the ship.

The captain sprang to the deck, ordered the mate to cut away the anchors, and get the cables overboard, to keep the ship from sinking. The mate ran to execute the orders, but succeeded only in relieving one anchor and getting one cable clear, the other having been fastened round the foremast. The ship was sinking rapidly.

The captain darted down into the cabin, where he found already three feet of water. It had become a question of moments. He caught up a chronometer, sextant, and chart, and again made his way to the deck. The ship was heeling over.

He ordered the boats to be cleared away, and, despatching his men to get water and provisions, descended to the cabin again. But so rapidly was the water rushing in, that he could procure nothing. Returning, he ordered all hands into the boats, and was the last to leave the ship, which he did by throwing himself into the sea, and swimming to the nearest boat.

The unfortunate *Ann Alexander* was now on her beam ends, her topgallant yards under water. The crew pushed off to a little distance, expecting her to sink in a short time. Upon an examination of the stores they had been able to save, it was found that they had only twelve quarts of water, and not a mouthful of provisions of any kind. Nor was this the end of their distress by any means. Darkness by this time had fallen. The boats contained eleven men each; and so leaky were they, that throughout the night the men had to bale continually to keep them above water.

Day broke. Looking about them they found that the *Ann Alexander* had not yet gone down. They drew near, no one but the captain venturing on board, for the intention was to cut away the masts, and there was a very considerable chance that as soon as these went the ship would go down. Captain Deblois, however, took the risk. Armed with a single hatchet, he clambered on board, and cut away the masts. The ship immediately righted.

It was now comparatively safe for the crew to come up, which they at once did. And the men, with a few spades that they had chanced to save, managed to cut away the chain cable from around the foremast. This put the ship nearly on her keel.

The men then tied ropes round their bodies, got into the sea, and cut holes through the decks to get out provisions. They could, however, procure nothing but about five gallons of vinegar and twenty pounds of wet bread. The ship threatened to sink, so, deeming it impossible to remain by her any longer, they set sail in the boats and left her.

Naturally, they were in a dreadful state of anxiety, for it was doubtful if they would be able to reach land, or catch sight of any vessel. With hopes exceedingly faint, they steered a northerly course, and, on the 22nd of August, at about five in the afternoon, had the indescribable joy of discerning a ship in the distance. They hoisted a signal, and were soon answered. The vessel proved to be the ship *Nantucket*, of Nantucket, Massachusetts, Captain Gibbs, who took them on board, clothed and fed them, and extended to these unfortunate whalers the greatest possible hospitality.

Next day Captain Gibbs went to the wreck of the *Ann Alexander*, for the purpose of procuring from her whatever could be saved. But the sea was so rough that he soon abandoned his project. The *Nantucket* then set sail for Paita, where she arrived on the 15th of September, and landed Captain Deblois and his men. "His story," says the chronicler, "created the deepest surprise and interest;" which is not improbable.

JUAN FERNANDEZ.

CRUSOE—AS A FACT.

I.

WHEN Enoch Arden returns to his native town, he has a deal to say (and says it very prettily) about "the mountain wooded to the peak," the "slender coco," and the flora and fauna in general of the desert island where he spent his time in watching for a sail. We know, too, by heart the entrancing scenery of Crusoe's island; we have heard that the luxuriant vegetation of that virgin paradise, the real Juan Fernandez, is no myth. But someone—a dull man—has said that Crusoeing "in reality is both physically unpleasant and mentally unprofitable." To this the obvious answer is, "Yes; to a dull man it would be both." And to save ourselves from suspicion of sharing his heresy, we say at once that the following examples of Crusoes in real life—which, of course, are lifeless beside the Crusoe of fiction—are intended as illustrations, rather than correctives, of Defoe's great tale.

The story of Juan Fernandez and its castaways is a curious one. The name is associated in our minds with Alexander Selkirk; but he was by no means the first who listened in that solitude in vain for "the sound of the church-going bell." Quite eighty years before his coming, a party of three soldiers—three gunners from the Dutch Admiral De Witt's fleet—were left here, it is said, at their own request. How long they remained, and what in time became of them, are alike unknown. In 1681, when that sturdy old buccaneer, Dampier, visited the island, he was told by his pilot that, many years before, a ship had been cast away on its rocks, and that one man only escaped, who lived alone there for five years. Oddly enough, Dampier was himself to supply, out of his crew, the next tenant of the spot.

Whilst he and his men loitered about the island, there appeared on the horizon the white canvas of a Spanish man-of-war bent on engaging and capturing the buccaneer who had wrought such havoc among Spanish shipping. The Englishmen had to pack off in such hurry, that one William, a Mosquito Indian, who had strayed off to hunt the wild goats of the place, was left behind.

The Spaniards landed, and found tokens of his presence. Time after time they endeavoured to get close to him; but always the Mosquito Indian eluded them. His belongings consisted only of his clothes, a knife, a gun, and some powder and shot. Naturally his ammunition was soon expended, and he was forced to subsist on seal-flesh, a diet that he appears to have loathed. But necessity, as ever, brought invention to birth. He converted his knife into a saw, and with this divided his gun-barrel into several pieces. With one of these and his gun-flint he managed to kindle a fire, and after a prodigious deal of heating and hammering, contrived to turn the rest of his steel into lance-heads and hooks, not to speak of a long hunting-knife. The lines for his hooks were supplied by strips of seal-skin; and, thus equipped, he kept his larder fairly full of fish, sea-fowl, and goat's flesh.

Being an Indian, he was not exacting about clothes. A waistband of seal-skin satisfied him very well. Seal-skin also he used for bedding and as a lining to his hut. And thus he lived, unmolested and unvisited, for three years, two months and eleven days, until Dampier, who had in the meantime cheated the Spaniards many a time, came once more to Juan Fernandez and took his old servant on board.

For three years the island appears to have enjoyed a little rest. (By the way, it is singular that the tenancies of these castaway men should never have clashed.) But in 1687 Captain Davis, another noted ruffian, came sailing along and put in at this spot. Five of his men that had gambled away their last groat, and were tired of a world in which gambling is impossible without either money or credit, now resolved to stay on the island here until some other adventurers came by with more appreciation for their I O U's. Davis consented very readily, and was good enough to leave four negro boys with them besides equipping them handsomely in some other respects, as a salt-pan and porridge-pot, guns, powder, shot, tools, ropes, and a small cannon. They brought their own dice, and having divided their territory into lots, gambled away their kingdoms to each other with great good-humour, feasting at not too protracted intervals on turnip-tops and goat's flesh. It is true they were not left entirely alone. Once or twice the Spaniards turned up and tried to oust them, but with the very poorest success. They continued, however, to make petty descents on the island at unexpected times, until the gamblers, annoyed at this vexatious interference with the calm current of dicing, gave it up after three years, and in 1690 consented to be taken off in the *Farewell.*

It was in 1704—fourteen years after—that the *Cinque Ports*, a consort of Dampier's, commanded by Stradling, put into Juan Fernandez. The master of this ship was one Alexander Selkirk, between whom and Stradling there was a certain amount of ill-feeling. At all events, matters were uncomfortable enough to make Selkirk determine upon remaining on the island. Stradling was willing; but Selkirk's resolution began to totter as he saw the ship moving away from the shore. He dropped upon his knees and begged the captain to take him on board again. Stradling wished he might be shot if he did any such thing, and sailed away, leaving his late master to wail and extend a pair of ineffective arms upon the shore.

This—for which Stradling may perhaps be forgiven—was for Selkirk a very lucky piece of cruelty; for his late messmates fell pretty soon into the hands of the Spaniards, and found mercy even scanter than they deserved. To the Scotchman, however, there seemed a gloomy prospect ahead, and none the less gloomy because chosen by himself. Day after day he passed by the beach, or on the rocks, with his gaze bent seaward, until hunger forced him to action, or darkness to his bed, where he would lie wakefully listening to the ceaseless, monotonous music of the breakers around his home.

In fact it took Selkirk at least eight months to reconcile himself in any degree to his lot. In the earlier days his thoughts fastened repeatedly upon suicide; and without giving him credit for all the namby-pamby sentimentalism with which the good Shenstone has dowered him in the still famous lines, "I am monarch of all I survey . . . ." we may agree that to a Scotchman, exile, without another Scotchman to share it, must be a dismal fate. Yet Selkirk was not so ill provided. He had a fair stock of clothes and boots, a tolerable amount of ammunition, a musket, a kettle, some pounds of tobacco, a Bible and other books, and a few mathematical instruments. The island was well stocked with fresh water, with seals, crayfish, and goats. He had vegetables, too—turnips, parsnips, radishes, cabbages, watercress, and parsley; and managed, by rubbing pimento sticks together, to kindle a fire and cook his dinner. Indeed, as he was already possessed of flint and steel, this rubbing together of sticks smacks of bravado. He had pimento pepper to season his food, and a climate to make a stay-at-home man's mouth water. Winter at Juan Fernandez is of the mildest description and lasts but two months.

Selkirk in fact was supplied with everything but snowballs, and remains, when reduced to fact, a showy theatrical grumbler. We need not imagine, as Steele imagines in his famous paper, the castaway reclining in a verdant bower, fanned by continual and fragrant breezes, and reposing, after the pleasures of the chase, on beds of tropical flowers. As a matter of fact, Selkirk found it extremely difficult to snatch any repose owing to the multitudes of rats that ate holes in his clothing and nibbled his toes. Nevertheless, the man grumbled too much. He grumbled because his clothes wore out; he was shocked (we have it on Shenstone's authority) at the tameness of the beasts of the island; he was vexed at the absence of a circulating library on Juan Fernandez. There was no satisfying the fellow.

Yet he seems to have kept down the vermin by means of a band of tame cats. He grew by practice so fleet of foot as to keep his larder supplied with goats' flesh long after his ammunition failed. The pimento-tree supplied him not only with pepper, but with candles and sweet-smelling firewood. He reared a large number of kids to ensure plenty of food in case illness interfered with his hunting—and, indeed, he was once laid up for almost a fortnight by tumbling over a precipice while pursuing a goat. He beguiled his idle moments by teaching his kids and cats any number of tricks. Clothes he provided out of goat-skins: but could not manage to make new shoes, so he had to go barefooted when his old ones were worn out.

During his long abode on the island he saw many ships pass, but of these only two put in to the shore. From them some Spaniards landed, who, perceiving Selkirk, gave chase. By this time, however, he had learnt to run down a goat, and had no difficulty in keeping his visitors at a safe distance. This was the only occasion on which the outer world invaded his solitude, until the arrival of the ship in which he left Juan Fernandez for ever, after a stay of four years and four months.

It happened in this way. In 1708 the restless Dampier persuaded some Bristol merchants to equip a couple of ships for the South Sea trade. Their names were the *Duke* and the *Duchess;* their captains, Rogers and Dover; and Dampier himself acted as pilot. On the last day of January, the two vessels arrived off Juan Fernandez, and while yet four leagues from the land, Captain Dover determined to go ashore in the pinnace. What followed shall be told in Captain Rogers' own words:—"As soon as it was dark, we saw a light ashore. Our boat was then about a league from the island, and bore away for the ships as soon as she saw the light. We put out lights aboard for the boat, though some were of opinion the light we saw was our boat's light; but as night came on, it appeared too large for that. We fired our quarter-deck guns and several muskets, showing lights in our mizzen and fore-shrouds.

"About two in the morning, our boat comes aboard. We are all convinced the light is on the shore, and design to make our ships ready to engage, believing them to be French ships at anchor; and we must fight them, or want water.

"All this stir and apprehension arose from one poor, naked man, who passed in our imagination for a body of French, a Spanish garrison, or a crew of pirates."

"HE OVERTOOK THE DEPARTING SHIP" (p. 184).

Of course the light was that of Selkirk's fire. He had kindled it, believing from their rig that the vessels were English. Next morning, as soon as the *Duke* and *Duchess* stood in towards shore, he advanced upon the beach, waving a white flag, and welcomed his countrymen with every expression of joy, pressing on them the best of everything that his larder could furnish. At first, however, he was unwilling to go aboard; and only consented upon a promise that he might go or stay, just as he chose. "But," says Captain Rogers, "he found such entertainment as made him no longer fond of his solitary retirement."

He is described as a man dressed in goat-skins and wilder in appearance than the goats themselves. Dampier, of course, knew him and spoke a word in his favour. He was offered, and accepted, the post of mate on board the *Duke.* The sailors immediately gave him the sobriquet of "The Governor," in allusion to his solitary sway over Juan Fernandez. Like most men who have lived long alone, he spoke with difficulty, forgetting, in most cases, the terminations of words: but language came back in time. He passed a quiet old age, and was buried in his native land.

With him the glory of Juan Fernandez passed into fiction and lives for ever on Defoe's page. The island, indeed, had other castaways. Ten years later it was occupied by four deserters from an English ship; but they remained two months only. Again, in 1720, the *Speedwell* was wrecked off its shores, and her crew remained there some months, until they built a boat in which they departed, leaving behind them a colony of eleven white men, thirteen blacks, and some Indians. But these are supposed to have surrendered or been massacred by the Spaniards; for two years after, when the island was again visited, no trace remained of them.

II.

A more thorough-going castaway than Selkirk was one Peter Serrano, a Spaniard, who has left his name to a sterile rock in the middle of the Caribbean Sea. Here was a man with no goats, no tame cats, no pimento-pepper: as Mr. Chadband would say, "without flocks and herds, without tents or dyed apparel." He lived for four years on a monotonous diet of cockles, shrimps, and turtle; and he made the best of it. He had a steel in his pocket, and dived in the sea until he fished up a couple of flints, and so procured a fire. He "provided for a rainy day" by drying strips of turtle-flesh while the sun shone. Water he obtained by setting out the larger turtle-shells to catch the rain, and the smaller shells he used for cups. He protected his fire—which was built out of seaweed and drift-wood—by a screen of turtle-shells. We all know from the books of our childhood how thoroughly useful an animal is the ox; but it was reserved for Peter Serrano to discover the possibilities that lurked in the turtle. Only he seems to have found the animal an inadequate parasol, and therefore betook himself to bathing when the sun's rays became unbearable.

His clothes wore out. Always fertile in resource, he hit on the happy expedient of doing without any, and lived naked for three years and eight months, scaring off the passing ships by the smoke signals he sent up to attract them. At the end of this time he received a shock. A visitor dropped in.

Peter stalked down the rock to welcome him, his body covered with coarse bristles and his face with a genial smile. His long beard waved over each shoulder in the sea-breeze.

"Signor, I bid you welcome!" Peter waved his hand pleasantly and advanced to kiss the new-comer.

The new-comer screamed "Satan! Satan!" and dropped on his knees.

"My territory is limited," Peter went on affably, "as is also my larder— but the Signor (whose acquaintance I have now the pleasure to make for the first time) will, doubtless, excuse deficiencies."

The Signor crossed himself several times, shut his eyes, and pattered off *Credos* by the dozen.

It was some time before Peter could persuade his guest to take heart and eat. But at length the two men fell into conversation, and by the end of the day were on the best of terms. By the end of the week they had quarrelled, and "cut" each other when they met. In three months' time they patched up their misunderstanding, and before they had time to quarrel again, a Spanish vessel came and took them off. Serrano had lived on the rock just four years. His companion died on the homeward voyage, but Peter himself reached Spain, where he attracted much notice and was presented to the Emperor Charles V., who gave him a pension. Upon this Peter retired to Panama, and died there some years after.

The next Crusoe on our list hails from Holland. In the days when the Island of St. Helena was an unpeopled waste, long before the coming of the great exile who has made its name famous, a Dutch vessel, returning from the West Indies, cast anchor off its coast. In a short while a boat was lowered. The occupants, besides the crew, were a dead officer in a coffin, and a downcast seaman in irons. This seaman, for some offence against discipline, had been condemned to death by the captain, but in consequence of an appeal for mercy signed by his mess-mates, was ordered to be marooned on this desolate island instead of being hung up to the yard-arm. It is probable that even this grace would have been denied him, but for the dead officer for whose burial the ship put into harbour.

The grave was dug; the officer buried; the crew departed; the ship weighed anchor. The Dutchman, on his side, lost no time. He opened the new-made grave, dragged out the coffin, tumbled his dead superior out of it, and carried it down to the shore, where, having launched his extemporised boat, he jumped in, in a trice, and using the lid as a paddle, quickly (thanks to a calm) over-took the departing ship. He was taken on board and pardoned, in consideration of his pluck.

III.

Said a grizzled seaman of about fifty to a crowd of admirers assembled in a Wapping alehouse, "My name's Lord. Since I was seventeen I've travelled up and down this world a bit; but I don't reckon to beat in the way of experiences a day or two that I passed in my seventeenth year; and what's more, I don't particularly care to.

"This is how it happened. I was aboard a South Sea whaler that put in for food and water at one of those small islands they call the Gallipagos group. Well, a few of us were sent ashore, and I among the number; and being a kind of cock-sure young man, and not afraid to wander off on my own account, I got myself pretty soon tangled up in a forest, and it was about the nastiest forest *I* ever set foot in. The remarkable fact about this particular forest was that there didn't seem any way out, to speak of. I tried to find one, and was still at it when night came on.

"Thought I to myself, 'It's all right. To begin with, there *must* be a way out, and I'll find it by daylight. The ship won't go till to-morrow; anyway, she won't go and leave me here without searching. I'll lie down and get a little sleep.' So I found a bit of turf under the trees and stretched myself out, and only woke at daybreak.

"I felt sure of getting out soon. But, as I didn't know what I might come across, thought it best before starting to provide myself with a good thick stick; which was lucky, as before ten minutes were out, I pulled up sharp and went cold all over. Another step and I should have trodden on a snake. As it was, I'd alarmed the varmint, and saw it lift its head, showing its white belly and flickering out its tongue, as nasty as you please, before I settled it with a crack of my stick.

"All the same, this gave me the shivers; and after this I was just as much on the look-out for snakes as to get clear of the forest. To save my life I couldn't help seeing one at every step, and kept my neck well back against my collar for fear one of them should come dropping down my back off the trees. You may laugh, sonnies; but wait till you've trodden on a healthy serpent and then you can *talk!*

"Well, on and on I went, hour after hour, looking this way and that, but seeing no escape, until I fairly lost heart. Towards sundown I seemed to remember the trees I was passing; and then, all of a sudden, I saw a snake indeed. It was the very one I had knocked down at daybreak.

"For a while I sat down beside it and cried. Aye, sirs, I hadn't cried for years, but I did then—like a baby. All that blessed day, you must remember, I had kept my ears well open, making sure to hear my comrades shouting for me; but all the while there was never a human sound to be heard, and I had been walking ever since dawn. So 'twasn't such a very odd thing to shed tears, after all.

"But presently I said to myself that crying was foolishness, and determined to lie quiet for the night and try again. However I didn't want any snakes fooling round, so I climbed up the nearest tree and there roosted like a bird all night.

"Next morning I dropped down from the tree. There was a branch underneath me, and before I knew what I was doing, I had knocked off an old owl that had taken up her quarters there—and stunned her too, so that I wrung her neck easily. And then it occurred to me that I was famished with hunger. You see, I had eaten nothing from the moment I left the ship.

"A raw owl isn't pretty feeding. But you have to be regularly in a corner as I was before you find out what a man *can* eat. I managed it, and set off again.

"Well, this day was just like the first. Not a shout, not a voice, was to be heard the whole time. But towards evening I found the ground rising. It grew steeper and steeper. I thought that if I could only gain the top of the hill I had a chance to

"'I CAUGHT THE SEAL ROUND THE THROAT'" (p. 186).

see my way. And sure enough, at length I did reach the top. But by this time it was dark; and I lay down, drenched with dew, to pass the night. Towards morning a heavy shower came down and finished the wetting. I woke up, so tired and stiff that 'twas as much as I could do to drag myself up the last few paces.

"I looked about. Below me lay the sea; but as for the ship, she was nowhere to be seen. Yet I could plainly make out the bay where she had been riding two days before. A brig was still there, evidently about to sail. I grew mad at the thought of losing my last chance of escape; and down the hill I plunged—panting, stumbling, catching my feet in thorns, sprawling among the undergrowth—yet running with all my powers and shouting with might and main.

"It took me a good two hours before I got another sight of the bay. It was empty—the brig by this time but a speck on the horizon!

"Well, sirs, I sat down. I sat and sat, and felt stupider and stupider as the day wore on. And then hunger began to fight with stupidity, and a rare tussle they had. Hunger won. I hobbled along the shore in search of shell-fish, but not one did I find, and finally had to put up with a few berries that I managed to pull from the shrubs that lined the beach.

"Next day, though, I had better luck. Somehow I had kept hold of my thick stick all the time—chiefly, I think, because it had never occurred to me to throw it away. And now in the early morning I came on a seal, sunning itself on the beach. I knocked it over, cut it open, and ate its liver ravenously. Before an hour was out, it turned me deadly sick. I lay down and thought that all was over.

"In two hours more I was so far recovered as to get on my feet again, and ramble a bit further. This time I knocked over a tortoise and, being empty again, made a good meal off him. This gave me heart to return to the seal. I set to work, cut it up, and spread the strips on the sand to dry.

"Well, sirs, I don't want to make this a long yarn. I lived for a week on that seal, and I passed just three weeks on that island. All day long I paced up and down the shore, and at night I crept back to the woods to sleep. As soon as the seal was eaten, I had to make my dinner off berries only. There were plenty of fish in the sea, and there were plenty of birds that time after time came close to me; but, you see, I had neither fish-hooks nor gun.

"One night, instead of returning to the woods, I lay down and slept on the beach. You may guess how I felt when I opened my eyes and saw a big seal lying cheek-by-jowl with me on the sand. By bad luck, I had before this mislaid my thick stick; but none the less I resolved to have a dinner at any risk. So I caught the seal round the throat, and about the sand we rolled—first one atop, then the other—until we soused into the sea together. And with that I found I was getting the worst of it, and was glad enough to scramble ashore with a whole skin.

"By the twenty-first day my strength was spent. 'If no help comes in twenty-four hours,' said I, 'why, then I must die;' and with that I crawled up-hill once more, with precious little hope of ever coming down again. Every step was pain, and I took the best part of the day in reaching the summit. I looked around.

"There was a dark speck on the horizon. It grew and grew, and at length I saw clearly it was a sail. What was more, I had no need to signal, for the ship was making straight for the island. Down the hill I tottered—Heaven knows how—and gained the beach, just as she entered the harbour. I saw her drop anchor and lower a boat; and that was all I saw before I fainted off.

" Well, I came round, and there were a dozen good British mariners standing round,—aye, sirs, and when I asked for water they gave me grog— which is the way they differed from the landlord here, who, when you ask for grog, brings you water—and—gentlemen, are your glasses charged? Then, here's to the memory of Captain Cook!—for 'twas he that saved me."

IV.

There is a tradition that, in the year 1615, the ordinary passage-boat between England and Ireland fell in with a French privateer and was taken. A stiff gale arose, however, and forced the Frenchmen to relinquish their prey. The tow-rope was cut, and the boat, with three occupants, was left to the mercy of the sea. The Frenchmen had left nothing but a little sugar on board; and death soon carried off one of the three unfortunate men. The two survivors rowed on desperately for a while, and then sank to the bottom of the boat, too feeble to do anything but wait for their doom.

The boat, however, was driven on a rock, close to a deserted island off the Scotch coast; and on this island the pair contrived to land. Not a tree, not a blade of grass was to be seen. A couple of long stones supporting a third might have given gratification to a modern tourist, but were viewed with in-difference by these enforced wanderers. However, they crept under these relics of antiquity for the night.

Next day they found strength enough to make an expedition, and lit on a few sea-birds' eggs hidden among the cliffs. On this fare and on such fresh water as they could find in fissures and cavities of the rocks they eked out a wretched existence, tempering their misery now and then with the flesh of sea-dogs and sea-mews that they managed somehow to entrap. Out of the shattered boat they patched up a rough dwelling-place, and thus lived for six weeks; at the end of which time one of the pair disappeared. He never returned: and his comrade could only conjecture him to have fallen into the sea when in quest of eggs.

The survivor soon after lost his only weapon, his knife, and was forced to fashion a substitute out of a nail taken from the wrecked boat. Before winter came, his clothes were worn out; and when snow fell, it obliged him to risk starvation and remain indoors. However, he managed to sustain life by poking out a baited stick through a crevice of his hut, and so catching a few hungry sea-birds. It was only after eleven months thus miserably passed that a Flemish timber-vessel, under the command of Pickman, the recoverer of the Armada guns, ran aground near the island. A few of the crew landed and began to search the rocks for eggs. While thus engaged they caught sight of a naked hairy man running towards them with joyful outcries. Taking him for a pirate, they rushed towards their ship. The castaway followed. At length looking back, they saw him drop on his knees, and took courage enough to approach him. His tale was soon told, and he was taken on board. Pretty soon the wind rose and sent the timber-ship into deep water; whereupon they made all speed for London, whence the castaway found his way safely home.

The truth of the above story is likely enough. But here is another more modern and better authenticated. It relates to the *Saint Abbs*, wrecked on a reef off San Juan de Nuova in 1855. Out of twenty-eight people on board, six contrived to reach the shore. The story shall be told by one of the castaways, Cadet (afterwards Captain) Ross:—

"It was," he says, "a low, flat island, about a mile in circumference; all sand, and covered with birds and their eggs. We sucked some raw eggs and passed a miserable night. Next morning, at daybreak, we went to see if we could render the other poor fellows any assistance; but during the night the ship must have broken up, and all the poor fellows doubtless perished. There was no water in the island, and we could not make a fire, so that we had to eat raw birds and suck eggs. The birds were in thousands and quite tame. We were four days without a fire, but at length succeeded in making one. We also picked up some wine and spirits, but had no water. However, we drank champagne, and so kept ourselves alive. Every morning, some men were sent on the reef, and picked up what they could; but we could get nothing eatable except a few preserves, which were not of much use.

"We lived in this manner for fourteen days, when (as it was full moon) we determined to try and walk across the reef at low water to the other island, which appeared larger and better. We set out early in the morning, and dragged a raft across the reef with all our stock of wine and spirits. The distance was about seven miles, over sharp coral rocks, and as we had no shoes on, it was fearful work. The island turned out to be a large one, about fifteen miles long. We then knew it to be Juan de Nuova. Next morning, we explored for water, and the skipper and another man came back with the news that they had found a well and a hut at the very end of the island. Next day we went there, and found a good well and a small hut built of bamboo and leaves. There were plenty of birds, and we found some turtle made fast in a hut in the sea. We had plenty of water now, and could cook broth and boil birds and eggs. We lived in this style for another fortnight, when a small schooner hove in sight; we made all the signals we could, with shirts, &c., and she observed us. She had come from the island of Mahé for the turtle. She remained six days at San Juan de Nuova, when we six embarked for Mahé, and arrived safe and sound."

"'MY MISTRESS MADE A SHORT SPEECH'" (p. 191).

CALDECOTE HALL.

THE STORY OF A SIEGE. August, 1642.

YOU know, of course, that 'twas on the 25th of August (1642) that the King raised his standard at Nottingham, and so began the strife that afterwards devastated England with fire and sword. My master, Colonel Purefoy, of Caldecote Hall, in Warwickshire, was a Parliament man and an ardent supporter of the Reformed religion. Master Richard Vines, the Vicar of Caldecote and a sturdy preacher, was used to call my master a "root and branch man," which, indeed, he was. He sat in Parliament for the borough of Warwick, and at the first breaking out of the troubles raised all the men upon his estate and led them off to Coventry, to be a reinforcement to Lord Brooke, and so had left us, little thinking that any mischief threatened us beside the quiet river Anker.

"I was a child at the time, but old enough to understand something of affairs; and, you may be sure, listened eagerly to all the news that reached us. We had heard that the King had tried to seize on the castle at Hull, and had sent his nephews, Prince Rupert and Prince Morris, wild devil-may-care fellows, harum-scaruming through the country, frightening honest folks and doing little good but to set them against the King. Well, the King got together a parcel of gentlemen and troopers and came to Coventry. And 'twas ' Open the gates forthwith!' with him, as bold as you please. But the honest citizens shook their heads and answered very civilly that they could not admit him, and would he please to go elsewhere? For his Majesty, they said, he was welcome to come in by himself: but they had no mind to entertain all the tag-rag of the country. On hearing this, the King flew into a mighty rage and hurried off to Stoneleigh, and sent his cannon across to batter Coventry gates down.

"This put us in a great quandary, for we could hear the thunder of the ordnance quite plain; and shook in our beds o' nights at the sound of it. And one afternoon a man, that was passing along the high-road, stopped and told us that the King's party had forced the gates and were setting fire to the city, besides killing and ravishing right and left. All of which we afterwards found to be a lie. But at the time we ran up to the top of the church tower, whence we could indeed espy a great smoke, but whether 'twas from the powder of the culverels or the burning houses we could not tell.

"Now on the 28th, which was Sunday, Colonel Purefoy posts over from Warwick Castle in a mighty sweat to see Master George Abbot. Master Abbot was his son-in-law, and managed the Hall for the time: and the reason of the Colonel's coming was to concert with him about the raising more men to join my Lord Brooke (who was by this time gone to Northampton), and also to see about sending more provision to Sir Edward Peto, then in command of Warwick Castle and daily expecting to be besieged. Now for provision, I believe we had a plenty: but as for fighting men, we were but women, children, and cripples— as you shall hear.

"I recollect that Sunday morning well — a fiery hot day. The sun was blazing on the leads as I climbed up the top of the church tower to see if I could mark anything of Coventry spires and the fire, for I was anxious about my father. My uncle Robin and three men had come over with the Colonel: but there were but nine altogether (including the Colonel and Master George) about the house, and some of these men had wives in the village.

"I, as I have said, went up the tower to look towards Coventry, but I could see nothing except a little smoke. I was looking at our river Anker, that shone very bright in the sunlight, and thinking how pleasant it looked, when, as I thought, I saw the river moving in the distance.

"Upon this I rubbed my eyes and looked again: and now I saw it was the steel jackets of a multitude of soldiers: and they wound along the road and glistened as 'twere a great silver serpent coming towards me. I stood looking at them for a minute: and this was time enough to tell me they were not men of our regiment. And with that I thought of the Devilskin prince, of whom we were all in such terror, and turned and ran down the staircase of the tower for dear life.

"I nearly flew down the steps, being young then and nimble, and ran towards the Hall: and caught sight of the Colonel and Master George walking up and down together with Master Richard Vines (the preacher) in front of the house above the river. They had their heads very close together, and were debating so earnestly that neither of them noticed me until I ran into their midst.

"'What's the matter with the boy?' says the Colonel, wheeling round with his hands deep in his pockets, and his brow knitted. 'Hey—hey— what's the matter now?' That was his way of speaking, very sharp and jerky. He thought of nothing but affairs of state, and often, before the war broke out, would sit at the head of the table, scarce tasting his food and taking no heed of the conversation but to say 'Hey—hey?'—very often when no one had spoken. In general I was afraid of him, but now spoke up very boldly and told what I had seen.

"The three men looked at each other, and Master George gave a long whistle. However, the Colonel patted my head and said I was a good boy. Master Vines began somewhat about the depravity of the human heart, and the sin of looking from the tower on the Sabbath: but the Colonel cut him short with a speech of which I caught nothing beyond the word 'Rahab,' and Master Vines muttered, 'Aye, aye—His ways are past finding out.'

"But of course there was no time to be lost in such discussions. Master George told me to run with the Colonel into the hop-garden and hide him there. For my master was, next after my Lord Brooke, the first leader of our party in Warwickshire, and there was no doubt 'twas he our enemies were after. I knew the hiding that Master George meant; for, some days before, we had contrived a snug pit in the middle of the garden and covered it over with long hop-poles. People called this cowardice afterwards: but that 'twas really wisdom and not cowardice is plain from the sequel. And in any case the Colonel's life was not to be thrown away in defending a poor country seat such as ours was.

"There were at this time only eight men inside the house, for we had not time to call the villagers, who did not know the Colonel was come home—so secret was he forced to be for fear of treachery. Master George said that all the men who were worth anything were away at Warwick or Coventry. So the bells went tinkling away for church as usual, for the Colonel would not have them taken away, though Master Vines tried again and again to persuade him to this, saying they were an invention of the devil and fit only for the service of the Scarlet Woman, &c. &c.

"Well, as soon as the Colonel was hid, Dame Purefoy (our dear mistress) and Master George called us together in the Hall, and my mistress made a **short** speech, saying that the King's men were coming for her husband, but she was resolved to resist them and prevent their entering the house. 'Twas an old-fashioned house then, for the Colonel had not begun the alterations you see now.

"We stirred ourselves bravely, getting out the good feather-beds and placing them in the windows. One or two of the men barricaded the door: and the mistress told Dolly, the cook, to make up a fire and bring the pewter spoons and plates to melt down for bullets: for we had some powder and several guns, but no bullets at all. And Master George showed the women-servants how to load the guns, so that the men might meanwhile keep a watch on the outside.

"Almost before we had all the guns loaded, we could hear the clattering of the horses' hoofs on the road. Good Lord, what a noise they made!—and though 'twas the Sabbath day they were singing snatches of profane songs, so that Master Vines marched up and down muttering the most horrible predictions for them in the midst of his business.

"Master George had stationed himself with four men at the great entrance just opposite the court-yard, but the mistress and I were at the porter's wicket at the side; the old steward and my uncle Robin were in the upper rooms. While we were waiting side by side, my mistress and I, I asked her if she were not terribly afraid. She answered, 'Not a whit!' My own heart was going pit-pat; yet I did not feel over-much fright. We did not know which way they would approach; but we heard the halt of the troopers, for there were eight or nine troops of horse—in all several hundred men.

"Soon after, a trumpet sounded, and about a dozen officers and men came to our wicket. My mistress, seeing them approach, called out in a commanding voice and asked who they were and what right they had to come disturbing godly people on the Sabbath. Whereupon an officer stepped forward and demanded entrance for the Prince Rupert in the King's name to search for a rebellious subject that had been levying war against his Majesty. My mistress replied that she knew of none such, and bade them begone for a pack of rascally marauders. They said they would have admittance, and were about to force the door, when the good dame lifted up one of the muskets, and saying, 'God forgive me!' under her breath—though I heard it clear enough—pulled the trigger.

"While the noise of the discharge was yet in my ears, I peeped out and saw that one of the officers had fallen and lay groaning on his side. And with this our ears were saluted with a storm of dreadful curses the like of which I have never heard. Immediately after came a volley of bullets against the wicket; but none passed through. Master George, on hearing the shots, came rushing to our side of the house, and we fired all the guns, at a signal, from the windows and loopholes. This was the first shot I had ever fired in my life, and it surprised me to feel the musket kick back against my shoulder so that

I staggered back almost across the room. I thought at first I was wounded; but learning the true state of the case, ran to my window again and saw those of the godless troopers that were unhurt running out of the court as fast as they could. But there were two now, besides the officer that my mistress had shot, writhing on the pavement of the court. So we all drew a long breath, while the women loaded the firelocks again.

"'THE WOMEN HANDED US THE RELOADED ARMS'" (p. 194).

"We could see there was some consultation going on, and in a few minutes were startled by the noise of firing, and a score or more of bullets came flying in through the windows. This hurt nobody, being no more than we expected. We were all behind shelter and did not mind; albeit the glass was shattered all about the room.

"Master George conjectured they were about to attack the court-yard entrance, and stationed us so as to cover it with our guns. He was right; for very soon after the court gates were burst open, and the troopers, shouting to one another, came rushing at the hall door with battering-poles.

"'Now then,' called out Master George, 'steady, all of you—and take good aim!'

"I think we all obeyed him; for as we all fired together, two or three officers dropped, and at least as many soldiers; so that nobody can have missed his mark. We had spare guns, and fired again. Then the women (that all this time were busy, though very white) handed us the reloaded arms, and we fired a third time before they cleared out of the court-yard, leaving their dead and wounded behind.

"We all thanked God, and some of us thought that they had gone, after so warm a welcome. But Master George knew better. He said they would try to make a diversion. Now at this time I did not take the meaning of his words, but this we pretty soon found out.

"Soon straw was brought to the front, out of the stable loft. This our enemies fired, and when the flame and smoke were at the highest, again made a rush at the hall door. We fired again, but though we did some execution 'twas not so much as on their former attempt. They pulled up for a moment, but soon came on again; and now our powder began to run short.

"Whilst we were cast down at this, and looking in each other's faces very grimly, there came a shout from one of the women at the back of the house that the stables were afire. Sure enough it was so. And though all our horses but two were with the Parliament troops, yet 'twas saddening to see the smoke curling out of the stable windows and the flames glowing within. Master George now goes up to my mistress, and, taking her by the hand, whispers that we shall be obliged to give in.

"My mistress sighed, but answered very submissively—

"'You know best, George; but 'tis a sore trial to me.'

"And just as the troopers, now headed by Prince Rupert himself (who had dismounted and was swearing the profanest oaths), were getting ready for another assault, the dame flung wide the hall-door—for the flames had already reached the manor-house—and, casting herself at the Prince's feet, besought him not to injure the hairs of the heads of a few poor women.

"'Why, to be sure I will not,' says he; 'but where be all the men?'

"'So please your highness, there are no men here, to speak of.'

"'No men!'

"'Seven or eight only,' says she.

"'And the Colonel Purefoy?'

"'He is not here.'

"The Prince was too much of a gentleman, for all his bad oaths, to give her the lie. Yet I could see he could barely believe her. So before replying 'yea' or 'nay,' he apologised and said he intended no harm, but to search the house for the Colonel, 'for form's sake,' as he put it. But when he really found that the bird was not there, he gave us all our lives, with many generous words about our courage. To Master George he offered the command, on the spot, of a troop of his horse. But at this offer Master George shook his head, acknowledging the honour in the gracefullest way, but declaring that 'twould be against his conscience to accept it. Which refusal the Prince in his turn took very politely, wishing him a better mind.

"The troopers were all for sacking the house. But at this proposal the Prince's language broke out worse than ever. They cowered before him like whipped dogs: and then, turning to us, he said we had acted bravely, and he knew how to respect brave men and women. They then took up their wounded, and went off in the direction of Coventry.

"The villagers from Weddington, Mancetter, and the neighbouring hamlets, came to help us extinguish the fire, which was soon done. We all fell to laughing at Dolly, who, now the excitement was over, flung her apron over her head and was lamenting for the broken and melted platters she had polished so bravely.

"When night fell the Colonel came in, very stiff from being so long shut up in the narrow pit; and before morning went off towards Northampton."

In this siege perished, on the Royalist side, Captain Mayford, Captain Shute, Captain Steward, and fifteen men. The old manor-house has long been replaced by a pile of more modern taste, though many relics of it are yet to be seen. In Caldecote Church, close by, is a monument to "Master George," erected by his mother-in-law, the Dame Purefoy of this story. The inscription runs :—

"Here lieth the body of George Abbot, late of Caldecott, in Warwickshire, Esquire, whose eminent parts, virtues, and graces, drawn forth to life in his exemplary walking with God, his tenderness to all the members of Christ, who frequently fled to his charity for their wants and counsel in cases of conscience: his exact observation of the Sabbath, which he vindicated by his pen, and on which, August 28th, 1642, God honoured him in the memorable and unparalleled defence of this adjoining house, with eight men (besides his mother and her maids) against the furious and fierce assaults of Princes Rupert and Maurice, with eighteen troops of horse and dragooners: his perspicuous paraphrases of the books of Job and Psalms, his judicious tracts of public affairs then emergent, his known integrity in public employments : rendered him one of a thousand for singular piety, wisdom, learning, charity, courage, and fidelity to his country, which he served in two Parliaments, the former and the present, whereof he died a member, February the 2nd, 1648, in the 44th year of his age. This monument was erected to his memory by his dear mother and executrix, Johan Purefoy, the wife of Colonel William Purefoy, his beloved father-in-law, the 28th day of August, Anno Domini 1649."

THE BASTILLE.

THE PRISONER OF THE BASTILLE.

Masers de Latude. 1750—1756.

MASERS DE LATUDE, son of the Marquis de Latude, a military officer of rank and distinction, was born in Languedoc, 1725. Like his father, he was educated for the military profession, and in his twenty-fourth year was studying engineering in Paris, when by his own folly he involved himself in misfortunes that may almost be termed monumental.

The Marquise de Pompadour was at this time in the meridian of her beauty and power. Latude had seen her and fallen a victim to her charms. In this he differed nothing from many hundreds of young men in Paris. But the means by which he tried to attract her notice were as original as they proved unfortunate.

He was sitting one sunny morning on a bench in the garden of the Tuileries, when two men in hot argument passed down the gravel walk before him. So deeply engaged were they in their discussion as to forget the likelihood of being overheard. Latude overheard them. Their theme was the iniquity of Madame de Pompadour; and it supplied the young man with a scheme.

It was original, but clumsy nevertheless. He placed in the post a small cardboard box containing a packet of harmless powder, addressed to the Marchioness. Then, donning his best suit, he went straight to Versailles and demanded admission to the Pompadour's apartments. She received him, and listened to his story. He had overheard (he said) a conspiracy against her life ; had seen the two men he suspected dropping a small packet into the post ; and had come straight to Versailles in the apprehension that the packet contained some subtle poison.

The Pompadour was all gratitude ; attempted to reward him with a purse of gold ; dismissed him with many kindly expressions, and then sat down to reflect. As a result of her reflections she took the trouble to procure a specimen of the handwriting of her *soi-disant* preserver, compared it with that of the address on the cardboard packet, and, finding them identical, flew into a passion and planned a revenge.

A few days later M. de Latude found himself in the Bastille.

He remained there four months, shut in a narrow cell in the Tour du Cour. Then, one day, three turnkeys entered his cell with the news that Madame la Marquise had relented, and that he was free. Joyfully enough Latude stepped across the threshold—and was carried off to a new prison, the Castle of Vincennes.

The Marquise, in fact, was inflexible : and Latude (though bestowed in a comfortable apartment and allowed to walk daily for two hours in the garden) began to think his imprisonment was intended to last for life. So he bent his thoughts on escape.

"I kept up my heart," says he, "in the hope that I should one day be free, and the conviction that this freedom would be due to my own efforts, not to the favour of my gaolers. I was for ever hatching plans.

"Among my fellow-prisoners was an aged priest, who used to appear every day in the castle garden. He had been deprived of his liberty a long while on account of his leanings to Jansenism. He was often visited by an Abbé of St. Sauveur, and devoted a great part of his leisure to teaching the officer's children their letters. When in the company of his little pupils he was permitted to go almost where he pleased ; and usually took his walk about the time when I was led into a small garden on the other side of the wall. Two turnkeys used to escort me on my leaving my cell, and again on my return ; but occasionally the senior of the two would await me in the garden, while his junior came up alone to let me out. By degrees I accustomed this man to see me run down the staircase in front of him and join his comrade in the garden, so that he always moved very leisurely when he came to fetch me.

"On a certain day I had resolved, at any cost, to make an attempt at escape. As soon, therefore, as he came into my cell, I ran downstairs for my life, and, hastily bolting the staircase door on the outside, left him a prisoner within. I had now four sentinels to deal with. The first stood on the other side of a door that led from the dungeon—a door that was always closed.

"I knocked : the door was opened.

"'Where is the Abbé of St. Sauveur ?' I asked rapidly. 'Our priest has been awaiting him in the garden for more than two hours. I've been looking for him everywhere.'

"As I spoke, I ran forward till I came to the second sentinel. To him I put the same question, and he allowed me to pass in the same way; and to a third, posted on the other side of the drawbridge, with whom I was just as successful. The fourth sentinel, seeing I had passed the others, did not for a moment suspect I was a prisoner. I crossed the threshold of the outside gate. I ran forward until out of sight. I was free!

"I made my way across the fields, keeping off the highway as much as possible; and at length I came to Paris, where I hired furnished lodgings, and tasted the pleasures of liberty to their full extent with a palate sharpened by fourteen months of captivity."

So far, so good. But though the escape was neat, how was Latude to remain in hiding? To escape from France was as difficult. Latude resolved to throw himself on the generosity of his persecutors. He drew up a memorial to the King, writing of Madame de Pompadour in respectful terms, and of his fault with contrition. He entreated that her vengeance might be satisfied with what he had already suffered, and concluded by naming his place of hiding.

Latude had been ill-advised to put his trust in princes. He was answered by a visit of the police, who promptly arrested and carried him off to the Bastille. They assured him he was merely in custody that he might explain his late escape. He did so, and was at once clapped in a strong dungeon. For eighteen months he endured the harshest treatment in this place, when M. Berryer, a lieutenant of police, and a former friend of Latude's, interposed on the side of clemency. The unfortunate young man was removed to a more spacious room, and even allowed an attendant. A young fellow named Cochar undertook the post of servant to the prisoner, but over-calculated his strength to bear up against the perpetual confinement for which he so heroically volunteered. He pined away, and though at last removed into freedom, tasted it only to die.

Latude at first was inconsolable. But after a while M. Berryer supplied a new comrade, this time a fellow-prisoner, D'Alègre by name, who also had offended the petulant Marquise. So sick was she by this at repeated petitions for the pardon of the two youths—for D'Alègre was about the same age as Latude—that she vowed their imprisonment should be perpetual. The lieutenant of police was forced to break the news to the pair, that, until her death or disgrace, hope for them was vain. And here Latude shall be left to tell his own story.

"Under these circumstances, young men could come to but one resolve—to escape or perish. But to anyone able to form the faintest idea of the Bastille, this project must seem little short of madness. As our eyes rested on its walls, which are above six feet thick, on the four iron bars in the windows of our cell, on the four iron bars in the chimney; and as we considered by how many armed men the prison is guarded, the height of its walls, the water in its moats, it seemed impossible for two prisoners, without human help, to make their escape. Yet in my project I knew what I was about, and hope, in the sequel, I shall be credited with a soul something above the ordinary.

"It was no use to think of escaping from the Bastille by the gates; and, the ground being thus denied me, there was but one other course—to mount into the air. Our room had a chimney that ran to the top of the tower; but this, like every other in the place, was (as I have hinted) so fortified with iron bars as scarce to leave a passage for the smoke. Moreover, anyone making his way to the top of the tower would find himself cut off from the surrounding buildings with a ditch, commanded by a high wall, about 200 feet below him.

"Here is a list of our necessities:—We must climb to the top of the chimney in spite of the iron bars; we must have 1,400 feet of cord and two ladders—one of rope, 250 steps in length, to reach the foot of the tower; and a second of wood, between twenty and thirty feet long, for mounting the ditch beyond. We must make these ourselves, and therefore must procure tools and materials; and having made, we must hide them, though the officers, with the turnkey, paid us a visit several times a week, and strictly searched our persons.

"Figure to yourselves ten years passed in a room where you can neither see nor speak with the prisoner above your head. Many times, and for many years, has a whole family—husband, wife, and children—been immured in the Bastille without either guessing that a relative was near. You never learn any news: kings die, ministries are changed, you hear not a syllable. The officers, the surgeon, the gaolers say, 'Good morning!' 'Good evening!' 'Do you want anything?' That is all.

"Well, my first care was to find out a hiding-place for my implements, &c., as soon as I should procure them; and at length I hit on a bright idea. I had been in several rooms in the Bastille, and had always known if the one above or below me were occupied, by the noise the prisoner made. On this occasion I heard sounds from above, but none from below; and yet I knew there was someone in the room beneath. This made me guess there must be a double thickness of boards between us. I determined to find out.

"There was a chapel in the Bastille where mass was celebrated once a day during the week, and on Sundays and holidays thrice. Permission to attend it is rarely granted; but I and my comrade enjoyed it, as did the prisoner below us. Now in the chapel are five small compartments: the prisoner is placed in one of these during the ceremony; he is taken back after the elevation; and so the priest never views the face of a prisoner, nor does the prisoner see more of the priest than his back. The prisoner below us went to mass on our days, descended the first, and returned to his cell after us. So now I told my companion I had a mind to take a view of the stranger's room on our return from mass.

"This was how I desired him to help me. He was to put his tweezer-case into his handkerchief, and on regaining the second storey to contrive, by pulling out the handkerchief, that the case should fall downstairs to the greatest possible distance. He must then immediately desire the turnkey, who attended us, to run back and pick it up.

"All this was perfectly managed. The turnkey descended to find the case: and I, being foremost, ran to our fellow-prisoner's room, shot back the bolt, and opened the door. I examined the height of the room, and found it about ten feet. I shut the door again, and had time to measure a step or two of the staircase. Then, counting the number of these steps between that chamber and our own, I found a difference of five feet. The ceiling was not of stone, so could not well be five feet thick. There must be a double partition!

"'My friend,' said I to D'Alègre on our return, 'we are saved! There is a drum between the room below us and our own.'

"'Drum!' said he: 'suppose all the drums in the army were there, how are they to help us to escape?'

"'Nonsense: we don't want the drums of the army; but if, as I am sure, there is a hollow to hide the ropes and other implements that I shall need, I will engage that we escape.'

"'This is pretty talk of hiding ropes,' he answered impatiently. 'First of all we must get them.'

"'Why, as to *getting* ropes, you need give yourself no trouble; for in my trunk here we have more than a thousand feet.'

"'Trunk! Rope!'—he thought me mad. 'I know what your portmanteau holds—not a single yard of rope, I'll be sworn.'

"'Indeed, yes,' I said, 'it holds twelve dozen of shirts, six dozen pairs of silk stockings, twelve dozen pairs of under-stockings, besides towels and drawers. Are these not enough for a rope of a thousand feet?'

"'True; but how are we to remove the iron bars in our chimney? We have no instruments.'

"Said I, 'The hand is the instrument of all instruments. Look at the iron hinges of our folding-table. I will put each of these into a handle, and sharpen it to an edge on the tiled floor. We have a steel, too; and by breaking this I will manufacture, in less than two hours, a good knife to make the handles.'

"So I did. With a hinge from our table we managed to prise up a tile in the floor, and set about digging, with such success that in six hours we had picked a hole through the brickwork beneath, and found that my hasty calculation had not misled me. There was a clear space of four feet between our floor and the ceiling below. Henceforward we considered our escape a certainty. But this was work enough for one day. We swept all the rubbish back into the hole, and carefully replaced the tile.

"Next day I broke our steel and made a penknife out of it. Our next operation was to unstitch two of my shirts and unravel them, drawing out one thread after another. These threads we carefully braided until we had a rope fifty-five feet long; and then, with the wood that was brought us for firing, we set rungs to our rope, which now became a ladder some twenty feet long, enabling us to move from place to place in the chimney while we were removing the iron bars.

"For we now came to this—the most painful and trying part of our task; and its execution cost us six months of agony that to this day I shudder to think of. We never struck a dozen strokes without covering our hands with blood; and our bodies were so bruised in the chimney that often we had to rest an hour for very anguish. The bars were fixed in extremely hard cement, on which we could make no impression till we had moistened it with water, and the water had to be carried up in our mouths. So slow was our progress that we were satisfied if we could remove a single square inch of cement in one night. As soon as we had loosened a bar we left it in its place, for fear the chimney should be examined before the moment of our escape.

"'I GAINED THE TOP OF THE CHIMNEY'" (p. 203).

"This hateful toil completed, we set to work to build a wooden ladder of twenty feet, to reach from the trench to the parapet, that would lead us into the governor's garden. To make this, we set apart the pieces of wood sent up for firing. But our two hinges were not suitable for the work I had in view, so I managed to rig up an excellent saw out of an old iron candlestick, and notched it with my penknife. With this and our knives, we began to shape our billets of wood to make first a kind of pole, fastened together with bits of metal and bolts of wood; and then to fit into this a series of rungs passing through holes and sticking out about six inches on either side. The whole could be taken to pieces easily, so we had no difficulty in hiding it beneath the flooring.

"As the officers and turnkeys often entered our chamber by day, when we least expected them, we were forced to hide not only our tools but also the rubbish down to the smallest chip; and to prosecute our work by night only. Still, guards have ears as well as eyes; and as we could not avoid discussing our projects together, we had to invent a language intelligible only to ourselves. This was easily done. The saw was called *Faunus;* the hinges, *Tubal Cain;* the hole in the floor, *Polyphemus;* the wooden ladder, *Jacob;* the ropes, *doves* (from their whiteness); the pocket-knife, *puppy,* and so on. When any person came near, he who was next the door whispered, ' *Cain !* ' or ' *Dove !* ' &c.; and the other would throw his handkerchief over whatever was to be concealed, or removed it. We were always on our guard.

" We now began to think about the ropes of our great ladder, which (we now calculated) must be at least 180 feet long. To find the material we sacrificed shirts, towels, stockings, flannels—nearly the whole of our underclothing, in short. As fast as we unravelled a clew of a certain length, we hid it in *Polyphemus.* When we had a sufficient number, we spent a whole night in twisting our main rope; and (for its size) I would defy any ropemaker to produce a stronger.

" At the top of every tower of the Bastille projects a ledge, or 'entablature,' of some four feet. This, we felt sure, would thrust our ladder out in the air and cause us at every step of the descent to vibrate from side to side. We should probably lose our hold from giddiness and fall to the ground. To steady this ladder, then, we made a second rope, 360 feet long (or twice the height of the tower), by which, though the working was too complicated to describe here, either one of us, whether above or below the tower, might steady his comrade during the descent. We also fashioned smaller ropes, to fasten to our ladder, to tie it to a cannon, and to meet other possible exigencies.

" When these ropes were all ready, we found them to measure 1,400 feet. Our ladders had 208 rungs, all counted ; and to prevent the steps of the ropeladder from rustling against the wall as we descended, we covered them with the linings of our bedgowns and under-waistcoats. These preparations cost eighteen months of toil, and yet the work was not complete.

" You know now our plans for ascending our chimney to the top of the tower; for descending to the trench; for climbing thence to the parapet of the governor's garden ; for crossing this garden and coming to the great moat or ditch of the Porte St. Antoine. It was at this point that two further difficulties would meet us.

" To begin with, the parapet between the garden and the ditch was always guarded by sentinels. We should choose a dark night, of course, and a stormy. But it might rain while we were leaving the chimney and yet be perfectly fine before we came to the parapet and the sentinels. And, besides these sentinels, there would be the guard going the grand rounds. To be seen by them was to be lost. Yet we must risk it.

" The second point was less of a danger but more of a difficulty. Let it be granted we gained the ditch : there was still a wall on the far side, separating it from the Porte St. Antoine, *i.e.* from our liberty.

"Reflecting on this wall, I resolved that we must bore a passage through it. I told D'Alègre that since the building the Seine had overflowed at least 300 times; that its waters must have dissolved the salts held by the mortar, to the depth, perhaps, of half an inch at each overflow; and therefore that to perforate the wall could not be extremely difficult. To do so would be a thousand times less hazardous than to climb it before the very eyes of the sentinels.

"So we pulled out a screw from our bedstead, and made a gimlet of it. With this we hoped to make some holes in the interstices of the mortar, which would allow us, with a couple of iron bars thrust in for levers, to lift as much as five tons weight.

"We were now ready, and fixed on Monday, the 25th of February, 1756, for our flight. The river had overflowed its banks, and the ditches of the Bastille held water to the depth of four feet. Besides my trunk, I had a large leathern portmanteau; and not doubting that every stitch of our clothing would be soaked as we worked in the water, we packed this portmanteau with a complete change of clothes, picking out the best of the garments that still remained to us.

"Next day, immediately after our dinner, we took our rope-ladder from its hiding-place beneath the floor, and having looked to the rungs and found them in order, hid it again beneath the bed, ready for instant use. We then adjusted our wooden ladder, made up the rest of our tools into several bundles, bound our crowbars in rags, as well to prevent the metal from knocking against the wall as to handle them more conveniently, and furnished ourselves with a bottle of usquebaugh to keep us warm during the nine hours that we were to pass for the most part in the ditches. And this proved a very needful precaution.

"This done, we sat down to wait, as patiently as we could, the hour of supper. It came at length, and our gaolers left us for the night.

"They were scarce out of the room when we started. I was the first, in spite of a rheumatic pain in my left arm, to set about climbing the chimney, and had a tough struggle to reach the top. I was almost suffocated with the soot, and, not being aware that chimney-sweepers wear pads on their loins and elbows, as well as a strip of sacking over their heads, was pretty near flayed as well against the brickwork. By the time I reached the top my knees and elbows were streaming with blood.

"At last I gained the top of the chimney, where, without thinking of my wounds, I placed myself astride, and thence unwound a ball of thread, to the end of which my comrade was to fasten the strongest rope. This I pulled up, and lowered for my portmanteau, which I pulled out at the chimney-top and let down to the roof. I now returned the rope and drew up, first the wooden ladder, and, in the same manner, the two iron bars and the rest of our packages.

"When I had these, I again lowered my pack-thread for the rope-ladder, drawing most of it out at the chimney-top, but leaving enough for D'Alègre, who was to make the ascent by its means. At his signal I fastened it. He came up with ease; and pulling the end after him, we hung the whole across

the chimney in such a manner that we descended both at once to the roof, one on each side of the chimney, and each serving to counterpoise the other

"We were on the roof of the Bastille, with luggage

"' I SWAYED ABOUT HORRIBLY '" (p. 205).

enough to tax two horses to move all together. We began by doubling up the rope-ladder till it formed a sort of bale, five feet in height, and a foot thick, and trundled this millstone (as I may call it) along the roof till we came to the Treasury tower, where we thought our descent would be easiest. Here we tied one end of the rope-ladder to a cannon, and let the other drop gently down into the ditch below. Next we made a journey to fetch our parcels; and then I got ready for the descent.

"I tied my thigh securely to the steadying-rope, got on the ladder, and went down step after step, holding my breath for terror. In proportion as I descended, my comrade let out the steadying-rope. But, notwithstanding his precautions, I swayed about horribly. Every time I moved, my body resembled a kite dancing in the wind. I became so giddy that once or twice I felt myself on the point of losing consciousness, and gave myself up for lost. Had this occurred by daylight, of a thousand persons who might have seen me not one would have doubted my destruction. Yet I reached the ditch without mishap.

"At once D'Alègre lowered my portmanteau, the crowbars, the wooden ladder, and all our equipment; and, finding a little bank that rose above the water by the foot of the tower, I placed them there, high and dry. He then fastened his end of the steadying-rope above his knee, and prepared to follow me.

"So as soon as he began, I steadied him from below as he had steadied me from above, only in this case with more success, as I managed to rest the weight of my thighs on the last rung of the ladder, and, sitting on it, to prevent any considerable vibration. He reached the bottom safe and sound.

"Now all this time the sentinel could not have been thirty feet from us, and I heard his steps distinctly as he tramped—for it was not raining—along the top of the parapet that shut us off from the governor's garden; which for a moment upset our plans, for it prevented our climbing into the garden as we had intended.

"We accordingly resolved to wade the ditch, and try the wall lower down, where it parts the trench of the Bastille from that of the Port St. Antoine. But, unfortunately, just at the spot which we were obliged to choose, the ditch was deeper, so that we were wetted up to our armpits instead of up to our breasts.

"A thaw had set in some hours before, and the ditch was full of lumps of ice. At the moment when I began with my gimlet to bore a hole for our levers, the grand round passed us. I saw the soldiers on the parapet, twelve feet above us. Their great lantern lit up the place where we hid. There was no way to avoid discovery but to bob down in the water up to our chins.

"As soon as they had passed, I set to work again, and in a short while had bored two or three small holes with my gimlet. We inserted our crowbars and took a large stone out: after which we attacked a second and a third stone. The second round of the watch now passed us, and down we slipped again up to our chins—an operation we were obliged to repeat at each visit—that is to say, every half-hour—during nine weary hours.

"Before midnight, however, we had loosened and removed two barrows-full of large stones; and after the ninth hour of toil and terror, by picking stone from stone (and the difficulty of it is inconceivable), we had succeeded in making a breach through the wall, which was four and a half feet thick.

"I bade D'Alègre crawl through and await me on the other side; and told him that should I meet with any mishap in fetching the portmanteau, he must flee at once. By Heaven's grace I fetched it without disaster. D'Alègre drew it through the breach, and I followed, leaving the rest of our now useless baggage behind us.

"For we were now in the trench of the Porte St. Antoine, and thought ourselves out of danger. Our souls were already lifted with joy, when we experienced a new and unforeseen mischance.

"D'Alègre was holding one end of the portmanteau, and I the other. In this fashion we began to wade the ditch in order to gain the road to Bercy. But hardly had we advanced twenty steps in the water, when we tumbled into the aqueduct, in the middle of the trench, with about ten feet of water above our heads. To make matters worse, we had underfoot some two feet of thick filtering deposit (for the most part salt) on which walking was impossible. But for this latter difficulty we might easily have gained the opposite bank, for the aqueduct was only six feet in breadth.

"As it was, D'Alègre, finding himself beyond his depth, was foolish enough to drop the portmanteau and clutch me convulsively. This, I saw, must infallibly end us both; for if we fell into the salt mud, we should never have strength to raise ourselves again.

"I therefore dealt my companion a heavy blow with my fist, which forced him to drop his hold; and thus disentangled, I managed by a vigorous push to gain the further side of the aqueduct, where for a moment I hung, clinging. Then, plunging my hand into the water, I drew him towards me by the hair of his head; and afterwards caught and saved my portmanteau, which luckily floated on the surface.

"It struck five as we clambered up and out of the trench, which, after a declivity of thirty paces, brought us to dry ground. The sound of the bell had hardly died out, when we stood side by side on the main-road—free men!

"We embraced each other, and dropped on our knees to thank God, who indeed had watched over us. Our rope-ladder had proved so exact as not to be a foot too short or too long: not an inch of it had we found out of place. The clothes on our back were wet through; but those in the portmanteau, having been carefully packed and covered with linen, were quite dry.

"Our hands were galled and bruised by pulling out the stones to make the breach; and, oddly enough, we felt the cold more severely now we stood on dry ground than we had in the ditch when up to our necks in water.

"With shivering hands we began to dress. But each of us had so little control over his fingers that I was forced to act as my comrade's *valet de chambre*, and he in return performed the same office for me.

"We were ready at last, however; and, walking briskly along the road, found a hackney coach : we jumped inside, and were driven straight to the house of M. de Silhouette, Chancellor of the Duc d'Orléans. Unfortunately he had gone to Versailles, so we hurried on to the Abbey of St. Germain-des-prés."

Here we may drop Latude's narrative. He and D'Alègre found friends at the Abbey, and there lay in concealment for a month, waiting till the hue and cry had died out. They then, to avoid suspicion, separated, and departed for Brussels by different ways. D'Alègre adopted the disguise of a peasant, and having reached Brussels in safety, sent word of his success to Latude, who prepared to follow.

Furnishing himself with a parish register of his host, who happened to be about Latude's age, and a bundle of old law-papers, our hero dressed himself up as a servant and set out. At first he walked; but having put a league or two between himself and Paris, he took the *diligence* for Valenciennes. Several times stopped, questioned, and even searched, he yet managed, by sticking to his story—that he was carrying law-papers to his master's brother in Amsterdam—to reach Valenciennes at last and get into the stage for Brussels. As they approached the post that marked the Netherland frontier, he descended and walked towards it. "My feelings," says he, "overcame my prudence; I prostrated myself on the ground and kissed it with transports. 'At length,' thought I, 'I can draw a free breath!' My fellow-travellers, in astonishment, demanded my reasons for this extravagant behaviour. I told them that it was the anniversary of my escape from a serious peril, and that I always expressed in this way my gratitude to Heaven as the day came round."

D'Alègre was to await his comrade in the Hôtel de Coffi, in Brussels. Thither Latude at once directed his steps—only to meet with an overwhelming disappointment. At first the host denied all knowledge of D'Alègre, but, on being pressed, grew embarrassed. Latude began to suspect. D'Alègre must have been seized! Or else how had he failed—knowing the probable hour of Latude's arrival—to keep his appointment? And if D'Alègre had been arrested, he himself could not remain in this territory without sharing a like fate.

Terribly dejected, Latude resolved to fly yet further from the vengeance of the implacable Marquise. He took his passage in a canal boat, which was that same evening to start for Antwerp. During the voyage, in conversation with the captain, the whole truth came out. One of two daring criminals (said the man) who had managed to break out of the Bastille had been arrested, three days back, at the Hôtel de Coffi, and transported to Lille under a strong escort. "Moreover," added the unsuspecting informant, "all this was kept very secret, in order not to alarm the other convict, who would be bound sooner or later to come inquiring for his fellow."

Latude's heart flew into his mouth. He remembered with a pang his inquisitiveness in the presence of the landlord of the hotel. The whole country seemed full of eyes and ears. He felt convinced that police-officers were

waiting at every halting-place to seize him.   Leaving the canal boat, he fled
to Bergen-op-Zoom.

Here fresh tribulation befell him.   His money was at an end.   At Brussels
he had missed a remittance that his father was to have sent, and afterwards
learnt it had fallen into the hands of the police who were employed to hunt
him down.   He paid the rent of his garret at Bergen, and his passage on a
boat to take him to Amsterdam, and had but a shilling or two left in his
pocket.   For some time he endeavoured to live on grass and wild herbs;
finding this impossible, he supplemented the diet with black rye-bread.

At length he summoned courage to embark for Amsterdam.   During the
voyage he kept, as far as possible, aloof from his fellow-passengers.   There
happened, however, to be travelling on the boat a certain Jan Teerhost, who
kept a tavern in Amsterdam.   This honest man took pity on the poverty-
stricken wanderer, approached him, learnt by degrees his history, and, on
arriving at the capital, gave him a hiding in his own cellar.

But Latude was not to escape.   The spies of the Pompadour were on his
track.   By means of a letter from his father, containing a draft on an Amsterdam banker, they decoyed him to his ruin.   He was walking from his hiding-
place to the bank; the Dutch police pounced upon him, and in a moment he
was fettered.   A large crowd gathered, and the policemen, dragging their prey
along, cleared a path to the Town Hall with their bludgeons.   One of these
blows fell on Latude's neck and stretched him senseless.

Here we will leave him, promising to pursue his adventures at some future
time, and tell a tale no less stirring than has been given in these pages.   But
two small details may be added here.

Fifteen years later, Latude (then a prisoner at Charenton) learnt that his
old friend D'Alègre was an inmate of the same gloomy building.   So earnestly
did he entreat permission to see his former comrade, that his gaolers at length
gave way.   He found D'Alègre in an iron cage, his hair matted, his eyes sunken,
his flesh shrunk around his bones.   Latude ran towards him.   The man growled
and broke into a yell.   He was a maniac!   In vain did his old fellow-prisoner
plead for a sign of recognition.   D'Alègre looked at him with blazing eyes.   " I
know you not!" he screamed; "be off!   I am God!"   He had been ten years in
Charenton.   On such horrors rested the charming edifice of the Pompadour's
sway.

On the 15th of July, 1789—the day after the capture of the Bastille, when
the said charming edifice had come down with a crash, dragging after it so
much that was base, and so much that was noble—Latude, a free man, visited
the prison from which, thirty-three years before, he had escaped.   Among the
archives he found the rope-ladder he had left dangling from the Treasury
tower, and with it a *procès-verbal*, dated the 27th of February, 1756, giving a
description of the escape, and signed by the Major of the Bastille and the
Commissary Rochebrune.

FEVER AND FIRE: TWO STORIES OF DELIVERANCE.

I.—A STRICKEN CREW.

I SAILED from Liverpool for Jamaica, and, after a pleasant voyage, arrived at my destination and discharged my cargo. My vessel was called the *Lively Charlotte*, a tight brig, well found for trading, and navigated by thirteen hands. I reloaded with sugar and rum for Halifax, intending to freight from that place for England before the setting in of winter. This object I could only achieve by using double diligence, allowing reasonable time for accidental obstacles.

"My brig was built sharp, for sailing fast; and I did not trouble myself about convoy (it was during war), as I could run a fair race with a common privateer. And we trusted to our manœuvring, four heavy carronades, and a formidable show of painted ports and quakers (dummy guns, so called because they will not fight), for escaping capture by any enemy not possessing such an overwhelming superiority of force as would give him confidence to run boldly close alongside and find out what were really our means of defence.

"I speedily shipped what provisions and necessaries I wanted, and set sail. A breeze scarcely sufficient to fill the canvas carried us out of Port Royal Harbour. The weather was insufferably hot; the air seemed full of fire, and the redness of the atmosphere, not long before sunset, glared as intensely as the flame of a burning city. Jamaica was very sickly; the yellow fever had destroyed numbers of the inhabitants, and three-fourths of all new-comers speedily became its victims.

"I had been fortunate enough to lose only two men during my stay of three or four weeks (Jack Wilson and Tom Waring), but they were the two steadiest and healthiest seamen in the brig. The first died in thirty-nine hours after he was attacked, and the second on the fourth day. Two hands besides were ill when we left, which reduced to nine the number capable of performing duty. I imagined that putting off to sea was the best plan I could adopt to afford the sick a chance of recovery, and retard the spreading of the disorder among such as remained in health; but I was deceived. I carried the contagion with me, and on the evening of the day on which we lost sight of land, another hand died, and three more were taken ill.

"Still I congratulated myself I was no worse off, since other vessels had lost half their crews while in Port Royal, and some in much less time than we had remained there. We sailed prosperously through the windward passage, so close to Cuba that we could plainly distinguish the trees and shrubs growing upon it, and then shaped our course north-easterly, to clear the Bahamas and gain the great ocean.

"We had seen and lost sight of Crooked Island three days, when it became all at once a dead calm. Even the undulation of the sea, commonly called the ground swell, subsided; the sails hung slackened from the yards; the vessel slept like a turtle on the ocean, which became as smooth as a summer millpond. The atmosphere could not have sustained a feather: cloudless and clear, the blue skies above and the water below were alike spotless, shadowless, and stagnant.

"Disappointment and impatience were exhibited by us all, while the sun, flaring from the burning sky, melted the pitch in the rigging till it ran down on the decks, and a beef-steak might have been broiled on the anchor-fluke. We could not pace the planks without blistering our feet, until I ordered an awning over the deck for our protection; but still the languor we experienced was overpowering.

"A dead calm is always viewed with an uneasy sensation by the seamen, but in the present case it was more than usually unwelcome. To the sick it denied the freshness of the breeze, that would have mitigated in some degree their agonies; and it gave the healthy a predisposition to imbibe the infection, lassitude and despondency being its powerful auxiliaries. Assisted by the great heat, the fever appeared to decompose the very substance of the blood; and its progress was so rapid that no medicine could operate before death closed the scene of suffering.

"I had no surgeon on board, and from a medicine-chest I in vain administered the common remedies. But what remedies could be expected to act with efficiency, where the disease destroyed life almost as quickly as the current of life circulated?

"I had now but five men able to do duty, and never can I forget my feelings when three of those were taken ill on the fourth day of our unhappy inactivity. One of the sick expired, as I stood by his cot, in horrible convulsions. His skin was of a deep saffron hue; watery blood oozed from every pore and from the corners of his eyes; he seemed dissolving into blood, liquefying into death. Another man rushed upon deck in a fit of delirium, and sprang over the ship's side into the very jaws of the sharks that hovered ravenous around us, and seemed to be aware of the terrible havoc death was making.

"I had now the dreadful prospect of seeing all that remained perish, and prayed to God I might not be the last; for I should then become an ocean solitary, dragging on a life of hours in every second. A day's space must then be an age of misery. There was still no appearance of a breeze springing up; the horrible calm appeared as if it would endure for ever. A storm would have been welcome. The irritating indolence, the frightful loneliness and tranquillity that reigned around, united with the frequent presence of human dissolution thinning our scanty number, was more than the firmest nerves could sustain without yielding to despair. Sleep fled far from me. I paced the deck at night, gazing upon the remnant of my crew in silence, and they upon me, hopeless and speechless. I looked at the brilliant stars, that shone in tropical glory, with feverish and impatient feelings, wishing I were among them, or bereft of consciousness, or were anything but a man. A heavy presentiment of increasing evil bore down my spirits. I regarded the unruffled sea, dark and glassy, and the reflection of the heavens in it, as a sinner would have contemplated the mouth of hell. The scene, so beautiful at any other time, was terrible under my circumstances. I was overwhelmed with present and anticipated misery. Thirty years I had been accustomed to a sea life, but I had never contemplated that so horrible a situation as mine was possible; I had never imagined that any state half so frightful could exist, though storms had often placed my life in jeopardy, and I had been twice shipwrecked. In the last misfortune, mind and body were actively employed, and I had no leisure to brood over the future. To be passive, as I now was, with destruction creeping towards me inch by inch, to perceive the most horrible fate advancing slowly upon me, and be obliged to await its approach, powerless, unable to keep the hope of deliverance alive by action—such a situation was the extreme of mortal suffering, a pain of mind language is inadequate to describe; and I endured in silence the full weight of its infliction.

"My mate and cabin-boy were now taken with the disease, and on the evening of the fifth day, Will Stokes, the oldest seaman on board, breathed his last just at the going down of the sun. At midnight, another died.

"By the light of the stars we committed them to the ocean; though, while wrapping the hammock round the body of the last, we found the stench of rapid putrefaction so overpowering and nauseous, that we with difficulty got it on deck and flung it into its unfathomable grave. The dull splash of the carcase as it plunged, I shall never forget. As it raised lucid circles on the dark unruffled water, and broke the obstinate silence of the time, it struck my heart with a thrilling chilliness—a rush of feeling came over me. Even now this sepulchral sound strikes at times on my ear during sleep, in its loneliness of horror, and I fancy I am again in that ship.

"These mournful entombments were viewed by us at last with that unconcern which is shown by men rendered desperate from circumstances. Disease and dissolution were become every-day matters to us, and the fear of death had lost its power; nay, we rather trembled at the thought of surviving. Thus does habitude fit us for the most terrible situations.

"The last precaution I took was to remove the sick to the deck, under the shelter of a wet sail, to afford them coolness. The next that died was my old townsman, Job Watson. Just after I had seen him expire, about ten o'clock in the evening, when all around was like the stillness of a dead world, I was leaning over the taffrail and looking upon the ocean's face, that, from its placidity and attraction to the eye, was to me and mine like an angel of destruction clothed in beauty, when on a sudden I became free from anxiety, obdurate, reckless of everything. I imagined I had taken leave of hope for ever, and an apathy came upon me little removed from despair. I was ready for my destiny, come when it might. I got rid of a load of anxiety that I could not have carried much longer.

"So that, even when the rising moon showed me the body of the mate, which we had thrown into the water, floating on its back, half disenveloped from its hammock when I distinctly saw its livid and ghastly features covered only by an inch of transparent sea, and a huge shark preparing his hungry jaws to prey upon it, I drew not back, but kept my eye coldly upon it, as if it had been the most indifferent object upon earth; for I was as insensible to emotion as a statue would have been.

"This insensibility enabled me to undertake any office for the sick, and to drag the bodies of the dead to the ship's side and fling them overboard; for at last no one else was left to do it.

"All, save myself, were attacked with the disorder; and, one by one, died before the ninth day was completed, save James Robson, the least athletic man I had, who, to judge from his constitution, was little likely to have survived. The disease left him weak as a child. I gave him the most nourishing things I could find. I carried him, a mere skeleton, into my cabin, and placed him on a fresh bed, flinging his own and all the other beds overboard. I valued him as the only living thing with me in the vessel; though, had he died, I should at the time have felt little additional pain. I regarded him as one brute animal would have looked at another in such a situation.

"How the ship was to be navigated by one man, and what means I possessed of keeping her afloat in case blowing weather should come on, gave me no apprehension. I was too much proof against the fear of the future, or any danger that it might bring. Robson could give me no assistance; I had therefore to rely upon my own exertions for everything. If the vessel ever moved again, I must hand and steer—though, from the continuance of the calm, it did not seem likely I should be called upon to do either.

"I kept watch at night upon deck, and could sleep, day or night, only by short snatches, extended at full length near the helm. On the tenth night,

"'ANOTHER MAN SPRANG OVER THE SHIP'S SIDE'" (p. 211).

while the sea was yet in the repose of the grave around me, I fell into a doze, and was assailed with horrible dreams, that precluded my receiving refreshment from rest. Millions of living things, which had ascended from the caverns of the deep, or been engendered from the stagnation and heat, seemed to play in snaky antics on the surface of the sea. I aroused myself, and the silence on every side seemed more terrible than ever. Clouds were rising over the distant sea-line, and obscuring the stars, and the ocean put on a gloomy aspect. No sailor was now pacing the deck on his accustomed watch. The want of motion in the ship, and her powerless sails hanging in festoons amid the diminishing starlight, added to the solitary feeling which, in spite of my apathy, I experienced. I thought myself cut off from mankind for ever, and that my ship, beyond where winds ever blew, would lie and rot upon the corrupting sea. I forgot the melancholy fate of my crew at this moment, and thought, with comparative unconcern, that the time must soon come when, the last draught of water being finished, I too must die.

"The next night, as I lay half slumbering, a thousand strange images would come before my sight. The countenance of my lost mate, or some one of the crew, was frequently among them, distorted and fitted upon uncouth bodies. I felt feverish and unwell on awakening. One moment I fancied I saw a vessel pass the ship, under full sail and with a stiff breeze—and then another— while no ruffle appeared on the ocean near mine, and I hailed them in vain. Now I heard the tramp of feet upon the deck, and the whisper of voices, as of persons walking near me, whom I uselessly challenged. This would be followed by the usual obdurate silence. I felt no fear. Nature had no visitation for mortal man more appalling than that which I had already encountered; and to the ultimate of evils with social man, as I have before observed, I was insensible. For what weight could social ideas of good or evil have with me at that moment?

"The morning of the eleventh day of my suffering, I went down into the cabin to take some refreshment to Robson. Though at intervals in the full possession of his senses, he would be exhausted by the shortest rational conversation, while talking in his incoherent fits did not produce the same debilitating effect.

"'Where is the mate?' he wildly asked me; 'why am I in your cabin, captain? Have they flung Waring overboard yet?'

"I contented myself with giving him general answers, which appeared to satisfy him. I feared to tell him we were the only survivors; for the truth, had he chanced to comprehend it in its full force, might have been fatal.

"On returning upon the deck, I observed that clouds were slowly forming, while the air became doubly oppressive and sultry. The intensity of the sun's rays was exchanged for a closer and even more suffocating heat, that indicated an alteration of some kind in the atmosphere. Hope suddenly awoke in my bosom again: a breeze might spring up, and I might get free from my horrible captivity!

"I took an observation, and found that I was clear of the rocks and shoals of the Bahamas, towards which I feared a current might have insensibly borne me. All I could do, therefore, in case the wind blew, was to hang out a signal of distress, and try to keep the sea until I fell in with some friendly vessel.

"I immediately took measures for navigating the ship by myself. I fastened a rope to secure the helm in any position I might find needful, so that I might venture to leave it a few minutes when occasion required. I went aloft and cut away the topsails which I could not reef, and reduced the canvas all over the ship as much as possible, leaving only one or two of the lower sails set; for if it blew fresh, I could not have taken them in, and the ship might perish, while by doing that I had some chance of keeping her alive.

"I now anxiously watched the clouds, which seemed to be in motion; and the sight was a cordial to me. At last the sea began to heave with gentle undulations: a slight ripple succeeded, and bore new life with it. I wept for joy, and laughed as I saw it shake the sails and gradually fill them. And when at length the brig moved, just at noon on the eleventh day of our becalming, I became almost mad with delight. It was like a resurrection from the dead: it was the beginning of a new existence with me. Fearful as my state then was in reality, it appeared a heaven to that which I had been in. The hope of deliverance aroused me to new energies. I felt hungry, and ate voraciously; for till that moment I had scarcely eaten enough to sustain life. The chance of once more mingling with my fellow-men filled my imagination and braced every fibre of my frame almost to breaking.

"The ship's motion perceptibly increased; the ripple under her bow at length became audible; she felt an additional impulse; moved yet faster; and at length cut through the water at the rate of four or five knots an hour. This was fast enough for her safety, though not for my impatience. I steered her large before the wind for some time, and then kept her as near as possible to the track of vessels bound for Europe, certain that, carrying so little sail, I must be speedily overtaken by some ship that could render me assistance.

"Nor was I disappointed in my expectation. After I had steered two days, with a moderate breeze—during which time I never left the helm—a large West Indiaman came up with me and gave me every necessary aid. By this means, I was at length enabled to reach Halifax, and finally the river Mersey, about five weeks later than the time I had formerly calculated for my voyage."

II.—MAXWELL, THE PILOT. 1827.

EARLY in the century a family of brave men, natives of Stirlingshire, finding little prospect of wealth in the tillage of the barren farm at home, moved westward in a body to Port Glasgow, intending to sail from the Clyde for Canada, as so many of their stout-hearted fellow-countrymen had sailed before them. But it was not to be. The man entrusted with the money they had managed to scrape together for the expenses of the voyage was not to be found in Glasgow. He had absconded. The poor men had but a shilling or two between them, and consequently remained, against their will, in Port Glasgow, where the majority embraced the only occupation that was to be had, and became sailors.

The Maxwells—for this was their name—were all steady, thrifty men, and in time were all in good situations, working as masters or pilots on different steamships, some at home in the coasting-trade, and some abroad. James, with whom our story deals, was pilot on board the *Clydesdale*, the master of which was a gallant fellow, though somewhat young for his post, by name Turner.

The *Clydesdale* plied with passengers between the Clyde and the west coast of Ireland. One evening in the year 1827, she started with about eighty on board. Maxwell as usual was on the bridge, his eyes fixed ahead, his right hand cast behind him giving its silent orders to the wheelman. They had gained the open sea, and his task was for the while a light one. All at once he lifted his head and sniffed the air suspiciously.

Surely there was an unusual smell in the air to-night.

Maxwell stood for a minute drawing the breeze through his nostrils, then quietly descended from the bridge. He was somewhat earlier than usual in leaving it, for, as a rule, he was inclined to be over-particular in this respect. But the man at the wheel knew that the dangers of the coast were passed, and was quite content to steer alone.

The pilot, his nostrils still dilated, stepped down on deck and drew Turner aside.

"Have you noticed a peculiar smell these last few minutes?"

The master nodded, and turned an inquiring look at Maxwell.

"Fire!"

"God help us! I thought something of the kind; but where?"

"That's for us to find out. Hush! don't alarm the passengers; it may be a mistake. We'd better go quietly about and find out what it is."

The two separated, and were about to investigate, when one of the passengers—a man more accustomed than the rest to the ways of steamers at sea—came up hurriedly and caught Turner by the arm.

"This smell—haven't you noticed it? Queer; it seems to have gone now. A moment ago I could have sworn the steamer was on fire somewhere."

Turner faced him, saying in a quick, low voice—

"Hush! Yes, I've noticed it; but, for God's sake, keep quiet! I'm just off to explore, and if it turns out to be anything serious, you shall all know fast enough."

The passenger, being a sensible man, nodded and walked calmly away. Indeed, as he had said, the smell seemed to have vanished. Nevertheless, Maxwell and Turner went below to satisfy themselves that all was safe.

At eleven o'clock that night, Maxwell, his investigations failing to discover aught amiss, had returned to deck, and taken the helm himself. The passenger, hearing no more, had gone to his berth, and was sound asleep. The *Clydesdale*, beneath the stars, was steadily cleaving her way across a dark and tranquil sea for the Irish coast.

Meanwhile, the master had not ceased his search for an instant. To his senses, as he moved rapidly from place to place, the air became thicker and

"AT INTERVALS THEY CATCH SIGHT OF HIM" (p. 219).

thicker, heavier and heavier with the smell of burning timber. But where was the fire ?

At length, however, he sprang on deck. The passengers by this time were all below, and he flew towards Maxwell, who stood, rigid as a statue, beside the wheel.

"Maxwell—may God help us ! The flames have burst out in the paddle-box!"

The pilot, under the shock, turned a steady face to the master, and asked gravely—

"Shall I put about ?"

"No, no; we are near half-way across. Better make a run for it."

"Very well." Maxwell for a moment appeared to be taking in the situation; then (for he was a devout man) he murmured, loud enough for Turner to hear, and no louder, "God Almighty, enable me to do my duty! And, O God, provide for my wife, my mother, and my child!"

There was a second's pause as his prayer ended. Then he turned to the master :—

"Tell them to keep up the fires."

As Turner went off on his errand, the brave man, still with his hand on the wheel, became once more as rigid as a statue.

It was the dangerous nature of the Galloway coast that had determined the master's decision against running back. This coast, even under favourable conditions, taxed all a pilot's skill and vigilance. But in a few moments Maxwell saw that it was less to be feared than the extra distance before them. Action followed decision, swift as lightning. On his own responsibility he put the steamer about; and in a minute or so the *Clydesdale* was flying back towards the coast she had left, the consuming death within her keeping pace with her utmost efforts.

By this time the word had passed, "The steamer is on fire !" Up on deck rushed the frightened passengers, and running to Maxwell, implored him to speak the truth to them and say if there were any hope.

"Keep back—keep back ! Forward, all of you, towards the bows!"

Turner, freshly arrived from the engine-room, helped with all his authority, and presently the crowd was huddled into a small space near the bows, where the rapid flight of the vessel kept them clear of the flames, that flew back by this time and seemed to wrap the pilot in a mantle of fire.

"Maxwell—you'll never do it ! Come away and take to the boats with the rest !"

It was the master's voice. The pilot hardly turned his eyes that were fixed across the dark miles of water on the spot where the Galloway coast must lie.

"Shut down the valves!" he called.

The crew were hurrying about with buckets in useless endeavour to keep the flames under. Down in the engine-room the men worked for dear life until absolutely stormed from their posts. With throbbing machinery the

Clydesdale—at that time one of the fastest steamers built—flew across the sea at incredible speed. And all the while the smoke and flames flew backwards to the quarter-gallery, where, now alone, stood the grim figure of the man who had to save the ship. And he *would* save it, or die.

The master and the crew still plied their buckets—no longer to subdue the fire (for that was clearly hopeless) but to drench the spot where Maxwell stood like a martyr at the stake. On flew the steamer, devouring the miles; and now it seems as if the intrepid man *must* give way; for the flames have reached the cabin beneath him, and the timbers are scorching and blistering his feet. Still he is immovable. At intervals, as a rush of wind blows aside the intervening curtain of fire and smoke for an instant, the multitude of passengers in the bows catch sight of him, standing upright and moving his wheel as coolly as if on a holiday trip beneath a serene sky.

Some find heart to cheer him; others stand silent and awed, between fear for themselves and wonder at this heroism; others again are on their knees, praying aloud that this dreadful task may be accomplished. Cowards. looking aft there, feel their hearts lifted with an undreamed knowledge; brave men tingle and feel their joy in living confirmed. He only seems to have no emotion.

And now as the coast draws nearer they are observed. The blazing steamer, glaring through the darkness, has attracted hundreds down to the shore. The danger, the struggle, the desperate attempt, the chances—all this needs no explanation. The flames tell all; and in a trice the wiser among these seafaring folk know that they can help.

They swarm along the rocks to the one place where destruction leaves a gap for safety—to a parting in the rocks, about twelve yards wide, that leads to a shingly beach where the steamer may ground without danger. But how can a steamer in that state hit off this narrow path to rescue? For the matter of that, how can she be steered at all? She is coming—straight as an arrow. And one exclamation springs to the lips of all these onlookers—

"God in heaven!—what a pilot!"

But, as we said, they too can help; nay, they *must* help. They light torches and crowd, with these in hand, on either side of the narrow passage. They have now done their part; will their signals be understood?

Nearer comes the steamer, flaming through the night. Someone on shore cries—

"She's the *Clydesdale!*"

"Who's the pilot?"

"Jim Maxwell."

"Aye—*or some angel!*"

For Maxwell had understood their signals. His feet are already roasted. The engines are throbbing as if to burst the *Clydesdale's* sides—they are red-hot. The valves are shut. Between her passengers and death lie one minute and a passage twelve yards wide. Five seconds pass—ten—twenty—and now is the supreme instant. Can he see to steer it? No!—Yes!

YES!

A shout leaps up to heaven. With flames shooting high against either ledge of rock and driving the torch-bearers there from their ground—with thundering engines and roaring flames—the *Clydesdale* shoots in through the narrow passage and lies alongside a ledge of rock.

Every soul on board is helped out by willing hands. Not a man, woman, or child is scathed, except the pilot to whom they owed all. What of him?

On leaving the deck one passenger turned:

"Hi!" he cried—"There's a trunk of mine on deck. I'm a ruined man without it. Five pounds to anyone who brings it ashore!"

The rescuers are engaged in more heroic work, and do not heed him. But Maxwell does, as he totters from the wheel. He takes a pace or two—paces full of agony—snatches the burning handle of the trunk and swings it ashore, leaving the skin of his hands and fingers sticking upon it. Then his roasted feet give way, and he tumbles, but is caught and dragged into safety.

The owner of the trunk wept when it was restored to him—and never paid a penny of the promised reward.

As for Maxwell, he was a broken man. Such had been the heat around and about him, that his hair, his large hair-cap, his thick dreadnought pilot-coat, crumbled into powder beneath the hands that pulled him from the deck. It took all the skill and enthusiasm of a clever doctor to save his life; beyond this, he had lost all. Henceforward he could walk only with a stick: his stalwart form withered around his bones, his hair was grey.

A subscription was raised in Glasgow, and produced £100; of this, £60 was divided between Maxwell and Turner, and the rest given to the crew. Maxwell, always independent, attempted to pursue his old work as soon as ever health allowed him; but, owing to the weakness of his feet caused by the injuries they had received, he fell and fractured his ribs. However, he recovered, and shortly before his death, received another public donation in recognition of his heroic deed.

Such is the story of the *Clydesdale*. We leave optimists and cynics to discuss its moral. For James Maxwell was a fact; but so unfortunately, was the man with the trunk.

THE ADVENTURES OF ALEXANDER HENRY.

I.—His Capture by the Chippeway Indians.

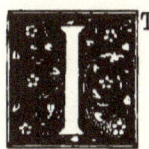T happened at the massacre of Michilimackinac, where I had lately opened a store. On my arrival there I had found several other traders gathered from different parts of the country, and their universal talk was of the hostility of the Indians. Many even dreaded an attack on the fort. M. Laurent Ducharme distinctly informed Major Etherington that a plan was on foot for destroying his garrison, and all the English in the upper country; but the commandant, who believed this and other reports of the same nature to be without foundation, at last lost his temper and swore he would send the next man to prison who came with a story of the kind. The garrison at this time consisted of ninety privates, two subalterns, and the commandant; and the English merchants at the fort were four in number. Thus strong, the majority of us felt little anxiety about the Indians, who had no weapons but small arms.

Meanwhile, the Indians from every quarter were daily assembling in unusual numbers, but with every appearance of friendship, frequenting the fort and disposing of their peltries in such a manner as to dissipate almost everyone's fears. For myself, on one occasion I took the liberty of observing to the Major that, in my judgment, no confidence ought to be placed in them, and that I was informed no less than four hundred lay around the fort. In return the Major only rallied me on my timidity; and it is to be confessed that if this officer neglected admonition on his part, so did I on mine.

Not long after my arrival at Michilimackinac, a Chippeway, named Wawatam, began to frequent my house, betraying in his demeanour strong marks of personal regard. After this had continued for some time, he came one day with his whole family, and at the same time brought a large present of skins, sugar, and dried meat. Having laid these in a heap he began a speech, in which he informed me that, some years before, he had observed a fast, devoting himself, according to the custom of his nation, to solitude and the mortification of his body, in hope to obtain from the Great Spirit protection through all his days; that on this occasion he had dreamed of adopting an Englishman as his son, brother, and friend; that, from the moment in which he first beheld me, he had recognised me as the person whom the Great Spirit had been pleased to point out to him for a brother; that he hoped I would not refuse his present; and that he should for ever regard me as one of his family.

Well, I could not do otherwise than accept the present, and declare my willingness to have so good a man for my friend and brother. I offered a present in return, which Wawatam accepted. And then, thanking me for the favour which he said that I had rendered him, he left me, and soon after set out on his winter's hunt.

Twelve months had now passed since his visit, and I had almost forgotten the person of my "brother," when, on June 2nd, Wawatam again appeared at my house, this time in a temper obviously melancholy and thoughtful.

He told me that he had just returned from his wintering-ground, and I asked after his health. Without answering my question, he went on to say he was sorry to find me returned from the Sault; he intended to go thither at once, and wished me to accompany him and his family. Here he paused for a while, and suddenly inquired if the commandant had heard any bad news; adding that, during the winter, he himself had frequently been disturbed by the noise of "evil birds"; and further suggesting that there were numbers of Indians about the fort who had never shown themselves within it.

Wawatam was about forty-five years of age, a chief, and of excellent character among his nation. Referring much of what I heard to the peculiarities of the Indian character, I did not pay to his remarks much of the attention that it will be found they deserved. I replied that I could not think of going to the Sault so soon (he had named next morning as the best time for starting), but would follow him there after the arrival of my clerks.

Finding himself unable to prevail upon me, he withdrew for that day; but early next morning he came again, bringing with him his wife, and a present of dried meat. At this interview, after stating that he had several packs of beaver, for which he intended to deal with me, he expressed a second time his apprehensions from the numerous Indians who were around the fort, and earnestly pressed me to agree to an immediate departure for the Sault. As a reason for this particular request, he assured me that all the Indians proposed to come in a body that day to the fort, to demand liquor of the commandant, and he desired me to be gone before they grew intoxicated.

I had made by this time so much progress in the language in which Wawatam addressed me, as to be able to hold an ordinary conversation in it; but the Indian manner of speech is so extravagantly figurative, that it is only a perfect master who can follow and comprehend it entirely. Had I been further advanced in this respect, I think that I should have gathered so much information from this friendly monitor, as would have put me in possession of the design of the enemy, and enabled me to save others as well as myself. As it was, I turned a deaf ear to everything, leaving Wawatam and his wife, after long and patient but ineffectual efforts, to depart alone, with dejected countenances, and not before they had each let fall some tears.

In the course of the same day, I observed that the Indians came in great numbers into the fort, purchasing tomahawks, and frequently desiring to see silver arm-bands, and other valuable ornaments, of which I had a large quantity for sale. The ornaments, however, they in no instance purchased; but after turning them over and over, left them, saying they would call again the next day. At night I turned in my mind the visits of Wawatam; but though they were calculated to excite uneasiness, nothing induced me to believe that serious mischief was at hand.

The next day, being the 4th of June, was the King's birthday. The morning was sultry. A· Chippeway came to tell me that his nation was going to play "Baggatiwag" with the Saes, or Saakies, another Indian nation, for a high wager. He invited me to witness the sport, adding that the Major was to be there, and would bet on the side of the Chippeways. In consequence of this information I went to the Major, and expostulated with him a little, representing that the Indians might possibly have some sinister end in view. But the Major only smiled at my suspicions.

I did not go myself to see the match which was now to be played without the fort, because, there being a canoe preparing to depart on the following day for Montreal, I employed myself in writing letters to my friends. And even when a fellow-trader, a Mr. Tracy, happened to call upon me, saying that another canoe had just arrived from Detroit, and proposing that I should go with him to the beach to inquire the news, it so happened that I still remained to finish my letters, promising to follow in the course of a few minutes.

Mr. Tracy had not gone more than twenty paces from the door, when I heard an Indian war-cry, and a noise of general confusion.

Going instantly to my window, I saw a crowd of Indians within the fort, furiously cutting down and scalping every Englishman they found. In particular, I witnessed the fate of Lieutenant Jemette. I had, in the room in which I was, a fowling-piece, loaded with swan-shot. This I immediately seized, and held it for a few moments, waiting to hear the drum beat to arms. In this dreadful interval I saw several of my countrymen fall, and more than one struggling between the knees of an Indian, who, holding him in this manner, scalped him while yet living.

At length, disappointed in the hope of seeing resistance made to the enemy, and sensible, of course, that no effort of my own unassisted arm could avail against four hundred Indians, I thought only of seeking shelter.

Amid the slaughter which was raging, I observed many of the Canadian inhabitants of the fort calmly looking on, neither opposing the Indians nor suffering injury. From this circumstance I conceived a hope of finding security in their houses.

Between the yard-door of my own house and that of M. Langlade, my next neighbour, there was only a low fence, over which I easily climbed. At my entrance I found the whole family at the windows, gazing on the scene of blood before them. I addressed myself immediately to M. Langlade, begging that he would put me in some place of safety, until the heat of the affair should be over—an act of charity by which he might perhaps preserve me from the general massacre.

But while I uttered my petition, M. Langlade, who had looked for a moment at me, turned again to the window, shrugging his shoulders, and intimating that he could do nothing for me.

This was a moment of despair. But, the next, a Paris woman of M. Langlade's household beckoned me to follow her. She brought me to a door, which she opened, desiring me to enter, and telling me that it led to a garret, where

"FOUR INDIANS ENTERED THE ROOM" (p. 226).

I must go and conceal myself. I joyfully obeyed her directions; and she, having followed me up to the garret door, locked it after me, and with great presence of mind took away the key.

This shelter obtained, if shelter I could hope to find it, I was naturally anxious to know what might still be passing without. Through an aperture which afforded me a view of the area of the fort, I beheld, in shapes the foulest and most terrible, the ferocious triumphs of barbarian conquerors. The dead were scalped and mangled; the dying were writhing and shrieking under the unsatiated knife and tomahawk, amidst the shouts of rage and victory. I was shaken not only with horror at the sight, but with terror for myself. The sufferings which I witnessed, I seemed to be on the point of experiencing. No long time elapsed before, everyone being destroyed who could be found, there was a general cry of "All is finished!" And, at the same instant, I heard some of the Indians enter the house in which I was!

The garret was separated from the room below only by a layer of single boards, at once the flooring of the one and the ceiling of the other. I could, therefore, hear everything that passed; and the Indians no sooner came in than they inquired whether or not any Englishmen were in the house. M. Langlade replied that he could not say: he did not know of any—answers in which he did not exceed the truth, for the Paris woman had not only hidden me by stealth, but kept my secret and her own. M. Langlade was, therefore,

"HIS EYES WERE FIXED ON MINE" (p. 227).

as I presume, as far from a wish to destroy me as he was careless about saving me, when he added to these answers that "they might examine for themselves and would soon be satisfied as to the answer to their question." Saying this, he brought them to the garret door.

The state of my mind will be imagined. When they arrived outside the door, some delay was occasioned by the absence of the key, and a few moments were thus allowed me in which to look around for a hiding-place. In one corner of the garret was a heap of those vessels of birch-bark which are used in maple-sugar making. The door was unlocked and opened, and the Indians ascended the stairs before I had completely crept into the opening which presented itself at one end of the heap.

An instant after, four Indians entered the room, all armed with tomahawks, and all besmeared with blood upon every part of their bodies.

The die appeared to be cast. I could scarcely breathe, but I thought that my heart with its throbbing made noise loud enough to betray me, and one of them approached me so closely that, at a particular moment, had he put forth his hand he must have touched me.

Still I remained undiscovered, a circumstance to which the dark colour of my clothes, and the want of light in the room (for it had no window, and I lay in the corner), must have contributed. In a word, after taking several turns around the room, during which they told M. Langlade how many they had killed, and how many scalps they had taken, they returned downstairs, and I, with sensations not to be expressed, heard the door, which was the barrier between me and my fate, locked for the second time.

There was a feather-bed on the floor; and on this, exhausted as I was by the agitation of my mind, I threw myself down and fell asleep. In this state I remained till the dusk of the evening, when I was awakened by a second opening of the door.

The person that now entered was M. Langlade's wife, who was much surprised at finding me, but advised me not to be uneasy, observing that the Indians had killed most of the English, but that she hoped I might myself escape. A shower of rain having begun to fall, she had come to stop a hole in the roof. On her going away, I begged her to send me a little water to drink: which she did.

As night was now advancing, I continued to lie on my bed, ruminating on my condition, but unable to discover a resource from which I could hope for life. A flight to Detroit had no probable chance of success. The distance from Michilimackinac was four hundred miles; I was without provisions; and the whole of the road lay through Indian countries, countries of an enemy in arms, where the first man I should meet would kill me. To stay where I was threatened nearly the same issue. As before, fatigue of mind, and not tranquillity, suspended my cares, and procured me further sleep.

But the respite which sleep afforded me during the night was put an end to by the return of the morning. I was again on the rack of apprehension. At sunrise I heard the family stirring, and, presently after, Indian voices informing M. Langlade that they had not found my body amongst the dead, and they supposed me to be somewhere concealed.

M. Langlade appeared, from what followed, to be by this time acquainted with the place of my retreat, of which, no doubt, he had been informed by his wife. The poor woman, as soon as the Indians mentioned me, declared to her husband, in the French tongue, that he should no longer keep me in his house, but deliver me up to my pursuers, giving as a reason for this measure, that should the Indians discover his instrumentality in my concealment, they might revenge it on her children, and that it was better that I should die than they.

M. Langlade resisted at first this sentence of his wife's, but soon suffered her to prevail, informing the Indians that he had been told I was in his house, that I had come there without his knowledge, and that he would put me into their hands. This was no sooner expressed than he began to ascend the stairs, the Indians following upon his heels.

I now resigned myself to the fate with which I was menaced; and regarding every attempt at concealment in vain, I arose from the bed, and presented myself full in view to the Indians who were entering the room.

They were all in a state of intoxication, and entirely naked, except about the middle. One of them, named Wenniway, whom I had previously known, and who was upwards of six feet in height, had his entire face and body covered with charcoal and grease, except that a white spot of two inches in diameter encircled each eye. This man walked up to me, seized me with one hand by the collar of the coat, while in the other he held a large carving-knife, as if to plunge it into my breast. His eyes meanwhile were fixed steadfastly on mine.

Second after second passed—each second an hour of suspense—and still I was returning his look defiantly. At length he dropped his arm.

"I won't kill you!" he said.

And then, turning to the others, he added that he had frequently engaged in wars against the English, and had brought away many scalps; that on a certain occasion he had lost a brother, whose name was Musingon, and that I should be called after him.

A reprieve upon any terms placed me among the living, and gave me back the sustaining voice of hope; but Wenniway ordered me downstairs, and there informed me that I was to be taken to his cabin, where—and indeed everywhere else—were Indians, now mad with liquor. Death was again threatened, and not as possible only, but certain. I mentioned my fears on this subject to M. Langlade, begging him to represent the danger to my new master. M. Langlade in this instance did not withhold his compassion, and Wenniway immediately consented that I should remain where I was until he found another opportunity to take me away.

Thus far secure, I re-ascended my garret stairs, in order to place myself as far as possible out of reach of insult from the drunken Indians. But I had not remained there more than an hour, when I was called to the room below, in which was an Indian, who said I must go with him out of the fort, Wenniway having sent him to fetch me.

This man, as well as Wenniway himself, I had seen before. In the preceding year I had allowed him to take goods on credit, for which he was still in my debt; and some short time previous to the surprise of the fort he had said, upon my upbraiding him with want of honesty, that he would pay me before long.

This speech now came fresh into my memory, and led me to suspect that the fellow had formed a design against my life. I communicated the suspicion to M. Langlade; but he gave for answer that "I was not now my own master, and must do as I was ordered." The Indian, on his part, directed that before I left the house I should undress myself, and declared that my coat and shirt would become him better than they became me. His pleasure in this respect being complied with, no choice was left me but either to go out naked or put on the clothes of the Indian, which he freely gave me in exchange. His motive for thus stripping me of my apparel was no other, as I afterwards learned; than this, that it might not be stained with blood when he should kill me.

I was now told to proceed, and my driver followed me close until I had passed the gate of the fort, when I turned towards the spot where I knew the Indians to be encamped. This, however, did not suit the purpose of my enemy, who seized me by the arm and drew me violently in the opposite direction, to the distance of fifty yards above the fort. Here, finding that I was approaching the bushes and sand-hills, I determined to proceed no further, but told the Indian that I believed he meant to murder me; and if so, he might as well strike where I was as at a greater distance.

He replied with coolness that my suspicions were just, and that he meant to pay me in this manner for my goods. At the same time he produced a knife, and held me in a position to receive the intended blow. This, and that which followed, took but a moment.

By some effort, too sudden and too independent of thought to be explained or remembered, I was able to arrest his arm and give him a sudden push. The push spun him round, and I broke from his grasp and ran for my life.

I sped towards the fort with all the swiftness in my power. The Indian dashed after at my heels. Every moment I expected to feel the stroke of his knife in my back. And so for a minute we raced.

I won. I managed to dart inside the fort as the Indian's knife missed me by six inches. I caught a glimpse of Wenniway standing in the midst of the area, and tottered towards him for protection. Wenniway called out to the other to keep off; but the fellow's blood was up, and he pursued me round my master, jobbing at me with his knife, and foaming at the mouth with rage at the repeated failure of his purpose. At length Wenniway, still screening me, moved backwards to M. Langlade's house. The door was open and into it I sprang—the Indian after me. But no sooner was I well inside than he voluntarily abandoned the pursuit.

Preserved so often and so unexpectedly, I now returned to my garret, with a strong inclination to believe that, through the will of an overruling Power, no Indian enemy could do me hurt.

"SO FOR A MINUTE WE RACED" (p. 228).

But new trials, as I believed, were at hand, when, at ten o'clock in the evening, I was roused from sleep and once more desired to descend the stairs. No less, however, to my satisfaction than surprise, I was summoned only to meet Major Etherington, Mr. Bostwick, and Lieutenant Leslie, who were in the room below. These gentlemen had been taken prisoners while looking at the game without the fort, and immediately stripped of all their clothes. They were now sent into the fort, under the charge of Canadians, because, the Indians having resolved on getting drunk, the chiefs were apprehensive that they would be murdered if they continued in the camp. Lieutenant Jemette and seventy soldiers had been killed, and but twenty Englishmen, including soldiers, were still alive. These were all within the fort, together with nearly three hundred Canadians belonging to the canoes.

These being our numbers, I and some others proposed to Major Etherington to make an effort for regaining possession of the fort and maintaining it against the Indians. The Jesuit missionary was consulted on the project; but he discouraged us by his representations not only of the merciless treatment which we must expect from the Indians, should they regain their superiority, but of the little dependence which was to be placed upon our Canadian auxiliaries. Thus the fort and prisoners remained in the hands of the Indians, though through the whole night the prisoners and whites were in actual possession, and the Indians outside the gates.

The whole night, or the greater part of it, was passed in mutual condolence; and my fellow-prisoners shared my garret. In the morning, being again called down, I found my master, Wenniway, and was desired to follow him. He led me to a small house within the fort, where, in a dark narrow room, I found Mr. Ezekiel Solomons with an Englishman from Detroit, and a soldier, all prisoners. With these I remained in painful suspense till ten o'clock in the forenoon, when an Indian arrived, and presently marched us to the lake-side. Here we saw a canoe lying, ready for departure, and found that we were to embark.

Our voyage, full of doubt as it was, would have begun at once but for the absence of one of the Indians who was to be of the party. So we awaited him in the bitter north-east wind. An old shirt was all that covered me. I suffered much from the cold; and in this extremity, catching sight of M. Langlade on the beach, I asked him for a blanket, promising that if I lived I would pay him any price he pleased. He said I could not have the blanket unless there were someone to be security for the payment. For myself, he observed, I had no longer any property in that country.

I had no more to say to M. Langlade. But presently, seeing another Canadian, I addressed to him a similar request and was not refused. Naked as I was, and rigorous as was the weather, but for the blanket I must have perished. At noon our party was all collected, the prisoners all embarked, and we steered for the Isles du Castor (Beaver Islands) in Lake Michigan.

II.—HIS VOYAGE AND RANSOM.

The soldier who was our companion in misfortune, was made fast to a bar of the canoe by a rope tied round his neck, as is the manner of the Indians in transporting their prisoners. The rest were left unconfined; but a paddle was put into the hands of each, and we were forced to ply it. The Indians in the canoe were seven in number, the prisoners four—Mr. Ezekiel Solomons, the soldier, the Englishman from Detroit, and myself. And this was the 6th of June, the third day of our distress.

We were bound, as I have said, for the Isles du Castor, which lie in the mouth of Lake Michigan; and we should have crossed the lake had not a thick fog come on, in which the Indians deemed it safer to keep the shore under their lee. We therefore approached the lands of the Ottawas, and their village, on the opposite side of the tongue of land on which the fort is built. Every half-hour the Indians gave their war-whoop four times, once for every prisoner in their canoe. This is a general custom, by the aid of which all other Indians within hearing are apprised of the number of prisoners they are carrying.

In this manner we reached Fox Point, a long spit of land, eighteen miles distance from Michilimackinac. Here the Indians repeated their war-whoop; and an Ottawa appeared on the beach, who made signs that we should land. We approached. The Ottawa asked the news, and kept the Chippeways in conversation till we were within a few yards of the land and in shallow water. At this moment, a hundred men rushed upon us from among the bushes, and dragged all the prisoners out of the canoe amid a terrifying shout.

We now believed that our last sufferings were approaching. But no sooner were we fairly on our legs than the chiefs of the party advanced, and gave each of us their hands, saying they were . our friends, whom the Chippeways had insulted by destroying the English without consulting them on the affair. They said, also, that they had laid this ambush to save our lives; for the Chippeways were carrying us to the Isles du Castor only to kill and devour us.

It was not long before we were again embarked, this time in the canoes of the Ottawas; and, that same evening, they re-landed us at Michilimackinac, where they marched us into the fort, in view of the Chippeways, who stood confounded to see the Ottawas espousing the opposite side. Our protectors, who had accompanied us in sufficient numbers, took possession of the fort. We were still prisoners, however, and were lodged in the commandant's house, under a strict guard.

Early the next morning, a general council was held, in which the Chippeways complained much of the conduct of the Ottawas in robbing them of their prisoners; alleging that all the Indians, the Ottawas alone excepted, were at war with the English; that Pontiac had taken Detroit; that the King of France had awoke, and repossessed himself of Quebec and Montreal; and that the English were meeting destruction in every part of the world. From all this they inferred that it became the Ottawas to restore the prisoners and to join in the war; and the speech was followed by large presents, being part of the plunder of the fort, which were previously heaped in the centre of the room. The Indians rarely make their answers till the day after they have heard the arguments offered. They did not depart from their custom now; and the council therefore adjourned.

We, the prisoners, whose fate was thus in controversy, were unacquainted at the time with this transaction, and therefore enjoyed a night of tolerable tranquillity, not in the least suspecting the reverse which was preparing for us. Which of the arguments of the Chippeways prevailed I cannot say; but the council was resumed at an early hour in the morning, and after several speeches had been made in it, the prisoners were sent for, and returned to the Chippeways. These, as soon as we were restored to them, marched us to a village of their own, situated at a point below the fort, and put us in a lodge, already the prison of fourteen soldiers, tied two and two, with each a rope about his neck, and made fast to a pole which might be called the supporter of the building.

I was left untied; but I passed the night sleepless and wretched. My bed was the bare ground, and I was again reduced to an old shirt as my entire apparel, my blanket having been taken from me. I was, besides, in want of food, having for two days eaten nothing. I confess that in the canoe with the Chippeways I was offered bread; but bread with what accompaniment? They had a loaf, which they cut with the same knives that they had employed in the massacre—knives still covered with blood. The blood they moistened with spittle, and rubbing it on the bread, offered this for food to their prisoners, telling them to eat the blood of their countrymen. Such was my situation on the morning of the 7th of June, in the year 1763; but a few hours produced an event which gave a new colour to my lot.

Towards noon, when the Great War-Chief, in company with Wenniway, was seated at the opposite end of the lodge, my friend and brother, Wawatam, suddenly came in. During the four preceding days I had often wondered what had become of him. In passing by he gave me his hand, but went immediately towards the Great Chief, by the side of whom and Wenniway he sat himself down.

The most uninterrupted silence prevailed. Each smoked his pipe; and, this done, Wawatam arose and left the lodge, saying to me as he passed, "Take courage!"

An hour elapsed, during which several chiefs entered, and preparations appeared to be making for a council. At length Wawatam re-entered the lodge, followed by his wife. Both were loaded with merchandise, which they carried up to the chiefs, and laid in a heap before them. Some moments of silence followed, at the end of which Wawatam pronounced a speech, every word of which to me was of extraordinary interest.

"Friends and relatives," he began, "what is it that I shall say? You know what I feel. You all have friends, and brothers, and children, whom, as yourselves, you love. And what would you suffer did you, like me, behold your dearest friend, your brother, in the condition of a slave—a slave exposed every instant to insult and menaces of death? This case is mine. See there"—he pointed to me—"my friend and brother among slaves, himself a slave! You all well know that long before the war began I adopted him as a brother. From that moment he became one of my family; and because I am your relative, so also is he; and how, as such, can he be your slave? On the day when the war began you were fearful lest, on his account, I should reveal

your secret. You requested, therefore, that I should leave the fort and even
cross the lake. I did so, but with reluctance, notwithstanding that you, Menehwehna, who led this expedition, gave me your promise to protect my friend and
render him safely to me. The performance of this promise I now claim. I
come not with empty hands. You, Menehwehna, best know if you have
kept your word. But I bring these gifts to buy off every claim that anyone
among you may have on my
brother as his prisoner."

As Wawatam ceased the
pipes were again filled. After
they were finished a period
of silence followed; at the
end of which Menehwehna
rose and gave his reply:—

"Kinsman and brother,"
said he, "what you have
spoken is the truth. We are
acquainted with the friendship which you hold towards
the Englishman on whose
behalf you have spoken. We
knew the danger of having
our secret discovered, and
the consequences which must
follow; and you say truly
that we requested you to
leave the fort. This we did
out of regard for you and
your family; for if the discovery of our design had
been made, you would have

WAWATAM'S SPEECH (p. 232).

been blamed, whether guilty or not. It is true, also, that I promised to take
care of your friend; and this promise I performed, by desiring my son, at the
moment of the assault, to seek and bring him to my lodge. He went accordingly
but could not find him. The next day, I sent him to Langlade's, where he
was informed that your friend was safe; and had it not been that our
folk were then drinking the rum which was found in the fort, he would have
led him home according to my orders. We accept your present, and you may
take him home with you."

Wawatam thanked the assembled chiefs, and taking me by the hand, led
me to his lodge, which was at the distance of a few yards only from the prison
lodge. My entrance appeared to give joy to the whole family; food was immediately prepared for me, and I now ate the first hearty meal which I had

made since my capture. I found myself one of the family; and but that I had still my fears as to the other Indians, I felt as happy as the situation would allow.

In the evening of the next day, a large canoe, such as those which came from Montreal, was seen advancing to the fort. It was full of men, and I distinguished several passengers. The Indian cry was raised in the village, a general muster ordered, and to the number of two hundred they marched up to the fort, where the canoe was expected to land. The passengers, who were English traders, suspecting nothing, came boldly to the fort: where they were seized, dragged through the water, beat, reviled, marched to the prison lodge, and there stripped of their clothes and kept under guard.

In the morning of the 9th of June, a general council was held, at which it was agreed to remove to the island of Michilimackinac, as a more defensible position in the event of an attack by the English. The Indians had begun to entertain apprehensions of want of strength, and consequently prepared for speedy retreat. At noon the camp was broken up, and we embarked, taking with us the prisoners that were still undisposed of. On our passage we encountered a gale of wind, and there were some appearances of danger. To avert it, a dog, of which the legs were previously tied, was thrown into the lake to soothe the angry passions of some offended Manito.

As we approached the island, two women in our canoe began to utter melancholy and hideous cries. Precarious as my condition still remained, I felt some sensation of alarm at these mysterious sounds, of which I could not then discover the occasion. Subsequently, I learned that it is customary for the women, on passing near the burial-places of relations, to denote their grief in this manner. By the evening we had reached the island in safety, and the women were not long in erecting our cabins. Several days now passed, during which a guard was kept day and night, and alarms were frequently spread; when, one morning, I heard a continued commotion, and saw the Indians running in a confused manner towards the beach. In a short time I learned that two large canoes from Montreal were in sight. All the Indian canoes were immediately manned, and those from Montreal were surrounded and captured as they turned a point behind which the flotilla had been concealed.

They contained a large quantity of liquor — a dangerous acquisition. Wawatam, always watchful, no sooner heard the noise of drunkenness that evening than he represented to me the danger of remaining in the village, and owned that he could not himself resist the temptation to join in the debauch. That I might, therefore, escape all mischief, he bade me accompany him to the mountain, where I was to remain hidden till the liquor should be drunk.

We climbed the mountain accordingly, which constitutes the high land in the middle of the island, and is considered to resemble a *turtle*, whence it derives its name—Michilimackinac. It is thickly covered with wood, and very rocky towards the top.   After walking more than half a mile, we came to a large rock, at the base of which was an opening, dark within, that seemed to be the entrance of a cave.   Here Wawatam recommended that I should take up my lodging, and by all means remain till he returned.

On going into the cave, of which the entrance was nearly ten feet wide, I found the further end to be rounded in its shape, like that of an oven, but with a further aperture, too small, however, to be explored.   After thus looking about me, I broke small branches from the trees, and spread them for a bed, then wrapped myself in my blanket and slept till daybreak.   On awakening, I felt myself incommoded by some object on which I lay, and, removing it, found it to be a bone.   This I supposed to be that of a deer, or some other animal, and what might very naturally be looked for in the place in which it was; but, when daylight visited my chamber, I discovered, with some feelings of horror, that I was lying on nothing less than a heap of human bones and skulls, which covered all the floor.

The · day passed without the return of Wawatam and without food.   As night approached, I found myself unable to meet its darkness in the charnel-house, which, nevertheless, I had viewed free from uneasiness during the day. I chose, therefore, an adjacent bush for this night's lodging, and slept under it as before.   But in the morning I awoke hungry and dispirited, and almost envying the dry bones, to the view of which I returned.

At length the sound of a foot reached me, and my Indian friend appeared, making many apologies for his long absence, the cause of which was an unfortunate excess in the enjoyment of his liquor.   This point being explained, I mentioned the extraordinary sight that had presented itself in the cave to which he had committed my slumbers.   He had never heard of its existence before, and upon examining the cave together, we saw reason to believe that it had been anciently filled with human bodies.

On returning to the lodge, I experienced a cordial reception from the family: Wawatam related to the other Indians the adventure of the bones. All of them expressed surprise at hearing it, and declared that they had never been aware of the contents of this cave before.   After visiting it, which they immediately did, almost everyone offered a different opinion as to its history.

It was soon after this that Menehwehna came one day to the lodge of my friend and advised that I should, to escape further insult, be dressed in future like an Indian.   I consented; and the chief was kind enough to help in effecting the metamorphosis.   My hair was cut off, and my head shaved, with the exception of a spot on the crown of about twice the diameter of a crown-piece.   My face was painted with three or four different colours, some parts of it red, and some black.   A shirt was provided for me, painted with vermilion mixed with grease.   A large collar of wampum was put round my neck, and another suspended on my breast.   Both my arms were decorated with large bands of silver above the elbows, besides several smaller ones on the wrists;

and my legs were covered with mitases, a kind of hose made of scarlet cloth. Over all I was to wear a scarlet mantle or blanket, and on my head a large bunch of feathers. I parted, not without some regret, with the long hair that was natural to it; but the ladies of the family, and of the village in general, appeared to think my person improved, and now condescended to call me handsome even among Indians.

"I DISCOVERED I WAS LYING ON A HEAP OF BONES" (p. 235).

III.—HIS HUNTING.

[*From Michilimackinac, Alexander Henry, now a naturalised Indian, migrated in time to the Island of St. Martin, and thence about the shores of Lake Michigan on several hunting expeditions, some of which we will now leave him to describe.*]

To kill beaver we used to go several miles up the rivers—especially the river Aux Sables, on the south side of the lake—before the approach of night, and, after the dark came on, to suffer the canoe to drift gently down the current without noise. The beaver on this part of the river came abroad to procure food, or materials for repairing their habitations, and, as they were not alarmed by the canoe, they often passed it within gunshot. I soon became as export as the Indians themselves in hunting of all kinds. Our lodge was fifteen miles above the mouth of the stream.   The principal animals which the country afforded were the red deer, the common American deer, the bear, raccoon, beaver, and marten.

The most common way of taking the beaver is that of breaking up its house, which is done with trenching tools, during the winter, when the ice is strong enough to allow of approaching them, and when also the fur is in its most valuable state.   Breaking up the house, however, is only a preparatory step.   During this operation the family make their escape to one or more of their *washes*.   These are to be discovered by striking the ice along the bank, and, where the holes are, a hollow sound is returned.   After discovering and searching many of them in vain, we often found the whole family together in the same wash.   I was taught occasionally to distinguish a full wash from an empty one by the motion of the water above its entrance, occasioned by the breathing of the animals concealed in it.   From the washes they must be taken out with the hands, and, in doing this, the hunter sometimes received severe wounds from their teeth.   In those days I thought that beaver-flesh was very good, but after again tasting that of the ox, I could not relish it.   The tail is considered a tit-bit.

The raccoon was another object of our chase.   It was my practice to go out in the evening with dogs, accompanied by the youngest son of my guardian, to hunt this animal.   The raccoon never leaves its hiding-place till after sunset. As soon as a dog falls on the fresh track of one, he gives notice by a cry, and immediately pursues.   His barking enables the hunter to follow.   The raccoon, which travels slowly, and is soon overtaken, makes · for a tree, on which he remains till shot.   In snow, however, one need only follow the track of his feet.   In this season he seldom leaves his habitation, and never lays up any food.   I have found six at a time in the hollow of one tree, lying upon each other, and nearly in a torpid state.   In more than one instance, to my know- ledge, they have lived six weeks without food.   The mouse is their principal prey.

I was growing used to my new life; and, but for the whispered notion that one day I should be released from it, could have extracted complete enjoyment from my hunting.

On the 20th of December we took an account of our spoils, and found we had a hundred beaver-skins, as many raccoons, and a large quantity of dried venison, all of which was safe from the wolves, being raised upon a scaffold. A hunting excursion into the interior of the country was resolved on, and early next morning our bundles were made up by the women.   I remarked that the bundle given to me was the lightest, and those carried by the women the largest and heaviest of the whole.

On the first day of our march we advanced about twenty miles, and then encamped.   Being somewhat fatigued, I could not hunt, but Wawatam killed a stag not far from our encampment.   The next morning we moved our lodge to

the carcase.   At this station we remained two days, employed in drying the
meat.   The method was to cut it into slices of the thickness of a steak, and
then hang it over the fire to smoke.   On the third day we removed, and
marched till two o'clock in the afternoon.   While the women were busy in
erecting and preparing the lodges, I took my gun and strolled away, telling
Wawatam that I intended looking out for some fresh meat for supper.   He
answered that he would do the same, and on this we both left the encampment in different directions.

The sun was visible, so I had no fear of losing my way; but in following
several tracks of animals, in momentary expectation of falling in with game, I
was led too far, and it was not till near sunset that I thought of returning.
The sky, too, had become overcast, and I was therefore left without the sun
for my guide.   In this situation I walked as fast as I could, always supposing
myself to be approaching our encampment, till at length it became so dark
that I ran against the trees.

I became convinced that I was lost, and was alarmed by the reflection that
I was in a country strange to me, and in danger from hostile Indians.   With
the flint of my gun I made a fire, and then laid me down to sleep.

In the night it rained hard.   I awoke cold and wet, and, as soon as light
appeared, I recommenced my journey, sometimes walking, and sometimes
running, not knowing whither to go, bewildered, and like a madman.   Towards
evening I reached the border of a large lake, of which I could scarcely discern
the opposite shore.   I had never heard of a lake in this part of the country,
and therefore felt myself more lost than ever.   To tread back my steps
appeared the most likely way to deliverance, and I accordingly determined to
turn my face directly from the lake, and keep this direction as nearly as I
could.   A heavy snowstorm began to descend, and night soon afterwards came
on.   On this I stopped and made a fire, and stripping a tree of its sheet of
bark, lay down under it for shelter.   All night, at small distances, the wolves
howled around, and, to me, seemed to be acquainted with my misfortune.

Amid thoughts the most distracted, I was able at length to fall asleep; but
it was not long before I awoke refreshed, and wondering at the terror to which
I had given way.   That I could really have wanted the means of recovering
my way appeared incredible.   How was it I had failed to remember the lessons
of my Indian friend, designed on purpose to meet difficulties of this kind?
These were that, generally speaking, the tops of pine-trees lean towards the
sunrise; that moss grows towards the roots of trees on the side which faces
the north, and that the limbs of trees are most numerous towards the south.

Determined to direct my feet by these marks, and persuaded that I should
thus, sooner or later, reach Lake Michigan, which I reckoned to be distant
about sixty miles, I began my march at break of day.   I had neither taken,
nor wished to take, any nourishment since I left the encampment; I had with
me my gun and ammunition, and was therefore under no anxiety in regard

to food. The snow lay about half a foot in depth. My eyes were now employed upon the trees. When their tops leaned different ways, I looked to the moss or to the branches, and by connecting one with another I found the means of travelling with some degree of confidence. At four o'clock in the afternoon, the sun, to my inexpressible joy, broke from the clouds, and I had now no further need to examine the trees.

In going down the side of a lofty hill, I saw a herd of red deer approaching. Desirous of killing one of them for food, I hid myself in the bushes, and on a large one coming near, presented my piece, which missed fire on account of the priming having been wetted. The animals walked along without taking the least alarm, and having reloaded my gun, I followed them and presented a second time.

But now a disaster of the heaviest kind had befallen me; for, on attempting to fire, I found that I had lost the hammer of my gun. I had previously lost the screw by which it was fastened to the lock, and to prevent this from being lost also, I had tied it in its place with a leathern string. The lock, to prevent it catching in the boughs, I had carried under my coat. Of all the sufferings which I had experienced, this seemed to me the most severe. I was in a strange country, and knew not how far I had to go. I had been three days without food; I was without the means of procuring myself either food or fire. Despair had almost overpowered me; but I soon resigned myself into the hands of that Providence whose arm had so often saved me, and returned on my track in search of what I had lost. My search was in vain, and I resumed my course, wet, cold, and hungry, and almost without clothing.

The sun was setting fast when I descended the hill, at the bottom of which was a small lake entirely frozen over. Drawing near, I saw a beaver-lodge in the middle, offering some faint prospect of food; but I found it already broken up. While I looked at it, it suddenly occurred to me that I had seen it before, and turning my eyes round the place, I discovered a small tree which I had myself cut down in the autumn. I was no longer at a loss. My course was to follow a small stream of water which came down to the lake here past the spot where my friends were encamped. The whole of that night and the succeeding day I walked up the rivulet, and at sunset reached the encampment, where I was received with delight. The family had searched for me long and vainly in the woods, and at length given me up for dead.

Some days elapsed, during which I rested and recruited my strength. After this I resumed the chase, secure that, as the snow had now fallen, I could always return by the way I went.

In the middle of January, I noticed that the trunk of a large pine-tree was much torn by the claws of a bear, made both by going up and coming down. On further examination, I saw that there was a large opening in the upper part, near which the smaller branches were broken. From these marks, and from the additional circumstance that there were no tracks in the snow, there was reason to believe that a bear lay concealed in the tree.

On returning to the lodge, I communicated my discovery; and it was agreed that all the family should go together in the morning to assist in cutting down the tree, the girth of which was not less than three fathoms. The women at first opposed the undertaking, because our axes, being only of a pound and a half weight, were not well adapted to so heavy labour; but the hope of finding a large bear, and obtaining from his fat a large quantity of oil, an article at the time much wanted, at length prevailed.

Accordingly, in the morning we surrounded the tree, both men and women, as many at a time as could conveniently work at it; and here we toiled like beavers till the sun went down. This day's work carried us about half-way through the trunk; and next morning we renewed the attack, continuing it until about two o'clock in the afternoon, when the tree fell to the ground. For a few minutes everything remained quiet, and I feared that all our expectations were disappointed; but as I advanced to the opening, there came out, to the great satisfaction of all our party, a bear of extraordinary size, which, before she had proceeded many yards, I shot.

The bear being dead, all my assistants approached, and all, but more particularly my old mother, as I was wont to call her, took her head in their hands, stroking and kissing it several times; begging a thousand pardons for taking away her life; calling her their kinswoman and grandmother; and requesting her not to lay the fault upon them, since it was truly an Englishman that had put her to death.

This ceremony was not of long duration; and if it was I that killed their grandmother, they were not themselves behind-hand in what remained to be performed. The skin being taken off, we found the fat in several places six inches deep. This, being divided into two parts, loaded two persons; and the flesh parts were as much as four persons could carry. In all, the carcase must have exceeded five hundredweight.

As soon as we reached the lodge, the bear's head was adorned with all the trinkets in the possession of the family, and then laid upon a scaffold, set up for its reception within the lodge. Near the nose was placed a large quantity of tobacco. The next morning no sooner appeared than preparations were made for a feast to the *manes*. The lodge was cleaned and swept; and the head of the bear lighted up, and a new blanket spread under it. Pipes were now lit, and Wawatam blew tobacco-smoke into the nostrils of the bear, telling me to do the same and thus appease her anger. At length, the feast being ready, Wawatam began a speech, deploring the necessity under which men laboured thus to destroy "their friends." He represented, however, that the misfortune was unavoidable, since without doing so they could by no means subsist. The speech ended, all ate heartily of the bear's flesh; and even the head itself, after remaining three days on the scaffold, was put into the kettle.

The fat was melted down, and the oil filled six porcupine-skins. A part of the meat was cut into strips and fire-dried, after which it was put into vessels containing the oil, where it remained in perfect preservation until the middle of the summer.

"THERE CAME OUT A BEAR" (p. 240).

February, among the people with whom I dwelt, is called the Moon of Hard or Crusted Snow:—for now the snow can bear a man, or at least dogs, in pursuit of game. At this season the stag is very successfully hunted, his feet breaking through at every step, and the crust upon the snow cutting his legs with its sharp edges to the very bone. He is consequently in sore distress, and it frequently happened that we killed twelve in the short space of two hours. Thus we were soon put into possession of four thousand pounds weight of dried venison, which was to be carried on our back, along with all the rest of our wealth, for seventy miles, the distance of our encampment from that part of the lake at which we had·left our canoes in the autumn.

IV.—His Departure.

· We stayed by the shore of the lake for some time, and then embarked for Michilimackinac. In the evening of April 27th we landed at the fort, which now contained only French traders. The Indians who had arrived before us were very few in number; and by all who were of our party I was used very kindly. I had the entire freedom both of the fort and camp. Wawatam and I settled our stock and paid our debts; and this done, I found that my share of the surplus consisted of 100 beaver-skins, 60 raccoon-skins, and 6 otter, of the total value of 160 dollars.

With these earnings of my winter toil, I proposed to purchase clothes, of which I was much in need, having been six months without a shirt; but on inquiring into the price of goods, I found that all my means would not go far. I was able, however, to buy two shirts at ten pounds of beaver apiece; a pair of leggings of scarlet cloth, which, with the ribbon to fasten them fashionably, cost me fifteen pounds of beaver; and some articles at proportionable rates. In this manner my wealth was soon reduced, but not before I had laid in a good stock of ammunition and tobacco. To the use of the latter I had become much attached during the winter.

Eight days had passed in tranquillity, when there arrived a band of Indians from the Bay of Saguenam. They had assisted at the siege of Detroit, and came to muster as many of their friends as they could against the English. As I was the only Englishman in the place, they proposed (I was told) to kill me, to make a mess of English broth to give their friends courage.

Wawatam came with a long face, bringing this news; and, in consequence, I desired him to carry me· to the Sault de Sainte Marie, where I knew the Indians to be peaceably inclined, and that a M. Cadotte there exercised a powerful influence over their conduct. They considered him as their chief; and he happened not only to be my friend, but a friend to all the English.

Wawatam consented. With his family we left Michilimackinac by night, and reached the Bay of Boutchitaouy, where we found plenty of wild-fowl, and spent three days in fishing and hunting. Leaving the bay, we made for the Isle aux Outardes, whence we proposed sailing for the Sault next morning.

But when the morning came, Wawatam's wife complained that she was sick, adding that she had had bad dreams, and knew if we went to the Sault we should all be destroyed. I could not argue against the infallibility of dreams, for I should have seemed guilty of an odious want of sensibility to the possible calamities of a family that had done so much to alleviate mine.

I was silent, although I believed my fate sealed, for the island lay in the direct route of the Indians bound for Detroit, and they were hourly expected to pass. Unable, therefore, to remonstrate, but in fear for my life, I passed all the day in the topmost branches of a tall tree, from which the lake on both sides of the island lay open to my view. Here I might hope to learn, at the earliest possible time, the approach of canoes, and be warned to conceal myself.

On the second morning, at daybreak, I returned to my watch-tower, and had not been there long before I discovered a sail coming from Michili-mackinac. It was a white one, and much larger than that usually employed by the Northern Indians. I therefore indulged a hope that it might be a Canadian canoe bound for Montreal. My hopes continued to gain ground; for I soon persuaded myself that the manner in which the paddles were being used was Canadian and not Indian. My spirits rose. I climbed down from my perch, and hastened to the lodge with my tidings and schemes for liberty.

The family congratulated me; and Wawatam, lighting his pipe, presented it to me, saying—

"My son, this may be the last time that ever you and I shall smoke out of the same pipe. I am sorry to part with you. You know the love I have always borne you, and the dangers which I and my family have run to preserve you from your enemies. I am happy that my efforts promise not to have been in vain."

Hereupon a boy ran into the lodge, bringing news that the canoe had come from Michilimackinac, and was bound for the Sault de Sainte Marie. It was manned by three Canadians, and was carrying home Madame Cadotte, the wife of my friend.

I resolved to accompany Madame Cadotte, with her permission, to the Sault. She cheerfully acceded to my wish. She was an Indian woman of the Chippeway nation, and was very generally respected. I returned to the lodge, where I packed up my wardrobe, my two shirts, my leggings, and my blanket; besides these I took a gun and ammunition, presenting what remained over to my host.

We now exchanged farewells with tenderness on both sides. I did not quit the lodge without the most grateful sense of the goodness I had experienced in it. All the family accompanied me to the beach; and the canoe had no sooner put off than Wawatam began an address to Kitchi-Manito, the Great Spirit, beseeching him to take care of me, his brother, till we should next meet. We were out of hearing before I ceased to wave my hand, or Wawatam to offer up his prayers.

Being now no longer in the vicinity of the Indians, I put aside the dress, and donned that of a Canadian. At daybreak, on the second morning of our voyage, we perceived several canoes behind us. As they approached we ascertained them to be the Indians bound for the Missisaki—the very fleet of which I had been so long in dread!

It amounted to twenty sail. On coming up with us and surrounding our canoe, and amid general inquiries concerning the news, an Indian challenged me for an Englishman, and his companions supported him by declaring that I looked very like one; but I affected not to understand any of the questions which they asked me, and Madame Cadotte assured them that I was a Canadian whom she had brought on this voyage from Montreal.

They left us in peace, and the following day saw us safely landed at the Sault, where I experienced a generous welcome from M. Cadotte.

"'HE BEAT HIS HEAD AND STOOD CRYING ALOUD'" (p. 246).

ROGUES ALL.

IT is a sorry fact that adventures befall the wicked as well as the good. And in case any of our readers should think that the truly virtuous have had it all their own way of late in these pages, we hasten to set matters right, and introduce them, not to a Chamber of Horrors, but to a Museum of Scamps.

Knavery being at least as old as tradition, our first specimen shall be exhibited by the Father of History himself, and the story given in his own words.

" Rhampsinitus, King of Egypt (says Herodotus), possessed a great quantity of money—such as no one of his successors could surpass, or even rival—and, wishing to store up his wealth in safety, he built a chamber of stone, of which one of the walls adjoined the outside of the palace. But the builder, having intentions of the treasure, hit on the following contrivance. He fitted one of the stones so that it could be easily moved by two men, or even one.

" When the chamber was finished, the king laid up his treasure in it. But in course of time, the builder, finding his end approaching, called his sons to him (for he had two), and that they might have abundant patrimony, described to them how he had contrived when building the king's treasury; and, having given them clear directions how to remove the stone, he gave them also its dimensions, saying that if they only observed his instructions they might become ' stewards of the king's treasure.'

" With this he died; and the sons were not long in applying themselves to the work. They visited the palace ·by night, and having found the stone, easily removed it and carried off a great quantity of treasure.

" When the king happened to open his chamber next, he was amazed to find the coffers deficient in treasure; but he was not able to accuse anyone, as the seals were unbroken, and the chamber well secured. So, finding on opening the room two or three times that the treasures each time were diminished— for the thieves did not cease plundering—he adopted the following plan. He ordered traps to be made, and placed them round the coffers in which the treasures lay. So when the thieves came as before, and one of them had entered, as soon as he went near a coffer he was straightway caught in a trap.

" Perceiving, therefore, his predicament, he called out at once to his brother, told him what had happened, and bade him enter as quick as possible and cut off his head, lest, if he were seen and recognised, he should ruin him also. The other thought that he spoke well, and did as he was advised; then having fitted the stone, he returned home, taking with him his brother's head.

" When day came the king entered the chamber, and was astonished to see the headless body of the thief within the trap, but the chamber secure, and without any means of exit or entrance. In this perplexity he contrived an expedient. He hung up the body of the thief from the wall, and having placed sentinels there, he ordered them to seize and bring before him whomsoever they should see weeping, or expressed commiseration at the spectacle.

" Now the mother was greatly grieved at the body being suspended, and, coming to words with her surviving son, commanded him, by any means he could, to contrive how he might take down and carry off the corpse of his brother. Should he neglect to do so, she threatened to go to the king and inform him that her son was the thief.

" When his mother treated him so harshly, and when with many entreaties he was unable to persuade her, he formed a scheme.

" He got some asses, which he loaded with skins full of wine, and then began to drive them along. But when he drew near the sentinels that guarded the suspended body, he pulled out two or three necks of the skins that hung down, and loosened them; and as soon as the wine began to run out, he beat his head and stood crying aloud, as if uncertain to which of the asses he should turn first.

" Now the sentinels, when they saw wine flowing in abundance, ran into the road, with vessels in their hands, and caught the liquor that was being spilt, thinking it all their own gain. But the fellow feigned to be angry, and railed bitterly against them all. However, as the sentinels soothed him, he at length became pacified, and consented to forego his anger; and at length drove his asses to the side of the road, and set them to rights again. More talk passed, and on one of the sentinels joking with him, and moving him to laughter, he gave them another of his skins; and they, just as they were, lay down and fell to drinking, and joining him to their party, invited him to stay and drink with them.

" He, if you please, was persuaded, and remained with them; and as they treated him kindly during the drinking, he gave them another of the skins; and the sentinels, having taken copious draughts, became exceedingly drunk, and being overpowered by the wine, fell asleep on the spot where they had been drinking. But he, as the night was far advanced, took down his brother's body, and, by way of insult, shaved the right cheeks of all the sentinels; then, having laid the corpse on the asses, he drove home, having performed his mother's injunctions.

" The king, when he was informed that the body of the thief had been stolen, was exceedingly indignant, and, resolving by any means to find out the contriver of this artifice, had recourse to a new device.

" He issued a proclamation, inviting suitors for his daughter's hand, and adding that each, to guide her in her choice, must in private confide to her what he had done in his life most clever and most wicked. And he agreed with her that whosoever should tell her the facts relating to the thief, him she was to seize, and not suffer to escape.

" The daughter did what her father commanded; but the thief, finding out for what purpose this trap was laid, acted as you shall hear.

" He cut off the arm of a fresh corpse at the shoulder, took it with him under his cloak, and presented his name as suitor for the king's daughter. Being admitted to her presence, he was asked the same question as the rest; and replied very readily that he had done the most wicked thing when he cut off the head of his brother, who was caught in a trap in the king's treasury; and the most clever thing when, having made the sentinels drunk, he took away the corpse of his brother that was hung up.

" The king's daughter, on hearing this, endeavoured to seize him. But the thief (for it was dusk) held out to her the dead man's arm, and she seized it and held it fast, imagining that she had got hold of the man's own arm. Then the thief, having let it go, made his escape through the door.

" When this also was reported to the king, he was astonished at the shrewdness and daring of the man; and at last, sending through all the cities, he caused a proclamation to be made, offering a free pardon, and promising great reward to the man, if he would discover himself. The thief, relying on this promise, went to the king's palace, and Rhampsinitus greatly admired him and gave him his daughter in marriage, accounting him the most knowing of all men; for that the Egyptians are superior to all others, and he was the best of the Egyptians."

As a pendant to this story from Herodotus, let us give an account of another treasure-robber, of later date. It is told by Camerarius, an old German essayist, who, in his turn, received it from Sabellicus.

A certain Cretan, called Stamat, happening to be in Venice when the treasures of that city were shown to the Duke of Ferrara, marched about so boldly with the crowd that he was taken for one of the Duke's body-servants; and whilst gazing his fill on the wealth displayed, instead of contenting himself with the sight, resolved to commit some notable piece of thievery.

"A FELLOW WAS QUIETLY DIPPING HIS HAND INTO THIS" (p. 250).

St. Mark's Church, gilded with pure gold very near all over, is built round the base, within and without, of pieces or tablets of marble. This Grecian thief, being marvellous cunning and nimble, devised to take out finely, by night, one of the marble tablets against that part of the church where the altar stands, called the "Children's Altar," and thereby to make himself an entrance to the treasure; and having laboured a night, because the wall could not in that time be wrought through, laid the stone handsomely back in its place, and fitted it so well that no man could perceive any show of opening. As for the small stones and rubbish that he took out of the wall, he carried it all away so clearly, and before day, that he was never discovered.

Having thus worked many nights, he got at length to the treasure, and began to carry away much riches of divers kinds. (I myself—says our author —did once see this treasure, being admitted amongst the train of Frederick, the Emperor. And besides an infinite number of precious stones set in work, I saw there twelve crowns, and as many breastplates, of gold, set with innumerable gems, whose brightness would have dazzled the eyes both of the body and the mind; moreover, pots of gold, agate, and other stones of price, also shrines, candlesticks, and many other implements for altars, which were not only of pure gold, but also garnished with so many stones of worth that the gold was nothing in comparison. I speak not of the unicorn's horn, which is infinitely estimated, nor of the Duke's crown, nor of the other pieces of exquisite work which this Greek carried away at leisure.) However, as is said, theft is never long hidden; and in this case the thief betrayed himself.

He had a friend at Venice, a gentleman of the same Isle of Candia, called Zacharias Grio, an honest man and of a good conscience. Stamat one day took him aside near the altar, and drawing a promise from him to keep the secret, told him from beginning to end all the tale of thievery, and then took him to his house. There he shows Grio all the inestimable riches that had been filched from the church.

Grio, being virtuous and conscionable, stood amazed at the sight, and quaked so at the horror of the sacrilege, that he began to reel, and could no longer stand. Whereupon, as they say, Stamat, like a desperate villain, was about to have killed him in the place. But Grio, divining his intention, stayed the blow by saying that his extreme joy at the prospect of such wealth had put him beside himself; and Stamat, content with this excuse, let him alone.

Grio, before they parted, received as a gift from Stamat a precious stone— the same which is now worn in the front of the Duke's crown. So making as if he had some weighty matter to despatch, forth Grio goes from the house, and hies him to the palace, where, having obtained access to the Duke, he revealed all the matter, adding that they had best look sharp, or Stamat might rouse himself, look about him, shift lodging, or save himself in some other way with the best of his booty. To give the more credit to his words, he drew forth from his bosom the precious stone that Stamat had given him.

This was no sooner seen than some men were sent off with all speed to the house, who laid hold of Stamat, and all that he had stolen, amounting to the value of two millions of gold. So he was hanged between two pillars; and the informer had a yearly pension for life out of the public treasury.

But Camerarius has other and better stories of thievery, and among them that of the "Duke's Cap," the worth of which he estimates at over two hundred thousand crowns. The tale he gives of this treasure is that it was brought to Venice by "four rich merchants; of whom two, thinking it unfit the treasure should have so many owners, resolved to poison the other pair; which pair

(not knowing the determination of their companions) proposed the same likewise on their part; so that they were poisoned all four, and died without heirs.
Whereupon the Seignory of Venice seized on all the wealth which they had
left; and this (they say) is signified by the four images of porphyry that stand
by the great gate of the common palace, embracing one another."

Here is another tale on the same authority.

King Francis the First of France was attending mass one day in Nôtre
Dame.   His Majesty, to say the truth, was not following the service very
closely, for it was a hot day.   He yawned and stretched out a leg, and winked
and stretched out an arm, and sighed and closed his eyes and dozed.   This
process he had repeated a dozen times with such variations as occurred to him,
when, happening to glance across at the spot where John, Cardinal of Lorraine,
was standing amid a small group of courtiers, His Majesty began to stare, and
then to be immensely interested and tickled.

John, Cardinal of Lorraine, wore a great pouch hanging from his belt.   And
into this a fellow at his side was quietly dipping his hand.   The man was
dressed like a courtier, and the king did not for an instant imagine him to be
any other.   Somebody was playing a trick on the Cardinal, and Francis laughed
softly to himself as he watched the success of it.

Suddenly the thief, stealing a glance round, saw the king's eyes fixed on
him, and a broad smile overspreading the royal countenance.

He was a man of contrivance.   In an instant he had his finger on lip and
nodded to the king to be silent.   His Majesty, on the other hand, was not a
man to spoil sport.   He nodded back, looked at the unconscious face of the
Cardinal, and chuckled.   One by one, the contents of the rich pouch were
transferred to the thief's pocket.

" A quaint fellow, that," thought the king; " I must make his acquaintance.
'Tis curious I don't remember his face."

The jest was played out; the yawning and stretching began again and
continued till the service was at an end.   Meanwhile, the thief had slipped away.

As the royal train passed out of the cathedral doors, it was besieged by
the usual crowd of beggars demanding "largess."

King Francis had a bright idea: he turned to the Cardinal beside him.

" Cousin, 'tis most unfortunate.   I have left my purse at home, and must
borrow of you, if you will lend."

The Cardinal dived his hand into his pouch.   It was empty.

" I have been robbed!"

The king began to laugh consumedly, and at length told the Cardinal that
one of the courtiers had been playing a trick on him.

" I am an accomplice," said he, " for I looked on all the while that the
fellow was at work."

" Oh!" said the Cardinal; " who was it, then?"

This was more than the king could tell.   He looked around.

"I cannot see him anywhere," said he.

"But you know his name."

"Indeed, I do not."

"My liege, it begins to strike me that a thief has been making a companion of you."

And so it proved.

A trick even cooler was once played on the Emperor Charles V., which Camerarius shall be left to tell:—

"The Emperor upon a day commanded a remove of his furniture. And while every man was busied in putting up his stuff, there entered a good fellow into the hall where the Emperor then was, being meanly accompanied, and ready to take horse. The thief, having made a great reverence, presently went about taking down the hangings, making great bustle and haste, as if he had much business to do; and though it was not his profession to set up and take down hangings, yet he went about it so nimbly that when he whose charge it was to take them down came to do it, he found that somebody had already eased him of this labour, and (which was worse) of carrying them away."

"But the boldness of an Italian thief was as great," says our author, "who played his part at Rome in the time of Pope Paul the Third. A certain Cardinal having made a great feast in his house, and the silver vessels being locked up in a trunk that stood in a chamber next to the hall where the feast had been, whilst many were sitting and walking in this chamber waiting for their master, there came a man in with a torch carried before him, bearing the countenance of the steward, and having a jacket on, who prayed those that sat on the trunk to rise up from it, as he was to use the same. Whereupon, the company having risen up, he made it to be lifted by certain porters that followed him in, and went clear away with it; and this was done while the steward and all the servants of the house were at supper."

History repeats herself; and the two preceding achievements were emulated, if not surpassed, a few years ago in the Dublin Law Courts, where one day, before the judge and barristers assembled, during the hearing of a case, a brisk fellow trotted in with a ladder, took down the big clock, handed it to a couple of white-aproned accomplices, and trotted out again with his spoil, under the very eyes of avenging justice!

But perhaps the king of the profession which we are now considering was a certain Captain Hanam, whose exploits are recorded in a little book that lately fell into our hands, entitled "The English Villain, or the Grand Thief," published at London, and printed for John Andrews at the "White Lion" in the Old Bailey.

This Captain Hanam is remarkable, however, rather for the mass than the quality of his rogueries, though if to fly at high game be the test of greatness, he has few rivals. Most of the crowned heads of Europe could boast of his patronage, as a few headings to the chapters of his biography will sufficiently prove. Here is a selection :—

> "*How Hanam passed beyond sea ; and how he first robbed the King of Denmark, and after passed into Sweden.*"
>
> "*How Hanam robbed the Queen of Sweden of all her rich jewels, with other great sums of money, to the value of five thousand pounds.*"
>
> "*How Hanam got into France, and then robbed the King of France of several great sums of money.*"
>
> "*How Hanam after this departed out of France into the Low Countries, and how he committed several robberies there : among others, how he robbed the King of Scots at the Hague in Holland.*"
>
> "*How Hanam came into England again ; and how he made an attempt to have robbed his Highness's Treasury of the Exchequer.*"
>
> "*How Hanam went to Rome, and there committed more robberies ; especially how he robbed the late Queen of Sweden in her nunnery,*" &c.

The man was also no mean prison-breaker, having escaped once from the prison at Stockholm, a dozen times in Holland, once from Newgate, where he lay under sentence of death; which latter escape is told by his biographer with quaint brevity :—

"Hanam being condemned to die, and the day of execution drawing near, he resolved to make one desperate attempt for to make an escape, quickly effected, to the wonder of all that beheld the same, the like having never been seen or done before; and this, his design, he made on little Grimes, formerly a prisoner in the same place, who had been condemned for having two wives, but was afterwards reprieved, and at the same time executed the place of an under-clerk in Newgate Prison. Now this Grimes, lying in the same room with Hanam, was made privy to his escape, which he willingly consented to, and so suffered him to take off the irons with which he was fettered, which (as the said little Grimes confessed before the Honourable Bench) he did use to do with ease every night, and put them on again in the morning. Now, Hanam, having taken off his iron chains, presently breaks open three or four great doors, and breaks asunder all the great chains and iron bars, and so escapes, leaving little Grimes to answer for his treachery, who afterwards, *contrary to his own expectation*, was hanged at Tyburn for the said fact."

Poor little Grimes!—so unkindly hanged "contrary to his own expectation!" But perhaps the charm of the captain's presence had been too much for him —a charm that the biographer frankly recognises. "The subject of my discourse," says he, "was a most proper, complete man for person; but for thieving, and picking of bolts and bars, and other such-like exploits, a *nonpareil.*"

He was recaptured, and again escaped when within sight of Newgate doors; was caught after a short but merry fling on the Continent, and at length clapped, strongly ironed, into the strongest cell in Newgate, "where multitudes daily flocked to see him, expecting his execution; which, *to give the gallows and hangman their due*" (sweet sarcasm!) "was performed in Smithfield on the

17th day of the present month. You have thus heard a brief but true account of the rude life and notable villanies committed by this wretched and unparalleled villain, with his desperate but deserved shameful death; the like to whom hath not been, nor, I hope, never will be again—

"Thus Hanam's dead and
    gone,
And bids the world ' adieu !'
And for his thefts and
    villanies
At the gallows had his
    due."

He was a bad, bad man; but probably he was better than the above verse after all.

Something more than a hundred years ago, a good likely sort of man stepped into a baker's shop in Arundel Street by the Strand, London, and addressed the baker, who stood behind his counter—

"You have lodgings to let, as I see by your card."

"I have."

"Good, clean lodgings ?"

"HE CONFIDED A SECRET TO THE BAKER" (p. 254).

"Not over-big, but clean as a pin, however."

"You are from Oxfordshire, I can tell it by your speech."

"To be sure I am," said the baker.

"What part ?"

"Banbury."

"Why, I come from Banbury too !"

"It's a very good place to come from, then."

"Aye—a very good town. How long since you left it ?"

"Near upon twenty years."

"A long time—a long time," mused the stranger, and then asked suddenly, 'I suppose you never heard of a Mr. Wickham, of those parts ?"

"The rich Mr. Wickham ? Why, of course !"

"Well—well," murmured the stranger with some show of confusion, "let's say passably rich—no more. Do you know him by sight?"

"Never saw him in my life; but I've heard tell of him often enough—a good man."

"Come, come!" put in the stranger, more confused than ever, "let's say passably good. You see I'm a modest man——"

"Hey?"

"And as I happen to *be* Mr. Wickham——"

"Bless my soul!" cried the baker; "and you mean to say you want——?"

"Lodgings; yes."

"But our small rooms would never suit the likes of you, sir."

"Hush!" The stranger looked mysteriously round the shop, and in a low voice confided a secret to the baker. "My servants," he said—"for doubtless you wonder at my coming thus unattended—are in a place where I can easily find them if I want to; but just now I have to be very careful against being known, for the fact is, I have come up to London on rather a delicate business, which is to arrest a certain merchant in Cheapside who owes me a large sum of money, and who, I have reason to believe, is going to break. So I must remain *incognito* for fear of missing my stroke. Therefore be so good as to mention my name to nobody."

The baker was thoroughly satisfied with this story. The family were called up that Mr. Wickham might see them, and the baker and his new lodger—for the lodgings were taken by this time—drank a glass together to their friends at Banbury and smoked a friendly pipe before retiring to rest.

Now so far this is but the story of an ordinary swindle. For of course the lodger was not Mr. Wickham. As a matter of fact, he had been a footman in that gentleman's family for some years, and thus had acquired the information which enabled him to impose on the unfortunate baker. But the distinction of this particular swindle lies, not in its originality, but rather in the earnestness with which it was carried through to the bitter end—an earnestness, a sincerity of acting that refused to relinquish the comedy when it was a comedy no longer, an artistic enthusiasm (call it what you will) that by sheer perseverance in absurdity gave absurdity the value of tragedy, and clothed a rather shabby trick with the glories of a lofty action.

The day after the lodgings were taken, "Mr. Wickham" (as we will now call him) went abroad to concert measures with a confederate of his own stamp, to play his little game out. It was agreed between them that the confederate should pass for Mr. Wickham's lackey, and come privately, from time to time, to see his master and wait upon him.

That same night the lackey arrived at the baker's; and Mr. Wickham, dressing before the glass, flew into a mighty rage with him for neglecting his cravats—he wore a dirty one at the time—and letting him be without money, linen, or any other conveniences, through a stupid neglect to carry his master's box to the waggon in due time, which would cause a delay of three days.

This was said aloud while the baker was in the next room, and on purpose that he might hear it. And what does this poor deluded baker, but run to his wardrobe, carry to Mr. Wickham the best linen in the house, beg him to wear it, and laying down fifty guineas on the table, entreat his lodger to accept this small loan also!

Mr. Wickham is greatly astonished at these proofs of confidence and generosity, and at first refuses to accept the loan; but after much ado, gives way to the baker's importunity. Not only does he pocket the money, but he lays it out to the best advantage. He purchases a suit of livery of the same colour as the true Mr. Wickham's, gives it to another pretended footman, and brings to his lodging a box of goods as coming from the Banbury waggon.

The baker, always fully convinced that he has to do with Mr. Wickham, and consequently with one of the richest and best-hearted men in England, made it more and more of his business to give his lodger fresh marks of his deep respect and affection. To be short, Wickham made a shift to get of him a hundred and fifty guineas besides the original fifty, for all of which he gave his I O U.

Now mark the event.

Three weeks after the beginning of this adventure, as the rogue was at a tavern, he was seized with a violent headache, a burning fever, and great pains in all parts of his body.

As soon as he found himself ill, he posted home to his lodgings and took to his bed. The illness grew more and more serious. Throughout he was waited on by one of his pretended footmen, and assisted in everything by the kind-hearted baker, who advanced whatever money was wanted, and passed his word to the doctors, apothecaries, and everybody else. Meanwhile Wickham's condition became desperate.

On the fifth day the doctors gave him over.

The poor baker, distracted at his patron's melancholy condition, thought himself bound to break the news, and informed the sick man, with every expression of regret, what the physicians thought of his case.

Wickham received the news like a good Christian. Never was calmer resignation to the will of God; never was greater zeal or piety, or deeper consciousness of unworthiness tempered by hope. He prepared himself for death; desired that a clergyman might be sent for; and received the Sacrament that same day.

On the morrow the distemper had increased, and life was but a question of hours. The swindler accepted the inevitable, and braced himself up to play the last act out. To be sure it was ending very differently from what he anticipated, but he was ready. Seriously, there is a touch of the heroic in this last act.

He sent for the baker, and told him that it was not enough to have taken care of his soul, he ought also to set his worldly affairs in order, and wished to make his will while he was yet sound in mind. A scrivener was therefore immediately summoned, and the will drawn up and signed in due form before several witnesses. Wickham by this disposed of all his estate, real and personal, jewels, coaches, teams, racehorses of such-and-such colours, packs of hounds, ready money, &c., and a house with all appurtenances and dependencies, to the baker; almost all his linen to his wife; five hundred guineas to their eldest son; eight hundred guineas to the four daughters; two hundred to the parson that had comforted him in his sickness; two hundred to each of the doctors, and one hundred to the apothecary; fifty guineas and mourning to each of his footmen; fifty to embalm him; fifty for his coffin; two hundred to hang the house with mourning, and to defray the rest of the charges of his interment; a hundred guineas for gloves, hat-bands, scarfs, and gold rings; such a diamond to such a friend, and such an emerald to another. Nothing was ever more noble or more generous.

This done, Wickham called the baker to him, loaded him and all his family with benedictions, and told him that after his decease he had nothing to do but to go to the lawyer mentioned in his will, who was acquainted with all his affairs, and would give him full instructions how to proceed.

The end came soon after. It came with a series of strong convulsions that left him just able to rise upon his elbow. He feebly wrung the hand of the baker, and, looking round with a slow smile upon the mourners around his bed, sank back gently on the pillows. The baker bent over him. He was dead. But the smile yet lingered on his face.

Well, at first the baker can think of nothing but interring his benefactor with all pomp and ceremonial, according to the will. He hangs all the stair-cases, all the rooms, the shop, the entry, with mourning sables; he gives orders to jewellers, tailors, undertakers; he sends for an embalmer. In a word, he omits nothing that the deceased has ordered, or would have wished.

Wickham was not to be interred till the fourth day after his death, and by the second evening all was ready. The baker, having got this hurry off his hands, had now time to look for the lawyer before he laid him in the ground. After having put the body into a rich coffin, covered with velvet and plates of silver, and settled everything else, he began to consider that it would not be improper to reimburse himself as soon as possible, and to take possession of his new estate. He therefore went to the lawyer's rooms, gained admittance, and announced Mr. Wickham's decease.

"Bless my heart and soul!" cried the lawyer; "why, 'twas only yesterday I had a letter from him, from Banbury!"

*   *   *   *   *   *   *

We will draw the curtain over the rest of this interview. Poor, confiding baker! He staggered out into the street and home in a kind of mental fog.

The sight of the coffin, silver-plated, pompous, elaborate, aroused him. He seized a hammer.

Twenty minutes after, the signs of mourning were a dismal wreck, and the poor knave lay on the boards, naked.

"THE SIGNS OF MOURNING WERE A DISMAL WRECK."

But why continue? The coffin was sold for a third of its value. The tradesmen employed for the burial took compassion and had their goods back again, though not without some loss to the baker. A hole was dug in a corner of St. Clement's Church-yard, and the body tumbled into it with the scantiest ceremony. As for the baker, he was recompensed to some extent by the generosity of the true Mr. Wickham, for whose sake he had been so open-hearted and open-handed. But he ceased to take lodgers without references.

THE TALE OF AN AVALANCHE.

BEING THE NARRATIVE OF AN ACCIDENT ON THE HAUT-DE-CRY. FEBRUARY 28TH, 1864. BY PHILIP C. GOSSET.

HAS often occurred to me, when walking on hard snow in winter, that a mountain ascent at that period of the year might be made with much less difficulty and trouble than in summer. My friend B. was familiar with mountains in winter; he had been up the Æggischhorn and Riederhorn in December, 1863. Easy as these points may be to reach in summer, in winter, if the snow is not hard, the question is very different. On February 28, 1864, we left Sion with Bennen to mount the Haut-de-Cry. We started at 2.15 a.m. in a light carriage that brought us to the village of Ardon, distant six miles. We there met three men that were to accompany us as local guides or porters, Jean Joseph Nance, Frederic Rebot, who acted as my personal guide, and Auguste Bevarde. We at once began to ascend on the right bank of the Lyzerne.

The night was splendid, the sky cloudless, and the moon shining so as to make walking easy without the use of a lantern. For about half an hour we went up through the vineyards by a rather steep path, and then entered the valley of the Lyzerne, about 700 feet above the torrent. We here found a remarkably good path, gradually rising and leading towards the Col de Chéville. Having followed this path for about three hours, we struck off to the left, and began zigzagging up the mountain-side through a pine-forest. We had passed what may be called the snow-line, in winter, a little above 2,000 feet.

We had not ascended for more than a quarter of an hour in this pine-forest before the snow got very deep and very soft. We had to change leader every five or six minutes, and even thus our progress was remarkably slow. We saw clearly that, should the snow be as soft above the fir region, we should have to give up the ascent. At 7 a.m. we reached a châlet, and stopped for about twenty minutes to rest and look at the sunrise on the Diablerets. On observing an aneroid, which we had brought with us, we found that we were at the height of about 7,000 feet; the temperature was 1° C.

The Haut-de-Cry has four arêtes: the first running towards the west, the second south-east, the third east, and the fourth north-east. We were between the two last-named arêtes. Our plan was to go up between them to the foot of the peak, and mount it by the arête running north-east. As we had expected, the snow was in much better state when once we were above the woods. For some time we advanced pretty rapidly. The peak was glistening before us, and the idea of success put us in high spirits.

Our good fortune did not last long. We soon came to snow frozen on the surface, and capable of bearing for a few steps and then giving way. But this was nothing compared to the trouble of pulling up through the pine-wood, so instead of making us grumble it only excited our hilarity. Bennen was in a particularly good humour, and laughed loudly at our combined efforts to get out of the holes we every now and then made in the snow. Judging from appearances, the snow-field over which we were walking covered a gradually rising Alp. We made a second observation with our aneroid, and found, rather to our astonishment and dismay, that we had only risen 1,000 feet in the last three hours. It was 10 o'clock; we were at the height of about 8,000 feet; temperature, 1° 5' C.

During the last half-hour we had found a little hard snow, so we had all hope of success. Thinking we might advance better on the arête, we took to it, and rose along it for some time. It soon became cut up by rocks, so we took to the snow again. It turned out to be here hard-frozen, so that we reached the real foot of the peak without the slightest difficulty. It was decidedly steeper than I had expected it would be, judging from the valley of the Rhone. Bennen looked at it with decided pleasure; having completed his survey, he proposed to take the eastern arête, as in doing so we should gain at least two hours.

Rebot had been over this last-named arête in summer, and was of Bennen's opinion. Two or three of the party did not like the idea much, so there was a discussion on the probable advantages and disadvantages of the north-east and east arêtes. We were losing time; so Bennen cut matters short by saying, "Ich will der Erste über die arête!" Thus saying he made for the east arête; it looked very narrow, and, what was worse, it was considerably cut up by high rocks, the intervals between the teeth of the arête being filled up with snow. To gain this arête, we had to go up a steep snow-field, about 800 feet high, as well as I remember. It was about 150 feet broad at the top, and 400 or 500 at the bottom. It was a sort of couloir on a large scale.

During the ascent we sank about one foot deep at every step. Bennen did not seem to like the look of the snow very much. He asked the local guides whether avalanches ever came down this couloir, to which they answered that our position was perfectly safe. We had mounted on the northern side of the couloir, and having arrived at 150 feet from the top, we began crossing it on a horizontal curve, so as to gain the east arête. The inflexion or dip of the couloir was slight, not above 25 feet, the inclination near 35°.

We were walking in the following order: Bevard, Nance, Bennen, myself, B. and Rebot. Having crossed over about three-quarters of the breadth of the couloir, the two leading men suddenly sank considerably above their waists. Bennen tightened the rope. The snow was too deep to think of getting out of the hole they had made, so they advanced one or two steps, dividing the snow with their bodies. Bennen turned round and told us that he was afraid of starting an avalanche; we asked whether it would not be better to return and cross the couloir higher up. To this the three Ardon men opposed themselves; they mistook the proposed precaution for fear, and the two leading men continued their work.

After three or four steps gained in the aforesaid manner, the snow became hard again. Bennen had not moved—he was evidently undecided what he should do; as soon, however, as he saw hard snow again, he advanced and

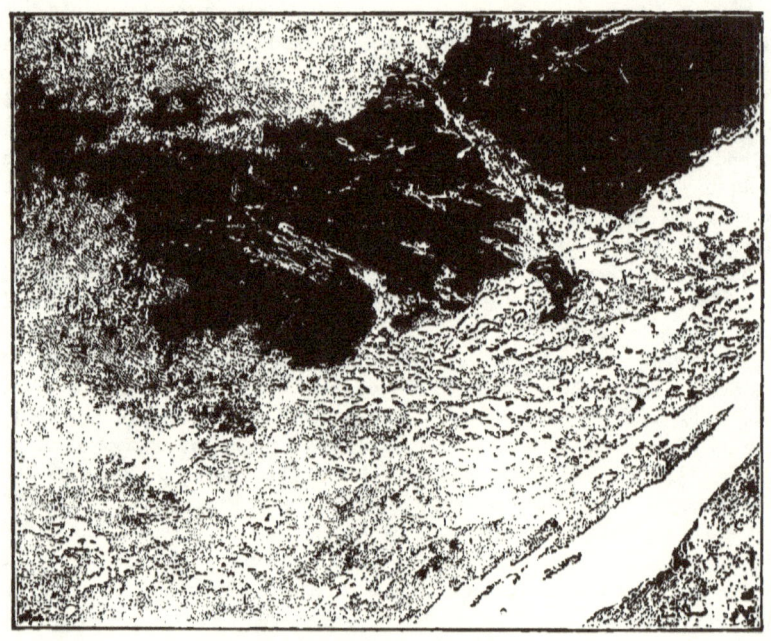

crossed parallel to, but above, the furrow the Ardon men had made. Strange to say, the snow supported him.

While he was passing I observed that the leader, Bevard, had ten or twelve feet of rope coiled round his shoulder. I, of course, at once told him to uncoil it and get on the arête, from which he was not more than fifteen feet distant. Bennen then told me to follow. I tried his steps, but sank up to my waist in the very first. So I went through the furrows, holding my elbows close to my body, so as not to touch the sides. This furrow was about twelve feet long, and as the snow was good on the other side, we had all come to the false conclusion that the snow was accidentally softer there than elsewhere.

Bennen advanced; he had made but a few steps when we heard a deep, cutting sound. The snow-field split in two about fourteen or fifteen feet above us. The cleft was at first quite narrow, not more than an inch broad.

An awful silence ensued; it lasted but a few seconds, and then it was broken by Bennen's voice, " Wir sind alle verloren ! " (*We are all lost !*) His words were slow and solemn, and those who knew him felt what they really meant when spoken by such a man as Bennen. They were his last words.

I drove my alpenstock into the snow, and brought the weight of my body to bear on it. I then waited.

It was an awful moment of suspense. I turned my head towards Bennen to see whether he had done the same thing. To my astonishment I saw him turn round, face the valley, and stretch out both arms. The ground on which we stood began to move slowly, and I felt the utter uselessness of any alpenstock. I soon sank up to my shoulders and began descending backwards.

From this moment I saw nothing of what had happened to the rest of the party. With a good deal of trouble I succeeded in turning round. The speed of the avalanche increased rapidly, and before long I was covered up with snow. I was suffocating when I suddenly came to the surface again. I was on a wave of the avalanche, and saw it before me as I was carried down.

It was the most awful sight I ever saw. The head of the avalanche was already at the spot where we had made our last halt. The head alone was preceded by a thick cloud of snow-dust; the rest of the avalanche was clear. Around me I heard the horrid hissing of the snow, and far before me the thundering of the foremost part of the avalanche.

To prevent myself sinking again, I made use of my arms much in the same way as when swimming in a standing position. At last I noticed that I was moving slower; then I saw the pieces of snow in front of me stop at some yards' distance; then the snow straight before me stopped, and I heard on a large scale the same creaking sound that is produced when a heavy cart passes over frozen snow in winter. I felt that I also had stopped, and instantly threw up both arms to protect my head in case I should again be covered up. I had stopped, but the snow behind me was still in motion; its pressure on my body was so strong, that I thought I should be crushed to death. This tremendous pressure lasted but a short time; I was covered up by snow coming from behind me.

My first impulse was to try and uncover my head—but this I could not do; the avalanche had frozen by pressure the moment it stopped, and I was frozen in. Whilst trying vainly to move my arms, I suddenly became aware that the hands as far as the wrist had the faculty of motion. The conclusion was easy, they must be above the snow. I set to work as well as I could; it was time, for I could not have held out much longer.

At last I saw a faint glimmer of light. The crust above my head was getting thinner, but I could not reach it any more with my hands; the idea struck me that I might pierce it with my breath. After several efforts I succeeded in doing so, and felt suddenly a rush of air towards my mouth. I saw the sky again through a little round hole.

A dead silence reigned around me; I was so surprised to be still alive, and so persuaded at the first moment that none of my fellow-sufferers had survived, that I did not even think of shouting for them. I then made vain efforts to extricate my arms, but found it impossible; the most I could do was to join the ends of my fingers, but they could not reach the snow any longer.

After a few minutes I heard a man shouting; what a relief it was to know that I was not the sole survivor! to know that perhaps he was not frozen in and could come to my assistance! I answered; the voice approached, but seemed uncertain where to go, and yet it was now quite near.

A sudden exclamation of surprise! Rebot had seen my hands.

He cleared my head in an instant, and was about to try and cut me out completely, when I saw a foot above the snow, and so near to me that I could touch it with my arms, although they were not quite free yet. I at once tried to move the foot; it was my poor friend's.

A pang of agony shot through me as I saw that the foot did not move. Poor B. had lost sensation, and was perhaps already dead. Rebot did his best; after some time he wished me to help him, so he freed my arms a little more so that I could make use of them. I could do but little, for Rebot had torn the axe from my shoulder as soon as he had cleared my head (I generally carry an axe separate from my alpenstock—the blade tied to the belt, and the handle attached to the left shoulder).

Before coming to me, Rebot had helped Nance out of the snow; he was lying nearly horizontally, and was not much covered over. Nance found Bevard, who was upright in the snow, but covered up to the head. After about twenty minutes the two last-named guides came up. I was at length taken out; the snow had to be cut·with the axe down to my feet before I could be pulled out.

A few minutes after 1 o'clock p.m., we came to my poor friend's face. . . . I wished the body to be taken out completely, but nothing could induce the three guides to work any longer, from the moment they saw that it was too late to save him. I acknowledge that they were nearly as incapable of doing anything as I was.

When I was taken out of the snow, the cord had to be cut. We tried the end going towards Bennen, but could not move it; it went nearly straight down, and showed us that there was the grave of the bravest guide the Valais ever had, and ever will have. The cold had done its work on us; we could stand it no longer, and began the descent. We followed the frozen avalanche for about twenty-five minutes, that being the easiest way of progressing, and then took the track we had made in the morning. In five hours we reached Ardon.

[For leave to insert Mr. Gosset's narrative, our thanks are due to the Editor of the "Alpine Journal," and the members of the Alpine Club.]

TALES OF THE DUEL.

E read," says an ancient writer, "that in the family of Limino, at Padua, there were once two brothers, who being on a summer's day in the country, went abroad after supper, talking together of many things. As they were standing and gazing upon the stars that twinkled in the sky, one of them began in merriment to say to the other, 'Would I had as many oxen as I see stars in yonder firmament!' The other answers him presently, 'And would I had a pasture as wide as the firmament!' And therewith turning to his brother, saith unto him, 'Where wouldst thou feed thy oxen?' 'Marry, in thy pasture,' quoth his brother. 'But how if I would not let thee?' saith the other. 'I would,' quoth the first, 'whether thou wouldst or not.' 'What,' replied the second, 'in spite of my teeth?' 'Yes,' said he, 'whatever thou couldst do to the contrary.' Hereupon their sport turns to outrageous words, and at last to fury, the one still offering to be louder than the other, that in the end they drew their swords and fell to it so hotly, that in a turn of the hand they ran one another through the body, so that the one fell one way and the other another way, both weltering in their blood. The people of the house, hearing the bustle, ran towards them, but came too late, and, carrying them into the house, they both soon after gave up the ghost."

It would be hard to beat the absurdity of the above, and the *reductio ad absurdum*, which is among the best weapons in the logical armoury, is peculiarly effective in the discussion of the duello, a practice that must be based solely on a fallacy. For if it be unreasonable to suppose that right dwells on the side that is handier with incisive or perforating instruments, it is almost as illogical to hold that when a man's nose has been pulled he gets a fair satisfaction out of an encounter in which aggrieved and aggressor equally stake their lives. The equation may be balanced if a nose be pulled on each side, but this is rare.

As far as logic goes, the absurdity of the above anecdote is equalled by the affair between Sir H. Bellasis and Mr. Thomas Porter, which took place in Covent Garden in 1667, and is thus related by the gossipy Samuel Pepys, who takes occasion to term it "a kind of emblem of the general complexion of the whole kingdom."

"The two," says he, "dined yesterday at Sir Robert Carr's, where it seems people do drink high, all that come. It happened that these two, the greatest friends in the world, were talking together, and Sir H. Bellasis talked a little louder than ordinary to Tom Porter, giving him some advice. Some of the company standing by said, 'What, are they quarrelling, that they talk so high?' Sir H. Bellasis, hearing it, said, 'No, I would have you know I never quarrel, but I strike; take that as a rule of mine.'—'How?' said Tom Porter, 'Strike? I would I could see the man in England that durst give me a blow.' With that Sir H. Bellasis did give him a box on the ear, and so they were going out to fight, but were hindered. And by-and-by Tom Porter went out, and meeting Dryden, the poet, told him of the business, and that he was resolved to fight Sir H. Bellasis presently, for he knew, if he did not, they would be friends to-morrow, and then the blow would rest upon him; and he desired Dryden to let him have his boy to bring him notice which way Sir H. Bellasis goes. By-and-by he is informed that Sir H. Bellasis' coach was coming; so Tom Porter went down out of the coffee-room, where he stayed for the tidings, and stopped the coach, and bade Sir H. Bellasis come out. 'Why,' said Sir H. Bellasis, 'you will not hurt me coming out, will you?' 'No,' says Tom Porter.

"So out he went, and both drew. And Sir H. Bellasis having drawn and flung away the scabbard, Tom Porter asked him whether he was ready. The other answered he was; and they fought, some of their acquaintances by. They wounded one another; and Sir H. Bellasis so much that it is feared he will die. And finding himself severely wounded, he called to Tom Porter and kissed him, and bade him shift for himself, 'for,' says he, 'Tom, thou hast hurt me; but I will make shift to stand on my legs till thou mayest withdraw, and the world not take notice of thee, for I would not have thee troubled for what thou hast done.' And so whether he did fly or not I cannot tell; but Tom Porter showed Sir H. Bellasis that he was wounded too, and they are both ill, but Sir H. Bellasis to the life. And this is fine example! And Sir H. Bellasis a Parliament man too! And both of them extraordinary friends!"

The upshot was that Bellasis lingered a few days and then died. Says Pepys, in noticing his death, "It is pretty to see how the world talks of them as a couple of fools, that killed one another out of love."

"A Parliament man too!", says Pepys. But in France and England, at any rate, politics seem to have been accountable for as many duels as love. Here is an account, and in its way an amusing one, of an encounter about a century later than the one just narrated. It was celebrated enough at the time, the combatants being both well-known men—Earl Talbot and John Wilkes. The dispute arose out of certain expressions injurious to the earl in the 12th number of the *North Briton* (Wilkes' famous newspaper), on the 21st of August, 1762. The aggrieved nobleman challenged Wilkes, who immediately wrote off the following sprightly letter to Colonel Berkeley, the earl's second :—

" Winchester, September 30th, 1762.

" Sir,—Lord Talbot, by your message, has at last brought this most important question to the precise point where my first answer to his Lordship fixed it, if he preferred that. Be assured that if I am between heaven and earth, I will be on Tuesday evening at Telbury's, the 'Red Lion,' at Bagshot, and on Wednesday morning will play this duel with his Lordship.

"It is a real satisfaction to me that his Lordship will be accompanied by a gentleman of Colonel Berkeley's worth and honour.

"This will be delivered to you by my adjutant, who attends me at Bagshot. I shall not bring any servant with me, from the fear of any of the parties being known. My pistols only, or his Lordship's, at his option, shall decide this point.

"I beg the favour of you to return me the letters, as I mean to leave Winchester this evening. I have Lord Bruce's leave of absence for ten days. I am, &c. &c.,   "JOHN WILKES.

"P.S.—I hope we may make a *partie carrée* for supper on Tuesday at Bagshot."

To this Colonel Berkeley replied thus :—

"Camp, near Winchester,
Sept. 30th, 1762.

"SIR,—I have sent all the letters, and shall depend upon the pleasure of supping with you at Telbury's, the 'Red Lion,' at Bagshot, Tuesday evening. My servant will attend me, as the going alone would give room for suspicion, but you may depend upon his following your directions at Bagshot, and that he shall not be seen where you would not have him. I am much obliged for your favourable opinion, and am, &c. &c.,

"H. BERKELEY."

And now we will add Wilkes' own description of the meeting, given in a letter that he wrote to Earl Temple :—

"'HE BADE HIM SHIFT FOR HIMSELF'" (*p.* 264).

"Red Lion, at Bagshot, Tuesday, 10 at night, Oct. 5th, 1762.

"My Lord,—I had the honour of transmitting to your Lordship copies of seven letters which passed between Lord Talbot and me. As the affair is now over, I enclose an original letter of Colonel Berkeley's, with a copy of mine previous to it, which fixed the particulars of our meeting, and therefore remained a secret, very sacredly kept by the four persons concerned.

"I came here at three this afternoon, and about five was told that Lord Talbot and Colonel Berkeley were in the house. Lord Talbot had been here at one, and was gone again, leaving a message, however, that he would soon return. I had continued in the room where I was at my first coming, for fear of raising any suspicion. I sent a compliment to Colonel Berkeley, and that I wished to see him. He was so obliging as to come to me directly. I told him that I supposed we were to sup together with Lord Talbot, whom I was ready to attend as became a private gentleman, and that he and Mr. Harris (my adjutant) as our seconds would settle the business of the next morning according to my letter to him from Winchester, and his answer.

"Berkeley said that his Lordship wished to finish the business immediately. I replied that the appointment was to sup together that evening, and to fight in the morning; that in consequence of such an arrangement, I had, like an idle man of pleasure, put off some business of real importance, which I meant to settle before I went to bed. I added that I came from Medmenham Abbey, where the jovial monks of St. Francis had kept me up till four in the morning: that the world would therefore conclude that I was drunk, and form no favourable opinion of his Lordship from a duel at such a time; that it more became us both to take a cool hour of the next morning, and as early a one as was agreeable to his Lordship. Berkeley said that he had undertaken to bring us together, and as we were both now at Bagshot, he would leave us to settle our own business. He then asked me if I would go with him to his Lordship. I said I would, any moment he pleased. We went directly with my adjutant.

"I found his Lordship in an agony of passion. He said that I had injured him; that he was not used to be injured or insulted. 'What did I mean? Did I, or did I not, write to the *North Briton* of August the 21st, which affronted his honour? He would know; he insisted on a direct answer; here were his pistols!' I replied that he would soon use them; that I desired to know by what right his Lordship catechised me about a paper that did not bear my name; that I should never resolve the question to him till he made out the right of putting it; that if I could have entertained any other idea, I was too well bred to have given his Lordship and Colonel Berkeley the trouble of coming to Bagshot. I observed that I was a private English gentleman, perfectly free and independent, which I held to be the character of the highest dignity; that I obeyed with pleasure a gracious Sovereign, but would never submit to the arbitrary dictates of a fellow-subject, a lord steward of his household, my superior indeed in rank, fortune, and abilities, but my equal only in honour, courage, and liberty. His Lordship then asked me if I would fight him that evening. I said that I preferred the next morning, as it had been settled before, and gave my reasons. His Lordship replied that he insisted on finishing the affair immediately. I told him that I should very soon be ready; that I did not mean to quit him, but would absolutely first settle some important business relative to the education of my only daughter, whom I tenderly loved;

that it would take up but very little time; and that I would immediately decide
the affair in any way he chose, for I had brought both sword and pistols.

"I rang the bell for pen, ink, and paper, desiring his Lordship to conceal
his pistols, that they might not be seen by the waiters. He soon after became
half frantic, and used a thousand indecent expressions, that I should be hanged,
d——d, &c. &c. I said that I was not to be frightened, nor in the least affected
by such violence; that God had given me firmness and spirit equal to his
Lordship's or any other man's; that cool courage should always mark me;
and that it would be soon how well bottomed he was.

"After the waiter had brought pen, ink, and paper, I proposed that the door
of the room should be locked, and not opened till our business was decided.
His Lordship, on this proposition, became quite outrageous; declared that this
was mere *butchery*, and that I was a wretch who sought his life. I reminded
him that I came there on a point of honour, to give his Lordship satisfaction;
that I mentioned the circumstance of shutting the door only to prevent all
possibility of interruption; and that I would, in every circumstance, be governed,
not by the turbulence of the most violent temper I had ever seen, but by the
calm determination of our seconds, to whom I implicitly submitted. His Lordship
then asked me if I would deny the paper. I answered that I would neither
own nor deny it; if I survived, I would afterwards declare, but not before.

"Soon after, he grew a little cooler, and in a soothing tone of voice said,
'I have never, I believe, offended Mr. Wilkes: why, then, has he attacked me?
He must be sorry to see me unhappy?' I asked him upon what grounds his
Lordship imputed the paper to me; that Mr. Wilkes would justify any paper
to which he had put his name, and would equally assert the privilege of not
giving any answer whatever about a paper to which he had not; that that
was my undoubted right, which I was ready to seal with my blood.

"He then said he admired me exceedingly, really loved me, but I was an
unaccountable animal—such parts! But would I kill him who had never
offended me, &c. &c. We had after this a good deal of conversation about
the Bucks Militia, and the day his Lordship came to see me on Wycombe Heath
before I was colonel. He soon after flamed out again and said to me, 'You
are a murderer, you want to kill me, but I am sure I shall kill you—I know
I shall, by ——! If you will fight, if you will kill me, I hope you will be
hanged. I know you will.'

"I asked if I was first to be killed and afterwards hanged? That I know
his Lordship fought me with the King's pardon in his pocket, and I fought
him with a halter about my neck; that I would fight him for all that, and
if he fell I should not tarry here a moment for the tender mercies of such a
ministry; but would directly proceed to the next stage, where my valet waited
for me; from thence I would make the best of my way to France, as men of
honour were sure of protection in that country. He then told me that I was
an *unbeliever*, and wished to be killed. I could not help smiling at this, and

observed that we did not meet at Bagshot to settle articles of faith, but points of honour; that, indeed, I had no fear of dying, but I enjoyed life as much as any man; that I am as little subject to be gloomy, or even peevish, as any Englishman whatever; that I valued life and the fair enjoyments of it so much that I would never quit it with my own consent, except on a call of honour.

"I then wrote a letter to your Lordship respecting the education of Miss Wilkes, and gave you my poor thanks for the steady friendship-with which you have so many years honoured me. Colonel Berkeley took the care of the letter, and I have since desired him to send it to Stowe; for the sentiments of the head at such a moment are beyond all politics, and indeed everything else except such virtues as Lord Temple's.

"When I had sealed my letter, I told his Lordship I was entirely at his service, and I again desired that we might decide the affair in the room because there could not be a possibility of interruption; but he was quite inexorable. He then asked me how many times we should fire. I said that I left it to his choice. I had brought a flask of powder and a bag of bullets. Our seconds then charged the pistols which my adjutant had brought. They were large horse-pistols. It was agreed that we should fire at the word of command, to be given by one of our seconds. They tossed up, and it fell to my adjutant to give the word.

"We then left the room, and walked to a garden at some distance from the house. It was near seven, and the moon shone brightly. We stood about eight yards distant, and agreed not to turn round before we fired, but to continue facing each other.

"Harris gave the word. Both our fires were in very exact time, but neither took effect. I walked up immediately to his Lordship, and told him that now I avowed the paper. His Lordship paid me the highest encomiums on my courage, and said he would declare everywhere that I am the noblest fellow God ever made. He then desired that we might now be good friends, and retire to the inn to drink a bottle of claret together, which we did with great good humour and much laughing.

"His Lordship afterwards went to Windsor, Colonel Berkeley and my adjutant to Winchester, and I continue here until to-morrow morning, waiting the return of my valet, to whom I have sent a message. Berkeley told me he was grieved at his Lordship's passion, and admired my coolness and courage beyond his farthest idea—that was his expression. I am, my Lord, &c. &c.,

"JOHN WILKES"

A more unhappy affair of a political, or rather electioneering, origin was that fought in 1810 between Mr. Colclough and Mr. Alcock. Perhaps no other contributed more to the disrepute into which the duel has fallen in England.

The facts of it are briefly these. Mr. John Colclough, M.P. for Wexford, was seeking re-election, and as certain noblemen had for many years monopolised a seat for the county, to put the sense of the electorate to the proof, he proposed

Mr. Sheridan as joint candidate with himself. With these gentlemen, Mr. Alcock, supported by several influential voters, contested the seat. The election began, the poll proceeded, and Mr. Alcock was winning, when ruder methods finished the contest.

It appears that several tenants of one of Mr. Alcock's supporters refused in the most determined manner to vote for that gentleman, and declared that, come what might, they would support Mr. Colclough and "the great Sheridan."

"ALCOCK'S FRIENDS HURRIED HIM OFF THE GROUND" (*p.* 270).

Mr. Alcock's partisans ascribed this behaviour to bribery on the part of Mr. Colclough. Mr. Colclough solemnly protested that he had not even canvassed for their votes. Alcock insisted that they should not vote, then. "How can I prevent them?" was the reply, and it seems a reasonable one; but it did not satisfy Alcock, who, after a hot discussion, required his opponent to decline the votes, or receive them at his peril. This threat was, of course, disregarded. Open defiance followed, and the two candidates agreed to settle their differences next Monday by single combat.

The affair was witnessed by many hundred people, including several magistrates. It happened that both candidates were exceptionally short-sighted, and Mr. Alcock determined to use spectacles. This was resented by

Mr. Colclough's adherents, and Mr. Colclough himself refused to take a like advantage. Alcock, however, persisted, and in the end did wear the glasses. The ground was paced, the seconds handed a couple of pistols to each combatant, and placing them about eight or nine paces apart, withdrew.

Then followed a pause—a dead silence for at least two minutes—as the crowd, each with heart beating for the success of his candidate, stood in suspense, and motionless. The pistols were raised; the word was given; one shot rang out.

It was Mr. Alcock's; and in a second his former friend and intimate comrade fell to the earth, his pistol exploding aimlessly. Men ran towards him. He was dead—shot through the brain.

For a moment the dead silence continued, and then, from every quarter of the field, broke out a wild yell, fierce and horrible. Alcock's friends seized and hurried him off the ground, and just in time to save him from the rush of the mob.

Within two hours the poll was read out. It proclaimed Mr. Alcock *duly elected.*

At the next assize the new member was tried before Baron Smith for murder. The judge openly declared against a conviction; and the jury, without leaving the box, indeed without five minutes' discussion, returned a verdict of *Not Guilty.*

We have said, however, that the two duellists had been intimate friends; and this reflection preying on the mind of the acquitted man, embittered his days, which ended in complete insanity. Nor did the tragedy end here. Miss Alcock, his sister, had known Colclough since her infancy, and was warmly attached to him. She was an amiable and light-hearted girl; but her friend's death and her brother's trial and subsequent melancholy deprived her also of reason. She died with heart and intellect alike broken.

But for some of the most extraordinary episodes of the duel we are indebted to America. Here is a story that emulates the ferocity of a Corsican *vendetta.* It is taken from the American papers of the time:—

"Benjamin Price was a grocer at Rhinebeck, and was considered the flower of the flock. He was at the theatre one evening with a beautiful woman, when a British officer, in an adjoining box, took the liberty of turning round and staring her full in the face. She complained to Ben Price, and, on a repetition of the offence, he turned round, seized the officer's nose, and, before the whole audience, wrung it most effectually.

"The officer, having disengaged his nose from the assaulting finger and thumb, came round and knocked on the door of Ben Price's box. Ben opened. The officer, whose name was Green, stood in the entrance and demanded of Ben what he meant by this behaviour, at the same time remarking that he had not meant to insult the lady by what he had done. 'Oh, very well,' replied Ben, 'neither did I mean to insult you by what I did.' Upon this they shook hands as sworn brothers, and some time after Mr. Green went to Canada to join his regiment.

"The facts of this affair, however, reached Canada as soon as Mr. Green did, and, of course, were bruited about. The officers of the regiment, one of whom had a pique against him, caused it to be brought under the notice of his brother-officers, and one of them, Captain Wilson, insisted that Green should be sent to Coventry, unless he went back directly and fought Ben Price.

"Green, on hearing this, set to work and practised for five hours every day, until he could hit a dollar at ten paces nine times out of ten. He then came to New York and challenged Ben Price. They fought at Hoboken, and Ben was killed at the first fire. The seconds ran off, and Green took a small boat, crossed the river, and boarded a vessel in the bay just about to sail for England. The body of Ben was found at Hoboken, with a piece of paper attached to his breast, on which were written the following words :—' This is Benjamin Price, boarding in Verney Street, New York—take care of him.' The body was brought to the city quietly, and he was buried in New York.

"Some years afterwards, Captain Wilson, of the British army, whom we have mentioned above, arrived in the city (New York) from England, on his way to Canada, and put up at the Washington Hotel. One day, at dinner, the conversation turned on Ben Price's death, and the manner of it. Captain Wilson remarked that he had been mainly instrumental in bringing about the duel, and detailed the circumstances. His story was carried immediately to the dead man's son, Stephen Price, who was lying at home, ill of the gout. His friends say that he henceforth implicitly obeyed the instructions of a physician, obtained thereby a short cessation of the gout, and was enabled to hobble out of doors, his lower extremities swaddled in flannel.

"His first course was to seek the Washington Hotel, and his first inquiry was, 'Is Captain Wilson within?' 'He is,' said the waiter. 'Show me to his room,' said Stephen, and he was shown accordingly. He hobbled upstairs with great difficulty, cursing at intervals the gout and the captain with equal vehemence; and at last entered the captain's room, his feet encased in moccasins, and his hand grasping a stick.

"Captain Wilson rose to receive him, when he broke out, 'Are you Captain Wilson?' 'That is my name,' replied the other. 'Then, sir, my name is Stephen Price. You see, sir, I can scarcely put one foot before the other. I am afflicted with the gout. My object in coming here is to insult you. Shall I have to knock you down, or will you consider what I have said a sufficient insult, and act accordingly?' 'Sir,' replied the captain, 'I shall consider what you have said quite sufficient. You shall hear from me.'

"In due time there came a message from the captain to Stephen Price. Time, place, and weapons were appointed, and early one morning a barge left

New York, in which were seated, face to face, Stephen Price and Captain Wilson, and two friends.

"They all landed at Bedlaws Island; the principals took their positions; the signal was given; and Captain Wilson fell at the first shot.

"His body was buried in the vault there, and the rest of the party returned to New York. But the captain's friends thought he had gone to Canada, and always believed that he had died suddenly, or had been killed on his way to England to join his regiment."   /

Even grimmer is the story of Dr. Smith and Dr. Jefferies, two medical men, who fought at Philadelphia in August, 1830. They began at eight paces distance, and exchanged shots without effect. Their friends then interposed and endeavoured to bring about a reconciliation; but Dr. Jefferies said he would not leave the ground until he had lost his own life or taken Dr. Smith's. Pistols were thereupon handed them a second time, and at this fire Dr. Smith's right arm was broken. Again the seconds interfered; but Dr. Smith declared that as he was wounded he might as well die. So they had a third shot at each other, the wounded man using his left hand. At this fire Dr. Jefferies was hit in the thigh, and his loss of blood so exhausted him that the contest was perforce delayed for a few minutes. On recovering, however, he desired that the distance should be shortened. Dr. Smith agreed; and they stood up, covered with blood, for the fourth time, at a distance of six feet. They were to fire between the words "one" and "five," and the discharge proved fatal to both. Dr. Smith died as he dropped, with a ball through his heart. Dr. Jefferies survived for four hours, with a ball in his breast. When he saw his adversary fall, he asked, "Is he dead?" and on being assured that he was, exclaimed, "Then I'm quite ready to die." Just before his death he said he had been a school-friend of Dr. Smith, and had lived on terms of great intimacy with him for fifteen years; and he bore honourable testimony to his character as a man of science and a gentleman. So, having adequately stultified himself on his death-bed, he passed away.

We must go to Germany to match the grotesque idiocy of the above. The following extract will do so, perhaps. It is told by the author of "Bubbles of the Brunnens" :—

"A couple of Germans, having quarrelled about some beautiful lady, met with sabres in their hands to fight a duel. The ugly one, who was of course the most violent of the two, after many attempts to deprive his hated adversary of life, at last aimed a desperate blow at his head, which, though it missed its object, yet fell upon and actually cut off the good-looking man's nose. It had scarcely reached the ground when its owner, feeling that his beauty was gone, instantly threw away his sword, and with both arms extended eagerly, bent forward with the intention to pick up his own property, and replace it; but.

the ugly German no sooner observed the intention than, darting forwards, with the malice of the devil himself, he jumped upon the nose, and before its master's face crushed it and ground it to atoms!"

Now these stories have not been given without a moral: a moral which any intelligent man who turns, say, to the concluding chapters of Sir Walter

"'GREEN TOOK A SMALL BOAT'" (p. 271).

Scott's "Talisman," may draw for himself. Or let him turn to the beginning of Shakespeare's *Richard II.*, where the Dukes of Hereford and Norfolk enter the lists against each other; or listen to this account of the preparations for that combat, taken from an old chronicle:—

"The Kinge demanded of them bothe if they wolde agree between themselves, w'ch they bothe refused; and then he granted them the battell, and assigned them ye place to be at Coventree citye, in ȳe monthe of Auguste next ensueinge, where he caused a sumpteous theatre and list Roiall to be prepared.

"At the day appoynted, the two valiaunt Dukes came to Coventree, accompaignied with ye nobles and gentiles of their linages, w'ch encouraged them to ye uttermost. At ye day of combate and fyghte, the Duke of Aumarle, that daye high marshall, entred into the list with a great compaignie of men, apparailed in silk sendale, embroudered with silver both richly and curiouslye, every man having a tipped staffe to keep ye field in order. About the time of prime, came to the barriers of the list the Duke of Hereford, mounted upon a whyte courser, barbed with blewe and greene velute [velvet] embroudered sompteouslye w'th swannes and anteloppes of goldsmithes woorke, armed at all points. The constable and marshall came to ye barriers demandinge of him what he was? Who answered, ' I am Henrye, Duke of Herefordo, wh'ch am come hether to do my devoyre against Thomas Mowbraye, Duke of Northefolke, as a traitor untrewe to God, the King, his realme, and me.' Then incontinente he sware upon the Holy Evangeliste that his quarrel was just and trewe. Then he put up his swordo (w'ch before he held naked in his hande) and put down his visor, and made a crosse in his forehead, and w'th speare in his hand entred into ye list and descended from his horse, and set him down in a chair of green velute, w'ch was set in a traves of green and blew velute at the one end of the list, and there reposed himselfe, expectinge the cominge of his adversarye. . . . . . The Duke of Northefolke hovered on horseback at the entrye of the list, his horse being barbed with crimson velute embroudered with lyons of sylver, and mulberry trees. And when he had made his othe before the constable and marshall, that his quarrell was juste and trewe, he entred ye field manfully, sayinge aloude, ' God ayde him yt hath ye righte!' and then he dismounted from his horse, and sate down in the chayre, w'ch was crimson velute, curtened aboute with whyte and red damask.

" The Lord Marshall vewed theyre spoares to see that they were at once equall lengthe, and then the heraulde p'claimed that the travesses and charges of ye champions should be removed, commanding them on ye King's behalf to mount on horsebacke and to addresse themselves to the battayle and combate.

The Duke of Heref orde was quicklye horsed, and closed his barrier, and caste his speare into ye reste, and (when ye trumpet sounded) sette forwardes courageouslye towarde his enemy six or seven paces. The Duke of Northefolke was not fully sette forwarde when ye Kinge caste down his warder, and the heraulds cried ' Ho, ho!' The Kinge then caused their spears to be taken from them, and commanded them to repair unto their chayres, where they remained two long houres while ye Kinge and his counsaile deliberately consulted what way was best to be taken in so weighty a cause. . . . . ."

Well, the rest may be read in Shakespeare. But what the reader is invited to notice is this—how fair and splendid may seem an illogical custom in an age that has not advanced beyond it; and how base and sordid is its recrudescence in a world that has outlived it. For in this combat at the close of the fourteenth century and in those we have quoted from the nineteenth century the aim is one and the same. And this, if we come to look at it, is where the unseemliness of prize-fighting will be found to lie. For two mere brutes to settle differences with the fists is quite right and proper; the impropriety lies in the fact that the world has existed long enough to have eliminated the mere brute. He is an anachronism, and for civilised man to delight in his ways is a yet more fatal anachronism. So the duel is out of date; and society, as well as politics, has long recognised that to be out of date may fairly (in most cases) be made a crime.

Burke's famous trope on the age of chivalry is in fact the silliest nonsense. Vice was never the better for losing all its grossness. And if we want an instance to refute him, it will be found in the history of the duel. The frank display of its grossness has ruined it in the more advanced societies. If anyone wishes to see how this tinsel of chivalry may dazzle a man, let him study the following sentence from Millingen, the historian of the Duel:—

"*As civilisation improved, the ladies were allowed to witness these exhibitions.*" . . . . .

"As civilisation improved," forsooth! Now mark an account of a combat which immediately follows these words in the History:—

"A curious duel is related by Brantôme. At the coronation of Henry the Second, a dispute arose between a Baron des Guerres and a certain Seigneur de Faudilles, and they applied for a 'field' to settle their quarrel. The sovereign, however, had made a vow not to sanction any duel, since the death of his favourite De la Chasteneraye; and they therefore met at Sedan, which is under the sovereignty of Monsieur de Bouillon. The combatants appeared after all due preparation, *Le Sieur de Faudilles having lighted a fire and set up a gallows, to the which he intended to suspend . the corpse of his antagonist.* They were both attended by their *parrains*, the baron being armed with a peculiar sort of sword called *épée bâtarde, the dexterous use of which had been taught him by a cunning priest.* The action commenced, when Faudilles ran his sword through the baron's thigh, and inflicted a large wound that bled most profusely; then on his throwing away the sword a wrestling match ensued, the baron being very expert in this exercise, *which had been taught him by a priest of Brittany, a chaplain of Cardinal de Lennicourt.* Both parties now belaboured each other furiously, although from loss of blood the baron was every moment becoming weaker; until a scaffolding, upon which was collected a vast throng of ladies and elderly gentlemen assembled to see the fight, broke down with a tremendous crash. The outcries and shrieks of the ladies, with limbs bruised and fractured, added to the general uproar, *the bystanders not knowing whom they should first assist—the combatants who, sprawling on the ground, were still pummelling each other, or the affrighted ladies. ˉ While the relations and friends of the baron, perceiving that he was becoming more enfeebled, roared out, 'Throw sand in his eyes and mouth!—sand—sand in his eyes and mouth!' Which advice they dared not have given but for the interruption of the fall of the scaffolding; for the bystanders were not allowed to speak, move, or even blow their noses. The baron took the hint, and lost no time in seizing a handful of sand and cramming it into the eyes and mouth of his opponent, who gave in, amidst the loud shouts of the spectators, some approving and others blaming the stratagem. The baron's friends asserted that his opponent had yielded, which his party as firmly denied; and had it not been for M. de Bouillon, the judge of the 'field,' both parties would have come to blows."*

The italics are ours. A leading daily newspaper lately raised a discussion as to whether "chivalry" had died out. We sincerely hope so; but as we

IN THE LISTS (p. 274).

write these lines a paragraph is going the round of the press that would seem to dispute our hopes. It is to the effect that a Hungarian nobleman has just issued challenges to about thirty of his peers; and it adds that Count Esterhazy, one of the challenged, has refused to fight, which he may well do, without suspicion of cowardice, having in his time been through close on seventy encounters, in six of which he has left his adversary dead on the field!

We will conclude our chapter with Mark Twain's account of the students' duels at Heidelberg, permission to include which in THE WORLD OF ADVENTURE has been kindly granted us by Messrs. Chatto and Windus. The accuracy of the account loses nothing by the bright and vivid language in which the author has clothed it:—

I.

One day in the interest of science my agent obtained permission to bring me to the students' duelling-place. We crossed the river and drove up the bank a few hundred yards, then turned to the left, entered a narrow alley, followed it a hundred yards, and arrived at a two-storey public-house; we were acquainted with its outside aspect, for it was visible from the hotel. We went upstairs and passed into a large whitewashed apartment, which was perhaps fifty feet long by thirty feet wide, and twenty or twenty-five high. It was a well-lighted place. There was no carpet. Across one end and down both sides of the room extended a row of tables, and at these tables some fifty or seventy-five students were sitting.

Some of them were sipping wine, others were playing cards, others chess, other groups were chatting together, and many were smoking cigarettes while they waited for the coming duels. Nearly all of them wore coloured caps; there were white caps, green caps, blue caps, red caps, and bright yellow ones; so, all the five corps were present in strong force. In the windows at the vacant end of the room stood six or eight long, narrow-bladed swords, with large protecting guards for the hand, and outside was a man at work sharpening others on a grindstone. He understood his business; for when a sword left his hand one could shave himself with it.

It was observable that the young gentlemen neither bowed to nor spoke with students whose caps differed in colour from their own. This did not mean hostility, but only an armed neutrality. It was considered that a person could strike harder in the duel, and with a more earnest interest, if he had never been in a condition of comradeship with his antagonist; therefore, comradeship between the corps was not permitted. At intervals the presidents of the five corps have a cold official intercourse with each other, but nothing further. For example, when the regular duelling-day of one of the corps approaches, its president calls for volunteers from among the membership to offer battle; three or more respond—but there must not be less than three; the president lays their names before the other presidents with the request that they furnish antagonists for these challengers from among their corps. This is promptly done. It chanced that the present occasion was the battle-day of the Red Cap Corps. They were the challengers, and certain caps of other colours had volunteered to meet them. The students fight duels in the room which I have described *two days in every week during seven and a half or eight months in every year.* This custom has continued in Germany two hundred and fifty years.

To return to my narrative. A student in a white cap met us and introduced us to six or eight friends of his who also wore white caps, and while we stood conversing, two strange-looking figures' were led in from another room. They were students panoplied for the duel. They were bare-

headed; their eyes were protected by iron goggles, which projected an inch or
more, the leather straps of which bound their ears flat against their heads;
their necks were wound around and around with thick wrappings which a
sword could not cut through; from chin to ankle they were padded thoroughly
against injury; their arms were bandaged and re-bandaged, layer upon layer,
until they looked like solid black logs.   These weird apparitions had been
handsome youths, clad in fashionable attire, fifteen minutes before, but now
they did not resemble any beings one ever sees unless in nightmares.   They
strode along, with their arms projecting straight out from their bodies; they
did not hold them out themselves, but fellow-students walked beside them and
gave the needed support.

There was a rush for the vacant end of the room now, and we followed
and got good places.   The combatants were placed face to face, each with
several members of his own corps about him to assist; two seconds well
padded, and with swords in their hands, took near stations; a student belonging
to neither of the opposing corps placed himself in a good position to umpire the
combat; another student stood by with a watch and a memorandum-book to
keep record of the time and the number and nature of the wounds; a grey-
haired surgeon was present with his lint, his bandages, and his instruments.
After a moment's pause the duellists saluted the umpire respectfully, then one
after another the several officials stepped forward, gracefully removed their
caps and saluted him also, and returned to their places.   Everything was
ready now; students stood crowded together in the foreground, and others
stood behind them on chairs and tables.   Every face was turned towards the
centre of attraction.

The combatants were watching each other with alert eyes; a perfect stillness, a breathless interest reigned.   I felt that I was going to see some wary
work.   But not so.   The instant the word was given, the two apparitions
sprang forward and began to rain blows down upon each other with such
lightning rapidity that I could not quite tell whether I saw the swords or only
the flashes they made in the air; the rattling din of these blows, as they struck
steel or paddings, was something wonderfully stirring, and they were struck
with such terrific force that I could not understand why the opposing sword
was not beaten down under the assault.   Presently, in the midst of the sword-
flashes, I saw a handful of hair skip into the air as if it had lain loose on the
victim's head and a breath of wind had puffed it suddenly away.

The seconds cried "Halt!" and knocked up the combatants' swords with
their own.   The duellists sat down; a student official stepped forward, examined
the wounded head, and touched the place with a sponge once or twice; the
surgeon came and turned back the hair from the wound, and revealed a
crimson gash two or three inches long, and proceeded to bind an oval piece of
leather and a bunch of lint over it; the tally-keeper stepped up and tallied one
for the opposition in his book.

Then the duellists took position again; a small stream of blood was flowing down the side of the injured man's head, and over his shoulder, and down his body to the floor, but he did not seem to mind this. The word was given, and they plunged at each other as fiercely as before; once more the blows rained, and rattled, and flashed; every few moments the quick-eyed seconds would notice that a sword was bent—then they called "Halt!" struck up the contending weapons, and an assisting student straightened the bent one.

The wonderful turmoil went on—presently a bright spark sprang from a blade, and that blade, broken in several pieces, sent one of its fragments flying to the ceiling. A new sword was provided, and the fight proceeded. The exercise was tremendous, of course, and in time the fighters began to show great fatigue. They were allowed to rest a moment, every little while; they got other rests by wounding each other, for then they could sit down while the doctor applied the lint and bandages. The law is that the battle must continue fifteen minutes if the men can hold out; and as the pauses do not count, this duel was protracted to twenty or thirty minutes, I judged. At last it was decided that the men were too much wearied to do battle longer. They were led away drenched with crimson from head to foot. That was a good fight, but it could not count, partly because it did not last the lawful fifteen minutes (of actual fighting), and partly because neither man was disabled by his wounds. It was a drawn battle, and corps-law requires that drawn battles shall be re-fought as soon as the adversaries are well of their hurts.

During the conflict, I had talked a little, now and then, with a young gentleman of the white cap corps, and he had mentioned that he was to fight next—and had also pointed out his challenger, a young gentleman who was leaning against the opposite wall smoking a cigarette, and restfully observing the duel then in progress.

My acquaintanceship with a party to the coming contest had the effect of giving me a kind of personal interest in it; I naturally wished he might win, and it was the reverse of pleasant to learn that he probably would not, because, although he was a notable swordsman, the challenger was held to be his superior.

The duel presently began, and in the same furious way which had marked the previous one. I stood close by, but could not tell which blows told and which did not, they fell and vanished so like flashes of light. They all seemed to tell; the swords always bent over the opponents' heads, from the forehead back over the crown, and seemed to touch, all the way; but it was not so—a protecting blade, invisible to me, was always interposed between. At the end of ten seconds each man had struck twelve or fifteen blows, and warded off twelve or fifteen, and no harm done; then a sword became disabled, and a short rest followed whilst a new one was brought. Early in the next round the white corps student got an ugly wound on the side of his head, and gave his opponent one like it. In the third round the latter received another bad wound

in the head, and the former had his upper lip divided. After that, the white
corps student gave many severe wounds, but got none of consequence in return.
At the end of five minutes, from the beginning of the duel, the surgeon stopped
it; the challenging party had suffered such injuries that any addition to them
might be dangerous. These injuries were a fearful spectacle, but are better left
undescribed. So, against expectation, my acquaintance was the victor.

II.

The third duel was brief and bloody. The surgeon stopped it when he saw
that one of the men had received such bad wounds that he could not fight
longer without endangering his life.

The fourth duel was a tremendous encounter; but at the end of five or six
minutes the surgeon interfered once more: another man so severely hurt as
to render it unsafe to add to his harms. I watched this engagement as I had
watched the others—with rapt interest and strong excitement, and with a
shrink and a shudder for every blow that laid open a cheek or a forehead;
and a conscious paling of my face when I occasionally saw a wound of a yet
more shocking nature inflicted. My eyes were upon the loser of this duel
when he got his last and vanquishing wound—it was in his face, and it
carried away his—but no matter, I must not enter into details. I had but
a glance, and then turned quickly away, but I would not have been looking
at all if I had known what was coming. No, that is probably not true; one
thinks he would not look if he knew what was coming, but the interest and
the excitement are so powerful that they would doubtless conquer all other
feelings; and so, under the fierce exhilaration of the clashing steel, he would
yield and look after all. Sometimes spectators of these duels faint, and it does
seem a very reasonable thing to do, too.

Both parties to this fourth duel were badly hurt; so much so that the
surgeon was at work upon them nearly or quite an hour—a fact which is
suggestive. But this waiting interval was not wasted in idleness by the
assembled students. It was past noon; therefore they ordered their landlord,
downstairs, to send up hot beefsteaks, chickens, and such things, and these they
ate, sitting comfortably at the several tables, whilst they chatted, disputed, and
laughed. The door to the surgeon's room stood open meantime, but the
cutting, sewing, splicing, and bandaging going on in there in plain view, did not
seem to disturb anyone's appetite. I went in and saw the surgeon labour
awhile, but could not enjoy it; it was much less trying to see the wounds
given and received than to see them mended; the stir and turmoil, and the
music of the steel, were wanting here—one's nerves were wrung by this grisly
spectacle, whilst the duel's compensating pleasurable thrill was lacking.

Finally the doctor finished, and the men who were to fight the closing
battle of the day came forth. A good many dinners were not completed yet,

"EVERYTHING WAS READY NOW" (p. 273).

but no matter, they could be eaten cold after the battle; therefore everybody crowded forward to see. This was not a love-duel, but a "satisfaction" affair. These two students had quarrelled, and were here to settle it. They did not belong to any of the corps, but they were furnished with weapons and armour, and permitted to fight here by the five corps as a courtesy. Evidently these two young men were unfamiliar with the duelling ceremonies, though they were not unfamiliar with the sword. When they were placed in position, they thought it was time to begin—and they did begin, too, and with a most impetuous energy, without waiting for anybody to give the word. This vastly amused the spectators, and even broke down their studied and courtly gravity, and surprised them into laughter. Of course the seconds struck up the swords and started the duel over again. At the word, the deluge of blows began, but before long the surgeon once more interfered—for the only reason which ever permits him to interfere—and the day's war was over. It was now two in the afternoon, and I had been present since half-past nine in the morning. The field of battle was indeed a red one by this time; but some sawdust soon righted that. There had been one duel before I arrived. In it one of the men received many injuries, while the other one escaped without a scratch.

I had seen the heads and faces of ten youths gashed in every direction by the keen two-edged blades, and yet had not seen a victim wince, nor heard a moan, or detected any fleeting expression which confessed the sharp pain the hurts were inflicting. This was good fortitude indeed. Such endurance is to be expected in savages and prize-fighters, for they are born and educated to it; but to find it in such perfection in these gently bred and kindly nurtured young fellows is matter for surprise. It was not merely under the excitement of the sword-play that this fortitude was shown; it was shown in the surgeon's room, where an uninspiring quiet reigned, and where there was no audience. The doctor's manipulations brought out neither grimaces nor moans; and in the fights it was observable that these lads hacked and slashed with the same tremendous spirit, after they were covered with streaming wounds, which they had shown in the beginning.

The world in general looks upon the college duels as very farcical affairs; true, but, considering that the college duel is fought by boys, that the swords are real swords, and that the head and face are exposed, it seems to me that it is a farce which has quite a grave side to it. People laugh at it mainly because they think the student is so covered up with armour that he cannot be hurt. But it is not so; his eyes and ears are protected, but the rest of his face and head is bare. He can not only be badly wounded, but his life is in danger, and he would sometimes lose it but for the interference of the surgeon. It is not intended that his life shall be endangered. Fatal accidents are possible, however. For instance, the student's sword may break, and the end of it fly up behind his antagonist's ear and cut an artery which could not be reached if the sword remained whole. This has happened sometimes, and death has resulted on the spot. Formerly the student's arm-pits were not protected—and at that time the swords were pointed, whereas they are blunt now—so an artery in the armpit was sometimes cut, and death followed. Then, in the days of sharp-pointed swords, a spectator was an occa-sional victim; the end of a broken sword flew five or ten feet and buried itself in his neck or his heart, and death ensued instantly. The student duels in Germany occasion two or three deaths every year now, but this arises only from the carelessness of the wounded men; they eat or drink imprudently, or commit excesses in the way of over-exertion; inflammation sets in, and gets such a headway that it cannot be arrested. Indeed there is blood and pain and danger enough about the college duel to entitle it to a considerable degree of respect.

All the customs, all the laws, all the details pertaining to the student duel are quaint and naïve. The grave, precise, and courtly ceremony with which the thing is conducted, invests it with a sort of antique charm.

This dignity and these knightly graces suggest the tournament, not the prize-fight. The laws are as curious as they are strict. For instance, the duellist may step forward from the line he is placed upon, if he chooses, but never back of it. If he steps back of it, or even leans back, it is considered that he did it to avoid a blow or contrive an advantage, so he is dismissed from his corps in disgrace. It would seem but natural to step from under a descending sword unconsciously, and against one's will and intent, yet this unconsciousness is not allowed. Again, if, under the sudden anguish of a wound, the receiver of it makes a grimace, he falls some degrees in the estimation of his fellows; his corps are ashamed of him, they call him "hare-foot," which is the German equivalent for chicken-hearted.

III.

In addition to the corps laws, there are some corps usages which have the force of laws.

Perhaps the president of a corps notices that one of the membership who is no longer an exempt—that is a freshman—has remained a sophomore some little time without volunteering to fight; some day the president, instead of calling for volunteers, will *appoint* this sophomore to measure swords with a student of another corps; he is free to decline—everybody says so—there is no compulsion. This is all true—but I have not heard of any student who *did* decline. He would naturally rather retire from the corps than decline; to decline, and still remain in the corps, would make him unpleasantly conspicuous, and properly so, since he knew, when he joined, that his main business as a member would be to fight. No, there is no law against declining—except the law of custom, which is confessedly stronger than written law everywhere.

The ten men whose duels I had witnessed did not go away when their hurts were dressed, as I had supposed they would, but came back, one after another, as soon as they were free of the surgeon, and mingled with the assemblage in the duelling-room. The white cap student who won the second fight witnessed the remaining three, and talked with us during the intermissions. He could not talk very well, because his opponent's sword had cut his upper lip in two, and then the surgeon had sewed it together and overlaid it with a profusion of white plaister patches; neither could he eat easily, still he contrived to accomplish a slow and troublesome luncheon while the last duel was preparing. The man who was the worst hurt of all played chess while waiting to see this engagement. A good part of his face was covered with patches and bandages, and all the rest of his head was covered and concealed by them. It is said that the student likes to appear on the street and in other public places in this kind of array, and that this predilection often keeps him out when exposure to rain or sun is a positive danger for him. Newly bandaged students are a very common spectacle in the public gardens of Heidelberg. It is also said that the student is glad to get wounds in the face, because the scars they leave will show so well there; and it is also said that these face-wounds are so prized that youths have even been known to pull them apart from time to time and put red wine in them to make them heal badly and leave as ugly a scar as possible. It does not look reasonable, but it is roundly asserted and maintained, nevertheless. I am sure of one thing—scars are plenty enough in Germany among the young men; and very grim ones they are, too. They criss-cross the face in angry red welts, and are permanent and ineffaceable. Some of these scars are of a very strange and dreadful aspect; and the effect is striking when several such accent the milder ones, which form a city map on a man's face; they suggest the "burned district " then.

We had often noticed that many of the students wore a coloured silk band or riband diagonally across their breasts. It transpired that this signifies that the wearer has fought three duels in which a decision was reached—duels in which he either whipped or was whipped—for drawn battles do not count. After a student has received his riband he is "free;" he can cease from fighting without reproach—except someone insult him; his president cannot appoint him to fight; he can volunteer if he wants to, or remain quiescent if he prefers to do so. Statistics show that he does *not* prefer to remain quiescent. They show that the duel has a singular fascination about it somewhere, for these free men, so far from resting upon the privilege of the badge, are always volunteering. A corps student told me it was on record that Prince Bismarck fought thirty-two of these duels in a single summer term when he was in college. So he fought twenty-nine after his badge had given him the right to retire from the field.

The statistics may be found to possess interest in several particulars. Two days in every week are devoted to duelling. The rule is rigid that there must be three duels on each of these days; there are generally more, but there cannot be fewer. There were six the day I was present; sometimes there are seven or eight. It is insisted that eight duels a week—four for each of the two days—is too low an average to draw a calculation from, but I will reckon from that basis, preferring an under-statement to an over-statement of the case. This requires about 480 or 500 duellists in a year—for in summer the college term is about three and a half months, and in winter

"HE PLAYED CHESS WHILE WAITING TO SEE THIS ENGAGEMENT" (p. 284).

it is four months and sometimes longer. Of the 750 students in the university at the time I am writing of, only eighty belonged to the five corps, and it is only these corps that do the duelling; occasionally other students borrow the arms and battle-ground of the five corps in order to settle a quarrel, but this does not happen every duelling-day. Consequently eighty youths furnish the material for some 250 duels a year. This average gives six fights a year to each of the eighty. This large work could not be accomplished if the badge-holders stood upon their privilege and ceased to volunteer.

Of course, where there is so much fighting, the students make it a point to keep themselves in constant practice with the foil. One often sees them, at the tables in the Castle grounds, using their whips or canes to illustrate some new sword-trick which they have heard about; and between the duels, on the day whose history I have been writing, the swords were not always idle; every now and then we heard a succession of the keen hissing sounds which the sword makes when it is being put through its paces in the air, and this informed us that a student was practising. Necessarily this unceasing attention to the art develops an expert occasionally. He becomes famous in his own university, his renown spreads to other universities. He is invited to Göttingen to fight with a Göttingen expert; if he is victorious, he will be invited to other colleges, or those colleges will send their experts to him. Americans and Englishmen often join one or another of the five corps. A year or two ago, the principal Heidelberg expert was a big Kentuckian; he was invited to the various universities, and left a wake of victory behind him all about Germany; but at last a little student in Strasburg defeated him. There was formerly a student in Heidelberg who had picked up somewhere and mastered a peculiar trick of cutting up under instead of cleaving down from above. While the trick lasted he won in sixteen successive duels in his own university; but by that time observers had discovered what his charm was and how to break it, therefore his championship ceased.

The rule which forbids social intercourse between members of different corps is strict. In the duelling-house, in the parks, on the street, and anywhere and everywhere that students go, caps of a colour group themselves together. If all the tables in a public garden were crowded but one, and that one had two red-cap students at it and ten vacant places, the yellow caps, the blue caps, the white caps, and the green caps, seeking seats, would go by that table and not seem to see it, nor seem to be aware that there was such a table in the grounds. The student by whose courtesy we had been enabled to visit the duelling-place wore the white cap—Prussian Corps. He introduced us to many white caps, but to none of another colour. The corps etiquette extended even to us, who were strangers, and required us to group with the white corps only, and speak only with the white corps, while we were their guests, and keep aloof from caps of the other colours. Once I wished to examine some of the swords, but an American student said, "It would not be quite polite; these now in the windows all have red hilts or blue; they will bring in some white hilts presently, and those you can handle freely." When a sword was broken in the first duel, I wanted a piece of it; but its hilt was the wrong colour, so it was considered best and politest to await a proper season. It was brought to me after the room was cleared. The length of these swords is about three feet, and they are quite heavy. One's disposition to cheer, during the course of the duels or at their close, was naturally strong, but corps etiquette forbade any demonstrations of this sort. However brilliant a contest or a victory might be, no sign or sound betrayed that anyone was moved. A dignified gravity and repression were maintained at all times.

When the duelling was finished, and we were ready to go, the gentlemen of the Prussian Corps to whom we had been introduced took off their caps in the courteous German way, and also shook hands; their brethren of the same order took off their caps and bowed, but without shaking hands; the gentlemen of the other corps treated us just as they would have treated white caps—they fell apart, apparently unconsciously, and left us an unobstructed pathway, but did not seem to see us or know we were there. If we had gone thither the following week as guests of another corps, the white caps, without meaning any offence, would have observed the etiquette of their order, and ignored our presence.

"'I AWAITED HIS ONSET'" (*p. 290*).

GREAT GAME.

I.—THE LION.

ONE day, when eating my humble dinner, I was interrupted by the arrival of several natives, who in breathless haste related that an *ongeama*, or lion, had just killed one of their goats close to the mission station, and begged of me to lend them a hand in destroying the beast. They had so often cried 'Wolf!' that I did not give much heed to their statements; but, as they persisted in their story, I at last determined to ascertain its truth. Having strapped to my waist a shooting-belt, containing the several requisites of the hunter, such as bullets, caps, knife, &c., I shouldered my trusty double-barrelled gun (after loading it with steel-pointed balls) and followed the men.

"In a short time we reached the spot where the lion was believed to have taken refuge. This was in a dense tamarisk-brake of some considerable extent, situated partially on and below the sloping banks of the Swakop, near to its junction with the Omutenna, one of its tributaries.

"On the rising ground, above the brake in question, were drawn up in battle array a number of Damaras and Namaquas, some armed with assegais, and a few with guns. Others of the party were in the brake itself, endeavouring to oust the lion.

"But as it seemed to me that the beaters were timid, and moreover somewhat slow in their movements, I called them back, and, accompanied by only one or two persons, as also by a few worthless dogs, entered the brake myself. It was rather a dangerous proceeding, for in places the cover was so thick and tangled as to oblige me to creep on my hands and knees; and the lion, in consequence, might easily have pounced upon me without a moment's warning. At the time, however, I had not obtained any experimental knowledge of the old saying, 'A burnt child dreads the fire,' and therefore felt little or no apprehension.

"Thus I had proceeded for some time, when suddenly, and within a few paces of where I stood, I heard a low angry growl, which caused the dogs, with hair erect in the manner of hog's bristles, and with their tails between their legs, to slink behind my heels. Immediately afterwards a tremendous shout of '*Ongeama! Ongeama!*' was raised by the natives on the bank above, followed by a discharge of fire-arms. Presently, however, all was still again; for the lion, as I subsequently learnt, after showing himself on the outskirts of the brake, had retreated into it.

"Once more I attempted to dislodge the beast. But finding the enemy awaiting him in the more open country, he was very loth to leave his stronghold. Again, however, I succeeded in driving him to the edge of the brake, where, as in the first instance, he was received with a volley. But a broomstick would have been as efficacious as a gun in the hands of those people, for out of a great number of shot that had been fired, no one seemed to have taken effect.

"Worn out at length by my exertions, and disgusted beyond measure at the way in which the natives bungled the affair, I left the tamarisk-brake, and rejoining them on the bank above, offered to change places with them; but my proposal was, as I expected, immediately declined.

"As the day, however, was now fast drawing to a close, I determined to make one more effort to destroy the lion, and, should that prove unsuccessful, to give up the chase. Accordingly, accompanied by only a single native, I again entered the brake in question, which I examined for some time without seeing anything; but on arriving at that part of the cover we had first searched, and when in a spot comparatively free from bushes, up suddenly sprang the beast within a few paces of me!

"It was a black-maned lion, and one of the largest I ever remember to have encountered in Africa. But his movements were so rapid, so silent and smooth withal, that it was not until he had partially entered the thick cover (at which time he might have been about thirty paces distant) that I could fire.

"On receiving the ball he wheeled short about, and, with a terrific roar, bounded towards me. When within a few paces he couched as if to spring, having his head embedded, so to say, between his fore-paws.

"Drawing a large hunting-knife, and slipping it over the wrist of my right

67

hand, I dropped on one knee, and, thus prepared, awaited his onset. It was an awful moment of suspense, and my situation was critical in the extreme. Still, my presence of mind never for a moment forsook me: indeed, I felt that nothing but the most perfect coolness and absolute self-command would be of any avail.

"I would now have become the assailant; but as, owing to the intervening bushes and clouds of dust raised by the lion's lashing his tail against the ground, I was unable to see his head, while to aim at any other part would have been madness, I refrained from firing.

"While I crouched, intently watching his every motion, he suddenly bounded towards me; but whether it was owing to his not perceiving me, partially concealed as I was in the long grass—or to my instinctively throwing my body on one side—or to his miscalculating his distance in making his last spring, he went clear over me, and alighted on the ground three or four paces beyond.

"Instantly, without rising, I wheeled round on my knee, and discharged my second barrel; and, as his broadside was then towards me, lodged a ball in his shoulder, which it completely smashed.

"On receiving my second fire, he made another and more determined rush at me, but owing to his disabled state I happily avoided him. It was, however, only by a hair's-breadth.

"He passed me within arm's-length, and afterwards scrambled into the thick cover beyond, where, as night was then approaching, I did not deem it prudent to pursue him.

"At an early hour on the next morning, however, we followed his *spoor*, and soon came on the spot where he had passed the night. The sand here was one patch of blood, and the bushes immediately about were broken and beaten down by his weight, as he had staggered to and fro in his effort to get on his legs again. Strange to say, however, we here lost all clue to the beast. A large troop of lions that had been feasting on a giraffe in the early morning had obliterated his tracks; and it was not until some days afterwards, and when the carcase was in a state of decomposition, that his death was ascertained. He breathed his last very near to where we were 'at fault'; but in prosecuting the search we had unfortunately taken exactly the opposite direction.

*　　*　　*　　*　　*　　*　　*

"We were on our homeward journey, but halted at a spot where a novel scene occurred, which was described by an individual who had witnessed it when a boy. Near a very small fountain, which was shown to me, stood a camel-thorn tree. It was a stiff tree, about twelve feet high, with a flat bushy top.

"Many years ago, the relater, then a boy, was returning to his village, and having turned aside to the fountain for a drink, lay down on the bank and

"'THE LION MISSED HIS GRASP'" (p. 291).

fell asleep. Being awakened by the piercing rays of the sun, he saw, through the bush behind which he lay, a giraffe browsing at ease on the tender shoots of the tree of which I have spoken—and, to his horror, a lion creeping like a cat only a dozen yards from him, preparing to pounce on his prey.

"The lion eyed the giraffe for a few moments; his body gave a shake, and he bounded into the air to seize the head of the animal, which instantly turned his stately neck. The lion missed his grasp, fell on his back in the centre of the mass of thorns, like spikes, and the giraffe bounded away over the plain.

"The boy instantly followed his example, expecting as a matter of course that the enraged lion would soon find its way to earth.

"Some time afterwards, the people of the village, who seldom visited that spot, saw the eagles hovering in the air; and as it is almost always a certain sign that the lion has killed game, or some animal is lying dead, they went to the place; but sought in vain, till, coming under the lee of the tree, their olfactory nerves directed them to where the lion lay dead in his thorny bed. I still found some of his bones under the tree, and hair on its branches, to convince me of what I could scarcely have credited.

"We were often exposed to dangers from lions, which, from the scarcity of water, frequent the pools or fountains; and some of our number had some hair-breadth escapes.

"One night, we were quietly bivouacked at a small pool on the Oup river, where we never anticipated a visit from his majesty. We had just closed our united evening worship, the book was still in my hand, and the closing notes of the song of praise had scarce fallen from our lips when the terrific roar of the lion was heard.

"Our oxen, which before were quietly chewing the cud, rushed upon us and over our fires, leaving us prostrated in a cloud of dust. Hats and hymn-books, our Bibles and our guns, were all scattered in wild confusion. Providentially, no serious injury was sustained; the oxen were pursued, brought back, and secured to the waggon, for we could ill afford to lose any. Africaner, seeing the reluctance of the people to pursue in a dark and gloomy ravine, grasped a firebrand and exclaimed, 'Follow me!' and but for his promptness and intrepidity, we must have lost some of our number; for nothing can exceed the terror of oxen at even the smell of a lion. Though they may happen to be in the worst condition possible, worn out with fatigue and hunger, the moment the shaggy monster is perceived, they start like race-horses, with their tails erect, and sometimes days will elapse before they are found.

"Passing along a vale we came to a spot where the lion appeared to have been exercising himself in the way of leaping. As the natives are very expert in tracing the manœuvres of animals by their foot-marks, it was soon discovered that a large lion had crept towards a short black stump, very like the human form. When within about a dozen yards, he bounded on his supposed prey, when, to his mortification, he fell a foot or two short of it. According to the testimony of a native who had been watching his motions, and who joined us soon after, the lion lay for some time steadfastly eyeing his supposed meal. He then arose, smelt the object, and returned to the spot from which he commenced his first leap, and leaped for several times, till at last he placed his paw on the imagined prize.

"On another occasion, when Africaner and an attendant were passing near the end of a hill, from which jutted out a smooth rock of ten or twelve feet high, he observed a number of zebras pressing round it, obliged to keep the path, beyond which it was precipitous. A lion was seen creeping up towards the path to intercept the large stallion, which is always in the rear to defend or warn the troop. The lion missed his mark, and while the zebra rushed round the point, the lion knew well if he could mount the rock at one leap, the next would be on the zebra's back, it being obliged to turn towards the hill. He fell short, with only his head over the stone, looking at the galloping zebra switching his tail in the air. He then tried a second, and a third leap, till he succeeded. In the meantime, two more lions came up, and seemed to talk and roar away about something, while the old lion led them round the rock, and round it again. Then he made another 'grand leap to show them what he and they must do next time. Africaner added, with the most perfect gravity, 'They evidently talked to each other, but, though loud enough, I could not understand a word they said; and fearing lest we should be the next objects of their skill, we crept away and left them in council.'

"The following fact will show the fearful dangers to which solitary travellers are sometimes exposed. A man belonging to Mr. Schmelen's congregation at Bethany, returning homewards from a visit to his friends, took a circuitous course in order to pass a small fountain, or rather pool, where he hoped to kill an antelope to carry home to his family. The sun had risen to some height by the time he reached the spot, and, seeing no game, he laid his gun down on a shelving low rock, the back part of which was covered with a species of dwarf thorn-bushes.

"He went to the water, took a hearty drink, returned to the rock, smoked his pipe, and, being a little tired, fell asleep. In a short time the heat reflected from the rock awoke him, and opening his eyes he saw a large lion crouching before him, with its eyes glaring in his face, and within little more than a yard of his foot.

"He sat motionless for some minutes till he had recovered his presence of mind; then eyeing his gun, he moved his hand slowly towards it. The lion, seeing him, raised his head, and gave a tremendous roar. He made another, and another attempt, but the gun being far beyond his reach, he gave it up, as the lion seemed well aware of his object, and was enraged whenever he moved his hand.

"His situation now became painful in the extreme; the rock on which he sat became so hot that he could scarcely bear his naked feet to touch it, and kept moving them, alternately placing one above the other.

"So the day passed and the night also, but the lion never moved from the spot. The sun rose again, and its intense heat soon rendered his feet past

"'THE LION TURNED IN A RAGE.'"

feeling. At noon the lion rose, and walked to the water only a few yards distant, looking behind as he went, lest the man should move, and seeing him stretch out his hand to take his gun, turned in a rage, and was on the point of springing on him.

"The animal went to the water, drank, and returning, lay down again at the edge of the rock. Another night passed. The man, in describing it, said he knew not whether he slept, but if he did it must have been with his eyes open, for he always saw the lion at his feet.

"Next day, in the forenoon, the animal went again to the water, and while there he listened to some noise, apparently from an opposite quarter, and disappeared in the bushes.

"The man now made another effort and seized his gun. But on attempting to rise, he fell, his ankles being without power. With his gun in hand, he crept towards the water and drank; but looking at his feet, he saw, as he expressed it, his toes 'roasted,' and the skin torn off with the grass.

"There he sat a few moments expecting the lion's return, when he was resolved to send the contents of the gun through his head; but as it did not appear, tying his gun to his back, the poor man made the best of his way on his hands and knees to the nearest path, hoping some solitary individual might pass. He could go no farther when, providentially, a person came up, who took him to a place of safety, whence he obtained help, though he lost his toes and was a cripple for life."

II.—THE GRIZZLY.

THE grizzly bear is the only really formidable quadruped (says Washington Irving) of North America. He is the favourite theme of the hunters of the Far West, who describe him as equal in size to the common cow and of prodigious strength. He makes battle if assailed, and often, if pressed by hunger, is the assailant. If wounded, he becomes furious, and will pursue the hunter. His speed exceeds that of a man, but is inferior to that of a horse. In attacking he rears himself on his hind-legs and springs the length of his body. Woe to horse or rider that comes within sweep of his terrific claws, which are sometimes nine inches in length, and tear everything before them.

At the time we are treating of, the grizzly bear was still frequent in Missouri and in the lower country; but, like some of the broken tribes of the prairies, he has gradually fallen back before his enemies, and is now chiefly to be found in the upper regions, in rugged fastnesses like those of the Black Hills and the Rocky Mountains. Here he lurks in caverns, or holes which he has dug in the sides of hills, or under the roots and trunks of fallen trees. Like the common bear, he is fond of fruits and mast and roots, the latter of which he will dig up in his fore-claws. He is carnivorous also, and will even attack and conquer the lordly buffalo, dragging his huge carcase to the neighbourhood of his den, that he may prey upon it at his leisure.

The hunters, both red and white men, consider this the most heroic game They prefer to hunt him on horseback, and will venture so near as sometimes to singe his hair with the flash of their rifle. The hunter of the grizzly bear, however, must be an experienced hand, and know where to aim at a vital part; for of all quadrupeds, he is the most difficult to be killed. He will receive repeated wounds without flinching, and rarely is a shot mortal unless through the head or heart.

That the dangers apprehended from the grizzly bear, at a certain night encampment, were not imaginary, was proved by us one morning.

Among the hired men of our party was one William Cannon, who had been a soldier at one of the frontier posts, and entered into the employ of Mr. Hunt, the leader of the party at Mackinaw.

He was an inexperienced hunter and a poor shot, for which he was much bantered by his more adroit comrades. Piqued at their raillery, he had been practising ever since he had joined the expedition, but without success.

One afternoon, he went forth by himself to take a lesson in venery, and to his great delight had the good fortune to kill a buffalo. As he was a considerable distance from the camp, he cut out the tongue and some of the choice bits, made them up into a parcel, and slinging them on his shoulder by a strap passed round his forehead, as the voyageurs carry packages of goods, set out all glorious for the camp, anticipating a triumph over his brother-hunters.

In passing through a narrow ravine, he heard a noise behind him, and looking round, beheld, to his dismay, a grizzly bear in full pursuit, apparently attracted by the scent of the meat.

Cannon had heard so much of the invulnerability of this tremendous animal, that he never attempted to fire, but slipping the strap from his forehead, let go the buffalo-meat, and ran for his life. The bear did not stop to regale himself with the game, but kept on after the hunter. He had nearly overtaken him when Cannon reached a tree, and, throwing down his rifle, scrambled up it. The next instant Bruin was at the foot of the tree; but, as this species of bear does not climb, he contented himself with turning the siege into a blockade.

Night came on. In the darkness Cannon could not perceive whether or not the enemy maintained his station; but his fears pictured him rigorously mounting guard. He passed the night, therefore, in the tree, a prey to dismal fancies. In the morning the bear was gone. Cannon warily descended the tree, gathered up his gun, and made the best of his way back to the camp, without venturing to look after his buffalo-meat.

While on this theme, we will add another anecdote of an adventure with a grizzly bear, told of John Day, the Kentucky hunter, which happened at a different period of the expedition. Day was hunting in company with one of the clerks of the Hudson Bay Company, a lively youngster, who was a great favourite with the veteran, but whose vivacity he had continually to keep in check. They were in search of deer, when suddenly a large grizzly bear emerged from a thicket about thirty yards distant, rearing itself upon its hind-legs with a terrific growl, and displaying a hideous array of teeth and claws.

The rifle of the young man was levelled in an instant; but John Day's iron hand was quickly upon his arm.

" Be quiet! be quiet!" exclaimed the hunter between his clenched teeth, and without turning his eyes from the bear. They remained motionless. The monster regarded them for a time, then lowering himself on his fore-paws, slowly withdrew. He had not gone many paces before he again turned, reared himself upon his hind legs, and repeated his menace.

Day's hand was still on the arm of his young companion, he again pressed it hard, and kept repeating between his teeth, "Quiet, boy! keep quiet! keep quiet!" though the latter had not made a move since his first prohibition.

The bear again lowered himself on all fours, retreated some twenty yards further, and again turned, reared, showed his teeth, and growled.

This third menace was too much for the game spirit of John Day. "By Jove!" exclaimed he, "I can stand this no longer!" and in an instant a ball from his rifle whizzed into the foe.

The wound was not mortal; but luckily it dismayed instead of enraging the animal, and he retreated into the thicket. Day's young companion reproached him for not practising the caution which he enjoined upon others.

"Why, boy," replied the veteran, "caution is caution, but one must not put up with too much, even from a bear. You wouldn't have me stand here all day and be bullied by a bear, would you?"

Here is another story of the grizzly:—

Mr. Palliser and an attendant of his, Boucharville by name, had just returned from a hunting expedition, and had stopped beside a stream while the latter cleaned his gun, when an incident befell that shall be told in Mr. Palliser's own words.

"Boucharville had his rifle-barrel in the stream and was sponging away diligently. Suddenly he shouted, "*Un Ours! Un Ours!*" and at the same instant a she grizzly bear emerged from a cherry-thicket, charging right at him.

"Boucharville, dropping his rifle-barrel, sprang back into a clump of rose-bushes, when the bear, losing sight of him, stood on her hind-legs, and I then saw she had a cub of good size with her.

"I at first ran to assist my companion, but seeing him safe, and the bear at fault, I rushed back to the horse to secure him, fearing that, were he to smell the bear, he would soon speed his way over the prairie, and be lost to me for ever.

"Seeing me run, the bear instantly charged after me, and when, having reached the horse and rolled the halter a couple of times round my arm, I turned about to face her, she rose on her hind-legs. I did not like, however, to venture so long a shot, as I had only a single-barrelled rifle in my hand, and paused a moment, when she altered her intention, turned aside, and followed the direction taken by her cub.

"I then caught a glimpse of her, as she ran to the left, and fired through the bushes, but only hit her far back on the flank; on which she immediately checked her onward career, and wheeling round and round, snapped at her side, tearing at the wound with her teeth and claws, and, fortunately for me, afforded me sufficient time to enable me to load again.

"My ball was hardly down when a shout from Boucharville warned me that the fight was only beginning:—

"'SHE ROLLED FROM THE TOP TO THE BOTTOM OF THE SLOPE'" (p. 298).

"'*Gardez-vous, gardez-vous, Monsieur! Elle fonce encore!*'"—and on she furiously rushed at me.

"I had barely time to put on my copper-cap, and, as she rose on her hind-legs, I fired, and sent my bullet through her heart. She doubled up and rolled from the top to the bottom of the slope, where she expired with a choking growl.

"Boucharville now found me, but we did not venture to approach the enemy until I had loaded, and we ascertained that she was safe dead by pelting sticks and stumps at the carcase. All this time, my noble horse stood as firm as a rock; had he reared or shied, I should have been in a serious scrape. I was greatly rejoiced at my good fortune. She proved a fine old bear, measuring seven and a half feet in length, with claws four and a half inches long."

THE LOSS OF THE "CENTAUR.

September 16, 1782.

HE *Centaur*, a line-of-battle ship of seventy-four guns, under the command of Captain Inglefield, was one of the sharers in the great British victory in the West Indies, when Rodney, with the fear of recall at his heels, raced across the Atlantic and beat the Count de Grasse. On the homeward voyage, after the engagement, many of the British fleet, besides a number of their prizes, and a large convoy, were either lost or disabled; and among them perished the *Centaur*, whose loss we are about to tell in the words of her commander:—

"The *Centaur* left Jamaica in rather a leaky condition, keeping two hand-pumps going; and when it blew fresh, sometimes a spell with a chain-pump was necessary. But I had no apprehension that the ship was not able to encounter a common gale of wind.

"In the evening of the 16th of September, when the fatal gale came on, the ship was prepared for the worst weather usually met in those latitudes; the mainsail was reefed and set, the top-gallant masts struck, and the mizzen-yard lowered down, though at that time it did not blow very strong. Towards midnight it blew a gale of wind, and the ship made so much water that I was obliged to turn all hands up to take a spell at the pumps. The leak still increasing, I had thoughts to try the ship before the sea. Happy I should have been, perhaps, had I in this been determined. The impropriety of leaving the convoy except in the last extremity, and the hopes of the weather growing moderate, weighed against the opinion that it was right.

"About two in the morning the wind lulled, and we flattered ourselves the gale was breaking. Soon after, we had much thunder and lightning from the south-east, with rain, when it began to blow strong in gusts of wind, which obliged me to haul the mainsail up, the ship being then under bare poles. This was scarcely done when a gust of wind, exceeding in violence anything of the kind I had ever seen or had any conception of, laid the ship on her beam-ends. The water forsook the hold and appeared between decks so as to fill the men's hammocks to leeward; the ship lay motionless, and to all appearance irrecoverably upset.

"The water increasing fast, forced through the cells of the ports, and scuttled in the ports from the pressure of the ship. I gave immediate directions to cut away the main and mizzen-masts, hoping, when the ship righted, to wear her. The mainmast went first, upon cutting one or two of the lanyards, without the smallest effect on the ship. The mizzen-mast followed, upon cutting the lanyard of one shroud; and I had the disappointment to see the foremast and bowsprit follow.

"The ship upon this immediately righted, but with great violence; and the motion was so quick that it was difficult for the people to work the pumps. Three guns broke loose upon the main deck, and it was some time before they were secured, several men being maimed in this attempt. Every

"PUMPING AND BALING AT THE HATCHWAYS" (p. 304).

movable was destroyed, either from the shot thrown loose from the lockers, or the wreck of the deck. The officers, who had left their beds naked when the ship overset in the morning, had not an article of clothes to put on, nor could their friends supply them.

"The masts had not been over the sides ten minutes, before I was informed the tiller was broken short in the rudder-head; and before the chocks could be placed, the rudder itself was gone. Thus we were as much disastered as it was possible, lying at the mercy of the wind and sea; yet I had one comfort, that the pumps, if anything, reduced the water in the hold; and as the morning came on (the 17th) the weather grew more moderate, the wind having shifted in the gale to north-west.

"At daylight I saw two line-of-battle ships to leeward; one had lost fore-mast and bowsprit, the other her main-mast. It was the general opinion on board the *Centaur* that the former was the *Granada*, the other the *Glorieux*. The *Ramillies* was not in sight, nor more than fifteen sail of merchant ships. About seven in the morning I saw another line-of-battle ship ahead of us, which I soon distinguished to be the *Ville de Paris*, with all her masts standing.

"I immediately gave orders to make the signal of distress, hoisting the ensign on the stump of the mizzen-mast, union downwards, and firing one of the forecastle guns. The ensign blew away soon after it was hoisted, and it was the only one we had remaining; but I had the satisfaction to see the *Ville de Paris* wear and stand towards us. Several of the merchant ships also approached us, and those that could hailed, and offered their assistance; but depending on the king's ship, I only thanked them, desiring, if they joined Admiral Graves, to acquaint him of our condition. I had not the smallest doubt but the *Ville de Paris* was coming to us, as she appeared to us not to have suffered the least by the storm, and having seen her wear, we knew she was under government of her helm; at this time, also, it was so moderate that the merchantmen set their topsails; but approaching within two miles, she passed us to the windward.

"This being observed by one of the merchant ships, she wore and came under our stern, offering to carry any message to her. I desired the master would acquaint Captain Wilkinson that the *Centaur* had lost her rudder as well as her masts, that she made a great deal of water, and that I desired he would remain with her until the weather grew moderate. I saw the merchant-man approach afterwards near enough to speak to the *Ville de Paris*, but am afraid that her condition was much worse than it appeared to be, as she continued upon that tack.

"In the meantime all the quarter-deck guns were thrown overboard. The ship, lying in the trough of the sea, laboured prodigiously. I got over one of the anchors, with a boom and several gun-carriages, veering out from the head door by a large hawser, to keep the ship's bow to the sea; but this, with a top-gallant sail upon the stump of the mizzen-mast, had not the desired effect.

"As the evening came on it grew hazy, and blew strong in squalls. We lost sight of the *Ville de Paris*; but I thought it a certainty that we should see her the next morning. The night was passed in constant labour at the pumps. Sometimes the wind lulled and the water diminished; when it blew strong again, the sea rising, the water again increased. Towards the morning of the 18th I was informed there was seven feet of water upon the keelson, that one of the winches was broken, that the two spare ones would not fit, and that the hand-pumps were choked. These circumstances were sufficiently alarming; but upon opening the after-hold, to get some rum up for the people, we found our condition much more so. --

"It will be necessary to mention that the *Centaur's* after-hold was enclosed by a bulk-head at the after-part of the well. Here all the dry provisions and the ship's rum were stored upon twenty chaldrons of coals, which unfortunately had been started on this part of the ship, and by them the pumps were continually choked. The chain-pumps were so much worn as to be of little use; and the leathers which, had the well been clear, would have lasted twenty days or more, were all consumed in eight. At this time it was observed that the water had not a passage to the well; for here there was so much that it washed against the orlop deck. All the rum—twenty-six puncheons— all the provisions, of which there was sufficient for two months, in casks, were staved, having floated with violence from side to side until there was not a whole cask remaining, and even the staves that were found upon clearing the hold were most of them broken into two or three pieces.

"In the fore-hold we had a prospect of perishing. Should the ship swim we had no water but what remained in the ground tier, and over this all the wet provisions and butts filled with salt water were floating, and with so much motion that no man could with safety go into the hold. There was nothing left for us to try but baling with buckets at the fore-hatchway and fish-room; and twelve large buckets were immediately employed at each. On opening our fish-room we were so fortunate as to discover that two puncheons of rum, which belonged to me, had escaped. They were immediately got up, and served out at times in drams; and had it not been for this relief and some lime-juice the people would have dropped.

"We soon found our account in baling. The spare pump had been put down the fore-hatchway, and a pump shifted to the fish-room; but the motion of the ship had washed the coals so small that they reached every part of the ship, and the pumps were soon choked. However, the water by noon had considerably diminished by working the buckets; but there appeared no prospect of saving the ship if the gale continued. The labour was too great to hold out without water; yet the people worked without a murmur, and indeed with cheerfulness.

"At this time the weather was very moderate, and a couple of spars were got ready for shears to set up a jury foremast; but as the evening came on, the gale again increased. We had seen nothing this day but the ship that had lost her main-mast, and she appeared to be as much in want of assistance as ourselves, having fired guns of distress; and before night I was told that her foremast was gone. The *Centaur* laboured so much that I had scarcely a hope she could swim till morning. However, by great exertions of the chain-pumps, and baling, we held our own; but our sufferings for want of water were very great, and many of the people could not be restrained from drinking salt water.

"At daylight (the 19th) there was no vessel in sight; and flashes from guns having been seen in the night, we feared the ship we had seen the preceding day had foundered. Towards ten o'clock in the forenoon the weather·

grew more moderate, the water diminished in the hold, and the people were encouraged to redouble their efforts to get the water low enough to break a cask of fresh water out of the ground tier, and some of the most resolute of the seamen were employed in the attempt. At noon we succeeded with one cask, which, though little, was a seasonable relief. All the officers, passengers, and boys, who were not of the profession of seamen, had been employed in thrumming a sail, which was passed under the ship's bottom, and I thought had some effect. The shears were raised for the foremast; the weather looked promising, the sea fell, and at night we were able to relieve at the pumps and baling every two hours.

"By the morning of the 20th the fore-hold was cleared of the water, and we had the comfortable promise of a fine day. It proved so, and I was determined to make use of it with all possible exertion. I divided the ship's company, with officers attending them, into parties, to raise the jury foremast, to heave over the lower deck guns, to clear the wreck of the fore and after holds, to prepare the machine for steering the ship, and to work the pumps. By night the after-hold was as clear as when the ship was launched; for, to our astonishment, there was not a shovel of coals remaining, twenty chaldrons having been pumped out since the commencement of the gale. What I have called the wreck of the hold, was the bulkheads of the after-hold, fish-room, and spirit-rooms. The standards of the cock-pit, an immense quantity of staves and wood, and part of the lining of the ship was thrown overboard, that if the water should again appear in the hold we might have no impediment in baling. All the guns were overboard, the foremast secured, and the machine, which was to be similar to that with which the *Ipswich* was steered, was in great forwardness; so that I was in hopes, the moderate weather continuing, that I should be able to steer the ship by noon the following day, and at least save the people on some of the western islands. Had we any other ship in company with us I should have thought it my duty to have quitted the *Centaur* this day.

"This night the people got some rest by relieving the watches; but on the morning of the 21st we had the mortification to find that the weather again threatened, and by noon it blew a storm. The ship laboured greatly, and the water appeared in the fore and after-hold and increased. The carpenter also informed me that the leathers were nearly consumed, and likewise that the chains of the pumps, by constant exertion and the friction of the coals, were considered as nearly useless.

"As we had now no other resource but baling, I gave orders that scuttles should be cut through the deck to introduce more buckets into the hold; and all the sailmakers were employed night and day in making canvas buckets; and the orlop deck having fallen in on the larboard side, I ordered the sheet-cable to be tossed overboard. The wind at this time was at west, and being on the larboard tack, we had practised many schemes to wear the ship, that we might drive into a less boisterous latitude, as well as approach the western islands; but none succeeded, and having a weak carpenter's crew, we found they were hardly sufficient to attend to the pumps, so that we could not make any progress with the steering machine. Another sail had been thrummed and got over, but we did not find its use; indeed, there was no prospect but in a change of weather. A large leak had been discovered and stopped in the fore-hold, and another in the lady's hold; but the ship appeared so weak from her labouring that it was clear she could not last long. The after-cockpit had fallen in, the fore-cockpit the same, with all the store-rooms down; the sternpost was so loose that, as the ship rolled, the water rushed in on either side in great streams, which we could not stop.

"Night came on with the same dreary prospect as on the preceding, and was passed in continual efforts of labour. Morning came without our seeing anything, or any change of weather, and the day was spent with the same struggle to keep the ship above water, pumping and baling at the hatchways and scuttles. Towards night, another of the chain-pumps was rendered quite useless by one of the rollers being displaced at the bottom of the pump, and this was without remedy, there being too much water in the well to get to it; we also had but six leathers remaining, so that the fate of the ship was not far off.

"Still the labour went on without any apparent despair, every officer taking his share of it; and the people were always cheerful and obedient. During the night the weather increased; but about seven in the morning of the 23rd, I was informed that an unusual quantity of water appeared all at once in the fore-hold, which, upon my going forward to be convinced, I found but too true. The stowage of the hold ground tier was all in motion, so that in a short time there was not a whole cask to be seen. We were convinced the ship had sprung a fresh leak. Another sail had been thrumming all night, and I was giving directions to place it over the bows, when I perceived the ship to be settling by the head, the lower deck bow-ports being even with the water. At this period the carpenter acquainted me the well was staved in, destroyed by the wreck of the hold, and the chain-pumps displaced and totally useless. There was nothing left but to redouble our efforts in baling; but it became difficult to fill the buckets, from the quantity of staves, anchor stocks, planks, and yard-arm pieces, which were now washed from the wings and floating from side to side with the motion of the ship. The people till this period had laboured as if determined to conquer their difficulties, without a murmur or without a tear; but now, seeing their efforts useless, many of them burst into tears and wept like children.

"Every time that I visited the hatchway I observed the water increased, and at noon washed even the orlop deck. The carpenter assured me the ship could not swim long, and proposed making rafts to float the ship's company, whom it was not in my power to encourage any longer with a prospect of their safety. Some appeared perfectly resigned, went to their hammocks, and desired their messmates to lash them in; others were lashing themselves to gratings and small rafts; but the most predominant idea was that.of putting on their best and cleanest clothes.

"The weather about noon had been something moderate; and as rafts had been mentioned by the carpenter, I thought it right to make the attempt, though I knew our booms could not float half the ship's company in fine

"'WE ENDEAVOURED TO PULL HER BOW ROUND'" (p. 306).

weather; but we were in a situation to catch at a straw. I therefore called the ship's company together, told them my intention, recommending them to remain regular and obedient to their officers. Preparations were immediately made for this purpose; the booms were cleared; the boats, of which we had three, viz., cutter, pinnace, and five-oared yawl, were got over the side; a bag of bread was ordered to be put in each, and any liquor that could be got at, for the purpose of supplying the rafts. I had intended myself to go in the five-oared yawl, and the coxswain was desired to get anything from my steward that might be useful. Two men, captains of the tops of the forecastle, or quartermasters, were placed in each of them, to prevent any person from forcing the boats, or getting into them till an arrangement was made.

"While these preparations were making, the ship was gradually sinking, the orlop decks having been blown up by the water in the hold, and the cables floated to the gun-deck. The men had for some time quitted their employment of baling, and the ship was left to her fate. In the afternoon the weather again threatened, and blew strong in squalls; the sea ran high, and one of the boats (the yawl) was staved alongside and sank. As the evening approached, the ship appeared little more than suspended in water. There was no certainty that she would swim from one minute to another; and the love of life, which I believe never showed itself later on the approach of death, began now to level all distinctions. It was impossible, indeed, for any man to deceive himself with a hope of being saved upon a raft in such a sea; besides, it was probable that the ship, in sinking, would carry everything down with her in a vortex, to a certain distance.

"It was near five o'clock when, coming from my cabin, I observed a number of people looking very anxiously over the side; and looking myself, I saw that several men had forced the pinnace, and that more were attempting to get in. I had immediate thoughts of securing this boat before she might be sunk by numbers. There appeared not more than a moment for consideration: to remain and perish with the ship's company, to whom I could not be of use any longer, or seize the opportunity which was the only way of escape, and leave the people, with whom I had been so long satisfied on a variety of occasions, that I thought I could give my life to preserve them. This, indeed, was a painful conflict, such as I believe no man can describe, nor any have a just idea of, who has not been in a similar situation.

"The love of life prevailed. Calling to Mr. Rainy, the master, the only officer upon deck, I desired him to follow me, and immediately descended into the boat at the after-part of the chains, but not without great difficulty got the boat clear of the ship, twice the number that the boat would carry pushing to get in, and many jumping into the water. Mr. Baylis, a young gentleman about fifteen years of age, leaped from the chains after the boat had got off, and was taken in. The boat falling astern became exposed to the sea, and we endeavoured to pull her bow round to keep her to the break of the sea, and to pass to windward of the ship; but in the attempt she was nearly filled, the sea ran too high, and the only probability of living was in keeping her before the wind. It was then that I became sensible how little, if any, better our condition was than that of those who remained in the ship; at the best it appeared to be only a prolongation of a miserable existence. We were altogether twelve in number, in a leaky boat, with one of the gunwales staved, in nearly the middle of the Western Ocean, without quadrant, without sail, without great-coat or cloak, all very thinly clothed, in a gale of wind with a great sea running. It was now five o'clock in the evening, and in half an hour we lost sight of the ship. Before it was dark a blanket was discovered in the boat. This was immediately bent to one of the stretchers, and under it as a sail we scudded all night, in expectation of being swallowed up by every wave, it being with great difficulty that we could sometimes clear the boat of the water before the return of the next great sea; all of us half drowned, and sitting (except those who baled) at the bottom of the boat; and, without having really perished, no people ever endured more.

"In the morning the weather grew moderate, the wind having shifted to the southward, as we discovered by the sun. Having survived the night, we began to recollect ourselves, and to think of our future preservation.

"Upon examining what we had to subsist on, I found a bag of bread, a small ham, a single piece of pork, two quart bottles of water, and a few French cordials. The wind continued to be southward for eight or nine days, and providentially never blew so strong but that we could keep the side of the boat to the sea; but we were always miserably wet and cold. We kept a sort of reckoning; but the sun and stars being sometimes hidden from us for twenty-four hours, we had no very correct idea of our navigation. We judged at this period that we had made nearly an E.N.E. course since the first night's run, which had carried us to the S.E., and expected to see the island of Corvo. In this, however, we were disappointed, and we feared that the southerly wind had driven us far to the northward. Our prayers were now for a northerly wind. Our condition began to be truly miserable both from hunger and cold; for on the 5th we had discovered that our bread was nearly all spoilt by salt water, and it was necessary to go on short allowance : one biscuit divided into twelve morsels for breakfast, and the same for dinner; the neck of a bottle broken off, with the cork in, served for a glass, and this filled with water was the allowance of twenty-four hours for each man. This was done without any sort of partiality or distinction; but we must have perished ere this had we not caught six quarts of rain-water; and this we could not have been blessed with had we not found in the boat a pair of sheets, which by accident had been put there. These were spread when it rained, and when thoroughly wet wrung into the kid with which we baled the boat. With this short allowance, which was rather tantalising than sustaining in the comfortless condition, we began to grow very feeble; and our clothes being continually wet, our bodies were in many places chafed with sores.

"On the thirteenth day it fell calm; and soon after a breeze of wind sprang up from the S.S.W., and blew to a gale so that we ran before the sea at the rate of five or six miles an hour under our blanket, till we judged we were to the southward of Fayal, and to the westward sixty leagues; but the wind blowing strong, we could not attempt to steer for it. Our wishes were now for the wind to shift to the westward. This was the fifteenth day we had been in the boat, and we had only one day's bread, and one bottle of water remaining of a second supply of rain. Our sufferings were now as great as human strength could bear, but we were convinced that good spirits were a better support than any great bodily strength; for on this day Thomas Matthews, quartermaster, the stoutest man in the boat, perished from hunger and cold. On the day before he complained of want of strength in his throat, as he expressed it, to swallow his morsel, and in the night he drank salt water, grew delirious, and died without a groan.

"As it became next to a certainty that we should all perish in a day or two in the same manner, it was somewhat comfortable to reflect that dying of hunger was not so dreadful as our imaginations had represented. Others had complained of these symptoms in their throats; and some, indeed all but myself, had drunk salt water. As yet despair and gloom had been successfully prohibited; and as evening closed in the men had begun by turns to sing a song, or relate a story, instead of supper; but this evening I found it impossible to raise either. As the night came on it fell calm, and about midnight a breeze of wind sprang up, as we guessed from the westward, by the swell; but there not being a star to be seen, we were afraid of running out of the way, and waited impatiently for the rising sun to be our compass.

"As soon as the dawn appeared we found the wind to be exactly as we had wished, at W.S.W., and immediately spread our sail, running before the sea at the rate of four miles an hour. Our late breakfast had been served with the bread and water remaining when John Gregory, quartermaster, declared with much confidence that he saw land in the S.E.

"We had so often seen fog-banks which had the appearance of land, that I did not trust myself to believe it, and cautioned the people (who were extravagantly elated), that they might not feel the effects of disappointment; till at length one of them broke into a most immoderate swearing fit of joy, which I could not restrain, and declared he had never seen land in his life if what he now saw was not land.

"We immediately shaped our course for it, though on my part with very little faith. The wind freshened, and the boat went through the water at the rate of five or six miles an hour, and in two hours' time the land was plainly seen by every man in the boat, at a great distance, so that we did not reach it till ten at night. It was at least twenty leagues from us when first discovered, and I cannot help remarking, with much thankfulness, the providential favour shown to us in this instance.

"In every part of the horizon, except where the land was discovered, there was so thick a haze that we could not have seen anything for more than three or four leagues. Fayal by our reckoning bore E. by N., to which port we were steering, and in a few hours, had not the sky opened for our preservation, we should have increased our distance from the land, got to the eastward, and of course missed all the island. As we approached the land, our belief was strengthened that it was Fayal. The island of Pico, which might have revealed it to us had the weather been perfectly clear, was at this time capped with clouds; and it was some time before we were quite satisfied, having traversed for two hours a great part of the island, where the steep and rocky shore refused us a landing.

"This circumstance was borne with much impatience, for we had flattered ourselves that we should meet with fresh water at the first part of the land we might approach; and being disappointed, the thirst of some had increased anxiety almost to a degree of madness, so that we were near making the attempt to land in some places where the boat must have been dashed to pieces by the surf.

"At length we discovered a fishing canoe, which conducted us into the road of Fayal about midnight, but where the regulation of the port did not permit us to land till examined by the health officers; however, I did not think much of sleeping this night in the boat, our pilot having brought us some refreshments of bread, and wine, and water.

"In the morning we were visited by Mr. Grahame, the English Consul, whose humane attention made very ample amends for the formality of the Portuguese. Indeed, I can never sufficiently express the sense I have of his kindness and humanity both to myself and my people; for I believe it was the whole of his employment for several days to contrive the best means of restoring us to health and strength. It is true, I believe, there never were more pitiable objects. Some of the stoutest men belonging to the *Centaur* were obliged to be supported through the street of Fayal. Mr. Rainy, the master, and myself were, I think, in better health than the rest; but I could not walk without being supported, and for several days, with the best and most comfortable provisions of diet and lodging, we grew rather worse than better."

"THE BEAR WAS REGALED IN THE USUAL WAY" (*p.* 313).

COLONEL STOBÉE.

IN the spring of 1710 a Russian army of 18,000 men lay before the old town of Viborg, the chief border fortress then left to Finland, for Nöteborg, Nyen, and Narva had been lost earlier in the war. Yet this fortress, also, lay all too near the newly founded Russian capital, St. Petersburg; and the Czar, when he left the army which had long been besieging it, gave the commander the strictest orders to take Viborg at any cost. But its governor was Magnus Stiernstrale, the brave defender of Ivangorod, and he was manfully supported by the young Lieutenant Laurence Stobée, an officer of engineers, and one of the best soldiers of King Charles XII. Although but thirty-four years of age, Stobée had already given proof of bravery and firmness worthy of a veteran, and in the daily skirmishes constantly exposed himself to the greatest risks. By perseverance, skill, and courage, these two brave men succeeded in holding the town for thirteen weeks, with a small garrison, against overwhelming numbers; but were at length compelled, on June 10th, 1710, to surrender the town, on the condition that all the soldiers should be allowed to return, without hindrance, to their homes. But the Czar, angered at their long resistance, treacherously broke the treaty, declared the garrison prisoners of war, and despatched them to confinement in the interior of Russia. Among the prisoners was Stobée, who, with his young wife, Catherine Aherhjelm, and their little boy, was sent to St. Petersburg.

Here Stobée was employed for five years in designing and drawing plans for the parks and public gardens of the town; and the Czar was so struck with his skill and capabilities, that at the end of this period he offered him a commission in the Russian army, with the rank of major-general. Stobée, animated by love for his king and his country, utterly refused to listen to the tempting offer. The Czar, angered at his refusal, sent the stubborn Swedish officer to Archangel, on the shores of the White Sea, and gave orders to the governor of that town to keep a strict watch upon him. In Archangel, Stobée met many other Swedish prisoners, and amongst them a captain of volunteers named Hans Dumky, who, being well acquainted with the Russian language, was of great use to his companions in misfortune, and eventually was the means of Stobée's liberation.

All the prisoners in this remote spot were kept far more strictly than those in other parts of Russia. Money sent to them from home was very uncertain and slow in its coming; and when it did arrive it was very hard to get it from the Russian authorities. In order to live as economically as possible, the Swedes did everything they could for themselves, dwelling close together so as to be better able to help one another, and to ensure their safety in the midst of such a barbaric people as the Russians then were. In order to obtain a little more than the bare necessaries of life, and to generally improve their circumstances, they practised various trades. Some became smiths, carpenters, builders, or turners; others knitted stockings, gloves, and hats; a few baked or brewed.

One of them, who knew something of medicine, could let blood, bind up wounds, and set fractures, was often summoned by the Russians as a physician in cases of illness. He had fitted up a small chemist's shop, where he sold medicines prepared by himself. This shop was shared with him by the above-mentioned Dumky, who brewed beer and distilled spirits, and soon got a good sale for his wares among the inhabitants of Archangel, as well as the Swedish prisoners.

The shop occupied by these two was divided by a counter, behind which, besides their wares, was a skeleton, which proved useful; not only as an apothecary's sign, but in depriving the superstitious Russians of any desire of loitering in the shop, and indulging their passion for spirituous liquors.

This skeleton was so arranged that whenever the door was opened it moved its legs and arms. Besides the skeleton, they had fastened to the floor a large compass, the needle of which was violently agitated whenever the apothecary or the brewer approached it, for they had small pieces of iron hidden in their clothes. These marvels inspired a respectful dread in the minds of their customers, who asserted that the owners of the shop were in league with the Evil One, and declared they had seen the skeleton skating with them. The truth was that they had taken the apothecary, who was very tall and thin, for the skeleton dressed in a short coat. These tales caused the shop to be unmolested by noisy and turbulent customers, while the business was rather improved by them than otherwise. The governor of the town became a very good customer, and often visited the shop.

The prisoners were often visited by spies, sent by the governor to gain information as to their behaviour, and to make sure that none of them attempted to escape. Occasionally the governor came himself, accompanied by a tame bear, which followed him about like a dog wherever he went. On these visits the bear was now and again allowed his share in the good cheer offered to the governor by the brewer, and gradually acquired such a liking for beer that he used to find the way to the alehouse by himself. Whenever Master Bruin felt inclined for something warm to line his coat, he used to take a constitutional on his own account as far as the abode of his delight, and would refuse to take his departure until he had been properly regaled.

This circumstance was the foundation of the plan of Stobée's escape. As we remarked above, the governor had orders from the Czar to keep the strictest watch upon this officer, so valued by his king and respected by his comrades; and he was consequently so strictly watched that he could not have been a single day absent from Archangel without being followed. Stobée was well aware of this fact, and had next to no hope of ever being able to escape, while his prayers to be allowed to return home on parole had been sternly refused. Hitherto he had borne his lot with patience, in spite of his keen anxiety for the welfare of his wife and child, who were by this time at home, without anyone to help or stand by them.

The boy had been sent home with a friend to his grandparents immediately after the surrender of Viborg. Stobée's wife had at first shared her husband's imprisonment and trouble, but being overcome by home-sickness, and on the point of falling ill, had been persuaded by her husband to return to Sweden with a Colonel Gyllensten, one of his fellow-prisoners who had been exchanged. To one of his friends at home, Andrew Gyllenroth, he had entrusted the care of assisting his wife in the management of his estate, and the despatch to him of letters containing the money he so sorely needed. This trust appeared at first to have been duly fulfilled, but latterly there had been an entire cessation of letters from home, and Stobée was left in the most anxious state of entire ignorance as to the fate of his wife and his friend. He had feared that one or the other of them, or perhaps even both, might be dead, until he was one day informed by one of his fellow-prisoners who had received a letter from home, that there was a report in Sweden that he himself had died. Upon this intelligence Stobée became more and more anxious, foreboding evils which he saw could only be averted by his immediate return home. He determined therefore to do his utmost to escape.

His most intimate and trustworthy friends, therefore, put their heads together and devised several plans of escape, but all except Dumky's were decided to be impracticable. Dumky's plan was founded upon the bear's taste for beer, and was carried out in the following manner. The bear was regaled in the usual

"THEY WERE COMPELLED TO TURN BACK" (p. 314).

way when he came upon his visits, but more and more spirits were mixed with his beer, so that he often grew tipsy and had to sleep off his drink. On one of these occasions he was hurriedly knocked on the head, and his dead body carefully hidden in the cellar. His owner made some attempt to find him, but no one could tell where he had gone, and most people thought he must have taken to the forest.

Stobée had meanwhile simulated intermittent attacks of illness, and his friends had busied themselves in procuring him the outfit of a common pedlar, for which part Stobée endeavoured to qualify himself by rehearsal before them of the usual manner and expressions of such traders. After a few weeks' practice he felt ready for the part, and about the time that the bear was killed, he pretended to fall ill again, but this time far more seriously; indeed the report was spread that he had the putrid fever. The governor, who had hitherto frequently come to see him, at once ceased his visits for fear of infection. Indeed it had been so arranged that whenever the governor, or one of his emissaries, came to visit the sick man, the atmosphere of his room grew more and more unbearable, in spite of careful fumigations with juniper hash, vinegar, and the like. Those of Stobée's friends, too, who pretended to keep watch by his sick-bed now began to appear unwell, as if they too were smitten with the malignant disease. Finally they gave out that the Swedish officer was lying at his last gasp.

On the following night the bear's body, already in a state of putrefaction, was removed from the cellar, dressed in Stobée's usual night attire, and laid in his bed with the night-cap pulled well down over its head, and its face turned to the wall. Stobée himself took refuge meanwhile in a well-planned hiding-place. On the following morning his death was announced to the governor, who sent two officials to certify to the fact. But they were met at the door by such an overpowering stench that they were compelled to turn back, and holding their noses with their left hand, pointed horror-struck to the bed with their right, and declared that they were only too well convinced of the death, and ordered the body to be buried as soon as possible to prevent infection; and their orders were carried out without delay; and Stobée's comrades, who seemed naturally desirous to render him the last offices, would let no one touch the body but themselves, nor indeed was there anyone who was anxious to; they laid the bear's body in the coffin they had made ready, and immediately nailed it down. The funeral took place upon the same day, and was attended by the governor and his officers, the leading citizens of Archangel, and all the Swedish prisoners, most of whom were under the impression that it was really Stobée who was being buried. The latter, while the ceremony was proceeding, stole away disguised as a Russian pedlar, the habits of which class he was compelled to adopt in order to escape detection. Instead, therefore, of making at once for Finland, he wandered about the by-roads of Russia, beset by many hindrances and difficulties, and often in danger of being captured. After wandering about for the space of a year and the distance of nearly twelve hundred miles, and losing all his wares, he at last arrived at St. Petersburg, where he narrowly escaped detection in the following way:—

A wealthy Finnish merchant called Harlin, who lived in St. Petersburg, had given him refuge in his house. While he was there, the merchant came home one day in the greatest anxiety, bringing the news that the wandering pedlar was suspected of being a Swedish officer, as he actually was. What was to be done? Harlin's wife suggested that as the officer was not remarkably tall, and had grown very thin with trouble and anxiety, he might be disguised as nurse to their little boy. Necessity knows no laws. In a couple of hours' time, when the police came to search for the suspected podlar, they found that he had disappeared, but in his stead there had arrived the Finnish nurse, whom the Harlins had long been expecting. They were thoroughly taken in by his dress and his Finnish accent.

Stobée remained with the Harlins some time in the above disguise—a somewhat strange one for one of Charles XII.'s heroes—and is said to have been the object of the tender attentions of a Russian officer. At last in 1716 he succeeded with the help of his friends in escaping, this time dressed as a man, into Finland, where he, curiously enough, heard read the Imperial announcement of his escape. From Finland he made his way without delay over to Sweden.

Long before this period the reports of his death, which were current in his native land, had been confirmed by official communication from the Russian authorities. His wife having had no news of him for many years, for his letters had been stopped by Gyllensten, was fully convinced of his death. On account of her solitary position and led on by considerations for her son's future, she had, though sorely against her will, accepted an offer of marriage from her husband's so-called friend Gyllensten, who had not ceased to pay his court to her ever since their return together from Russia.

The young widow was at this period at her husband's estate in Vestergötland, where she had just received a visit from Gyllensten, and yielding to his entreaties, had consented to marry him within a few weeks' time. At this very moment, just in time to save the fortune of his house, Stobée suddenly entered the room like one risen from the dead. A cry of pain and anger burst from his lips at the sight which met his eyes. His wife sank fainting upon the sofa, believing him to be a ghost, while Gyllensten, who had started up, stood as if turned to stone, smarting with shame at being detected by the friend whose trust he had so shamefully betrayed. The cowardly wretch, taken in the very act, sought in vain for courage to meet the accusations poured upon him by the cruelly wronged husband in his righteous wrath. Stobée is said to have ignominiously expelled him from the house of which he had been on the point of being the lord.

"Whoever," says the chronicler, "has passed through similar trials, can picture to himself the overwhelming emotions of Stobée's wife, at the return of the husband whom she had long given up for lost, and by whose opportune arrival she was freed from the snares which had gone so near to ruin for ever their mutual happiness." Stobée spent several happy years with his wife, during which he did not forget his comrades in misfortune at Archangel. He kept them supplied with money as far as his income allowed him, for it had been considerably diminished by the self-seeking management of his treacherous friend. Yet it was not until several years after his escape that the money arrived and his friends got news of his fate. They had at first been delighted at the unnoticed escape of Stobée, and waited patiently to hear news of him.

More than a year passed by without their hearing of him. Rumours of his capture were spread abroad, but no one pretended to know anything of his ultimate fate. In the meanwhile, however, they hoped for the best. At last, after three years' waiting, the Swedes in Archangel received the news that all had gone well when the money arrived from Sweden, although the sender did not mention his name. After another year's waiting they obtained full particulars of his adventures, and discovered in a very unpleasant way that the Russian authorities had also learnt the fact of his escape. One fine day the governor commanded the pretended grave of Stobée to be opened, and found therein the remains of his long-lost bear.

His wrath can be better imagined than described. The prisoners were treated with far greater severity than before, and all who were known to have assisted in Stobée's escape, including Dumky, were sent to Siberia, where they remained until the peace of Nystad, in 1721, put an end to their troubles, and allowed them to return at last to their homes.

Of Stobée's further adventures we will give the following brief account:— Soon after his return home he again hastened to place his sword at the service of his country, then sorely in need of the help of all her sons. Charles XII., who had lately returned, after fifteen years' absence, to find his country impoverished by war, famine, and pestilence, was now in Skåne, awaiting the attack of 50,000 Russians and Danes from Själland.

Stobée betook himself thither, and found constant occupation in repairing ruined fortresses, and erecting new defensive works. In the following year he was summoned by the king to Norway, and led the attack on Fredrikshald, in which the king was killed. In 1719 he was made colonel, and the year after that he was for the second time the object of an infamous plot on the part of his traitorous friend Gyllensten, who had never been able to forget the ignominious manner in which Stobée had expelled from his house the betrayer of his home and of his trust.

Far from trying to atone for his shameful treachery by an altered line of conduct, this "monster of cruelty and iniquity," as he is called by his biographer, attempted by underhand means to deprive Stobée of his life and property. Even before Stobée's journey to Skåne he had essayed to carry out his designs, but being prosecuted by Stobée, had been exiled from the kingdom. Having now returned with a safe-conduct, he commenced a law-suit against Stobée; but the tools he made use of for the purpose, two women of evil reputation, were found out, and punished for giving false witness. Defeated in this attempt, Gyllensten formed a design of wider scope against his hated rival, in which he had the assistance of Gyllenroth, whom he persuaded, since Stobée had impugned his testimony at the former trial, to accuse him of high treason. He was declared to have given expression in an inn to the most injurious imputations against King Frederick and his Queen, coupled with noisy threats. Witnesses were procured who were ready to declare that they

"STOBÉE SUDDENLY ENTERED THE ROOM" (p. 315).

had themselves seen and heard a person who asserted that he was Colonel
Stobée, and who was so called by his companion, an officer unknown to them,
uttering treasonable expressions accompanied by oaths and curses. Stobée
was at once arrested, and was on the point of being declared guilty, when he
persuaded the judge to allow him to take his place among the spectators in
the body of the court previous to the examination of the witnesses. These
were then summoned separately, and asked if they felt certain of recognising
the person whom they had supposed to be Colonel Stobée. On their replying in the affirmative, they were requested to carefully examine the figures of
the spectators, and declare upon their conscience whether they saw anyone
among them who resembled the man against whom they had borne witness.
One and all declared upon their honour that there was no one among those
present who resembled the person they had seen, of whom they gave a description which did not in the least fit the real Stobée. Moreover, on examining
into their account, it was discovered that there could be no reasonable doubt
that it was Gyllenroth who had played the part of the colonel. He was
arrested and charged with bearing false witness, condemned to death, and
hanged at Stockholm, on the 23rd of April, 1722. Two of the false witnesses were branded and imprisoned at Marstrand, two others were exiled.

Gyllensten, the chief contriver of the plot, being warned in time of the
failure of his schemes, fled the country and wandered about abroad. In
Denmark he killed the Danish Admiral Fordenskiold in a duel; in Hamburg
he hanged a Jew in a wardrobe in the latter's own apartment; in Saxony he
gave himself out to be an adjutant-general, proposed to a lady of rank, on
being refused insulted her shamefully, and, what was worse, presently broke into
her house by night and murdered her and her mother in their beds. Caught
while trying to escape, he was brought to judgment and condemned to death.
As he refused to prepare himself for death by prayer, he was taken to the
scaffold as a blasphemer and denier of the existence of God, tied to a chain,
with a gag in his mouth, and ignominiously executed.

Stobée, after his fortunate deliverance from so threatening a danger, was
regarded with increased respect and admiration by all honourable men, and
lived to a good old age in full enjoyment of his sovereign's favour and confidence, and with no small benefit to his country.

He was promoted in 1740 to be Major-General, and Director of Fortifications:
in 1741 he was made Governor of Gothenburg, with which post he held that
of President of the Commission for the defence of the frontier towards Russia
till 1747, when, on being made a Knight Commander of the Order of the
Sword, he begged leave to resign his charges. He died in 1756, at the age of
eighty, on his estate of Agard in Vestergötland. He left no descendants, and was
the first and last noble of his name. The bride of his youth had died shortly
after his return from captivity, but he had since married twice: his second wife
was Anna Katarina Francke; his third, Maria Loos.

Stobée was the son of the famous Professor Andreas Stobœus, of Stöby in Skåne, whence he derived his name, and was born in 1676. In his youth he applied himself chiefly to mathematics, and at the age of twenty became land surveyor of his native province, the duties of which post gave him constant occupation till 1699, when he was given a commission as lieutenant of engineers, and despatched to Lifland to construct works of defence for the war which was then threatening. In 1701—2 he was employed on similar work at Vaxholm, the entrance to the port of Stockholm; in 1702 he became captain and was sent to Finland to assist in constructing the defensive earthworks of Kexholm and Viborg. In the following year he took part in the campaign in Negermanland, and in 1706, though only thirty years of age, he had contrived so to distinguish himself that he was made Quartermaster-General and raised to noble rank. He continued his work on the fortifications of Viborg until the second siege of that town by the Russians in 1710, where we first made his acquaintance. Though he passed through many trials and troubles, such as fall to the lot of few, he retained throughout a spotless character and an unshaken trust in the guidance of Providence, in which he never was deceived. Stobée stands forth as one of the brightest of the many shining stars in the history of Sweden's greatness and misfortunes during the reign of Charles XII.

A FROZEN CREW.

T was in the middle of August, 1775—I have cause enough to remember the date—that I, John Warrens, captain of the Greenland whaler *Try Again*, ran across the experience that I am going to tell, word for word, just as it happened. I can't say I expect to be believed, though reckoned a truthful man; but I'm growing accustomed to *that*. My private consolation is that I never had half the wits enough to invent it; so if you don't believe what I tell you for gospel, why, in a way, you're only paying me a compliment after all.

"We had sailed that spring, and been hanging about after whales ever since, and precious poor luck we had. But one evening—I won't swear to the day, but it was about the middle of August, as I said—we had a finish put to our disgust. The wind fell dead calm, and left us to drift.

"This was in about 77° north latitude. There's not much fun in lying becalmed at the best of times, but hereabouts there wasn't any at all. For, mark you, we were stuck in among the healthiest crop of icebergs you ever saw in your born days. There was a pile about a mile to starboard that made a man cold down the back to look at them. Tall? They made the *Try Again* look no bigger than a mouse, and were wedged together so that they looked like a continent. Over their shoulders you could see others peeping, and then more again—range after range of great snowy peaks, mostly glittering white, but in places like hollow green glass; and on the evening I'm talking about they were pretty enough to stop your breath—that is if you happened to be a judge of landscape. For the sky had turned to a great flush of red, without clouds, but hazy, so that distance was not to be judged; and the peaks wore a flaming rose-colour, and the sea all lilac and green, except where the reflections fell in great splashes. But there, I can't describe it if I sat down and tried for a week.

"However, this was not what bothered me at the time. I've seen this sort of sky before, though never so brilliant; and I didn't like the look of it It's bad enough, thought I, if this calm holds on and the current takes us on that pack; but it's going to be a deal worse if it blows a gale. I've no notion of bumping on an ice-pack that seems to have been here since the Flood. We shan't chip it enough to be proud of; and we shan't get home to talk about it even if we do. And either I'm a Dutchman, or there's a stiffish gale lying by for us.

"But as there was no wind yet, you see, there was nothing to be done. We couldn't move one way or another; and so I had to be content with keeping a strict watch, for I soon found there was nothing of a current, and I knew that as long as the icebergs stayed where they were, and we did the same, it was all right.

"Well, this lasted for a couple of hours, maybe, and I stood on deck all that time, watching the sight, and feeling my spirits go down. By-and-by the red glow turned paler, and changed slowly to a livid blue; and then I saw a cloud coming up on the larboard side. It hadn't been in sight a minute before a gentle heave came over the sea, gliding and swelling towards us.

"'It's coming,' said I; and before the words were out of my mouth there came an icy puff in my face, and the wind began to hum and mutter in the rigging.

"By good luck, though, the squall didn't take us at one blow; and so I had time to get matters snug. But it gathered, and gathered, and with it the haze all about us began to thicken up to a regular wall of fog, and we looked in each other's faces and found them very pale. Well, so it went on, the wind increasing all the time; and by midnight it was blowing half a gale. There was a deal of snow, too, in the wind; but even this was not the worst. The worst, I think, was the noise made by the ice. We could not see the great blocks in the haze; but we knew well enough that it was in motion. From minute to minute it creaked and groaned, crashed, thumped, and thundered, till our hearts jumped into our mouths—and stayed there. Every ten minutes or so it would shriek—yes, shriek—exactly like a human creature. I tell you, it was bad; for the thickness of the weather, of course, prevented us from discovering in what direction the open water lay. Indeed, we could not tell that there was any open water at all.

"So, first on one short tack and then on another, we passed that night, sheering off sharp as soon as the look-out on the bows caught sight of a lump of ice threatening us ahead. How we got through the time I don't know. But we did, by Providence, as I guess; and towards morning the wind dropped again.

"You may fancy my joy when I came to examine the *Try Again* and found her safe and sound, without an injury, even of the smallest. And this was the more curious as I now found that the storm must have been far more violent than we had any notion of at the time. The icebergs that, the evening before, had formed one solid wall on the starboard side, had been burst asunder, and driven this way and that way by the wind—so much so, that at one point a regular canal of open water led through the barrier.

"We steered for it, of course. The sky was clear again by this time, and a bright sunshine sparkling and twinkling on every point and pinnacle of the ice. Ahead of us, so far as the eye could trace, the canal wound away, its waters green and quiet between the cliffs formed by the wrenching asunder of the pack. It led us due south, and we glided down it, with a gentle breeze following at our backs.

"It was an odd bit of voyaging, and, to a nice eye, a very pretty one. The uncertainty, too, as to where we should be led, or if we could get through, lent to it a spice of adventure. Whether 'twas this, or the bright weather, or the cheerful northerly breeze, I don't know. It may have been due to all three; but at any rate, we were in the best of spirits—when suddenly the canal took a slight bend, and showed us a reach of still clear water for about two miles before it took another turn and was hidden from our sight.

"The mate was standing at my shoulder (we were all on deck, of course, and as keen as schoolboys), and says he—

"'Now Heaven send the channel ain't closed down yonder!'

"I was just going to answer, when I stopped short, and caught him by the arm—

"'Stop! No, it isn't, for look—look! What's that down yonder?'

"'Bless my soul! It looks like a ship's masts.'

"'Now, Lord knows how a ship can have come thereabouts; but a ship it is, and, what's more, she's moving!'

"There was a pretty excitement on deck by this time, and all eyes were turned on the two needle-points, as it were, that I had caught sight of; for of course the ice hid all besides, and presently they passed behind a lump that hid them completely.

"I sent a couple of fellows skimming up to the fore-top to see if they could discover any more of her; and presently one bawls down—

"'She's a brig, sailing down the channel ahead of us.'

"'What's her pace?' I shouted back.

"'No pace at all. Darn me if I ever saw—Look here, cap'n, I don't like the looks of her. Blest if I don't reckon she's a ghost!'

"Well, I thought the whole thing very queer myself; for I couldn't puzzle it out how that brig came there, ahead of us, sailing the same course as we, in a spot that only yesterday was packed with ice tight as a cheese. I couldn't make out how it was we hadn't seen her. True, there was the thick weather last night, but not too thick to see her lantern as she entered the canal—and she couldn't have done that long before us.

"We gave chase now, and it wasn't hard to see that we were overhauling her, 'hands down.' The bend of the canal down which she was driving was so narrow, and lay between cliffs of ice so deep, that up to the moment we entered it, the look-out men could hardly see more than we on deck, and that was just the tops of her masts.

"But when we turned into it and I saw her plain, I saw also that something was desperately amiss.

"Her rigging was just anyhow—torn, tangled, and dropping. Her sails were tattered and hung in strips from the yards. Whenever a puff of wind took her aslant she came to a pause, like as if she shivered, and went off before it helplessly, bumping and grazing the ice, first on this side, then on that. There was no steering in it, and I cried out—

"'I don't believe there's a soul on board.'

"The words were hardly out of my mouth when she plunged straight for a bank of low ice, was brought up short with a thump and a quiver, and stood still. She was fast aground.

"You may think I was pretty well excited by this time. . I ordered out a boat, jumped into it with six of my crew, and rowed towards the brig for dear life.

"As we drew near I could examine the hull more closely, and such a weather-beaten ruin I never saw in my life. There was an ice-line round her so deep that I wondered the timbers were not cut through, and a hundred odd gashes and wounds where she had driven against loose blocks. Her deck was white, heaped—covered with snow; and a line of snow was frozen along each of her yards. I stood up in the boat and shouted—

"'Ahoy, there! *Gloriana* ahoy!' For I had read the name in tall faded letters on her blistered stern. Not a soul answered.

"I shouted again and again, but never got any reply. So at last I was stepping aboard, when an open port-hole near the main-chains happened to catch my eye. I peered in.

"As I'm a master mariner, I saw a man inside.

"There was a table before him, covered with papers, charts, and inkpot. He was leaning back in his chair as if thinking, only I couldn't see very well for the dimness of the light. But I thought it odd he hadn't answered my hail, so I shouted in again through the port-hole—

"'Ahoy, there! Wake up and answer!'

"The man in the cabin never moved—never even turned his head.

"I stood for a moment wondering; then climbed on deck, with my party at my heels. The hatchway was covered deep with frozen snow. We prized it open and descended the cabin stairs.

"They were dark, and a horrible mildewed smell came up them, choking the breath out of our throats. A shiver ran over me as I put my hand to the cabin door. I conquered my feelings and flung it open.

"The man in the chair was still in the same attitude. As we entered he moved not an inch. I stepped forward and peered into his face.

"It was a corpse.

"Over his cheeks and forehead a green damp mould had spread. It coated his eyeballs, which were wide open, half veiling his horrible stare. In the hand that hung over the arm of the chair was a pen, frozen to the fingers. A log-book lay before him, open, on the table. I bent over it, and in the dim light read the last entry:—

"'November 11th, 1762. We have now been seventeen days in the ice. The fire went out yesterday, and our master has been trying ever since to kindle it again, without success. His wife died this——'

"The writing ended in a scratch, as though the hand had dropped in the very act of wrestling with the frozen ink.

"I caught up the book and we hurried out of the place without another word. I am half-sorry I began this tale, for the thought of that frozen corpse turns me queer to this day. But we saw other sights in that ship—oh, yes. We saw, in the principal cabin, the body of a woman, half-sitting, half-lying on a bed. She almost seemed as if she would speak to us as we

"'I PEERED INTO HIS FACE'" (p. 323).

entered. Her face was fresh as life itself; only we knew her to be dead at once by the way in which her limbs were shrunk.

"We saw on the floor, beside the bed, a man seated. He had a steel in one hand and a flint in the other. He was bending over them, as if in the very act of striking a spark. The tinder lay all ready in a heap beside him. He had held that flint and that steel for thirteen years.

"We saw, in the fore-part of the vessel, half a dozen sailors lying dead in their berths. We saw at the foot of the gangway stairs a small figure, a cabin-boy, huddled up into a ball for warmth. But we saw no provisions, no fuel; and we felt that our nerves were going.

"Once on deck again we looked at one another, and went, without speaking a word, into our boat, I with the log-book under my arm. We had seen enough to last us in bad dreams for a lifetime; and I drew not a clear breath again till, steering southward, we left the canal for open sea, and behind us the dead ship lay hidden by the icebergs. Of course you disbelieve me; I said how it would be. But the owners believed me, right enough, when they saw the log-book of the *Gloriana* there, and read the story of the brig that for thirteen years had been lost to them."

A HUNT FOR A MURDERER.

By Dick Donovan.

ONG years ago, when I was a young man, and new to the profession in which I have grown grey, I was stationed in London. I was full of zeal and energy, and particularly anxious to distinguish myself; but for some time I had to kick my heels in obscurity, as nothing occurred to give me the chance I panted for. Of course, I railed against fate, and thought that she had specially singled me out as a victim of her spite, and I began to think I would emigrate, try to discover the North Pole, find the philosopher's stone, fly through the air, or set to work upon some equally quixotic quest, when my old and respected chief, under whom I then served, called me into his room one morning and said—

"Here, youngster, I'm going to set you on a job that will test your mettle. A brutal murder was committed the night before last by a ferocious ruffian—a returned convict—who will stick at nothing. He has managed to get clear, and as he has baffled the police before, he is likely to do it again, for he is as cunning as a fox, as dangerous as a poison-snake. We have reason to believe he is lurking somewhere in the East End. You will join the East End division of the staff, and use every individual effort to capture the brute."

As I heard these orders my heart beat violently, and I felt somehow as if my opportunity had come at last. Moreover, at the time, though I know now it was not so, I thought my chief spoke in rather a contemptuous tone to me, as though he was of opinion that I was a fool, and he would not have put me on this job if he had not been compelled, owing to there being an unusual pressure of business just then, which taxed the resources of our department very severely. This idea fired me, and I resolved to do or die.

With a respectful salute to the chief, and merely remarking quietly, "I will do my best, sir," I took my departure, feeling eager for the fray, and hoping and praying that the merit of capturing this human brute might fall to me.

It appeared that two evenings before, about eight o'clock, a policeman was called to quell a row in a public-house, not of the best repute, and situated in Ratcliff Highway, for ever rendered notorious by the diabolical crime of Williams, the murderer, who has been immortalised by the genius of De Quincey, in that gem of English literature, "Murder Considered as One of the Fine Arts."

The cause of the row was a well-known character named Peter Mogford, then a man of about fifty years of age, and quite thirty of those years he had served in prison. He was, in fact, one of those born criminals who, like the fierce and untameable hyenas, should either be caged or killed.

Mogford had commenced life as a soldier. Both his parents had passed a considerable portion of their lives in prison, and a brother had been transported for a terrible outrage on a woman. Peter's antecedents, therefore, were by no means calculated to create an impression in his favour, and he soon showed that he intended to beat the record. He proved to be the most troublesome man in the regiment. He drank, he stole from his comrades, he was mutinous; and, though he was flogged, imprisoned, flogged and imprisoned again, he did not improve, and was at last drummed out of the army.

Subsequently he became a sailor, but soon gave that up, and his career from that time was one of outrage of almost every conceivable kind, and he was no sooner out of prison than he was in again. His last term had been penal servitude for ten years, and at the time he committed the double murder which sent a shudder through the land, he had only been released two months.

On the night in question he had gone into a public-house in the "Highway," where a number of sailors and their sweethearts were carousing. Mogford had insulted one of the women, which had led to a fight between him and a sailor, during which he struck his opponent over the head with a quart pewter pot, and rendered him insensible.

The row had then become general, and Mogford, who, although a little man, was possessed of a giant's strength, created great havoc, and the son of the landlord rushed out for a policeman. One happened to be close at hand, and, with the aid of some of the sailors, Peter was secured, bound with a rope, and in a state bordering on frenzy with drink and baffled rage, he was conveyed to the nearest "lock-up." It was a place never intended for desperate criminals, but was used principally for "drunk and incapables."

As Mogford complained that the rope hurt him, it was taken off, and he was then put into a cell and locked up for the night, and it was supposed that he had gone to sleep, as for three hours nothing was heard of him.

The station was then in charge of an old sergeant of police, whose duty it was to book any night cases, and a young constable was on duty with him. About midnight Mogford succeeded in noiselessly forcing the lock of his cell door, which was of the most flimsy kind. The old sergeant was nodding at his desk, and the constable was standing with his back to the fire, when Mogford suddenly appeared.

The constable sprang forward to try and stop his exit; but the ruffian seized a poker from the fire-grate, and with one tremendous blow felled the constable like an ox. The old sergeant then tackled him, but Mogford beat him about the head with the poker until he too fell insensible. The criminal then rifled the desk of the small amount of money it contained and made off.

In a few minutes the sergeant · had so far recovered consciousness as to be able to realise what had happened, and, though he was terribly injured, part of his head being almost beaten to a jelly, he managed to crawl to the street and raise an alarm.

When help came a local doctor was immediately summoned, but he found the constable dead, and the sergeant in such a dangerous state that he had him removed immediately to the hospital. There he was able to make a full and detailed statement of the tragic affair, but he soon after lapsed into unconsciousness again, and never rallied, but expired at eight o'clock in the morning.

As Mogford was so well known, it was considered that there would be no difficulty in effecting his arrest; but hour after hour went by and no tidings came of his capture. That night a house was broken into at Bow, and a considerable quantity of valuables carried off, including about ten pounds in cash, also a suit of clothes. A handkerchief that was found on the premises was recognised as one belonging to Mogford, and it was then felt that as he had succeeded in obtaining clothes and money, his capture might be difficult.

When the news spread the excitement was tremendous, and orders were given that every outlet in London was to be watched as far as possible, and every haunt of criminals scoured. And so effectual did the cordon seem, that it was deemed impossible that he could long remain uncaptured. Nevertheless there was a prevailing opinion that the desperate ruffian would never be taken alive, and that anyone attempting to take him would run the risk of losing his own life. Public excitement, therefore, was worked up to the fullest pitch, and from one end of the country to the other people were painfully anxious to hear of the capture of this savage human animal.

I have already indicated what my own feelings were when I heard that I was to be allowed to join in the hunt for the murderer. And though I was young and inexperienced at the time, I was bold enough, and, as many would have said, egotistical enough, to think that the steps then being taken to cut off the retreat of the fellow were not calculated to secure the object aimed at.

When I got my orders the first thing I did was to make myself acquainted with the habits of the man, as well as learn every detail of his personal appearance. Although I kept my thoughts to myself I came to the conclusion that he was possessed of the most extraordinary and ingenious cunning, and so daring that he might succeed in altogether baffling his pursuers, even as a fox can sometimes baffle the best-trained hounds.

Instead of joining in the full chase that was then going on, I ventured to think it might be as well first of all to try and find a track to follow up, and I quietly went to work to discover something about his relations. The most that I could learn was that he had an aunt living at Ratcliff Highway; but, as will presently be seen, that "most" was to prove of great service. I was informed that one of the force had already visited this woman, but could make nothing of her. That, however, did not deter me, and I was conceited enough to smile to myself as I thought the policeman must have bungled, for it wasn't likely that such a creature would give any information about her precious nephew, for she herself had been in prison, and bore a very bad character. I therefore did not. visit her as one of the force, but in the character of a Jew crimp. It was not an enviable character to assume, but

"'ARE YOU STRAIGHT?'" (p. 330).

the end justified the means, and the end was to try and bring to justice a cold-blooded murderer, and to prevent him, if possible, from shedding more blood.

The woman was known in the neighbourhood as "Mother Mogford," and she was then nearly eighty years of age, but looked much younger. She was a hideous specimen of womankind—in fact, about as repulsive a person as one could well picture. She occupied three small rooms and a kitchen in a very wretched house. As I entered she was sitting in a large chair, smoking a short, dirty, cutty pipe.

"Well, what the devil do you want?" she growled. "You ain't one of those police blokes, are you?" she asked as she scrutinised me with her bleared eyes, and grinned horribly.

"No, mother, I ain't," I answered; "I'm a pal of your nephew."

She broke into a screeching laugh as she exclaimed—

"I ain't going to be caught with that kind of chaff, you know."

"What kind of chaff?"

"Look here, give it to me straight. What do you want?" she demanded, as she banged her bony fist on the table to emphasise her words.

"Why, mother, you don't know your friends," I answered with a laugh. "I want to do you a good turn. You know that the traps are after Pete."

"Yes," she growled. "A bloke came here and thought himself mighty clever, but he did not screw much out of this child."

She laughed cunningly, and I laughed in chorus, and drawing a little flat flask of gin from my pocket, I remarked, going to the door first of all and listening—

"We'll have a drop o' the comfort together." I spoke in a mysterious sort of whisper, and taking up a handle-less cup that was on the table, I poured some gin into it and handed it to her. She poured the fiery stuff down her throat at one gulp, and wiping her thin lips with the back of her scraggy hands, she said—

"Ah, that's good for the stummick!"

I saw that I had gained a point, and being strongly impressed with the idea that she could give me some valuable information—for I ought to have stated that Peter lived, when not in prison, in his aunt's house—I said, still in a mysterious and confidential whisper—

"I know what Pete's done, and that the cops are after him, but I want to put him right. You see he owes me three pounds, and I know there ain't much chance of my getting it unless I can ship him. Now, I've got to put some hands on board a New Yorker that's lying in the river, and leaves to-morrow for San Francisco. This is a chance for Pete to get away, and if you can tell me where I'm likely to find him, I can ship him on the quiet, and will get his advance note, and pay myself the three pounds he owes me, and before anything can be known about it he'll be well out to sea."

As I told her this pardonable crammer I watched her narrowly, and I saw that her shrivelled face and beery eyes lighted up with an expression of delight and cunning, and my heart rejoiced as she asked, "Can you do this?" for the question assured me she knew of his whereabouts.

"Yes," I answered, "and I'll do it if I can find him, for I ain't agoing to lose my three quids if I can help it."

She struggled out of her chair with the aid of a stick, and hobbling to me, seized my hand, and said—

"Are you straight?"

"True as death," I answered.

"Well now, look here," she continued, "I've got some quids, and I'll give you ten of 'em if you'll get Pete clear."

"But where is he?" I asked, scarcely able to conceal the agitation I experienced as I began to dream of succeeding where the more practised men had failed.

She grinned hideously as she answered—

"He was here the day after he done the thing. He came 'cause he wanted some money. I saw something was up and I asked him what it was, and he told me he had killed a bloke. But he said he'd never be tuk."

"If I do what I have said there is no fear of his being taken," I answered.

"And you'll do it?" she asked with great eagerness.

"Yes, if I can make anything out of it."

"And you're straight?" she asked again.

"I've already told you," I returned, trying to keep down the excitement that was making my heart thump at my ribs.

She seemed to hesitate, and a fear came over me that after all she would refuse the information I was craving for. As it was, the old hag kept me on tenter-hooks by saying with a hideous laugh, that almost seemed to have something fiendish about it—

"Aha! he's where all the cops in London won't find him." Then she once more seized my hand, and, putting her face so near to mine that her hot gin-reeking breath caused me to turn away, she continued, "You put Pete on board a ship, so that he can get off, and I'll give you ten quid; but you needn't think you can bluff me. You see Pete knows how to write. They learnt him in the prison, and before you get your ten quid you'll have to bring some writing from Pete to tell me that he is all right."

"Well, well!" I exclaimed a little impatiently, and feeling disgusted with the cunning old wretch.

"Well, well!" she echoed, before I could say anything else, and startling me into a fear that she was after all going to withhold the information. "But, supposing I say it ain't well—well?" she continued; "I ain't agoing to take your word for it; and if you don't bring the writing, devil a halfpenny will you get from me."

"Look here, mother," I said, advancing to her and laying one of my hands on each of her shoulders in a familiar sort of way, "you've promised me ten pounds, and I am not such a fool as to miss the chance of getting a haul like that, if it's possible to get it. Ten, and the three sovereigns Pete owes me, makes thirteen. That's a big lump. Now do you think I'm such an idiot as to miss that when it's in my way to pocket it? No, no, mother; I know how many beans make five, you bet. Now, tell me where I am going to find Pete?"

She grinned diabolically, and then almost made me betray my exasperation by asking—

"Is there any more gin in the bottle?"

I drew out the flask from my pocket again, and emptied the contents of it into the cup, which I handed to her, and she drained it greedily. The fiery potion drew the tears from her red and raw-looking eyes, and for a moment she gasped for breath. She looked so horrible and repulsive that I fairly recoiled from her. Then, as I restored the flask to my pocket I said—

"Well, I can't lose any more time; so if you don't tell me where to find Pete, I'm off."

"Hold on, you fool," she cried. "I'm going to tell you. He's in the marshes."

My heart leapt into my mouth as I heard this, and I asked—

"What marshes?"

"Plumstead," she answered, with a leer.

I did not wait to hear another word, but almost bounded out of the house, and with breathless speed went off to my chief, and requested him to place a dozen stalwart and tried men absolutely under my control. He looked at me incredulously and smiled. There was irony in his smile, and it annoyed me, so I said warmly—

"If you do this, sir, I pledge myself to have the man, dead or alive."

This was a bold statement, because, after all, the old hag might have deceived me, or, assuming that the murderer had gone to the marshes, he had perhaps left again. However, it was do or die with me, and I felt that I was either to distinguish myself or for ever after remain unknown.

"Well, what do you want with the men?" the chief asked.

"I have got undoubtable information," I answered, "that the fellow is hiding in the marshes below Woolwich, and that means that he must be hunted down like a jungle tiger. A desperate man might baffle a regiment of soldiers in such a wilderness, but trust me, give me a chance, place me in charge of twelve good men, and I'll have him or perish myself."

The chief looked at me approvingly now, and said slowly—

"I admire your zeal and enthusiasm, and I'll give you the chance you ask for. The brute must be taken, dead or alive; but remember, we prefer to have him alive. The dozen men are at your disposal. Lose no time, and report progress to me as soon as possible."

I could scarcely find words to thank him. My heart throbbed violently with suppressed excitement, and I felt that this hunt in the wilderness for a desperate human wretch, whose hands were recking with the blood of his fellows, would put into the shade all the tiger hunts of which I had ever read.

The marshes below Woolwich, at the time I speak of, were as dreary a wilderness as any to be found in the British Islands. The wild wastes of sand stretched for seeming interminable miles, and were broken up into a bewildering maze by thousands of tidal streams, some mere tiny rivulets, others broad and deep. Great patches of swamp and dangerous quicksands added to the risks which anyone venturing into this region of desolation had to face. The bittern boomed in the sedges, and the marsh herons, solitary and gaunt, looked spectral as they stood silently on the banks of the streams. Overhead the sea-mews, curlews, and gulls screeched in chorus with the wind, which piped weirdly as it blew coldly over the great expanse of grey sand-dunes, which were unrelieved by a single tree or even a shrub. The only things that seemed to grow were sedges and a stunted wiry grass.

In this region of desolation a fugitive well provided with food, and at all acquainted with the intricacies of the streams and the lie of the swamps and quicksands, might long have defied capture; in fact, might even have escaped altogether if he could have reached the river or got on board of a ship or a barge; or a bold swimmer could have dared the river, landing on the other side.

"I SAW A MAN ON A SAND-RIDGE" (p. 335).

Under any circumstances the hunt in such a place for a desperate criminal who knew that his life was forfeited to the law could not fail to be exciting, and attended with no inconsiderable risk to the pursuers.

Of course I had no means of knowing how Mogford was situated for provisions, or whether he had provided himself with firearms. But I divined that his intention was to get on board of a passing ship, or a barge that would take him down to Greenhithe, where, as he was well furnished with money, he might succeed in obtaining a passage in an outward-bound vessel. In planting my men, therefore, I did not lose sight of the necessity there was for cutting off the fugitive's escape by the river.

In making my plans, I could not shut my eyes to the possibility, and even probability, there was that Mother Mogford had after all deceived me, or it might even be that she herself had been put off the scent by her precious nephew; and if it so chanced that I was wrong, and while I was pursuing a phantom the desperado should be captured elsewhere, I was perfectly well aware that disgrace, if not absolute ruin, would fall upon me.

But when I weighed all the *pros* and *cons* of the case it seemed to me that it was in the highest degree likely that the criminal had fled to the marshy wilderness, being well aware that no other place in that part of the kingdom could offer him so much security. This reflection consoled me, and I made a mental vow that if he had sought refuge there he should only leave the place as a prisoner or a corpse. Probably it would be the latter, for a savage and bloodthirsty tiger at bay is not usually taken alive.

The men who had been placed under my charge were discontented and lacking in zeal. This arose from jealousy and a contempt for me that they were at no pains to conceal. They thought I was an upstart, and that I had been guilty of arrogance in venturing to take any independent course in this hunt for the murderer.

"If you suppose, Donovan," said one fellow, "that you are going to find Mogford in this desert you must be a very simple young man. He ain't such a fool as to run into a trap like this."

There was a chorus of laughter, of course, at these words, but when it died away I remarked, without displaying a trace of irritation—

"I *am* a simple young man, but simple people have occasionally been known to do great deeds."

More laughter followed, and another man said—

"It seems to me this expedition is very like trying to put salt on a bird's tail. Mogford, you may depend upon it, will be safely caged before we even reach the marshes."

"Possibly," I answered, and then, after a pause, added, "and possibly not. Anyway, you have been placed under my orders, and all you have got to do is to obey my orders and do your duty. For any failure it is I who am responsible, not you."

To the general dead-set that was made against me there was an exception in the person of a shrewd, keen-witted, and determined little Irishman named Michael Owen.

"Howld yer wish, boys," he exclaimed, "for maybe the laugh will go agin ye before ye've taken the shine aff of yer brogues, and a foine figure ye'd cut,— all of yess, if Donovan happens to pot the fellow we're arter, won't yer?"

"Yes, fine figures," retorted one in a tone that was meant to be sarcastic.

"Bogorra, yes," cried Owen, "and you'll be the foinest of them all, and will get promotion backwards."

This caused a laugh at the expense of the man who had made the remark, and after that they did not venture upon any further criticism.

It was but natural that I should feel some partiality for the good-natured Irishman who had thus championed me, and, in disposing of my little force, I kept him near me. I instructed the others to form a cordon, so far as practicable; but four of them were gradually to work towards the river, keeping within touch of each other, and exercising the utmost vigilance.

It will readily be understood that from the very nature of the ground it was impossible to follow any fixed route. As I have already said, the place was a maze, owing to the innumerable streams that bisected and intersected, and crossed and re-crossed, running from and into each other, and twisting about at every conceivable angle. The high dunes and the long ridges prevented any extensive survey of the ground before me, while the many hollows afforded capital hiding for a fugitive.

Having giving my instructions, we separated, and had soon lost sight of each other. Each man was provided with a shrill whistle, and two short, sharp blasts were to be given by any man who might sight the fugitive. These blasts were to be taken up by the other members of the force, and so passed on.

Owen and I kept together as near as possible, but for many weary hours we tramped through the swamps and over the sand-hills, and waded through the shallow streams, but we saw nothing to relieve the melancholy monotony of sand and water. Night began to fall, and, with the fading of daylight, my hopes went down to zero, and I could not help thinking then that the expedition would be a failure.

I had previously arranged with my comrades that, if night overtook us, we were to pass the hours of darkness as best we could. This, of course, had caused a great deal of grumbling, but I was inflexible, being unwilling to give up the search until we had traversed the marshes in such a manner as to render it certain that no man was concealed within them.

Michael Owen and I scooped out a large hollow in a hillock, and ensconced ourselves there to try and get a few hours' sleep, and await the coming dawn.

I managed to doze in fitful snatches only, for my mind was too disturbed; but Owen slept like the proverbial top, and snored like the traditional trooper.

As the steely light of the coming day began to spread itself over the wilderness, the effect was almost startingly weird. Everything looked so cold, ghastly, and lifeless; while the silence, like the silence of a dead world, made itself felt. But as the light increased, the sea-birds rose from their watery resting-places, and began to wheel and scream overhead, and their shrill, harsh cries were a positive relief, for they, at least, broke the horrible stillness, which was not the stillness of repose, but of death and desolation.

I arose from my hole in the sand and shook myself, and then let my eyes wander all round the great expanse, and suddenly I started, for I saw, some distance away, a man on a sand-ridge.

He might have been half a mile off, but his figure was clearly cut against the eastern sky. It was impossible to distinguish any of the details of his appearance, excepting that he was not one of our comrades. I had brought a pair of small but powerful binoculars with me, and whipping them out of

my pocket, I adjusted them to my eyes, and then with a cry I exclaimed,
"Owen, by heaven, there's our man!"

The Irishman started to his feet, snatched the glasses from my hand, looked
in the direction I had pointed, and then exclaimed, "Be jabers, you are right!"

The binoculars revealed his features, showed that he was bare-headed, that
his hair was unkempt, and that he was dressed in a nondescript way.

Without waiting to partake of a frugal meal of biscuit and cheese, with
which we were provided, we started off at a quick pace. I was full of excitement, and the blood tingled in my veins. Our course was necessarily a devious
one, owing to the streams, but as far as we could we kept our eyes on the
spot where we had seen the man. We had lost sight of him for a time, but
suddenly he appeared again, scanning the horizon, and shading his eyes with
his hands. Then it became evident that he had seen us, for, like a startled
animal, he bounded away.

There was now no longer room to doubt that we had traced the fugitive,
and were on his heels. We blew our whistles, and the sounds were taken up
and passed on, and echoed and re-echoed, and they must have fallen upon
the ears of the hunted man like a knell of doom.

We made out the figures of others of our comrades now, far off and
scattered about, and we knew that the chase had been taken up. Then we
saw the criminal double back, and, for a while, lost sight of him. Owen and
I rushed along as well as the nature of the ground would permit, plunging
through the streams, and sometimes sinking above the knees in marsh, ooze,
and quicksand. For some time we had lost sight of our quarry, when suddenly
we were startled by his springing up within two dozen yards of us. He had
got on to a ridge to take a rapid survey, and seeing us he started off, and we
went in full chase after him.

My companion and I were in a state of great excitement. In my own case
every nerve and fibre in my body seemed stretched to its uttermost extent.
Again we lost sight of the fugitive as he was hidden in a hollow, but as we
mounted we descried him again, and saw that we had gained upon him. A
broad creek interposed itself in his course, but without hesitation he plunged
in and swam across, and as he climbed out on the opposite bank he stood still
for some minutes.

We saw that when he came out of the water he had something between
his teeth. It proved to be a double-barrelled pistol, and, taking deliberate aim,
he fired twice. The first shot went away into space; at the second I saw my
comrade fall, and sprang to his aid. He had been hit on the very top of the
left shoulder.

"Go you on," he said; "I'm not kilt yet."

I satisfied myself that the wound was not serious, and I told him to plant
himself in a conspicuous spot where he could be seen, and to try and staunch
the bleeding with a wet handkerchief. Then I darted off once more, and I

"HE HURLED THE PISTOL AT MY HEAD" (p. 338).

saw three or four of my little force converging towards me, so that it became evident we were hemming our man in. They had heard the pistol-shot, and asked excitedly if either of us had been hit. I told them that Michael had, and sent one of them to look after him. Then we searched about for our man, but found him not. We had last seen him darting down into a hollow formed by two ridges of sand, but when we rushed for the spot he had gone.

The chase had become exciting now, and the scent hot; and the very men who a few hours ago had treated me with such contempt began to sing my praises; but I cut them short and told them there was business to do. Then each seemed desirous of gaining the honour of having it said that he was the first to capture the villain.

In different directions we saw others of our comrades, and we apprised them by our whistles that we had found the scent. Then I told my men to spread themselves out, but to keep within easy distance, for the hunted murderer, as we now knew, was armed, and would sell his worthless life dearly. I felt sure that he could not escape, and I confess to a burning desire to be able to capture him myself. But in the meantime where had he gone? He had for the time being given us the slip. I managed to gain a sand-hillock, which enabled me to command a pretty wide area, and my heart leapt to my mouth as I caught sight of the fellow running along with his head bent low.

I blew my whistle, and waved my hands in his direction, so as to convey an intimation to my comrades of the quarter he was in. Right ahead of him were two of my hunters, and I saw if I missed him he would run into their arms, so I made a wild plunge after him. But in a few minutes he evidently caught sight of those in front of him, and doubled back. He came within a dozen yards of me, and I could see that his eyes were starting from his head while his face was ghastly and horrible in its greenish pallor. As he caught sight of me he uttered an oath, and, turning off sharply at an angle, plunged into a broad stream and swam across. I followed him, and when he landed on the other side he turned, and in his foaming rage he looked like some savage beast rather than a human being.

He covered me with his pistol and fired, but there was no discharge. He raised the hammer and fired again, with the same result, and it became evident that the weapon was soaked with water. With a fierce shriek of disappointment, he hurled the pistol at my head with all his might; but it fortunately fell short, and he turned and fled again.

I scrambled out of the water and followed. As luck would have it, the ground was pretty flat hereabouts, and I was enabled to keep him in sight; but he was fleeter than I, and I saw he was gaining in the race, so I sounded my whistle as I ran, and in a few moments I beheld one of my men ahead. The fugitive saw him too, and I heard a cry escape from his lips as he turned on a curve, which brought him to a river that was broad and deep, and running pretty strong. He plunged in and sank for a moment out of sight. When he rose it was obvious he was fagged, and I fancied he turned his eyes upon me with a look of despair and yet defiance.

I paused to blow a long, loud warning blast on my whistle. I heard it answered and I blew again; then in I went after him. I was fresher than he, made more rapid strokes, and gained upon him until I could almost touch him, when, with a sudden movement, he faced round and grappled me.

He had realised that his game was up—that he was at bay; but he was determined if possible to have more blood on his guilty soul, although he was within the shadow of death.

Amongst the few accomplishments that I really excelled in at school was that of swimming, and it was to serve me in good stead now, although at first I thought my last hour had come, for he seized me by the hair and held me under the water.

I managed, however, to get my head free; how I really don't know. Then I grappled him, and we struggled frantically together.

"You shall never get out alive!" he hissed in gasps.

But he was wrong. I had managed by some means, which I can scarcely describe, to drag him near enough to the edge to enable me to grasp the bank with one hand, while I held him with the other. I turned my eyes anxiously to see if help was coming, for I knew only too well that I could never hope to get him out of the water alone. We were both exhausted, and it was a question which would give in first. Although a maddening desperation lent him a certain strength, it would not hold out long, and I believe he would have succumbed before me, but that meant that he would be drowned, and I was particularly anxious to capture him alive.

It was a terrible and thrilling situation—one of those situations when a man's hopes, his future, his very life may be said to hang upon a hair, and it is impossible to predict if the hair will break or not.

I heard the gurgling of the water, and it mingled with the stertorous breathing of the wretch I was anxious to save, in order that the law might take its vengeance. I saw his fierce eyes glaring at me with something of fiendish hate in their expression.

Moments under such an awful strain seemed minutes, and minutes hours. The whole terrible scene was enacted in a very brief space of time, and yet it seemed interminable. Then I heard a rush and a plunge, and saw a third man in the water. It was one of my comrades, who, as if to make up for the way he had treated me on the previous day, did not hesitate to jump to my rescue. Then a third man appeared on the scene, and by our united efforts we dragged the half-drowned wretch on to the bank, where he lay prostrated for some little time. Presently he recovered, and we helped him to his feet and handcuffed him.

Never to my dying day shall I forget the look of utter despair that came into his pallid face as he felt the cold steel close on his wrists. His exhausted state had caused us to somewhat relax our watchfulness. He saw this, and with one mighty effort he threw himself backwards and fell with a great splash into the water again. We saw his feet appear above the surface for an instant or two; then he disappeared, and I have a notion that he must have literally dug his hands into the bottom of the river. In a few minutes his back showed on the surface; he was hanging limp down, with his head entirely covered. He was close to the bank, and we managed to grab him and land him.

But it was too late. Consciousness had fled, and though I could detect the beating of his heart for some minutes, it gradually ceased, and Peter Mogford, the most desperate ruffian of his time, was dead. He had at least succeeded in cheating man of his vengeance, and had robbed the public of a spectacle. We bore his worthless body back to London, and in due course it was consigned to a dishonoured grave.

My companion Michael Owen speedily recovered from his wound, and he, in common with all of us who had taken part in that memorable man-hunt, received a share of a considerable subscription that was raised by a grateful public; and in process of time the authorities were pleased to recognise the service I had rendered by awarding me promotion. I thus gained something, but I do not think that anything could ever have tempted me to again engage in such an awful and sickening duty as was that hunt for a murderer in the Woolwich marshes.

[Our thanks for permission to use the above story are due to Messrs. Chatto and Windus.]

ROZIERS' BALLOON.

TRAVELS IN THE AIR.

IN 1783 the two brothers Montgolfier had made their great discovery, the first considerable step, as it may be called, in aërostatics. Joseph Montgolfier, as a result of a series of minor experiments, had become convinced that air when heated to 180° became so highly rarefied as to occupy twice its original space, or, to put the fact differently, that this degree of heat diminished the weight of air by one-half. As a consequence he set his wits to work to invent a structure that, being filled with air thus heated, would triumph over its own weight and rise from the earth.

The structure was invented and became the parent of the modern balloon. A number of trials proved its success. Paris went wild over the new toy, Songs were sung about it in the streets; all the drawing-rooms discussed it; the libraries held models of it; learned societies issued pamphlets upon it to show its latent possibilities, its conceivable uses as an instrument of warfare, of locomotion, of scientific discovery, of criminal investigation, &c. &c. Society, from the noble to the *gamin*, trooped to the Champ de Mars, to Versailles, to the gardens of the Faubourg St. Antoine, whenever an ascent was to be exhibited. A new era, according to some, was beginning, and France of course led the way. "Then, as now," said a writer, "the voice of Paris gave the cue to France, and France to all the world."

This was all very well, but as yet the new invention had risen into the air alone. No man had been found daring enough to trust himself to the dismal luck that attends the pioneer of progress. The question was—Could a man go up with this new machine and come down alive? And before this could be answered came another question—Who cared to try?

A man whose name was destined to be famous—Pilâtre de Roziers—was the first volunteer. The balloon was a new one, constructed by the Montgolfiers. Its form was oval, its height 70 feet, its diameter 46 feet, its cubic capacity 60,000 feet. The top was embroidered with *fleurs-de-lis*, and with the signs of the Zodiac worked in gold. Below came the monogram of King Louis XVI., alternating with the device of the sun; and the bottom part was elaborately worked with festoons, masks, and eagles. A wicker basket, draped and elaborately ornamented, was attached to the bottom of the balloon by cords. This basket was three feet wide, and the sides were three feet in height. The whole structure weighed 1,600 pounds. It was completed on the 10th of October, 1783, and on the 15th Roziers made his ascent.

It was a small but interesting experiment. The balloon was inflated; stout ropes were fastened to it, which allowed it to rise to the height of 80 feet. To this height it accordingly soared, and remained there four minutes, twenty-five seconds. The crucial point to be tested was the manner in which it would descend when the hot air was exhausted. It descended quietly, distending as it dropped. Roziers jumped quietly out; and after touching the ground, the balloon, relieved of his weight, rose again a foot or two before it finally settled.

Two days later the same experiment was repeated with success before a vast concourse of people. There was a trying wind, the ropes were severely strained, and the balloon swayed unsteadily. Still the result was encouraging, and on the Sunday—a fine day—three bolder trials were made.

First Ascent: On October 19th, at half-past four, in presence of two thousand spectators, the machine was filled with gas in five minutes, and Roziers, being placed in the basket, with a ballast of 110 pounds to trim the car, was carried aloft to the height of 200 feet. The machine remained six minutes at this elevation, without any fire in the grating. (It must be explained that under the neck of the balloon was suspended a grating of iron wire, upon which the occupant of the car could kindle a fire and heat up the air afresh when the balloon began to be exhausted.)

Second Ascent: The machine, a fire being lit in the grating, carried Roziers and his ballast to the height of 200 feet. Here it remained stationary eight and a half minutes. As it was pulled back to earth, a wind from the east carried it against a clump of very tall trees in a neighbouring garden, when it became extricated, without, however, losing its equilibrium. Roziers renewed the fire, and the balloon, again rising majestically into the air, extricated itself from among the branches and soared aloft, followed by the acclamations of the public. This second ascent was highly instructive, for it had been often asserted that if ever a balloon fell upon a forest it would be destroyed, and would place those who travelled in it in the greatest peril. This experiment proved that the balloon does not *fall*, it *descends;* that it does not overturn; that it does not destroy itself on trees; that it neither causes death, nor even damage, to its passengers; that, on the contrary, by making fresh gas, they can give it the power of detaching itself from the trees; and that it can resume its course after such an event. The intrepid Roziers gave in this ascent a further proof of the facility he had in ascending and descending at will. When the machine had again risen to the height of 200 feet it began to descend lightly, and just before it came to earth the aëronaut very cleverly and quickly threw on more fuel and produced more smoke, at which the balloon, to the astonishment of every-one, suddenly soared away again to its former elevation.

Third Ascent: The balloon rose again with Roziers, who discarded his ballast, and was accompanied instead by another aëronaut, Gerond de Villette; and as the cords had been lengthened, the adventurers were carried up to the height of 324 feet. At this elevation the balloon rested in perfect equilibrium for nine minutes. It was the first time that human beings had ever been carried to an equal altitude, and the spectators were astonished to find that they could remain there without danger and without alarm. The balloon had a superb effect at this elevation; it looked down upon the whole town, and was seen from all the suburbs. Its size seemed hardly diminished, though the men them-selves were barely visible. By the aid of glasses, Roziers could be seen calmly and industriously manufacturing new gas.

Says de Villette, writing on this experiment:—"I found myself in a quarter of a minute raised 400 feet above the surface of the earth. Here we remained six minutes. My first employment was to watch with admiration my intelligent companion. His intelligence, his courage and agility in attending to the fire enchanted me. Below I could see the Boulevards, from the Porte St. Antoine to the Porte St. Martin, all covered with people, who seemed to me to be a flat band of flowers of various colours. Glancing at the distance, I beheld the summit of Montmartre, which seemed to me much below our level. I could easily distinguish Neuilly, St. Cloud, Sèvres, Issy, Ivry, Charenton, and Choisy. At once I was convinced that this machine might be very useful in war to enable one to discover the position of the enemy, his manœuvres and his marches, and to announce these by signals to our own army. I believe that at sea it is equally possible to make use of it. All that I regret is that I did not provide myself with a telescope."

There was one aim in these experiments—to test the possibility of navigating the air in the newly invented machine. It was quickly resolved that a voyage should be attempted.

But the scheme was opposed. King Louis at first forbade it; and on being pressed, would only grant permission on the condition that two condemned criminals should be placed in the car. Roziers was prettily indignant. What!

Were two vile malefactors to have the glory of first ascending the skies? He petitioned, agitated by every, means in his power, to bend the royal will. Paris supported him, and at length he found friends at Versailles to back his cause. The Duchess of Polignac, the King's favourite, pleaded for him. The Marquis d'Arlandes, a major of infantry, and an enthusiastic supporter of the aëronauts, who had been up with Roziers in one of his experiments, himself sought Louis, assured him there was no danger, and, in proof, professed himself ready to accompany Roziers.

The King, in face of this entreaty, gave way. D'Arlandes and Roziers ascended from the gardens of La Muette, at one o'clock in the afternoon of October 21st. All Paris was there to see, and the Dauphin attended with his suite. The story of the voyage shall be given in D'Arlandes' own words:—

"It is my intention," he writes to his friend, Faujas de Saint Fond, "to describe as well as I can the first journey attempted by man through an element which, previous to MM. Montgolfier's discovery, seemed but little fitted to support him.

"We ascended on October 21st, 1783, at near two o'clock: M. Roziers on the west side of the balloon, I on the east. The wind was nearly north-west. The machine, people say, rose majestically; but in fact the position of the balloon altered so that M. Roziers was soon on the east side, and I on the west.

"I was surprised at the silence and absence of movement among the spectators, and conceived them to be astonished, and perhaps awed at the strange spectacle. They might well have reassured themselves. I was still gazing, when M. Roziers cried out—

"'You are doing nothing, and the balloon is scarce rising a fathom!'

"'I beg your pardon,' I answered, placing a bundle of straw on the fire, and slightly stirring it. This done, I turned quickly. Already we had passed out of sight of La Muette. In astonishment I glanced down towards the river. I could perceive the confluence of the Oise. And naming the principal bends of the river by the places nearest them, I cried, 'Passy, St. Germain, St. Denis, Sèvres!'

"'If you look at the river in that way you will find yourself bathing in it soon,' called out Roziers. 'Some fire, my dear friend, some fire!'

"We travelled on; but instead of crossing the river, as our direction seemed to promise, we bore towards the Invalides, then returned towards the principal bed of the river, and travelled to above the barrier of La Conférence, thus dodging about the Seine, but not crossing it.

"'That river is very difficult to cross,' said I to my comrade.

"'So it seems,' he answered; 'but you do nothing. I suppose you are braver than I, and don't mind a tumble.'

"I stirred the fire, and seizing a truss of straw with my fork, pitched it into the middle of the flames. Immediately I felt myself lifted, as it were, into the heavens.

"'For once we move,' said I.

"'Yes,' said my comrade; 'we move.'

"At that instant I heard, from the top of the balloon, a sound which made me believe it had burst. I watched, but saw nothing. My companion had gone into the interior, no doubt to make some observations. As my eyes were fixed on the top of the machine I experienced a shock, and it was the only one I had yet. The direction of the movement was downwards from above. I said—

"'I SAW HIM CREEPING OUT'" (p. 346).

"'What are you doing there? Are you having a dance to yourself?'

"'I'm not stirring.'

"'So much the better. It is only a new current that I hope will carry us from the river.'

"I turned to see where we were, and found we were between the École Militaire and the Invalides.

"'We are getting on,' said Roziers.

"'Yes, we are travelling.'

"'Let us work, let us work,' said he.

"I now heard another report in the machine, which I believed was produced by the cracking of a cord. This new intimation made me carefully examine the inside of our habitation. I saw that the part that was turned towards the south was full of holes, of which some were of a considerable size.

"'It must descend!' I cried.

"'Why?'

"'Look!' I said. At the same time I took my sponge and quietly extinguished the little fire that was burning some of the holes within my reach; but at the same moment I noticed that the bottom of the cloth was coming away from the circle which surrounded it. .

"'We must descend,' I repeated.

"He looked below.

"'We are upon Paris,' he said.

"'It does not matter,' I answered; 'only look! Is there no danger? Are you holding on well?'

"'Yes.'

"I examined from my side and saw that we had nothing to fear. I then tried with my sponge the ropes that were within my reach. All of them held firm. Only two of the cords had broken.

"I then said, 'We can cross Paris.'

"During this operation we were rapidly getting down to the roofs. We made more fire, and rose again with the greatest ease. I looked down, and it seemed to me we were moving towards the towers of St. Sulpice; but, as we rose, a new current made us quit this direction and bear more to the south. I looked to the left and beheld a wood, which I believed to be that of Luxembourg. We were traversing the boulevard, and I cried all at once—

"'Get to ground!'

"But the intrepid Roziers, who never lost his head, but judged more accurately than I, prevented me from attempting to descend. I threw a bundle of straw on the fire. We rose again, and another current bore us to the left. We were now close to the ground, between two mills. As soon as we drew near to the earth I raised myself over the wicker gallery, and leaning there with both hands, felt the balloon pressing softly against my head. I pushed it back, and leapt down to the ground. Looking round and expecting to see the balloon still distended, I saw it to my astonishment quite flattened and empty. On gazing about for Roziers, I saw him creeping out from under the mass of canvas. He was in his shirt-sleeves. Before attempting to descend he had taken off his coat and put it in the basket. We were all right.

"As Roziers was without his coat I begged him to go to the nearest house. On our way thither we met the Duc de Chartres, who had followed us very closely, for I had the honour to converse with him the moment before we ascended."

It may be imagined that this ascent was soon emulated. Another took place on the 1st of December. The balloon this time was built by Professor

Charles, to be inflated with hydrogen gas, and to carry a car with one or two passengers; and it contained an invention which marks the second great step in the science of ballooning—the invention of a valve, to give escape to the gas and thus render the descent easy and readily checked. Besides this, the new balloon contained other important discoveries, notably the ballast of sand, to regulate the ascent and moderate the fall, the coating of caoutchouc that makes the structure air-tight and prevents loss of gas, and finally the barometer, to mark at any given instant the elevation attained by the aëronaut. If Montgolfier invented the balloon, Charles discovered the safeguards of ballooning.

All was ready for the ascent. The subscribers, who had paid four louis for their seats, were in their places, the roofs and windows were crowded, the throng covered the Square of Louis XV., and lined the Pont Royal. Around the balloon, in the Tuileries Gardens, were gathered (it was computed) near on 600,000 people.

All at once, at midday, a rumour spread that the King had forbidden the ascent. Charles, hearing it, ran off to the Chief Minister of State, burst into his room, and announced a bold determination. "My life," said he, "is the King's, but my honour is my own. I have pledged my word, and I will ascend." It was true that the King had issued a veto; but the professor triumphed, and wrung an unwilling permission.

The crowd in the Tuileries Gardens, meanwhile, was discussing the respective merits of Montgolfier and Charles; and each professor had his following of hot partisans. Charles, on returning to the gardens, heard the war of words raging. He walked up to Montgolfier and said, with admirable tact—

"It is for you, Monsieur, to show us the way to the skies."

Such a speech as this can only be fully comprehended by a Frenchman. The crowd shouted vociferous admiration. Montgolfier bowed to his rival, and threw up a small balloon that sailed gracefully away to the north-east, its emerald colours lit up by the radiant, winter sunshine.

And now let us follow Charles's narrative:—

"The balloon that escaped from the hands of M. Montgolfier soared into the air, and seemed to bear with it the testimony of friendship and regard between that gentleman and myself. Acclamations followed it. We, on our part, hastily prepared for departure. The fresh wind that was blowing did not allow us to have at our command all the arrangements that we had intended. To prepare them would have detained us too long on earth. As soon as the balloon and the car were in equilibrium, we threw over nineteen pounds of ballast, and we rose amid silence, the result of emotion and surprise on all hands.

"Nothing will ever match that moment of glad excitement which filled my whole being as I felt myself soaring away from the earth. It was not mere pleasure, it was perfect bliss. Escaped from the torments of persecution and calumny, I felt that I was answering all in rising above them.

"To this sentiment one even livelier succeeded—the admiration of the majestic spectacle that spread itself out before us. On whatever side we looked, all was gorgeous; a cloudless sky above, around a most delicious view. I turned to my companion, M. Robert (the mechanician of the balloon). 'My friend,' said I, 'how great is our good fortune! I care not what may be the condition of the earth: it is the sky that is for me now. What a serene heaven! What a ravishing scene! Would that I could bring here the last of our detractors, and say to the wretch, Behold what you would have lost had you arrested the progress of science!'

"As we rose with a progressively increasing speed, we waved our bannerets in token of cheerfulness, and to give confidence to our sympathisers below. M. Robert made an inventory of our stores. Our friends had provided us for a long voyage—champagne and other wines, garments of fur and other articles of clothing.

Said I, 'Good: throw that last article out of window.' He took a blanket and launched it into the air, through which it floated down slowly, and fell upon the dome of L'Assomption.

"As soon as the barometer

"MONTGOLFIER BOWED TO HIS RIVAL" (p. 347).

had fallen 26 inches, we ceased to ascend. We were at an elevation of 1,800 feet. This was the height to which I had promised myself to attain; and from this moment to the time when we disappeared from the eyes of our friends, we kept a horizontal course, the barometer registering between 26 inches and 26 inches 8 lines.

"According as the almost insensible escape of the hydrogen gas caused us to sink, we threw out ballast and recovered our elevation. If circumstances had allowed us to measure the quantity of ballast we threw over, I doubt not we should have found our course almost absolutely horizontal.

"Our car, after remaining for a few moments stationary, changed its course and was carried at the will of the wind. Soon we passed the Seine, between

St. Ouen and Amières. We crossed the river a second time, leaving Argenteuil on our left. We passed Samois, Franconville, Eau Bonne, St. Leu-Taverny, Villiers, and finally Nesles. This was about twenty-seven miles from Paris, and we had reached this distance in two hours, although now there was hardly enough wind to stir the air.

"Throughout this delightful voyage, not the slightest apprehension for our fate or that of the balloon entered my head for a moment. The balloon underwent no alteration, beyond the successive changes of dilatation and compression, which allowed us to mount and descend at will. The thermometer was, during more than an hour, between ten and twelve degrees above zero; this being to some extent accounted for by the fact that the interior of the car was warmed by the rays of the sun.

"At the end of fifty-six minutes, we heard the report of a cannon, that told us we had at that moment disappeared from view at Paris. We rejoiced that we had escaped, as we were no longer obliged to observe a horizontal course or to regulate the balloon for that purpose. We surrendered ourselves to the contemplation of the views presented by the vast stretch of country beneath us. From that time, though we had no opportunity of conversing with the inhabitants, we saw them running after us from all parts: we heard their cries, their exclamations of solicitude, and knew their alarm and admiration.

"We cried '*Vive le Roi!*' and the people responded. We heard very distinctly 'My good friends, have you no fear? Are you not sick? How beautiful it is! Heaven preserve you! Adieu, my friends!' And I was touched to tears by this true and tender interest awakened by our appearance.

"We continued to wave our flags without cessation, and we perceived that these signals greatly increased the cheerfulness and relieved the anxiety of the people below. Often we descended low enough to hear what they shouted to us. They asked us whence we came, and at what hour we had started.

"We threw over successively frock-coats, muffs, and habits. Sailing on above the Île d'Adam, after having admired the splendid view, we made signals with our flags, and demanded news of the Prince of Conti. One cried up to us in a stentorian voice, that he was at Paris and that he was unwell. We regretted to miss such an opportunity of paying our respects, for we could have descended into the Prince's gardens had we wished; but we preferred to pursue our course, and we re-ascended. Finally we arrived at the plain of Nesles.

"We saw, in the distance, groups of peasants running on before us across the fields. 'Let us go,' I said, and we descended towards a vast meadow.

"Some trees and shrubs stood round its border. Our car advanced majestically in a long inclined plane. Arriving near the trees, I feared their branches might damage the car, and threw over two pounds of ballast. We rose again, and ran along more than 120 feet, at the distance of one or two feet from the ground, so that we had the appearance of travelling in a sledge.

The peasants ran after us without being able to catch us, like children pursuing a butterfly in the fields.

"At last we stopped, and were instantly surrounded. Nothing could equal the simple and tender regard of these country-folk, their admiration and their lively emotion.

"I called at once for the curés and magistrates. They came round me on all sides ; there was quite a fête on the spot. I prepared a short report, which the curés and syndics signed. Then arrived a company of horsemen at a gallop. These were the Duke of Chartres, the Duke of Fitzjames, and M. Farrer. By a singular chance we had come down close by the hunting lodge of this last gentleman. He leapt from his horse, and threw himself into my arms. 'Monsieur Charles,' he cried, 'I was first!'

"The Duke of Chartres also embraced us both, covering me with caresses. I told him the incidents of our voyage.

"'But,' I wound up, 'this is not all, Monseigneur. I am going away again.'

"'What! going away?' exclaimed the Duke.

"'Monseigneur, you shall see. When do you wish me to come back again?'

"'In half an hour.'

"'Be it so. In half an hour I will be with you again.'

"M. Robert now descended from the car, and I was alone in the balloon.

"I said to the Duke, 'Monseigneur, I am off.' I said to the peasants who were holding down the balloon, 'My friends, go away, all of you, from the car the instant I give the signal.' I then shot up like a bird, and in ten minutes I was more than 3,000 feet above the ground. I no longer perceived terrestrial objects ; I only saw great masses of nature.

"In order to observe the barometer and thermometer, which were placed at different extremities of the car, and to avoid endangering the equilibrium, I now sat down in the middle, a watch and paper in my left hand, a pen and the cord of the valve in my right.

"I waited for what should happen. The balloon, which was quite soft and flabby when I ascended, had now become taut and fully distended. Soon the hydrogen gas began to escape in considerable quantities from the neck of the balloon, and then from time to time I pulled open the valve to give it two outlets at once. And I continued to mount upwards, all the time losing the inflammable air, which, as it rushed past me from the neck of the balloon, felt like a warm cloud.

"I passed in ten minutes from the temperature of spring to that of winter. The cold was keen and dry, but not insupportable. I examined all my sensations calmly ; *I could hear myself live*, so to speak, and I am certain that at first I experienced nothing disagreeable in this sudden passage from one temperature to another.

"When the barometer ceased to move, I noted very exactly 18 inches, 10 lines. The mercury did not suffer any sensible movement.

"After some minutes the cold began to catch my fingers. I could hardly hold the pen, but I had no longer any need to do so. I was stationary, or rather moved only in a horizontal direction.

"I raised myself in the middle of the car, and abandoned myself to contemplation of the spectacle below me. At my departure from the meadow the sun had sunk to the people in the valleys. Soon he shone for me alone, and poured his rays upon the balloon and the car. From horizon to horizon I was the only creature in sunshine. Before long, however, the sun disappeared, and thus I had the pleasure of seeing him set twice in the same day. I contemplated for some moments the mists and vapours that rose from the valley and the rivers. The clouds seemed to come forth from the earth, and to accumulate, the one upon the other. Their colour was a monotonous grey, a natural effect, for there was no light save that of the moon.

"I observed that I had tacked round twice, and felt currents that called me to my senses. I found with surprise the effect of the wind, and saw the cloth of my flag stretched out, tight and horizontal.

"From the midst of this ecstatic contemplation, so inexpressibly pleasurable, I was awakened by an extraordinary pain which I felt in the interior of my ears and in the maxillary glands. I attributed it to the dilatation of the air contained in the cellular tissue of the organ, as much as to the cold outside. I was in my vest, with my head uncovered. I immediately covered my head with a bonnet of wool which was at my feet, but the pain only disappeared with my descent to the ground.

"It was now seven or eight minutes since I had arrived at this elevation, and I now began to descend. I called to mind the promise I had made to the Duke of Chartres, to return in half an hour. I quickened my descent by opening the valve from time to time. Soon the balloon, empty now to one-half, presented the appearance of a hemisphere.

"Arrived at twenty-three fathoms from the earth, I suddenly threw over two or three pounds of ballast, which arrested my descent, and which I had carefully kept for this purpose. I then slowly descended upon the ground which I had, so to speak, chosen."

Curiously enough, Professor Charles never trusted himself to a balloon again. He writes in enthusiastic language; but it is said that, on alighting from the car, he swore he would never again expose himself to such terror as he experienced when the peasants let go the ropes and he shot up into the sky. His was the last ascent of 1783, the *annus mirabilis* of aëronautics.

In 1784 the whole world seemed to have gone ballooning; but of the innumerable ascents that were made in France, England, Austria, Italy, Germany, America, we will select one only. It shall be that of our old friend Roziers, who, together with a M. Proust, ascended from Versailles on June 23rd in the balloon *La Maria Antoinette*, and alighted at Compiègne, forty miles away.

"The Montgoltière," says Roziers, "rose at first diagonally and very gently. It was an imposing sight. Like a ship let loose from the stocks, this amazing machine hung balanced in the air for some time, and seemed to be beyond man's control. These erratic movements intimidated many of the spectators, who, fearing that, should there be a fall, their lives would be in danger, scattered right and left from under us with all speed.

"After having fed my fire I saluted the people, who answered me in a most cordial manner. I had even time to notice some faces that expressed mingled feelings of apprehension and pleasure. Still rising upwards, I remarked that an upper current of air made the Montgolfière bend, but on increasing our fire we rose above it. The size of objects on the earth now began perceptibly to diminish, which gave us a notion of our distance from them. It was about this time that we became visible to Paris and its suburbs, and so great was our elevation that many in the capital thought we were over their heads.

"We reached the clouds; the earth disappeared from our view. Now a thick mist would envelop us; now a clear space showed us where we were; and again we rode through a cloud of snow, portions of which stuck to our gallery. Being curious to know how high we could ascend, we resolved to increase our fire and raise the heat to the highest degree, by raising our grating, and holding up our fagots on the ends of our forks.

"Having gained this snowy elevation, and being unable to mount higher, we wandered about for some time in regions in which we perceived beneath us only enormous masses of snow, which, reflecting the sunshine, filled the firmament with glorious light. We remained eight minutes at this height, 11,732 feet above the earth. This situation, however agreeable it might have been to painter or poet, promised little to the man of science in the way of acquiring knowledge; and therefore we made up our minds, eighteen minutes after our departure, to return through the clouds to the earth. We had scarcely left these regions of snow, when the most pleasant scene succeeded the most dreary one. The broad plains appeared beneath us in all their magnificence. No snow, no clouds were to be seen, except around the horizon, where a few clouds seemed to rest on earth. We passed in a minute from winter to spring. We saw the immeasurable earth covered with towns and villages, which at that distance appeared only so many isolated mansions surrounded with gardens. The rivers, which wound about in all directions, seemed no more than rivulets for the adornment of these mansions; the largest forests looked mere clumps or groves, and the meadows and broad fields seemed but garden plots. These marvellous pictures—pictures beyond the reach of painters—reminded us of the metamorphoses of fairy-land; only with this difference, that we were beholding upon a gigantic scale what the imagination could only portray in little.

"Travelling at this altitude we had no need to bestow constant attention on our fire, and we could easily walk about the gallery. Upon our lofty balcony we were as much at peace as we should have been upon the terrace of a mansion, enjoying all the pictures which continually unrolled themselves, and yet experiencing no giddiness.

"I had broken my fork in my efforts with the fire, and went to fetch another. On my way I encountered my companion, M. Proust. We ought

"HE LOOKED IN TERROR TO HIS TWO FRIENDS" (p. 355).

never to have been on the same side of the balloon, for a capsize and the escape of all our gas might have been the result. As it was, so well was our balloon ballasted, that the only effect of our being on the one side made the balloon incline a little in that direction. The winds, though very considerable, caused us no uneasiness, and we only knew the swiftness of our progress by the rapidity with which the villages seemed to fly away from under us; so that it seemed, from the tranquillity with which we moved, that we were borne along by the diurnal movement of the globe. Often we wished to descend in order to hear what the people were shouting to us. The simplicity of our arrangements enabled us to rise, descend, move in horizontal or oblique lines, as we pleased, and as often as we thought necessary, without actually landing."

They finally landed in safety, and with ease. They had ascended, as we have read, to the height of 11,732 feet. All this had been accomplished in a year after Montgolfier's great invention. It seemed that man's triumph over the atmosphere was to be brief and easy. Never—perhaps not when Columbus brought America to light—was any discovery wafted to such a height on the breath of popular applause. Benjamin Franklin, then at the French Court, being interrogated on the possibilities of the balloon, had answered simply, " C'est l'enfant qui vient de naître."

It was a non-committal sort of reply ; and a century has shown the wisdom of it. More than a hundred years has passed ; and has ballooning made any great strides since 1783? We may perhaps find an answer in the account of an ascent made in 1875, and with that we will conclude our chapter.

On March 2nd, 1874, the French Society of Aërial Navigation resolved to organise an ascent with the balloon *Étoile du Nord*, for the purpose of testing the restorative powers of oxygen breathed in place of ordinary air in a rarefied atmosphere. The expedition was a failure. The aëronauts attained to no great altitude, and yet, according to their report, experienced severe derange-ment of the system, a derangement which the oxygen hardly succeeded in alleviating.

The Society determined to try again. "There are certain extremely systematic minds," says M. de Fonvielle, in commenting upon the experiment, "that have an unhappy tendency to believe that in physiological experiments we may substitute for natural conditions certain artificial preparations or operations made upon the subjects. It was in obedience to this disastrous idea that the future aëronauts of the *Zenith* submitted to experiments made under a pneumatic bell, for the purpose of accustoming themselves to this in rarefied air. The " bell ascent " having given satisfactory results, it was believed that no obstacle could arrest the intrepid men who set out to repeat it in infinite space."

At any rate, in the April of 1875, a new balloon, the *Zenith*, set out from the La Villette gas-works, in Paris. It was a bright spring day. The sky was cloudless ; in the loftier regions of the air a cold dry current blew from the Pole. The car contained three persons, M. Sivel, M. Crocé-Spinalli, and M. Gaston Tissandier. The last-mentioned had come for the express purpose of carrying out a particular experiment. His purpose was to analyse the dust of the air ; and to this end he had brought an aspirator containing a large reservoir of petroleum oil. The apparatus was heavy, but to prevent accidents it was fastened to the car by cords which could be easily cut. The bags of ballast also were so arranged outside the car that by a stroke of the knife they could be at once emptied.

The ascent was gradual. An E.N.E. wind was blowing, and the sky was blue but vaporous. The rate of ascent was calculated at nine feet per second, but slowly lessened. By one o'clock, or soon after, the three aëronauts were at an altitude of 22,800 feet. They were weak and languid, but felt otherwise well. The inhalation of the oxygen produced good effects.

A consultation was held, and it was desired to mount higher, the *Zenith* being in equilibrium. A quantity of ballast was thrown overboard. Up soared the balloon; and at this point M. Tissandier fainted.

At eighteen minutes past two he was awakened by M. Crocé-Spinalli, who begged him to heave over ballast as the balloon was rapidly descending.

He obeyed in a mechanical sort of way. At the same time M. Crocé-Spinalli threw overboard the aspirator, which weighed eighty pounds.. M. Tissandier then scribbled a few disconnected words in his note-book and, while doing so, dropped off into a state of stupor for about half an hour. When he awoke, the balloon was descending at a terrific rate. All the ballast was exhausted.

He looked in terror to his two friends for help. Their faces were black. They were dead—suffocated. Blood was flowing from their mouths and noses.

It was a terrible situation. Down hurled the balloon. Tissandier's sole resource was to cut the grapnel rope an instant before the car struck the ground. He did so with amazing coolness. The force of the wind had increased. Tissandier tore open the balloon to stop it. It was caught on a hedge, at Ciron, a commune of Indre, 190 miles S.S.W. of Paris. M. Tissandier escaped serious injury; the others were dead of course. The survivor was picked up by a family of the neighbourhood and treated with every kindness.

SCENE IN GOTLAND (WISBY).

THE GOTLAND MAIL.

(1830.)

IN 1855 there appeared in the *Gotland Journal* the following minute and harrowing account of one of the many perilous journeys undertaken by the Gotland mail-carriers in the performance of their duties. The island of Gotland, from which the heroes of this story set out, lies almost in the middle of the Baltic. Oeland, to which they carried the post, lies to the south-west of Gotland, separated from the Swedish mainland only by a narrow strait.

The mails are still carried over Oeland during the winter, as the sea to the north of Gotland is invariably frozen over, so that it is impossible to carry them directly to Stockholm, as is done during the summer.

To those who have never attempted to propel a boat through floating masses of ice, it seems almost incredible that the heroes of this tale should have lain for a whole day actually within sight of their houses, yet wholly unable to make their way to them, and without those on the shore being able to convey to them any help. But the difficulties of such a passage are enormous. Rowing is out of the question; and if an attempt be made to propel the boat by means of boat-hooks, or poles, as soon as one has the end of the pole fast on the ice, and gives a push, the ice goes under, without the boat being helped on its way.

If the boat be sufficiently near the land, help can be sometimes conveyed in the following way:—A few brave men set out from the shore on the hard frozen ice with a small flat-bottomed boat, which is subsequently propelled over the floating ice, with the help of boards laid out on either side of the boat. These both serve to support the boat and to give a firm foothold to the men who laboriously push it along. When they get near enough to the belated boat they cast out to it a rope which they have brought with them, the other end of it being made fast to the shore. Horses are then attached to the shore end of the cable, and the boat is gradually drawn to land. During the winters in Gotland this method has frequently to be put into practice.

Our story, which might be called "A Scene from a Gotland Winter, sketched from Nature," runs as follows:—

On the 14th of January, 1830, the ordinary mail-boat left Klinte, a port in Gotland, directly opposite the northern end of Oeland, with a crew consisting of three men—Anders Wallin, Jonas Hasselquist, and Nicholas Mårbeck. The passage was swift and uneventful; the mails were landed in Oeland on the same day.

A week later another post started from Klinte in an ordinary fishing-boat, the crew of which consisted of three men, Peter Wahlgren, Jonas Carlson, and Peter Magnus Fagerstrom. When they got as far as Karlsö, a small island a little distant from the coast of Gotland, they saw that the sea beyond it was covered with ice. They were unwilling to abandon the voyage, but as they needed at least four men to drag the boat over the ice, they returned to Klinte to get the necessary addition to their crew. They found the man they needed in Karl Löfquist, a young man of twenty years, the eldest of six children of a poor widow, whose chief support he was. Giving less thought to the danger of the voyage than to his mother's needs, he eagerly accepted their offer. So ill-equipped was he for the journey that he had to borrow a pair of seaman's boots from Wahlgren and a jersey from Fagerstrom.

On the following day they set out again from Klinte, and worked their way through a band of ice and floes to Karlsö. Beyond that the sea was fairly free from ice, and the wind being favourable, they arrived on the same afternoon within a short distance of Euggjersudden, in Oeland, where they stuck fast in the floating ice. But as they were no great distance from land, the crew of the mail-boat, which had arrived a week earlier, came out with some of the inhabitants of the coast to their assistance, and after considerable trouble managed to get a rope out to the boat, and drag it safely to land.

The next day the ice closed up around Oeland, so that there was no open water in sight. But a south-westerly wind arising again dispersed it, and the crews of the two boats, in the hope of getting open water, at least as far as Karlsö, agreed to return together, and to take with them a passenger, one

Wilhelm Måg, a journeyman saddler from Berlin, who had passed some time in Sweden, and spoke the language fluently.

On the 26th of January they started on their return journey from Enggjer-sudden. The larger boat was placed on sledges and dragged over the hard frozen ice, which bordered the coast, by horses; the smaller boat was pushed along by its crew. But soon after the start the ice broke under the foremost horses, which were promptly rescued, and sent back with the sledges to Oerland. The boats were pushed on to the edge of the ice and launched; but as the wind went down, and the ice began to look threatening, they returned again to land. At four o'clock on the morning of January 27th, they made a fresh start. The smaller boat, although with its sail set, was tied by a tow-rope to the larger one, which went at a faster rate. With a favourable wind they steered their course for Karlsö, which they hoped to reach by evening. Everything seemed to promise for the best, and they talked of taking their morning glass in their homes.

Owing to their stay of some days in Oeland, their provisions had run rather short, and in the hope of a swift and favourable voyage home, they had not cared to obtain any on credit. They had with them, by this time, barely enough for two days, and their provision of spirits was exceptionally small.

The boat sped on its way amid the joyous converse of the two crews; but towards the afternoon, Wallin, who was steering the large boat, called his comrades aft, and pointed out to them three lights, which seemed to be shining in the water beneath the rope which joined the two boats. Although intercourse with the wonders of the deep usually begets superstition, yet our travellers attached no great importance to this curious appearance. As will be seen, they discovered its meaning only too well later on.

In the evening they began to experience the unpleasant feeling of moving through floating ice. They hoped that it would not come to much, and that they would soon regain the open water; but their hopes were utterly frustrated, and about eight o'clock the boat stuck fast in the floes. The wind changed from south-west to south-east, and a dark winter's night, with gloomy clouds and whistling wind, closed upon the day which had been so full of bright hopes. All night long they toiled and strove to make their way through the floating ice and get nearer to land, or at any rate, hold their course. But their toil was all in vain.

Day rose on the 28th of January only to show the sea covered with ice as far as the eye could reach. All hope of reaching Karlsö was gone, for the ice was driving northward and bore the boat along with it. Yet the faster the boat was driven along the higher their spirits rose, for they saw a chance of working their way to the promontory of Vestergarn, which lies north of Karlsö. Clambering on to the blocks of ice which surrounded them, they tried to work the boat in the direction which they wished; and the drops of sweat which trickled from their brows, in spite of the cold, bore witness to the intensity of their efforts. Their courage was unshaken, nor was their strength diminished, for the one was inspired, and the other increased, by the sight of the well-known shores of their island home. They could even distinguish the larger buildings in Wisby, but they knew only too well that no rescue could be expected thence. Save from God they could expect no rescue but by their own unaided efforts. Unceasingly the hardy strugglers continued their work; night swept over them and concealed from their view the buildings they held so dear, yet did they not relax from their efforts, but rather increased them. The rifts and holes, the fissures in the ice, were all hidden in the darkness.

Their stock of provisions, which during the fair promise of their first day's voyage had been unsparingly dealt out, was now exhausted. Their last morsel, a cake which Hasselquist had received from his sister who lived in Ocland, as a present to take home with him, was divided up and eaten. Even their stock of water and spirits was exhausted, and they had to slake their thirst with sea-water, or water collected in holes on the ice.

Daylight dawned on the 29th of January, and showed our wanderers the impossibility of their reaching the promontory of Vestergarn. They had already been driven past it, and now set their hopes on reaching some more northerly point nearer Wisby. It had frozen hard during the night, and the ice was now closing up into a continuous mass, through which the boats could no longer be propelled, and over which the larger boat could not possibly be dragged. They therefore determined to abandon it, and placing all necessaries in the smaller boat, anchored the larger one through a hole in the ice. They fastened the mast across the smaller boat, and three men taking hold of it on either side thus pushed the boat across the ice. They had no thought of resting or taking turns at the work. The passenger, the saddler, had before partaken in the work, but was now exhausted and sat motionless in the boat. Wallin, too, was compelled to spare his strength, and now seldom left the boat, which at first vexed his comrades, until they took it into consideration that he was eldest and most experienced of them, and was still of use to them in keeping a good look-out as he stood up in the boat. Moreover he had started from Klinte as skipper of the larger boat, and had therefore some right to command the whole party.

During the toils of this day's journey they bethought themselves of invoking the help and protection of Him without whom all their efforts would be in vain; and resting about four o'clock in the afternoon, stood with bared heads while Fagerstrom read prayers, and took up the 119th Psalm at the 6th verse, in which they all joined. The solemnity of this simple service may be realised when one considers that these men, thus struggling for their lives, were so near land that they could see the buildings of Wisby, nay, even the waggons passing along the shore, and yet could expect no rescue save by God's help and their own efforts.

After their prayers they set out again on their wanderings with courage refreshed and strength still unfatigued. But their conversation, which had before been brief enough, was from this moment at an end. Not a word was exchanged which did not bear on the work in hand. It seemed as if they had come to a tacit agreement to keep their thoughts, from this time forward, within their breasts.

As long as the ice was firm and continuous they sped briskly over it, but soon they met with rifts, and had to embark and take to their oars. Towards evening, the ice entirely broke up again, they were fixed in the floes, and driven at great speed past Wisby, and came so near the shore at Toftashaudek that they could see the people getting hawsers ready on shore in hopes of rescuing them. They attempted to row towards land, but their efforts were as vain as an attempt to row in a sand-hill. Another cold winter's night swept over them and caused them to desist from their efforts. As the stars lit up their lamps in the frosty sky, the saddler, who had remained all day in silence, his head sunk upon his breast, lifted up his eyes to the stars, and spoke as in a trance—

"How fair and bright is the heaven above! Let us rather go in thither than stay out here and fare ill." Thus spake he as in a trance, but with clear and distinct utterance. His head sank down upon his breast; he was no more. Silently his comrades laid out his corpse in the bows of the boat. The stars faded away, and black darkness overspread them.

During the night the cold increased to such an extent that shortly after midnight they were able to walk on the ice around the boat. They thought they must be near the fishing village of Ginsvärd, and discussed whether they should leave the boat and try to walk to land. But on considering the heaviness of the mail-bags, and the difficulty of seeing the obstacles before them in the dark, they decided to send Wahlgren to land to get some food for them, and for the rest to wait in the boat till daylight.

Wahlgren set out accompanied by Löfquist, but had not gone far before his boat-hook slipping warned him that he stood upon the brink of a fissure in the ice. Shouting to his comrades, he turned back, followed by Löfquist, who threw himself down by the side of the boat. A horrible presentiment filled all their hearts, but not a word of it escaped their lips. They heard the young man mutter a few disconnected words concerning his brothers and sisters, and his poor mother. Presently he rose of his own accord, and stepped into the boat, where, after a few moments, he departed this life without a pang. His corpse was laid beside the saddler's. The poor mother's prayers for the welfare of her beloved son had been answered—but how?

After this long and terrible night, day dawned at last on the morn of the 30th of January. All eyes were strained to catch a glimpse of the land, which they thought so near. But though it was broad daylight, not a glimpse of land could be seen, not one sign. Wind and stream had carried the weary strugglers far out to sea. They thought they could catch a glimpse of Karlsö, but were not certain about it. They thought the saving land so near that it

"THEY LIFTED OUT THE THREE BODIES" (*p.* 362).

was a terrible blow to have their hopes thus frustrated, yet they bore their trouble in silence, and not a word of complaint or despair was uttered. They had now been driven so far westward that they could no longer set their hopes on landing on their island home, but spent the day in toiling to get the boat's head round to the west in the hope of reaching Oeland, or the mainland, and by the evening all felt need of rest. They laid themselves down in the boat close to one another for the sake of warmth. Night spread its starry mantle over the weary wanderers. Wahlgren, Carlson, and Fagerstrom were lying side by side, when suddenly Carlson, who lay in the middle, began to move his legs and arms about violently, and broke out into harsh words and curses against his old master, a peasant who had turned him out of his service, and forced him to seek the employment in which he was now starving and freezing to death. His words were borne unanswered on the whistling wind. He turned over in silence, and slept the sleep of death. Without a word his comrades laid his dead body beside the two other corpses.

The morn of the 31st of January dawned, and showed a field of ice stretching as far as the eye could reach. The wanderers recommenced their toils, but had to rest more frequently than before, for their strength was beginning to give out. For two days and nights they had not tasted food, if we except some salt, which had been brought from Klinte in the larger boat, for use in case of ice freezing around the boat during the voyage. This salt was now their most valued possession. They made holes in the rough ice, took a few grains of salt in their mouths, filled them with sea-water, and thus let the salt melt. Strange as it may seem, they felt wonderfully strengthened by it.

Tobacco had at first been their chief consolation for the lack of food, and had consequently been used up all the sooner. After it was all gone, they cut up and shared their waistcoat pockets, in which they always carried it. Of these they had now only threads left.

The boat now began to feel heavy to pull. Hitherto no one had raised the question of leaving the three corpses behind, but by this time they could no longer hide from themselves that this measure was necessary, and it was therefore carried out. This was the most painful moment of the whole of their journey. In the three corpses they seemed to have still something left to them of their lost comrades. The bonds of unselfish brotherly affection which united the living, seemed also to include the dead. None of them wished to be the first to lay his hands upon the dead bodies to remove them: it seemed like inflicting an injury on men unable to defend themselves. Silently, and with one accord, they lifted out the three bodies, and laid them upon the ice. The youthful Löfquist's fate awakened the warmest feelings, both for his own and his poor mother's sake. Someone suggested that they should take off his sea-boots, but his suggestion was met with mute dissent. His jersey, however, might help to save another's life, and was accordingly taken off his body; the men consoling themselves with the thought that he still had a coat on beneath.

They seemed to think that the dead man needed some protection against the cold, which was chilling the living. Danger, sorrow, and privation had steeled their spirits and-filled their breasts with a strong courage, but had at the same time made their hearts more feeling, although they dropped no tear, nor uttered any word of sorrow as they performed the last sad offices for their comrades.

As soon as the dead had been laid out, they began to clear the boat of ice so as to make it as light as possible. Suddenly a noise like thunder was heard beneath the ice, the meaning of which they knew only too well. The mail-bags and other luggage were thrown hurriedly into the boat, and the men leapt in after them, leaving behind them in their haste two oars and a boat-hook. The ice was fast breaking up, and although the floe on which the corpses had been laid did not break, yet an under-current drove mass after mass of ice up on to it, so that the dead men soon lay buried beneath an enormous mound of ice.

The survivors continuing on their way reached firm ice again, but were much impeded in their course over it by icebergs (which they were not strong enough to climb over, and had to go round. Their strength of mind as well as their bodily vigour had been terribly shaken by want of food and sleep, and by the emotions they had experienced on abandoning the dead bodies of their comrades. They imagined that the dead still shared in their wanderings, and scarcely dared to look behind them; it terrified them to think of their being near. They had abandoned their bodies, and had not the heart to face their ghosts.

By midday on February 1st, the boat was in such a damaged condition from being pushed over the ice, that, seeing that it would be of no use to them in the event of their again meeting with open water, they determined to abandon it. Of the seats and other easily detached boards they made a kind of sledge, using the halyards for tow-ropes. The mail-bags, the precious package of salt, and other necessaries were placed on the sledge, the rest was left to its fate. They began their march at night-fall, Wallin going ahead with the only compass. The numerous icebergs and rifts around which they had to go, made their journey all the harder. Wallin guarded himself against the danger of taking a wrong course by laying the compass upon the ice whenever he took his bearings.

By this time they scarcely felt their hunger any longer; their bodies had grown weary of being reminded of their need of food, now so long endured. Nor had they any special sense of fatigue; their frames were as dead mechanism, their legs seemed to bear them along mechanically without any connection with their bodies. They seemed to have lost all power of speech, and their minds grew duller every moment. At times they looked upon themselves as already doomed to die. Again they would try to conceive the hope that it was the intention of Providence to bring them safe home after their long wanderings.

So the night went by, and when the 2nd of February came, still was there no land in sight, nothing but ice on every side. They were compelled to lighten the slodge as much as possible; and even to relieve themselves of the weight of some of their clothing. Fagerstrom wore a double set of underclothing, of which he took off the greater part, leaving only enough to keep his back and stomach warm, in the hope that he would find it easier to get along with less on. During one of their halts Mårbeck suddenly sat down, and complained of his head feeling queer. He hoped for a quick and painless death such as his three comrades had met with. But one of them was carrying a shirt with him, which he bound tightly round Mårbeck's head, and in a few moments the hardy youth's strength and courage returned. After a short rest he rose and went on with the others.

The 3rd of February dawned. In the distance a bluish line could be seen. If it were land, they might yet be saved; but if it were open sea, then indeed were they hopelessly lost. Not a word was exchanged, for none of them wished to deceive his comrades with false hopes, or crush them with useless despair. The growing light answered their mute inquiries. It was land!

Wallin, who went in front, strained his eyes so keenly to view the distant land, that he suddenly fell through a hole in the ice up to his shoulders, but was quickly drawn out by his comrades, and regained the firm ice.

Early in the forenoon they broke up the sledge, for though the sight of land had raised their courage, and braced their strength, they would not hear of carrying the mail-bags to land. Some of them were to set out for the land and fetch some men, or if possible a waggon, for the ice seemed quite safe here, while Wallin and Mårbeck waited by the mail-bags for their return. They had kept the saddler's bag with them conscientiously hitherto; they would not touch another's property. But now Wallin, who had got wet through, took some clothes from it and changed. Hasselquist was the first to set out for land; he was followed immediately by Wahlgren, and after a while by Fagerstrom. As snow had fallen during the night, Fagerstrom followed in their tracks at first, but it was not long before he lost them. Hasselquist and Wahlgren came ashore at Ideloe, on the Swedish mainland; Fagerstrom reached land rather further south at Handelsoe.

He was received at once into a cottage, and after taking a little nourishment muttered a few words, trying to ask for help for the men left on the ice with the mail-bags. But the warmth of the room seemed to have deprived him of the last remnant of strength. He fainted with pain from his frost-bites, and was lifted up and carried to bed. Hasselquist and Wahlgren are said to have met with similar adventures at Ideloe.

Meanwhile Mårbeck and Wallin kept watch by the mail-bags, straining their eyes after help from the shore. A Gotland postman thinks before all things of the safety of the mails entrusted to him, but next to that he must think of preserving his own life. These two now felt that they could not survive another night on the ice, especially if they sat still in silent watch over the mails, which would not be saved by their dying beside them. They determined therefore to set out together for land, and seek for help to bring up the mails, as the others did not seem to have succeeded in finding it. So they decided and started on their way. Mårbeck must about this time have been overtaken with some kind of delirium and seized with delusions, for during his journey to land—so he tells the story, and such is his firm conviction—he was met on the ice far out from land by a child, who stretched out his hand to him and gave him a piece of bread. Mårbeck devoured the bread greedily and felt his strength wondrously increased. But the child he saw no more.

He got to land with Wallin in the afternoon, at Handelsoe, where they heard to their sorrow of Fa-

"HE WAS DRAWN OUT BY HIS COMRADES" (p. 364).

gerstrom's collapse, an experience which they were soon to suffer themselves. They too met with a hospitable reception, and were at once supplied with food. Wallin was given a glass of spirits with his food, but Mårbeck seemed so weak that they dared only give him a few drops, which caused him at once to feel a terrible pain in his leg. He tried to move from his seat, but was unable to stir an inch, and had, like Fagerstrom, to be carried off to bed.

Wallin fell into a deep refreshing sleep, but was so weak the next morning that he could not unlock his door.

Meanwhile messengers had been sent with the news to Westervik, the nearest large town, and the mail-bags were sought after and brought to land. On February 4th the five postmen were removed to Westervik and received into the hospital. Wallin was able to walk upstairs by himself, the other four had to be carried.

They met with the greatest care and attention at the hospital, but amputation was in all cases, except Wallin's, necessary in order to save their lives. Fagerstrom, who was the first to be operated upon, on February 22nd, lost all the toes of his right foot. Mårbeck on March 2nd had his right leg taken off below the knee, and lost three toes from the left foot, part of his left heel, and the first joint of one finger on the left hand. Wahlgren escaped with the loss of two fingers on each hand, and a piece of his right heel. During the amputation of his fingers he stood up and held out his hand as if it had merely been a matter of bandaging. Hasselquist had both legs taken off below the knee on the same day, one in the morning and the other in the afternoon. During the second operation the brave fellow seized a towel which lay near him, crammed it into his mouth and fastened his teeth into it, but not a cry or complaint escaped him. The reason why Wallin was enabled to come off whole was that he had taken care to keep himself dry, and until the last day had succeeded in doing so. The others had got wet through early in the journey, and their clothes had frozen hard to their feet and legs. Wallin and Wahlgren were the first to return home. Fagerstrom and Mårbeck came next in the beginning of July. Hasselquist got home about the middle of the same month.

It seems hard to believe that any human frame could support such toils and hardship without tasting food for six days. Yet their departure from Oeland on January 27th, and their arrival at Handelsoe on February 3rd, their stay at the hospital in Westervik, are all confirmed by unimpeachable authority. On the 29th of January they were seen from the Gotland shore, at Vestergarn, and hawsers were brought there from Klinte, but night came on, and by the following morning, as we said above, they had been driven far out of sight of land. Our authorities for the incidents of the journey are its two remaining survivors, from whose simple and undeviating account the above has been compiled. Fagerstrom, who knows how to write, made notes of the chief events of their wanderings soon after his return home. But even without notes, such days and nights would not easily be obliterated from their memory. It is, however, a pity that the story was not written immediately after their return home, for there may be by this time some slight confusion in the episodes of which the stars shining in the winter nights were the only witnesses.

Mårbeck's meeting with the child appeared to the compiler of the above story to be an incident of such touching beauty, that he had not the heart to omit mentioning this wondrous mystery.

When the above story appeared in the *Gotland Journal* in 1855, Mårbeck and Fagerstrom were still alive, and it is not to be imagined that any of these men who underwent such hardships subsequently suffered in health or strength. Quite the contrary is the case. Wallin and Wahlgren continued their work as postmen until they died, the former at the age of fifty-seven, the latter sixty-one. Hasselquist got about on his wooden legs until he died at the age of fifty-two. Mårbeck lived to be sixty-two, and Fagerstrom to be over eighty years old.

THE STORY OF A WATCH.

BEING THE NARRATIVE OF AN ACCIDENT ON THE PIZ MORTERATSCH, JULY, 1863
BY PROFESSOR TYNDALL.

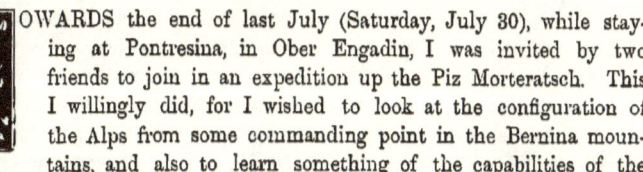 OWARDS the end of last July (Saturday, July 30), while staying at Pontresina, in Ober Engadin, I was invited by two friends to join in an expedition up the Piz Morteratsch. This I willingly did, for I wished to look at the configuration of the Alps from some commanding point in the Bernina mountains, and also to learn something of the capabilities of the Pontresina guides. We took two of them with us—Jenni, who is the man of greatest repute among them, and Walter, who is the head of the bureau of guides.

We proposed to ascend by the Roseg, and to return by the Morteratsch glacier, thus making a circuit, instead of retracing our steps. About eight hours of pleasant healthful exertion placed us on the Morteratsch Spitze, where we remained for an hour, and where the conviction forced on my mind on many another summit was renewed—namely, that these mountains and valleys are not, as supposed by the renowned President of the Geographical Society, ridges and heaps tossed up by the earth's central fires, with great fissures between them, but that ice and water, acting through long ages, have been the real sculptors of the Alps.

Jenni is a heavy man, and marches rather slowly up a mountain, but he is a thoroughly competent mountaineer. We were particularly pleased with his performance in descending. He swept down the slopes and cleared the "schrunds" which cut the upper snows, with great courage and skill.

We at length reached the point at which it was necessary to quit our morning's track, and immediately afterwards got upon some steep rocks, which were rendered slippery here and there by the water which trickled over them. To our right was a broad couloir, which was once filled with snow, but this had been melted and refrozen, so as to expose a sloping wall of ice.

We were all tied together at this time in the following order—Jenni led, I came next, then my friend H., an intrepid mountaineer, then his friend L., and last of all the guide Walter. L. had had but little experience of the higher Alps, and was placed in front of Walter, so that any false step on his part might be instantly checked.

After descending the rocks for a time, Jenni turned and asked me whether I thought it better to adhere to them or to try the ice-slope to our right. I pronounced in favour of the rocks, but he seemed to misunderstand me, and turned towards the couloir.

I stopped him before he reached it, and said, "Jenni, you know where you are going; the slope is pure ice." He replied, "I know it; but the ice is quite bare for a few yards only. Across this exposed portion I will cut steps, and then the snow which covers the ice will give us a footing."

He cut the steps, reached the snow, and descended carefully along it—all following in apparently good order. After a little time he stopped, turned, and looked upwards at the last three men. He said something about keeping carefully in the tracks, adding that a false step might detach an avalanche.

The word was scarcely uttered when I heard the sound of a fall behind me, then a rush, and in the twinkling of an eye my two friends and their guide, all apparently entangled together, whirred past me. I suddenly planted myself to resist their shock, but in an instant I was in their wake, for their impetus was irresistible. A moment afterwards Jenni was whirled away, and thus all five of us found ourselves riding downward with uncontrollable speed on the back of an avalanche which a single slip had originated.

When thrown down by the jerk of the rope, I turned promptly on my face and drove my bâton through the moving snow, seeking to anchor it in the ice underneath. I had held it firmly thus for a few seconds, when I came into collision with some obstacle and was rudely tossed through the air, Jenni at the same time being shot down upon me. Both of us here lost our bâtons. We had, in fact, been carried over a crevasse, had hit its lower edge, our great velocity causing us to be pitched beyond it. I was quite bewildered for a moment, but immediately righted myself, and could see those in front of me half buried in the snow, and jolted from side to side by the ruts among which they were passing.

Suddenly I saw them tumbled over by a lurch of the avalanche, and immediately afterwards found myself imitating their motion. This was caused by a second crevasse. Jenni knew of its existence and plunged right into it—a brave and manful act, but for the time unavailing. He is over thirteen stone in weight, and he thought that by jumping into the chasm a strain might be put upon the rope sufficient to check the motion. He was, however, violently jerked out of the fissure and almost squeezed to death by the pressure of the rope.

A long slope was below us, which led directly downwards to a brow where the glacier suddenly fell in a declivity of ice. At the base of this declivity the glacier was cut by a series of profound chasms, and towards these we were now rapidly borne.

The three foremost men rode upon the forehead of the avalanche, and at times were almost wholly immersed in the snow; but the moving layer was thinner behind, and Jenni rose incessantly, and with desperate energy drove his feet into the firmer substance underneath. His voice shouting "Halt! Herr Jesus, halt!" was the only one heard during the descent.

A kind of condensed memory, such as that described by people who have narrowly escaped drowning, took possession of me; and I thought and reasoned with preternatural clearness as I rushed along. Our start, moreover, was too sudden and the excitement too great to permit of the development of terror. The slope at one place became less steep, the speed visibly slackened, and we thought we were coming to rest; the avalanche, however, crossed the brow which terminated this gentler slope, and regained its motion.

Here H. threw his arm round his friend, all hope for the time being extinguished, while I grasped my belt and struggled for an instant to detach myself. Finding this difficult I resumed the pull upon the rope.

"I WAS TOSSED THROUGH THE AIR" (p. 368).

My share in the work was, I fear, infinitesimal; but Jenni's powerful strain made itself felt at last. Aided probably by a slight change of inclination, he brought the whole to rest within a short distance of the chasms, over which, had we preserved our speed, a few seconds would have carried us.

None of us suffered serious damage. H. emerged from the snow with his forehead bleeding, but the wound was superficial. Jenni had a bit of flesh removed from his hand by collision against a stone; the pressure of the rope had left black welts on my arms; and we all experienced a tingling sensation over the hands, like that produced by incipient frost-bite, which continued for several days. I found a portion of my watch-chain hanging round my neck, another portion in my pocket; the watch itself was gone.

This happened on the 30th of July. Two days afterwards I went to Italy, and remained there for ten or twelve days. On the 16th of August I was again at Pontresina, and on that day made an expedition in search of the lost watch. Both the guides and myself thought the sun's heat might melt the snow above it, and I inferred that if its back should happen to be uppermost, the slight absorbent power of gold for the solar rays would prevent the watch from sinking as a stone sinks under like circumstances. The watch would thus be brought quite to the surface; and, although a small object, it might possibly be seen from some distance. I was accompanied up the Morteratsch glacier by five friends, of whose conduct I cannot speak too highly. One of them in particular, a member of the British Legislature, sixty-four years of age, exhibited a courage and collectedness in places of real difficulty which were perfectly admirable.

Two only of the party, both competent mountaineers, accompanied me to the scene of the accident, and none of us ventured on the ice where it originated. Just before stepping upon the remains of the avalanche, a stone some tons in weight, detached by the sun from the snow-slope above us, came rushing down the line of our glissade. Its leaps became more and more impetuous, and on reaching the brow near which we had been brought to rest, it bounded through the air, and with a single spring reached the lower glacier, raising a cloud of ice-dust in the air.

Some fragments of rope found upon the snow assured us that we were upon the exact track of the avalanche, and then the search commenced.

It had not continued for twenty minutes when a cheer from one of the guides—Christian Michel, of Grindelwald—announced the discovery of the watch. It had been brought to the surface in the manner surmised, and on examination seemed to be dry and uninjured. I noticed, moreover, that the position of the hands indicated that it had only run down beneath the snow. I wound it up, hardly hoping, however, to find it capable of responding. But the watch showed instant signs of animation. It had remained eighteen days in the avalanche, but the application of its key at once restored it to life, and it has gone with unvarying regularity ever since.

NOTE.—We have to thank the author of the above narrative—Professor Tyndall—for permission to include it in THE WORLD OF ADVENTURE.

TALES OF THE NORTH AMERICAN INDIANS.

I.—A CRUEL ENEMY.

(1759.)

HE first of our stories under this title shall be extracted from an old volume of the *Naval Chronicle*. It is a testimony at once to the savagery of Indian warfare and to the gallantry of British troops under fire.

Captain Ochterlony and Ensign Peyton were both officers in the regiment of Brigadier-General Monckton. They were nearly of an age, which did not exceed thirty. Captain Ochterlony was a Scot; Ensign Peyton an Irishman. Both were handsome, stalwart young soldiers; and the pair were close friends.

On the day before the famous battle off the Falls of Montmorency, Captain Ochterlony had been obliged to fight a duel with a German officer. He had wounded and disarmed his antagonist, but had nevertheless caught in the encounter a dangerous wound under his right arm. His friends, fearing the nature of his hurt, had for a long while insisted on his remaining in camp during the action of the next day; but the captain's spirit was too ardent to comply with their remonstrances. He declared that it should never be said that a scratch, received in a private encounter, had prevented him from doing his duty when his country required his service; and he took the field with a fusil in his hand, though he was hardly able to carry his arms.

In leading up his men to the enemy's entrenchments, he was shot through the lungs with a musket-ball, an accident which obliged him to part with his fusil; but he still continued to advance, until by loss of blood he became too weak to proceed further.

Almost at the same instant, Mr. Peyton was lamed by a shot, which shattered the small bone of his left leg.

The two friends lay on the ground but a few paces from each other, and within reach of the enemy's fire. Their men went on, and after a plucky assault were driven back. As they passed in good order, the soldiers earnestly begged, with tears in their eyes, that Captain Ochterlony would allow them to carry him and the ensign off the field. But he was so bigoted to a severe point of honour that he refused to quit the ground, though he desired them to take care of his ensign. Mr. Peyton, for his part, with a generous disdain, rejected their good offices, declaring that he would not leave his captain in such a situation. The soldiers entreated and expostulated, but without effect. And in a little while the pair were the only survivors left on that part of the field.

The enemy's bullets still continued to whiz by them, or to patter into the turf around. Immediate death seemed certain. Captain Ochterlony raised himself painfully on his fists, staggered across to his friend and sat down beside him.

" Good-bye, old fellow ! " he said.

The two friends shook hands, and awaited their fate ; but in a second or two the captain uttered an exclamation of hope. There was yet a chance that they might be protected as prisoners ; for the firing suddenly ceased and presently three figures were seen approaching from the entrenchments. They were a French soldier and two Indians ; and they advanced straight towards the spot where the wounded officers lay.

" THE TWO MEN CLOSED " (p. 373).

Captain Ochterlony at once got upon his feet, and accosting them in the French language, which he spoke perfectly, expressed his hope that they would treat him and his companion as officers, prisoners, and gentlemen.

The two Indians, however, seemed to be entirely under the conduct of the Frenchman, who, without answering the captain, walked up to Mr. Peyton as he lay, snatched his lace hat from his head, and then turning, robbed the captain of his watch and money.

This outrage was the signal to the Indians for murder and pillage. One of them, clubbing his firelock, struck at the captain from behind, to knock him down. The blow missed his head indeed, but took effect on his shoulder. At the same instant the other Indian poured his shot into the captain's breast, who cried out, "Peyton, the villain has shot me!" and dropped down on his knee.

Not yet satiated with cruelty, the Indian followed up the shot by springing forward and stabbing him. The captain had parted with his fusil, and was thus left without a single weapon of defence, as none of the officers wore swords in this action. The three ruffians noting this, and finding him still alive and struggling on his knees with surprising tenacity, caught at his sash, and with this attempted to strangle him.

At this juncture, Mr. Peyton, having a double-barrelled musket in his hand, and seeing that all was up with his friend unless prompt assistance came, took good aim at a distance of four yards, fired at one of the Indians, and shot him dead.

The other wheeled round, and imagining that the ensign, now that his piece was discharged, would be an easy prey, sprang forward upon him. Peyton lifted his musket, took aim, and fired his second barrel; but the shot did not seem to take effect.

It was now the savage's turn; he fired and wounded the ensign in the shoulder; then rushing in, thrust his bayonet through his body. He repeated the blow, and Peyton, in parrying it, received another wound in his left hand; nevertheless he seized the Indian's musket with it, pulled him forwards, and whipping out a small dagger that hung at his belt, drove it into the savage's side. The two men closed in a desperate grapple, which lasted for a full minute.

From it the Irishman emerged victorious. He managed to get his knee on the Indian's chest, and with repeated strokes of the dagger killed him outright. He stood up, panting with the struggle, and suffering excruciating pain in his wounded leg. Nevertheless at this moment—with a trivial inconsequence familiar to those who have lived through a desperate piece of warfare —as he stood, swaying weakly, the uppermost desire in his mind was to discover if his second shot had taken effect on the Indian.

"I'll be sworn I hit him," said the ensign to himself.

He turned the body over, stripped off the blanket that clothed it, and perceived, with a childish pleasure, that his ball had penetrated quite through the cavity of the breast.

Thus satisfied, he turned to look after his companion, and saw Captain Ochterlony standing, sixty yards away, close by the enemy's breastwork, with the French soldier attending him. Peyton called out—

"Ochterlony, glad to see you're under protection. Take care of that villain, though. God bless you, dear fellow! I see a pack of Indians coming; so it's all up with me."

It was true. A number of these savages, who had for some time been employed on the left in scalping and pillaging the dead and dying on the field, were now coming straight towards him. They were thirty in all, and Peyton saw that his time was come. Even should his life be spared for the moment, it would only be that they might afterwards sacrifice him to propitiate the spirits of their brethren whom he had slain, and in that case he knew he would be put to death by the most excruciating tortures. Full of this idea, he snatched up his musket, and, notwithstanding his shattered leg, ran about forty yards without halting. Then, feeling himself totally disabled, and incapable of proceeding one step further, he loaded his piece and presented it at the two foremost Indians, who stood aloof, waiting to be joined by their fellows.

A minute passed, and still Peyton stood facing his enemies, while the French from their breastworks kept up a continual fire of cannon and small arms upon this poor solitary and maimed gentleman.

Another sixty seconds dragged by. He turned his head, and saw in the distance a Highland officer with a party of his men skirting the field of battle. He waved his hand in signal of distress. The officer perceived him.

He was a Captain Macdonald, of Captain Frazer's battalion, who, understanding that a young officer, his kinsman, was lying on the field of battle, had put himself at the head of this party, penetrated to the middle of the field, driven back a crowd of French and Indians, and finding his kinsman still unscalped, carried him off in triumph. He was returning to the British lines when he caught sight of Peyton standing at bay before the crowd of Indians.

Captain Macdonald did not hesitate, but immediately detached three Highlanders to the rescue. These brave fellows hastened towards Peyton through the midst of a perfect storm of fire, caught him up and bore him back on their shoulders. Strange to say, in time he recovered of his wounds.

Poor Captain Ochterlony was carried by the French to Quebec, where he lingered but a few days. After the reduction of that place, the French doctors who had attended him declared that in all probability he would have recovered of the two shots he had received in his breast, had he not been mortally wounded in the belly by the Indian's scalping-knife.

"As this remarkable scene," winds up the *Naval Chronicle*, "was acted in sight of both armies, General Townshend, in the sequel, expostulated with the French officers upon the inhumanity of keeping up such a severe fire against two wounded gentlemen who were disabled and destitute of all hope of escaping. They answered that the fire was not made by the regulars, but by the Canadians and savages, whom it was not in the power of discipline to restrain."

II.—RACING THE FLAMES.

"I was riding, one day, across a prairie in the Upper Missouri, where the grass is seven or eight feet high. I had three companions, one an Indian guide of the name of Pah-me-o-ne-qua, or 'Red Thunder.' We had just halted for our mid-day meal, and were stretched at full length enjoying it, when I noticed that the Indian was standing aloof, quiet and thoughtful. I asked him why he did not join us.

"'This is the plain of *fire-grass*,' answered he, 'where the fleet-bounding

"'I SAW . . . HIS FOAMING HORSE LEAPING UP THE STEEP FACE
OF THE BLUFF'" (p. 375).

wild horse mingles his bones with those of the red man, and the eagle's wing is melted as he darts over the surface.'

"Notwithstanding these ominous words, to which, being accustomed to Indian hyperbole, I paid little attention, he presently came near and sank gracefully down on the grass beside us.

"The rest of us were in high spirits, and as the meal proceeded our tongues were unloosed, and we chatted glibly and merrily. Suddenly, with a bound Red Thunder was on his feet—his long arm was stretched over the grass.

"'White man,' said he, 'see you that small cloud lifting itself from the prairie?—He rises! The hoofs of our horses have waked him!—The Fire Spirit is awake—the wind is from his nostrils, and his face is this way.'

"No more: in a moment his swift horse was dashing under him, and he seemed to slide over the waving grass as it was bent by the wind. We sprang up, left our food, our cups, to lie, vaulted into our saddles, and in less than a minute were racing swiftly on his trail.

"The extraordinary leaps of his wild horse occasionally raised his red shoulders to view, and again he sank into the waving billows of grass. The tremulous wind had risen. It overtook and outstripped us. On it was borne the agitated wing of the eagle. I saw his neck as he beat above us, stretched out for the towering bluff, miles ahead. I heard the thrilling screams of his voice, and it told the secret that was behind him.

"Our horses were swift, and we struggled hard. But our hopes were feeble. Far ahead of us the bluff was yet blue in the distance, and in the long grass our pace would quickly be spent. The sunshine was dying; or if not, what was the shadow sweeping over the plain? We dared not look back.

"We dared not look back, but we strained every nerve. For now a hum arose, far behind, a mutter, a roar as of a distant cataract. It was gradually advancing on us, catching us up. The wind increased, until it seemed that a mad tempest howled behind us.

"The beetles, the heath hens, instinctively drew their straight lines over our heads. The antelopes passed us also, and the still swifter, long-legged hare, which leaves but a shadow as he flies. Here was no time for thought; but I recollect that the heavens were overcast, and a red glare sprang up behind, throwing our shadows far along our path. The hot air breathed on our necks, and the smell that came on it made my heart sick as we drew nearer and nearer to the headland.

"We were almost at the foot of it. I strained my eyes ahead.

"As I did so a piercing yell rang in my ears. It was the yell of our guide. I saw his robe flapping in the air, and his foaming horse leaping up the steep face of the bluff.

"We followed. Our breath and our sinews, in this last struggle for life, were just enough to bring us to its summit. I turned now for the first time in my saddle.

"We had risen from a sea of fire. Below, an immense cloud of black smoke filled the plain from horizon to horizon. It rushed round the headland, swaying giddily on a bed of liquid fire. Higher yet, around us, enveloping and swamping us, the white smoke, pale as death, was streaming and rising up in magnificent cliffs to heaven.

"I stood secure, but trembling. I heard the maddened wind hurl the flames like billows around the bluff. I saw a thousand lightnings flashing. And then it was gone, and I looked on nothing but black and smoky desolation."

III.—THE COLONEL'S STORY.

A MAN of gigantic stature; his chest broad and prominent; his countenance full of courage, enterprise, and perseverance. A man who, when he spoke, conveyed by the very motion of his lips that an untruth was impossible to him. Such was Colonel Boone, the narrator of the following story:—

"I was once on a hunting expedition on the banks of the Green River, when the lower parts of Kentucky were still in the hand of nature, and none but the sons of the soil were looked upon as its lawful proprietors. We Virginians had for some time been waging a war of intrusion upon them, and I, amongst the rest, rambled through the woods in pursuit of their race, as I now would follow the tracks of any ravenous animal.

"The Indians outwitted me one dark night, and I was as unexpectedly as suddenly made a prisoner by them. The trick had been managed with great skill; for no sooner had I extinguished the fire of my camp, and laid me down to rest in full security, as I thought, than I felt myself seized by an indistinguishable number of hands, and was immediately pinioned, as if about to be led to the scaffold for execution. To have attempted to be refractory would have proved useless and dangerous to my life; and I suffered myself to be removed from my camp to theirs, a few miles distant, without uttering a word of complaint.

"You are aware, I dare say, that to act in this manner was the best policy, as you understand that by so doing I proved to the Indians at once that I was born and br'd as fearless of death as any of themselves.

"When we reached the camp, great rejoicings were exhibited. Two squaws and a few papooses appeared particularly delighted at the sight of me, and I was assured by very unequivocal gestures and words that on the morrow the mortal enemy of the red-skin would cease to live.

"I never opened my lips, but was busy contriving some scheme which might enable me to give the rascals the slip before dawn. The women immediately fell a-searching about my hunting-shirt for whatever they might think valuable, and, fortunately for me, soon found my flask filled with *monongahela* (strong whisky). A terrific grin was exhibited on their murderous countenances, while my heart throbbed with joy at the anticipation of their intoxication.

"The crew immediately began to beat their bellies and sing, as they passed

"'THEY WERE BECOMING MORE AND MORE DRUNK'" (p. 378).

the bottle from mouth to mouth. How often did I wish the flask ten times its size, and filled with aquafortis! I observed that the squaws drank more freely than the warriors, and again my spirits were about to be depressed when the report of a gun was heard at a distance.

"The Indians all jumped on their feet; the singing and drinking were both brought to a stand; and I saw, with inexpressible joy, the men walk off to some distance and talk to the squaws. I knew that they were consulting about me, and I foresaw that in a few moments the warriors would go to discover the cause of the gun having been fired so near the camp. I expected that the squaws would be left to guard me.

"Well, sir, it was just so. They returned; the men took up their guns and walked away. The squaws sat down again, and in less than five minutes had my bottle up to their dirty mouths, gurgling down their throats the remains of the whisky.

"With what pleasure did I see them becoming more and more drunk, until the liquor took such hold on them, that it was quite impossible for these women to be of any service. They tumbled down, rolled about, and began to snore; when I, having no other chance of freeing myself from the cords that fastened me, rolled over and over towards the fire, and after a short time burned them asunder.

"I rose on my feet, stretched my stiffened sinews, snatched up my rifle, and, for once in my life, spared that of Indians. I now recollect how desirous I once felt to lay open the skulls of the wretches with my tomahawk; but when I again thought upon killing things unprepared and unable to defend themselves, it looked like murder without need, and I gave up the idea.

"But, sir, I felt determined to mark the spot, and walking to a thrifty ash sapling, I cut out of it three large chips and ran off. I soon reached the river, crossed it, and threw myself deep into the cane-brakes, imitating the tracks of an Indian with my feet, so that no chance might be left for those from whom I had escaped to overtake me."

IV.—AUDUBON'S ADVENTURE.

"On my return from the Upper Mississippi, I found myself obliged to cross one of the wide prairies which, in that portion of the United States, vary the appearance of the country. The weather was fine; all around me was as fresh and blooming as if it had just issued from the bosom of Nature. My knapsack, my gun, and my dog were all I had for baggage and company. The track that I followed was an old Indian track; and as darkness overshadowed the prairie, I felt some desire to reach at least a copse in which I might lie down to rest. The night-hawks were skimming over and around me, attracted by the buzzing wings of the beetles which form their food; and the distant howlings of wolves gave me some hope that I should soon arrive at the skirts of some woodland.

"I did so; and almost at the same instant a fire-light attracted my eye. I moved towards it, full of confidence that it proceeded from the camp of some wandering Indians. I was mistaken. I discovered by its glare that it was from the hut of a small log-cabin, and that a tall figure passed and repassed between it and me, as if busily engaged in household arrangements.

"I reached the spot, and presenting myself at the door, asked the tall figure, which proved to be a woman, if I might take shelter under her roof for the night. Her voice was gruff, and her attire negligently thrown about her. She answered in the affirmative. I walked in, took a stool, and quietly seated myself by the fire.

"The next object that attracted my attention was a finely formed young Indian, resting his head between his hands, with his elbows on his knees. A long bow rested against the log wall near him, while a quantity of arrows and two or three raccoon-skins lay at his feet. He moved not—he apparently breathed not.

"Accustomed to the habits of the Indians, and knowing that they pay little attention to the approach of civilised strangers (a circumstance which in some countries is considered to evince the apathy of their character), I addressed him in French, a language not unfrequently partially known to the people in that neighbourhood.

" He raised his head, pointed to one of his eyes with his finger, and gave me a significant glance with the other. His face was covered with blood. The fact was that about an hour before this, as he was in the act of discharging an arrow at a raccoon in the top of a tree, the arrow had split upon the cord, and sprung back with such violence into his right eye as to destroy it for ever.

"Feeling hungry, I inquired what sort of fare I might expect. Such a thing as a bed was not to be seen, but many large untanned bear and buffalo hides lay piled in a corner. I drew a fine timepiece from my breast, and told the woman that it was late, and that I was fatigued. She had espied my watch, the richness of which seemed to operate upon her feelings with electric quickness. She told me that there was plenty of venison and jerked buffalo meat, and that on removing the ashes I should find a cake.

"But my watch had struck her fancy, and her curiosity had to be gratified by an immediate sight of it. I took off the gold chain that secured it from around my neck, and presented it to her. She was all ecstasy, spoke of its beauty, asked me its value, and put my chain round her brawny neck, saying how happy the possession of such a watch would make her.

"Thoughtless, and as I fancied myself in so retired a spot secure, I paid little attention to her talk or her movements. I helped my dog to a good supper of venison, and was not long in satisfying the demands of my own appetite.

"The Indian rose from his seat as if in extreme suffering. He passed and repassed me several times, and once pinched me on the side so violently that the pain nearly brought forth an exclamation of anger. I looked at him; his eye met mine, but his look was so forbidding that it struck a chill into the more nervous part of my system. He again seated himself, drew his butcher's knife from its greasy scabbard, examined its edge as I would do that of a razor suspected dull, replaced it, and again taking his tomahawk from his back, filled the pipe of it with tobacco, and sent me expressive glances whenever our hostess chanced to have her back towards us.

"Never until that moment had my senses been awakened to the danger which I now suspected to be about me. I returned glance for glance to my companion, and rested well assured that, whatever enemies I might have, he was not one of their number. I asked the woman for my watch, wound it up, and under pretence of wishing to see how the weather might probably be on the morrow, took up my gun and walked out of the cabin. I slipped a ball into each barrel, scraped the edges of my flints, renewed the primings, and returning to the hut, gave a favourable account of my observations. I took a few bear-skins, made a pallet of them, and calling my faithful dog to my side, lay down, with my gun close to my body, and in a few minutes was to all appearance fast asleep.

"A short time had elapsed, when some voices were heard, and from the corner of my eyes I saw two athletic youths making their entrance, bearing a dead stag on a pole. They disposed of their burden, and asking for whisky, helped themselves freely to it. Observing me and the wounded Indian, they asked who I was, and why that rascal (meaning the Indian, who, they knew, understood not a word of English) was in the house. The mother—for so she proved to be—bade them speak less loudly, made mention of my watch, and took them to a corner, where a conversation took place, the purport of which it required little shrewdness in me to guess. I tapped my dog gently; he moved his tail, and with indescribable pleasure I saw his fine eyes alternately fixed on me, and raised towards the trio in the corner. I felt that he perceived danger in my situation. The Indian exchanged a last glance with me.

"The lads had eaten and drunk themselves into such condition, that I already looked upon them as *hors de combat;* and the frequent visits of the whisky-bottle to the ugly mouth of their dam I hoped would soon reduce her to a like state. Judge of my astonishment, reader, when I saw this incarnate fiend take a large carving-knife and go to the grindstone to whet its edge. I saw her pour the water on the turning machine, and watched her working away with the dangerous instrument, until the cold sweat covered every part of my body, in despite of my determination to defend myself to the last. Her task finished, she walked to her reeling sons, and said, "There, that'll soon settle him. Boys, kill you him, and then for the watch!"

"I turned, cocked my gunlocks silently, touched my faithful companion, and lay ready to start up and shoot the first that might attempt my life. The moment was fast approaching, and that night might have been my last in this world, had not Providence made preparations for my rescue. All was ready; the infernal hag was advancing slowly, probably contemplating the best way of despatching me whilst her sons should be engaged with the Indian. I was several times on the eve of rising and shooting her on the spot: but she was not to be punished thus. The door was suddenly opened, and there entered two stout travellers, each with a long rifle on his shoulder. I bounced up on my feet, and making them most heartily welcome, told them how well it was for me that they should have arrived at that moment. The tale was told in a minute. The drunken men were secured, and the woman, in spite of her defence and vociferations, shared the same fate. The Indian fairly danced with joy, and gave us to understand that, as he could not sleep for pain, he would watch over us. You may suppose we slept much less than we talked. The two strangers gave me an account of their once having been themselves in a somewhat similar situation. Day came, fair and rosy, and with it the punishment of our captives.

"They were now quite sobered. Their feet were unbound, but their arms were still securely tied. We marched them into the woods off the road, and having used them as regulators were wont to use such delinquents, we set fire to the cabin, gave all their skins and implements to the young Indian warrior, and proceeded well pleased towards the settlements.

"During upwards of twenty-five years, when my wanderings extended to all parts of our country, this was the only time at which my life was in danger from my fellow-creatures. Indeed, so little risk do travellers run in the United States that no one born there ever dreams of any to be encountered on the road; and I can only account for the occurrence by supposing that the inhabitants of the cabin were not Americans."

V.—THE STORY OF A WOLF-SKIN CAP.

"THE first day I came to Boone's station," said James Harrod, a stalwart and mighty hunter, "the Colonel was off making salt at the Licks, and had taken with him the better part of his company. Them that were left I found in a bad way. The Shawanees, it seems, had found out the state of the case, and had attacked the station time after time, killing the cattle, driving in the hunting parties, and very nearly cutting off supplies. It was as much as the poor fellows could do to keep their eyes open and alert, let alone going for provisions. They were in great straits, and I cast about in my mind how I could relieve them.

"Well, first of all I proposed that some of the fellows remaining should come with me to one of the nearest spots where I had my season's game stored and hidden, the fruit of my hunting. They thanked me, but shook their heads. The risk was too great, they said. All the same I could tell they were dying of starvation, and in the end, finding they were unwilling to go, I offered to leave the station that night alone. I told the women to keep a good heart, and promised that, if alive, I would soon return with plenty of meat.

"I took my gun and set out; and before morning broke I was pretty well on my way. Game was very shy, and I could see plenty of Indian signs about. So I made up my mind to have the first meat I could get, and run back with it as soon as ever I could to the relief of the station.

"At length I caught sight of a small herd of deer. They were moving alone as if somebody had lately roused them, and were still on the look-out. I didn't like the look of this.

"'There are Indians somewhere about,' said I to myself, 'or else I'm much mistaken.' I felt certain, too, that they were pretty close at hand. I stopped still for a moment and cast up the odds; and the end was I made up my mind to have one of those deer or lose my scalp. Unfortunately, the odds seemed in favour of the latter. But I said to myself, 'I never turned aside for a red man yet, and I'm not going to begin at *my* time of life.' You see, I looked on these hunting-grounds as my own preserves.

"So I followed up the deer, and pretty soon my suspicions were turned into certainty. I came on the marks of moccasins following up the trail of the deer. However, I had the advantage, for I was on the look-out for the Indians, and they weren't in the least on the look-out for me. You see, they had frightened those poor folk at the station to such a degree that they hadn't the least idea that anyone would come out after game, and I could tell from their slip-shod trail that they didn't guess I was close.

"On I went then, mile after mile, taking care to expose myself as little as possible. Indeed, I stepped from tree to tree all the way, just as if it were a bush fight. I thought no one saw me, when all of a sudden something whistled by my head, so close that I put my hand up to my ear.

"There was no doubt about it now. It was a bullet. I had been spied, and there was business ahead. A couple of rifles rang out almost before I could get to shelter. They came from the left, and luckily they missed. But I was in a tight fix.

"The Indians kept close. I should think that quite five minutes passed as I crouched behind my tree, and I heard nothing more. I made up my mind to take a peep round the trunk.

Ping!

A rifle spoke out. You see I wear my hair rather long over my shoulders. Well, the bullet clipped off a lock of it neatly and grazed my neck as it passed, stinging me pretty sharply.

"I had enough of reconnoitring. Down I crouched again, and for minute after minute all was still as death. I saw how the land lay. I had an Indian on my right and two on my left. The latter had been lying close, and the fellow on the right now did the same, reloading his rifle and waiting for his next chance.

"It began to be a case of tiring me out. My heart was going *thump-thump* on my ribs as I crouched. The foot of the tree luckily was surrounded with bushes and undergrowth about three feet high, so that they could not see to hit me; but, on the other hand, I couldn't see to hit them without lifting my head into view.

"One thing was certain. It wouldn't do to lie here all day, even if I cared for it; for as soon as night fell, between these three savages, my game would be up. I thought the case over and over, and for a long time couldn't see how to help myself. And then all of a sudden a notion struck me.

"I had on my head a cap made out of wolf-skin, a piece of clothing that had served me for more than half a dozen good years. It had flaps to keep the ears warm in cold weather; and I won't say but it had a hole or two in it, where bullets had whizzed through in these border scrimmages. Anyway, it was a good cap yet, and had done good service, but never a better than I intended it to do now.

"I fixed up my plans, and making sure that this was my only chance of getting a sight of the Indians, I pulled out my ramrod and stuck my cap on top of it. I didn't hoist it up at once, but first of all rustled up and down a bit in the bushes, just to give the fellows a notion that I was getting restless. When I thought I had played this game enough, I very gingerly lifted up the cap in my left hand, keeping my right on my rifle, and peering out through the bushes.

"*Ping—Ping—Ping!*

"The three rifles rang out, one after another, as fast as you can clap your hands. And then before the echoes had finished came the death-howl of the Indian on the right. I fancied all along that he was the least cautious of the three, and he had exposed just half his head as he took aim.

"'Number one,' said I, dropping on my knee and reloading. I felt pretty cheerful, and almost inclined to whistle, for now, as far as I knew, all my enemies were on one side. I thought it a pity if I couldn't account for a couple of Indians whose whereabouts I knew.

"It was some time before I repeated the trick, for I didn't want them to smell a rat. And so the old waiting game went on. But at length I took heart to lift up the cap once more.

"I only drew one fire this time; for the Indians were sharper than I fancied, and had taken warning. I didn't hit a man either—didn't try to. I wasn't going to waste powder and ball' till I found out where exactly they were—I only knew the direction before—and this was just what I learnt by this fire.

"I kept my eyes on the spot, and in half a minute the fellow who had just fired reloaded. In sending home his rod he exposed part of his breast. It was only for a second, but it was long enough. I shot him through the heart.

"Next minute the survivor was running for his life, dashing here and there among the bushes. I sent my remaining ball after him, though; and I think he took it home. I verily believe the fellow was entirely taken in by the cap, and fancied there must be half a dozen white men at least among the bushes.

"Perhaps the best of the fun was that they had killed my deer for me already, and the last fellow was in too much of a hurry to fetch it along with him. I dressed the deer—there was a couple—at my leisure, and went home to the station that night with plenty of meat. You should have seen the joy of the famished folk when I came trudging in with it.

"And the cap? Oh, yes. I brought home the cap too. But, you see, it wasn't much of a *cap* any longer. I think I told you it had a hole or two before. Well, after this it wouldn't cover the head—wouldn't cover it anything to speak of. It would fix on to half a dozen heads at once in a sketchy sort of way—but not to keep the rain off. I didn't mind that much, however; it did pretty well as a curiosity.

"'I LIFTED UP THE CAP IN MY LEFT HAND'" (p. 383).

A FEDERAL SCOUT.

BEING A STORY OF CAPTAIN CHARLES LEIGHTON : TOLD BY HIMSELF.

T happened in Western Virginia.

I had been personally acquainted with our chief, General Rosencrantz, before the war commenced, and was by him engaged to act in a scouting expedition.

"Listen," said the General. "My only trusty scout, Mackworth, was killed last night at the Lower Ford; and General Forrest (the Confederate) has his headquarters at the Sedley Mansion, on the Romney road."

"Very well," I rejoined, beginning to feel a little queer.

"I want you to go to the Sedley Mansion," was the General's next sentence.

"To go *there!*" I exclaimed. "Why, it's in the very heart of the enemy's position!"

"Just the reason I want it done," resumed the General. "Listen. I attack to-morrow at daybreak. Forrest knows it, or half suspects it, and will mass his troops either on the centre or left wing. *I must know which.* The task is a dangerous one—regular life and death. Two miles from here, midway to the enemy's outposts, and six paces beyond the second milestone, are two rockets propped on the inside of a hollow stump. Mackworth placed them there yesterday. You must slip into Forrest's quarters to-night, learn what I want, and hurry back to the hollow stump. If he masses on the centre, let off one rocket; if on the left, let off both. This duty, I repeat, is fraught with peril. You will have to start immediately and alone. Will you go?"

After a slight struggle, I answered in the affirmative, and immediately left the General's tent to make ready.

It was nearly ten o'clock when, having received a few additional instructions from the chief, I started on my dangerous ride. As the country was quite familiar to me, I had fortunately little fear of losing my way.

Riding slowly at first, as soon as I had passed our last outpost I put spurs to my horse—a glorious thorough-bred-grey, which the General had lent me for the occasion—and flew down the mountain at a tremendous pace.

It was a cool, misty, uncertain night, almost frosty, and the landscape was wild and desolate. Mountains and ravines were the prevailing features, with now and then that variety of the broomy undulating plateau which occasionally softens our mountain scenery. I continued my rapid pace without much caution, until I arrived at the farther extremity of one of these plateaux. Here I pulled up sharply beside a block of granite, which I recognised as the second milestone.

Dismounting, I proceeded to the hollow stump which the General had spoken of; and finding the rockets there, examined them to make sure of their efficiency, remounted, and was away again. But now I proceeded with much more watchfulness. I rode more slowly, kept my horse on the turf at the edge of the road, in order to deaden the hoof-beats, and also shortened the chain of my sabre, binding the scabbard with my knee to prevent its jingling. Still I was not satisfied, but tore my handkerchief in two, and fastened to either heel the rowel of my spurs, which otherwise kept up a little tinkle of their own.

" IN FRONT OF A GROUP OF HORSEMEN " (p. 387).

In this way I kept on the alert, with my eyes roaming all round, in the hope of catching a glimpse of some clue or landmark— the glimmer of a camp-fire, a tent-top in the moonlight, which now began to shine faintly, or to hear the snort of a steed, the signal of a picket, anything that might guide me, or give warning of the lurking foe. But no: if there had been any camp-fires, they were extinguished; if there had been any tents, they were struck. Not a sign —not a sound. All was quiet as a tomb.

The great mountains rose around me in their shrouds of pine and hoods of mist, cheerless, repelling, silent, as if their solitude had never been broken. The moon was driving through a weird and ragged sky, with a certain something of desolation and gloom in her pallid face that seemed to foretoken evil. And in spite of all my resolve, I felt the chill of loneliness and sense of danger creep through my flesh and smite my very bones.

None but those who have actually experienced it can form any real idea of the apprehensions that haunt even the bravest of the brave if he feels himself alone in the midst of *unseen* enemies. The lion-hunter of Abyssinia is surrounded with dangers when he makes a pillow of his gun in the desert. Our own pioneer of the wilderness can slumber but lightly when he knows that the bloodthirsty Indian is prowling in the neighbourhood of his cabin.

But the lion is only ferocious when famished. The Indian may often be conciliated. The hunter confronts his savage antagonist with something deadlier than ferocity. The hand that levels and the eye that guides the unerring rifle are animated by—

"The mind, the spirit, the Promethean spark,"

which is more than a match for the Indian's vengeful astuteness. But to the solitary scout, at midnight, every turn of the road may conceal a finger on a hair-trigger; behind every stump or bush may lurk a foe. If he ride through a forest, it is only in the deepest shadow that he dare ride upright. Should he traverse an open glade, where the starlight or moonshine falls fully, he crouches low on the saddle, and scours across, for every second he feels he may be the target of an invisible foe. His senses are painfully alive; his faculties strained to their utmost tension.

Here I may introduce a digressive paragraph.

I knew a very successful scout—who met his death in the early years of the war—who always required a long sleep immediately after an expedition of peril, though it might have lasted but a few hours, and had apparently called forth no more muscular exertion than was necessary to, sit in the saddle. Yet, strange as it may seem, he would complain of overpowering fatigue, and immediately drop into the most profound slumber. And I have been informed that under similar circumstances this frequently occurs. I can only attribute it to the fact that, owing to the extreme and most abnormal tension of the faculties and senses, a man on these momentous occasions lives twice or thrice as fast as he ordinarily does; and the nerve-play and mental action usually spread over a day and night may thus be concentrated in the brief period of a few hours.

But to resume—

I felt to the full this apprehension, this anxiety, this exhaustion; but the knowledge of my position and the issues at stake kept my blood alive.

I had come to the termination of the last plateau or plain, when the road led me down the side of a ravine with a prospect ahead of nothing but darkness. Here, too, I was compelled to make more noise, as there was no sod for my horse to tread on, and the road was rough and flinty in the extreme. I was moving on as warily as possible, when suddenly, just at the bottom of the ravine, where the road began to ascend the opposite acclivity, I came to a dead halt in front of a group of horsemen, who seemed to have started from the earth like shadows.

"Why do you return so slowly?" said one of them impatiently. "What have you seen? Did you meet Colonel Craig?"

For a moment, a brief one, I gave myself up for lost; but, with the rapid reflection and keen invention that a desperate strait will sometimes stimulate, I seized the language of the speaker, and formed my plans accordingly.

Why do you return so slowly? I had been sent somewhere then.

What have you seen? I had been sent as a spy.

Did you meet Colonel Craig? Oho, I thought, *I* will be Colonel Craig; but no, I will be the Colonel's orderly. So I spoke out boldly—

"Colonel Craig met your messenger, who had seen nothing, and advised him to scout down the edge of the creek for half a mile. But he despatched me, his orderly, to say that the enemy appear to be retreating in heavy masses. I am also to convey this intelligence to General Forrest."

The troopers had started at the tones of a strange voice, but seemed to listen with interest and without suspicion.

"Did the Colonel think the movement a real retreat, or only a feint?" asked the leader.

"He was uncertain," I replied, beginning to feel secure and roguish at the same time; "but he bade me say that he would ascertain, and in an hour or two, if you should see one rocket up to the north there, you might conclude that the Yankees were retreating: if you should see two, then you might guess they were not retreating, but stationary, and would probably remain inactive for another day."

"Good!" cried the Confederate. "Do you know the way to the General's quarters?"

"I think I can find it," said I, "although I am not familiar with this side of the mountain."

"It's a mile this side of the Sedley Mansion," said the trooper. "You will find some pickets at the head of the road. You must there leave your horse and climb the steep, when you will see a farm-house, and fifteen minutes' walk towards it will bring you to the General's tent. I will go with you to the top of the road."

And setting off at a gallop the speaker left me to follow.

Now, owing to their mistake the countersign had not been thought of; but the next picket would not be likely to swallow the same dose of silence, and it was a lucky thing that the trooper led the way, for he would reach them first, and I should have a chance of catching the password from his lips.

But he passed the picket so quickly, and dropped the precious syllables so indistinctly, that I only caught the first two of them—"*Tally*"—while the remainder might as well have been Greek. *Tally—tally—tally*, what? Good heavens! thought I, what can it be? *Tally—tally*—here I am almost up to the pickets—what *can* it be? "Tally-ho?" no, that's English. "Tallyrand?" no, that's French. Heaven help me! *Tally—tally——*

"*Tallahassee!*" I yelled with the inspiration of despair as I dashed through the picket, and their levelled carbines sank harmlessly before that wonderful spell—the countersign.

Blessing my stars, and without further mishap, I reached the place indicated by the trooper, which was high up on the side of the mountain—so high that clouds were forming in the deep valley below. Making my bridle fast, I clambered with some difficulty the still ascending slope on my left. Extraordinary caution was required. I almost crept towards the farm-house, and soon perceived the tent of the rebel chief. A solitary guard was pacing between it and me—probably a hundred yards from the tent. Perceiving that boldness was my only chance of safety, I sauntered towards him with as free-and-easy an air as I could muster.

"Who goes there?"

"A friend!"

"Advance, and give the countersign!"

I advanced as near as was safe and whispered "Tallahassee," with some apprehension as to the result.

"It's a confounded lie!" said the sentry, bringing his piece to the shoulder in the twinkle of an eye. "That answers the pickets, but not me."

Click, click—with an awful sound—went the rising hammer of the musket.

"I am a dead man," I thought to myself; "I am a dead man unless the cap fails. And wonderful, marvellous to relate, it *did* fail. The hammer fell with a dull harmless thud on the nipple.

Swift as thought, and stealthily as a panther, I glided forward and clutched his throat, forcing him to his knees, while the gun slipped to the ground. A fierce but silent struggle ensued. The Confederate could not speak, for my hand grasped his throat too tightly; but he was a powerful man, with a bowie-knife in his belt, could he but lay hold of it. But I got it first—hesitated a moment—and then sheathed it in his midriff to the hilt. Just at that instant his teeth closed on my arm and bit to the bone. Restraining a cry with the utmost difficulty, I dealt him another blow, and this time—*home.*

Breathless with exhaustion I lay still to collect my thoughts, and listened to know if the inmates of the tent had been disturbed. But no! a light was streaming through the canvas, and I could catch the low murmur of voices within as of men engaged in serious consultation. I looked at the dead soldier remorsefully. His slouched hat had fallen off in the struggle, and his ghastly pale face was upturned towards the pitying heaven. A handsome face it was —young, and with a noble air—and I observed that his hands and feet were small and finely shaped; while the whole appearance of the body showed that it had been the tenement of a brave and gallant spirit.

Was it a fair fight? Was I justified in attacking him? thought I; and in the sudden contrition of my soul I almost bowed myself to the ground. But the sense of imminent peril returned to me, stifling every other feeling, however worthy. I stripped the dead man of his overcoat and put it on, threw my cap away, and wore in its stead the slouched sombrero, and then dragged the corpse behind a neighbouring outhouse.

Returning to the sentry's post, I seized his gun and began to march to and fro with apparent composure, but a keen observer would have detected an anxiety in my frequent glances at the tent, which would not have augured well for my safety.

At every turn I drew nearer to the tent, until I could almost distinguish what was said within; and presently, after a minute survey of the ground, I crept up to it, crouched down to the bottom of the trench, and listened eagerly. By lifting up the canvas I could even see into the tent.

Half a dozen Confederate Generals were seated within, and a map was spread on the table, around which they had assembled. At length their council came to an end, and the company rose to depart. I ran back to my place, and resumed the sentry's vigilant pace with as indifferent an air as possible, drawing the hat well over my eyes.

The Generals came outside the tent and looked about a little before they disappeared. Two of them came close to me, and passed almost within a yard of the dead sentinel's body. But they moved away, and I drew a deep sigh of relief. A light still glimmered in the tent, but that, too, vanished shortly, and all was still, except that occasionally I could hear the voice of some distant sentry, or perhaps the rattle of a halter in some distant manger.

I looked at my watch. It was two o'clock, would be five before I could give the signal, and the attack was to be delivered at daybreak.

As stealthily as before, I started on my return, and reached my horse without accident. Here I abandoned the gun and grey overcoat, remounted, and rode rapidly down the mountain.

By the aid of "Tallahassee" I got through the first picket; but something was evidently wrong when I drew near the troopers to whom I had been so confidentially despatched by Colonel Craig. Probably the true scout, or, it may be, the gallant Colonel himself, had paid them a visit during my absence. At all events, something critical had taken place, and I prepared to incur some imminent hazard.

"Tallahassee!" I cried, as I swept through the ravine.

"Halt, or you're a dead man!" shouted the leading trooper.

"He's a Yank! Cut him down!" exclaimed the others.

"Tallahassee! Tallahassee!" I yelled.

And with one brief prayer to Heaven, I galloped furiously onward, with sabre and revolver in either hand.

"*Click—bang!*" Something grazed my cheek like a hot iron. "*Click—bang*" again! Something whistled by my ear with a terrible intonation. And then I was in their midst, shooting, stabbing, slashing, swearing like a fiend. The rim of my hat flapped over my face from a sabre-cut, and I felt blood trickling down my neck. But I burst away from them, dashed up the banks of the ravine, and scudded along the bare plateau, all the time shouting, I knew not why, "Tallahassee! Tallahassee!"

I could hear the alarm spread back over the mountain by halloos and rattling drums, and soon I caught the clang of pursuing steeds. But I sped onward like a whirlwind, almost fainting from excitement and loss of blood, until I reeled off my horse at the hollow stump.

Fiz—fiz! *One—two!* My heart leaped with exultation as the rushing rockets rose after each other in rapid flight towards the zenith, and flung their fiery showers out upon the darkness.

Emptying the remaining tubes of my pistol at the nearest pursuer, now less than fifty yards distant, I was in the saddle and off again without pausing to

FIRING THE ROCKETS.

watch the result of my fire. For a few moments it was literally a ride for life, but I bestrode as gallant a steed as ever galloped. I soon outstripped my pursuers, and as we neared the Federal lines they gradually dropped off.

On attaining the summit of the first ridge of our position, and as the rosy day broke brightly over the pine-tops and along the crags, I felt the solid earth quiver beneath my feet—a swift wind seemed to pass before my face, and a hundred heavy cannon opened above, around, below me. Serried masses of men were sweeping irresistibly down the mountain towards the opposite slope; flying field-pieces were dashing into position; long lines of cavalry gleamed in the shadowy hollows or hung like eagles on the brink of the steep. And above the deadly din of the artillery echoed the wild blare of the exultant bugle.

Yes ; the two rockets had been seen and understood ; and while the Confederate General was gathering his strength upon his left wing, our veterans were swooping down upon his weakened centre in a storm of fire and flame. The victory was with the Stars and Stripes, and another leaf was that day added to the glorious chaplet of General Rosencrantz.